VINDOLANDA

ADRIAN GOLDSWORTHY studied at Oxford
and became an acclaimed historian of Ancient
Rome. He is the author of several books,
including *Anthony and Cleopatra*,
Caesar, and *The Fall of the West*.
Visit adriangoldsworthy.com

ADRIAN GOLDSWORTHY
VINDOLANDA

HEAD of ZEUS

First published in the UK in 2017 by Head of Zeus Ltd.

Copyright © Adrian Goldsworthy, 2017

9 7 5 3 1 2 4 6 8

A catalogue record for this book is available from
the British Library.

ISBN (HB) 9781784974688
ISBN (XTPB) 9781784974695
ISBN (E) 9781784974671

Typeset by Ben Cracknell Studio, Norwich
Printed and bound by CPI Group (UK) Ltd, Croydon, CR0 4YY

Endpaper image: akg-images / Peter Connolly

Head of Zeus Ltd
First Floor East
5–8 Hardwick Street
London EC1R 4RG

WWW.HEADOFZEUS.COM

For Siân

PLACE NAMES

Bremenium: High Rochester
Bremesio: Piercebridge
Coria: Corbridge
Corinium: Cirencester
Eboracum: York
Gades: Cadiz in Spain
Londinium: London
Lugdunum: Lyon in France
Luguvallium: Carlisle
Magna: Carvoran
Trimontium: Newstead

PROLOGUE

11 September AD *98*

THE RIDERS CAME from the north, black shapes in the darkness, and the few people who saw them kept out of their way and did not dare to call out a challenge. A band of men abroad at this hour were more than likely warriors or thieves or both. These ones moved with purpose, and that could mean many things. They came suddenly into a dell, scattering the dozen sheep that were grazing there, and the shepherd yelled out in anger before fear made him fall silent. The horsemen rode past, ignoring him and his animals. Half an hour later they came to a shallow valley, and the men urged their tired mounts into a canter. It was nearly dawn.

There was a Roman outpost in the valley, but the sentry standing on the tower over its single gateway did not see them for some time. He was a Thracian, tired at the end of a long watch and not expecting anything to happen because nothing much ever happened here. There might be the odd feud and murder, and the inevitable thefts of livestock, but not any real trouble. With twenty-three years' service under his belt, that was why the Thracian had applied for the posting. He had two more years left to go before his discharge. That meant becoming a Roman citizen, freedom from the army's rules, and... After such a long time it was hard to picture life outside the army. He was not quite sure what it would mean, but wanted to live to find out, which meant that quiet was good, and at times it was so quiet here that it seemed the army and the wider world had forgotten all about them.

The outpost was as small and insignificant as any he had ever seen. For an army whose units loved to proclaim that they had built anything, the painted sign above the gate was unusual and merely stated that Legio II Adiutrix had made this *burgus* – they did not say when or why, neither did any officer claim credit for supervising the work. The notice was plain and the lettering small, giving the impression that the legionaries were not proud of the deed, and the Thracian did not blame them, neither did he wonder why the whole legion had left Britannia and cleared off to the Danube soon afterwards. This was a half-forgotten dunghill in the middle of nowhere in the empire's most northerly province, and II Adiutrix had not even bothered to do a decent job.

It was supposed to be eighty-five feet square, but the side walls were nearly a double pace different in length and the front and back not much better. Long hours of guard duty, day after day and night after night, meant that the Thracian knew every inch of the place, and every creak in the walkway and crack in the timber where the legionaries had used green wood because they had wanted the job over with and had not waited for seasoned supplies to arrive. One of the planks of the tower's platform was spongy underfoot and would give way sooner or later. He had the happy hope that the new acting *curator* Crescens would be standing on it when it did. The Thracian smiled at the thought, turned to face the east and then raised hand to forehead and promised to pour a libation to the Rider God of his people if only it would happen.

As if in answer a sliver of burning orange light appeared over the top of the hill behind the fort and made him blink. Dawn was coming, and the Horseman was galloping through the heavens, his hound running alongside as they drove the stars from the sky and let the sun bring a fresh day to the world. A moment later he heard Crescens' voice raised in anger, bawling at one of the slaves for no good reason.

'That's him, lord,' the Thracian muttered. 'Know you're busy, but the bastard has it coming.'

The little garrison was stirring, apart from the centurion whose quarters were set up against the far wall. No one had seen the officer for three days – or heard him since the last burst of singing on the second morning. It happened every month or so, and by now the Thracian knew the pattern, and guessed that the centurion Flavius Ferox would be half sober by tonight, or maybe tomorrow morning.

Most of the time Ferox did not drink a lot by army standards, and did his job well. He was *centurio regionarius*, the centurion in charge of the region around here, tasked with keeping the peace and the rule of law, so that the army knew what was going on and the locals were content and willing to settle their disputes without lopping each other's heads off. Ferox was a Briton, albeit from a tribe living far away in the south-west, and although men said that this was why the locals trusted him, the Thracian doubted that it was the main reason. The centurion was a hard man, grim-faced, but was known for keeping his word and never giving up. They told stories of how he had chased fugitives for weeks on end and over hundreds of miles and almost always got them. Once he went to the far north in the dead of winter and came back with a young warrior accused of raping and murdering the wife of a Roman trader – and then testified at the trial on behalf of the captive and proved that he was innocent and the Roman guilty. Not everyone thanked him for that, but the warrior's relatives did, and word spread that the centurion prized the truth. It did not matter too much, for they never caught the husband, who had slipped away to Gaul, protected by influential friends.

The Thracian did not know whether any of this was true, for the army always had far more rumours than it had soldiers. Men also said that Ferox had once been a great hero and perhaps that *was* true, for the harness he occasionally wore over his mail was heavy with disc-shaped *phalerae*, torcs and other awards for valour. Others whispered that he was unlucky, and that disasters seemed to happen when he was around, with legions cut to pieces by the Dacians and Germans.

3

All that was long ago. Ferox had been at this outpost for seven years and nothing bad had happened. Nothing much had happened at all. The Thracian did not know whether a weakness for drink was why the centurion had been sent here in the first place or whether the damp monotony since had turned him to it. Still, Ferox was a Briton and they were an odd lot, so perhaps he liked this hole and was just prone to melancholy. When he arrived, he had had someone paint a much bigger sign with the word SYRACVSE in tall elegant letters, and had had this nailed above the message left by II Adiutrix. No one even pretended to know why.

The light was growing, and it was nearly day, which meant that the Thracian's four hours on guard would soon be over. Built for some fifty men and a dozen horses and mules, the outpost Syracuse now had less than half that number, and so Crescens had decided to inflict double watches on everyone since Ferox had shut himself away. The curator was parading his little power as garrison commander, picking on all those he did not like. Fortunately, that was just about everyone, so that the burden was shared. The man had barely served five years, but looked eager and could write in a clear hand, so would probably get promotion sooner or later, instead of this temporary post, which did not grant a man any permanent rank.

Stamping his feet to bring them back to life – and taking care to step over the soft plank – the Thracian went to the parapet on the outer side of the tower and looked out across the valley. The small village on the far side seemed quiet, although no doubt the women were stirring the hearth fires back into life. A few boys drove little clusters of cattle down to the stream.

'*Omnes ad stercus,*' the Thracian groaned, too tired for anger, but not for fear. 'Boy,' he hissed at the young sentry standing outside the little fort. The pair of them had shared this long watch, and as the senior man he had taken the ramparts and tower. The regulations for the army set down by the divine Augustus and repeated by every Caesar since then stated that a picket must always be maintained in the open outside each gate of a camp. Men on that duty were oath-bound to stand their ground even in the face of overwhelming odds, and were there to warn the garrison of danger. 'What if the barbarians come?' asked the new recruit in one of the army's oldest jokes. 'Just make plenty of noise while they're killing you,' was the centurion's answer.

The young sentry did not move, so was true to his pledge at least. He was also just where he should be, standing three paces in front of the ditch and to the right of the track leading up to the gate, but he was far too still.

'Boy!' the Thracian tried again, a little louder.

The lad stayed as he was, the butt of his spear planted firmly on the ground, the shaft against his shoulder to rest his weight. With his dark cloak gathered around him and shield propped against his legs, only his stillness and the slump of his helmeted head gave him away. The Thracian knew every soldier's trick and this was an old and dangerous one. One of the most important things a recruit had to learn was to nap whenever and wherever he got the chance, because the army never minded getting you up at all hours. Sleep was precious, almost as precious as food. A knack for sleeping while standing up was rare and sometimes useful, but a dangerous curse for a man on sentry duty.

'Wake up, you daft sod, or they'll have the skin off your back!' The Thracian spat the words out and then looked nervously back into the courtyard in case someone had heard. There were half a dozen men out in the street, fiddling with their equipment and adjusting buckles, but no one was paying him particular attention. The closed gate meant that they could not see the lad outside, but once the sun cleared the crest of the hill then it was the Thracian's duty to ring the brass bell to mark the end of the night watches and the beginning of a new day. As the garrison was roused and the gate opened, he would shift the wooden peg on the board beside it to show that it was now the third day before the Ides of September. A pair of sentries would come to relieve them, morning parade would be held, orders and a new password issued, and only after that was there a chance of some food. Nothing much changed whether the garrison held a whole legion or a couple of dozen men, so even here the army's day started in the same way as it did everywhere else.

He had to act quickly, for Crescens was bound to blame him for not keeping the youngster awake. He could tell that the curator was itching to lay formal charges against someone and earn them a beating or worse.

'Sonny!' the old soldier tried again, calling as loud as he dared. His foot kicked something across the floor. It was an apple core, left by one of the earlier sentries – probably that mucky bugger Victor. Propping his spear against the wooden parapet, he bent over to grab it.

As the Thracian straightened up, movement out in the valley caught his eye, and at last he saw the horsemen, no more than half a mile away, coming on at a brisk trot. There were little dots in his eyes as he stared at the rapidly approaching figures – at least ten and not more than twenty. The rising sun glinted red off helmets and spear points, which meant that they were well armed, but they did not ride in a neat column – more like a swarm – and that surely meant that they were Britons.

The Thracian had not seen an enemy since he had come here, back in the winter. He strained to see more clearly, in case this was about to change, while praying that it was not. The Britons swept past the herd boys and their cows, ignoring them, and the children did not seem to be afraid of them, which was a good sign.

The leading rider was a tall man on a big horse and even though he could not make out his face, the Thracian recognised him and breathed a sigh of relief. It was Vindex, leader of the scouts who served with the army. He and his men were frequent visitors, and the centurion often rode out with them, but they had not been here for nearly a month.

'Tower, there!' Crescens yelled up from the courtyard, interrupting his thoughts. 'Anything to report?'

'*Omnes ad stercus*,' the Thracians said wearily. There was no more time. Taking just a moment to aim, the Thracian lobbed the apple core, and felt considerable satisfaction when it struck the shallow neck guard of the boy's iron helmet. The young sentry jerked awake with a grunt, still groggy as he turned and looked up, his face very pale.

'Do your job, boy,' the Thracian shouted, pointing at the horsemen. It no longer mattered if he made any noise. He looked back over his shoulder. 'Riders coming in!'

Below him the lad was still sluggish as he looked in that direction. He stared for a moment, and then gasped, dropping his spear. The Thracian laughed as the boy, gaping, raised his own arm to point, the movement making his shield fall flat on the grass.

'Yes, I know,' the old soldier said under his breath, 'I see 'em. And how's your laundry doing, sonny-boy?'

The horsemen were close enough to count fourteen riders and three more horses carrying burdens. The sun had cleared the hill and cast long shadows behind them as they pounded up the path towards the gate. The Thracian stepped over to the bell and rang it six times to announce the rising of the sun. He waited for three breaths before ringing it again to sound the alarm, not that he thought there was anything to worry about, but because that was the rule.

'Scouts coming in,' he shouted down into the courtyard. 'Open the gate!'

Crescens glared up because the order was given without consulting him, but the Thracian knew exactly what the regulations said. Vindex kicked his horse and cantered past the flustered young sentry and through the entrance way just as the gate opened. The Thracian grinned, poking his fingers through the little gap where the cheek pieces of his helmet met and scratching his beard. They had style, some of these Britons, you had to give them that.

The rest of the horsemen halted outside. Like their leader the scouts were Brigantes, warriors from the big tribe that held a great swathe of northern Britannia, and loyal allies of Rome for some time now. Slim-faced, tall and rangy, they sat straight-backed as statues in their saddles, staring impassively down at the young sentry. Most of them had thick moustaches, although none as full as the great brown whiskers of their leader. Each wore an old-fashioned army-issue helmet, the bronze types with a straight neck guard, modest peak and topped by a blunt spike, the style that the legions had stopped wearing half a century ago. Only the leader had a mail shirt, but every man had a sword on his right hip, though these were every shape and size from long local blades to infantry- and cavalry-issue patterns. The shields were even more mixed and painted in bright colours, some with pictures of animals on them.

The young sentry looked as if he was trembling as he stared at the silent warriors, and at last one grinned, and then they were all laughing and talking while some swung down to the ground. Brigantes talked a lot – at least compared to other Britons. The Thracian noticed that two of them had been riding double – never a comfortable thing, especially for the one behind – and then saw that two more of the scouts were heading into the fort on foot, each one leading a pack horse.

With much stamping of hobnailed boots, the Thracian's relief arrived.

'Longinus reporting as guard to the gate-tower,' the man announced. He was a thickset Tungrian, his broken nose and scarred face hiding a gentle character. 'Anything to report, brother?'

The Thracian was not really listening. As the two pack horses came towards the gateway he saw that each bore a corpse hidden under a blanket. The side of one of the animals was caked with dried blood. It seemed that things were not so quiet after all.

'What?' he said after a moment, realising that Longinus was staring. 'Oh, you know, the usual – *omnes ad stercus.*'

His relief blinked, but the Thracian did not bother to explain. He went down the ladder on to the rampart and headed for the steps down into the courtyard, where Vindex sat his horse in front of the curator, staring down at the man.

'I need the centurion.' The Brigantian's Latin was clear in spite of an accent that gave the words a brusque, guttural tone. 'Is he here?' Vindex's face was long, almost horse-like, the skin so tight that every muscle and each line of his skull and jaw was stark. It was a face to terrify children and unsettle most men, the face of a ghost or devil, only softened a little by the luxuriant and well-combed moustache. Crescens hesitated, and the Thracian did not blame him.

The *stationarii* not on guard duty were paraded in a line on one side of the road. Temporarily detached from half a dozen parent units and stationed at this outpost, they wore a range of uniforms and carried shields of different shapes, but were ready for inspection – except that this Briton was between the curator and his morning parade.

'He is ill,' Crescens said at last.

Vindex sniffed, while his horse started to urinate. Crescens stepped back to avoid the splashes from the long and noisy yellow stream.

The Thracian joined the parade and watched the confrontation with amusement. Ferox's orders were for any scouts with information to be brought to him as soon as they arrived, and the curator must know that. Of course, the Thracian had to admit, the orders had not covered what to do when the centurion was drunk off his skull, so that was a knotty little problem for the curator to solve. It was hard not to smile.

'Ill?' Vindex's expression did not change, until with the tiniest twitch of his legs he sent his horse straight into a canter. Crescens gaped, unsure what to do.

The Brigantian brought his big bay horse to a dead stop in front of the water trough, pushed up from the saddle and jumped down in one fluid movement. As he strode up to the centurion's quarters, the mare was already lapping water. The Britons leading the pack horses followed him, ignoring the Roman soldiers as they followed their leader. Bare legs, shoeless and filthy, swung slowly from side to side as the leading mount passed the line of soldiers.

'I need to see the centurion.' Vindex's deep voice echoed around the small courtyard.

'My Lord Ferox regrets that he is unable to receive visitors.' That was Philo, the centurion's slave, a sleek easterner who looked far too civilised for a place like this.

'I need to see the regionarius,' the Brigantian repeated, his voice still loud. 'And I need to see him now.'

'I am sorry, my Lord Vindex, but that is not possible.'

The Thracian was at the right of the line of soldiers, and could see the tall Briton towering over the little slave, thumbs looped in the belt of chains around his waist that supported his long sword. Philo's skin was smooth and dark, his eyes such a deep brown that they were almost black. He wore no cloak, and his tunic was so bleached that the white shone. There did not seem to be a speck of dirt or dust anywhere on him, even though he stood in the mud in front of the doorway. He could not have been much more than a boy, barely five feet tall, and yet he stood firm against this barbarian who looked as if it would trouble him less to kill someone than waste time talking to them. The Thracian was impressed.

'This is important.' Vindex, the head scout, lowered his voice, although it still carried around the outpost.

'I am sorry, my lord, truly sorry.' Philo's left hand gripped his right wrist and rubbed it, but this was the only sign of nervousness.

'Which day is this?' Vindex spoke softly now, and smiled, though in his cadaverous face it looked more like a leer.

Philo's shoulders slumped and he clasped his hands together. 'This will be the fourth day,' he admitted.

Vindex grunted. He took a step forward and the slave straightened up again, still blocking the doorway. Crescens tried to force his way to join them, but was blocked by the two horses and the scout holding their reins.

'Look, Greek,' Vindex said, his tone combining reason with menace. 'We both know that I am going in there and that you cannot stop me. Your master will not blame you.' He was head and shoulders bigger than the slave, and at last Philo gave up and stepped aside. The Brigantian gestured to his remaining man to follow, pushed the door open and went inside.

There was a crash from inside the centurion's quarters, then another, and then the sound of pottery shattering.

'You mongrels!' The Thracian recognised Ferox's voice, although he had never heard him so full of rage.

More shouts, more smashing, then a sharp cry of 'Taranis!' suggesting someone in pain. Crescens again tried to push past the Briton, but the man and horses blocked him.

'I want two men, now!' he yelled, but his voice cracked and sounded weak. The Thracian and the man beside him stepped out of the rank to join the curator.

The struggle inside the building redoubled with even greater noise of violence and destruction. Philo winced at the sound of what must have been a whole shelf or table full of plates and vessels being struck by something heavy and smashed into ruin. The door burst open and the scout who had followed Vindex staggered out, his face bruised and blood pouring from a split lip.

Then the centurio regionarius Titus Flavius Ferox appeared, held in a lock by Vindex. The Brigantians loved their wrestling, although all that the Thracian had seen suggested more brute force and low cunning than true art. In this case he could not doubt its efficacy. Ferox was only a little shorter than the tall Brigantian, and much wider around the chest and shoulders, but he was bent over, arm twisted back so that all his strength was useless and he had to go forward if bone was not to break. Vindex drove him at the trough.

With a grunt of sheer effort the Brigantian lifted the centurion over its wooden side and plunged him head first into the cold water. He said something in his own tongue and the man with the split lip joined him, holding the Roman down as he fought them.

They pulled the centurion out of the water. Ferox was coughing up water, shaking his head and still struggling.

'Mongrels!' he spluttered. 'Sons of—'

Vindex and the other Briton thrust him back into the water. Crescens' mouth hung open as he watched, but still the curator did nothing.

11

The Britons lifted the centurion up again. This time he looked limp and exhausted, all the fight gone. His tunic was the dull off-white army issue, loosely belted so that it hung down to his shins, and the seam along one shoulder had been torn completely so that the material hung down. There were bruises growing on his bare skin, and a couple of old scars, one of them long. His dark hair was soaked and filthy, several days' worth of beard on the chin of his slim face, and his usually clear grey eyes stared out blankly. There were traces of dried vomit on his torn tunic and on his skin, wine stains and dirt on his hands, bare legs and feet.

'There, are you quiet?' Vindex had switched back to his accented Latin. 'I need you, and I need you now.' He saw Philo standing near the door, staring aghast at his master. 'Greek. Get him some *posca*.' That was the cheap drink of soldiers and slaves, more water than sour wine and very bitter in taste. 'And get him ready. He has a long way to ride and he may need to fight.'

With a nod at the other scout, they began to assist Ferox back into his quarters, until he shook them free. The centurion stared around him, eyes bleary. He noticed the gaping Crescens and looked at him for what seemed a long time.

'Ah, curator,' he said at last. His voice had a rich musical quality so that everything he said sounded almost like verse. 'Do not let us keep you from your duties.'

Vindex shrugged as he followed the centurion back into his quarters. The other Briton went back to the trough and started dabbing water on his cut lip.

Crescens rallied, took a roll call and issued the new watchword of 'Mercury Sanctus', but his heart was not in the parade and he dismissed them after only a cursory inspection. Several men, including the Thracian, decided to eat their breakfast out in the courtyard to see what happened. At first there was no sign of Ferox or Vindex and the only change was that the scouts had taken the corpses down and laid them side by side on the grass. Two more Britons came into the outpost and started to fill waterskins for the men and animals outside, walking past the dead bodies without visible signs of interest or concern.

One of the dead was an old man, with thin grey hair and a straggling beard, dressed only in a ragged tunic with a checked pattern so faded that it was only just visible. He had a few light cuts about the face, but no serious wound. The other body was younger, taller and fitter, wearing dark wool trousers, a striped tunic and a pair of shoes that still had plenty of wear left in them. His right leg was twisted, the lower bones obviously broken. Otherwise the young man looked unhurt, save that his head and his left hand had been cut off.

After a while Ferox and Vindex reappeared, and the soldiers moved back a little, but stayed close enough to listen. The centurion did not show any sign of noticing them. Ferox was pale, his eyes bloodshot and sunken. He was wearing closed boots, trousers and a deep red tunic with a padded jerkin on top. The centurion walked like an old man, but there was some trace of his normal hard-eyed gaze as he stared at the body of the old man.

'Any sign of the boy?' he asked Vindex. The regionarius was frowning, giving the impression that thought was a great effort, and talking an even greater feat of strength and will.

Vindex shook his head.

With a grunt, the centurion went to the other corpse and prodded it with his boot. 'Don't think I know this one,' he said, his voice flat.

'Nor me,' Vindex agreed. 'But I reckon he used to be taller.'

After a while Ferox leaned over to inspect the broken leg and the other wounds. The centurion studied the corpse in silence, his skin taking on a green tinge as a wave of nausea swept through him. The Thracian did not think that it was because of the grisly sight. The centurion swayed, rubbed his chin and mouth with one hand and straightened up.

'Hmm,' he muttered, and then added something that did not sound like Latin, all the while massaging his thick stubble.

Vindex said nothing and so they waited.

'Bad business,' Ferox said at the end. 'But do you truly need me?'

'Yes.' Vindex was standing very still, looking straight and unblinking at the centurion, who struggled to meet his gaze. 'This is your patch.'

'Huh.' Ferox prodded the corpse again with the toe of his boot.

'He's still dead,' Vindex said.

'Huh.'

Crescens appeared, coming from the small stable on the far side of the courtyard. There were four horses at the burgus, but one of the mares was not in good shape.

'Good morning, curator,' Ferox said, as if seeing Crescens for the first time that day. 'How is the grey?'

'The leg is coming on, but still lame.' Crescens' reply was confident, for he was a cavalryman and this was something that he did understand. 'I would not trust her for more than a mile or two.' That meant that Syracuse boasted just three horses fit for duty, for the centurion and the four cavalrymen among the stationarii, including the curator himself.

'Today is the Nones?' There was no more than the slightest trace of doubt in the centurion's tone. He looked at Vindex, who said nothing.

'No, sir. The third before the Ides,' Crescens said, surprised that the centurion was fully six days out of reckoning. 'In September, sir,' he added maliciously.

'Huh.' Ferox was still trying to meet Vindex's unflinching stare, as if Crescens was not there. 'And you are sure that you need me?'

'Yes, I need you. It will be easier to have a Roman with us, and you can follow a trail better than anyone I have ever met.'

'Is it my fault that you don't know many people?' the centurion said with a shrug. 'Are you truly certain?'

For the first time the Brigantian looked weary as he nodded. 'I swear by the god my tribe swears by, and by Sun and Moon, that you must come.'

Ferox said nothing and did not even grunt. He started to sway once again, and they could see the effort it took for him to stop.

'I also swear by our friendship that you should do this.'

Ferox sighed and seemed to sag. 'Curator,' he said, 'have the other horses saddled and ready to leave. I'll take Victor and you with me.'

As Crescens walked away Ferox spoke again, talking to the Brigantian.

'We are not friends,' the centurion said. 'I just haven't got around to killing you yet.'

I

I T WAS CLOSE to noon, only a few fat white clouds in an
otherwise bright sky, and Ferox pulled the brim of his
felt hat down to shade his eyes from the glare. He would
have preferred rain and wind, weather suited to his mood, but
the day was a fine one and he resented it, just as he resented
everything else. At least his gelding was behaving, and he gave
the horse a loose rein, trusting him to pick the best path down
this rocky valley. Ferox needed to think, but each thought came
grudgingly.

'Drink before a battle if you must,' his grandfather, the Lord
of the Hills, had told him when he was young, 'although not
too much if you hope to live. Never drink before a raid.' His
grandfather had forgotten more about raiding than most men
would ever know.

They were not on a raid this morning, but they were surely
hunting marauders who were and that needed the same cold
head and colder heart. Ferox had led plundering expeditions
and chased raiders more times than he could remember, and he
knew that this was true, just as he knew that today his spirit and
power were weak. So was the ability to reason, drummed into
him by his teachers all those years ago. His mind was not clear,
which meant that he would likely make mistakes, and perhaps
he would lead them into an ambush and he would die. At least
that would be a release.

He could almost feel his grandfather's scorn, and tried to break free from his black and hopeless mood.

Vindex had taken some precautions without waiting for him. Two of the Brigantian scouts rode ahead of them, two more hovered in the rear, and the rest, including the two Roman troopers, came a couple of horse's lengths behind him. They kept their distance and it was hard to blame them. Now and again Victor hummed a tune Ferox did not know. The rest of them were silent, watching him and waiting to see what happened. He sensed their doubt of his judgement and once again could not blame them. They rode for an hour, dismounted and led their horses for the next hour before remounting and pressing on at a gentle trot. They might have to go a long way and could not afford to wear out their mounts. At least the thick-limbed ponies favoured by the Brigantes were strong beasts, for they had already spent two days searching the country.

Ferox envied the animals their stamina and their lack of care, when he just wanted to lie down for a hundred years. His head throbbed, his belly churned and he could not rid his mouth of the taste of vomit. He worried that he might throw up again, as he had when they started to trot for the first time. He had not fallen off, but when he had tried to mount up back at Syracuse he had not been able to make his limbs work. Ferox had grabbed the horns on his saddle, ready to jump up, but could not. Instead he had just stood there, staring dumbly as the gelding turned its head and stared back. His legs had felt like lead – heavy, ready to bend or crack as soon as he put weight on them. He had bounced slightly, unable to do more. It was a sign of how bad he felt that the snort of laughter from one of his men and the contemptuous sniffs of the Brigantes had not cut deeper. They had to help him on, one of the soldiers cupping his hands and bracing them against his knee so that Ferox could step on it, while another man lifted and shoved him from behind.

Vindex was already on his own horse and had looked at him with a pity in his eyes that cut deeper than the laughter and contempt. Then his bony face became hard.

18

'She is gone,' the Brigantian had whispered. 'She's not coming back.'

It was like being thrust into the cold and dirty water of the horse trough again, and for a moment the old pain burned bright and fierce. Ferox hated the scout, hated himself for what he had become, hated the whole world and the gods who had brought him to this place and the great emptiness inside him. Rage and pain filled him with strength.

'Let's go,' he had said, and urged the gelding towards the gate. Once he was outside the ramparts he had given a gentle nudge and the animal willingly trotted – the whole move only spoiled when the nausea took over and he vomited. It left him empty and weak once again as he led the straggling column south. Vindex had left the trail of the men who had killed the old man to come to Syracuse, and rather than retrace his path they hoped to find it again further on. It was a gamble, but time was precious. The scouts had lost half the night coming to fetch him, and it had taken a good half-hour before they were ready to leave the outpost.

Now that it was too late, Ferox wished he had let Philo shave him. It was always easier to think with a smooth chin to rub, and somehow it made him feel more alive. The Alexandrian boy fussed over him – 'Like a good Jewish mother,' he always said, even if Ferox doubted that the slave had spent much of a childhood with either of his parents. Philo set high standards, clearly determined to make his master almost as neat and well groomed as he was, and looked so disappointed at the centurion's constant failure to match this ideal. Ferox liked the boy and indulged him a little, if only because he was a reminder of better times and of her. He had bought the boy as a slave for her, but then she had vanished and he was left with this fussy servant. That meant there was always a struggle for he could not be too hard on the boy.

The centurion had refused the mail shirt when the slave brought it out, knowing that if he had taken it the lad would surely have wanted him to wear his harness and decorations as well. He also

19

turned down the helmet with its high transverse crest of feathers, demanding this old felt hat instead. Master and slave compromised in the end, and he had left wearing the hat, but with the helmet strapped to the rolled blanket tied behind his saddle. Ferox also allowed the slave to pin a deep blue cloak around his shoulders. It might prove useful if the weather changed or they were out for a night or more. Philo was no doubt pleased that it partly covered the old padded jerkin, a garment that he was convinced shamed his important master.

'You should send a man and have the beacon lit.'

Ferox had not noticed Vindex come up beside him and was surprised at this interruption to his thoughts. It was the second time the Brigantian had made the request. There was a watchtower only a couple of miles away, built on one of the highest peaks in the line of hills, with a good view, especially of the lands to the south. There were rarely more than half a dozen soldiers there, enough to keep watch from the top of the tower and tend the beacon.

'We haven't found any sign of your *latrones* yet.'

'Have we not?' Vindex looked around him. 'Anyway, isn't that all the more reason to give the alarm? They could be anywhere.'

The black smoke of the beacon was visible for many miles and informed army and civilians alike that trouble was abroad. Once it was seen, riders would gallop from the garrisons to find out was happening, strong patrols would go out along the main routes and even larger forces prepare to move as soon as detailed reports came in. It warned the attackers just as it warned everyone else, letting them know that they were hunted, and that the danger would steadily increase for every hour they remained in the area.

'Not yet.' Ferox repeated his answer to the earlier request. The first time Vindex had dropped back and followed with the others. Now he said no more, but kept riding alongside the centurion.

Ferox was tempted, for there was certainly something not right. They had passed several farms and the people in them were courteous, nodding or waving at them as they went by. Yet they looked watchful, as if unsure what was happening and sensing danger. They met some drovers urging a small herd onwards in quite a hurry, but the men claimed to have seen and heard nothing untoward. To Ferox their faces were even more wary than men's faces often were when confronted by Romans asking questions. He suspected that if his mind were not so dulled by his hangover he would have seen more.

There were a few signs by the wayside of the sort used by the tribes to send simple messages. Among the Textoverdi of these lands, one stone piled on another meant that there were warriors or soldiers abroad, and he had seen several of these that looked fresh. A mile or so back there were three flat stones piled on top of each other, the highest one much lighter coloured than the others. That meant a large force of warriors, well armed, with the bright stone marking them as enemies, although in truth some of the locals signified the Roman army in that way. It meant that the group were not Textoverdi, and probably not from one of the other Brigantian clans like Vindex's Carvetii. Ferox wished that he had taken the time to read the fresh bundle of letters back at Syracuse and to check through the latest orders as that should have told him if a large army patrol or other detachment was in the area. He doubted that there was, as the nearest garrisons were stretched pretty thin these days, but it was still just summer, the time for training and shows of force, so it was possible that something was on.

Ferox knew that he did not believe it and wondered whether it was stubbornness or fear that stopped him from sending a man to raise the alarm. He could not pretend that the fear was not real. His was once a promising career, as the first young nobleman of the Silures to be given Roman citizenship, educated at Lugdunum in Gaul with the aristocratic children of the three provinces, commissioned as centurion in a legion, and decorated for valour by the Emperor Domitian himself. All of that had turned sour long ago and some of it was his fault. He had spent the last seven years here in the north of Britannia, without leave or promotion, serving away from his legion who never gave any suggestion that they

21

wanted his presence. His political importance had long vanished now that the Silures were said to be peaceful, and he was posted to Syracuse because he did not matter and neither did the duties he carried out – at least not to any senior man in the province, let alone anyone at Rome. Ferox was regionarius of a district of little importance and if he wanted to rot there or drink himself into an early grave then no one much minded. Neither were they much inclined to trust his judgement, for his stubborn pursuit of the truth had made him few friends and plenty of enemies.

The truth mattered. 'Lie to others,' his grandfather used to say, 'but don't be fool enough to lie to yourself.' Last summer, and then again at the start of this year, he had sent in reports of serious trouble brewing in the north. Everything he saw and heard had convinced him that it was only a matter of time before the tribes broke their alliance with Rome, but his superiors had scoffed at his fears, and nothing had happened so far, so he was now marked down as an alarmist, possibly unreliable. If he roused the garrisons with stories of great raiding bands of barbarians and it all proved to be nothing then he was finished. Crescens for one would happily testify to his drunkenness at the time of the alarm and there were bound to be others who would back up his story. After all, it was the truth. He would be broken, dishonourably discharged and lose the last faint traces of purpose and meaning in his life. Ferox could not face that, for he had nowhere else to go.

'It is a bit early for a big raid,' Ferox said, trying to delay the decision.

Vindex looked more than usually gaunt. 'Depends who they are,' he said. 'And what they want.'

Most bands came for livestock. There might be a few of them, especially if they were horse thieves, or several dozen. If it was a bigger attack, a chieftain with the warriors oath-bound to serve him and any others who wanted to come along, then they wanted more than to take a few animals. The best time was in a month or so, when autumn was truly here. That meant sheep and cattle fat and strong from summer pastures, ground frosted and hard so that the going was good, and the sheltering darkness of longer nights.

Ferox wondered if this was a murder raid. They were rarer these days, with all the tribes and clans allied to Rome and encouraged to be friendly to each other. A big part of Ferox's job was to hear complaints and arbitrate in disputes so that men were less tempted to go and burn someone else's house down. Much depended on the chieftains, whether they sent their clansmen to him, settled the matter themselves or refused to get involved. There were still warriors out there eager to take heads and add to their reputations as dangerous men. Some of the chieftains were as keen for glory or to prove their power, and then there was always hatred and vengeance.

'Someone took that young bugger's head,' Vindex said.

Ferox wanted to think, and needed quiet to do it, but had learned to value the Brigantian's judgement.

'Didn't take the Goat Man's, though, did they?'

Vindex was unimpressed. 'Well, would you want that ugly old sod staring at you?'

Ferox did not know the old man's real name, and wondered whether anyone really knew it or knew him. They called him the Goat Man, or sometimes just Goat, and even men who were grandfathers could only ever recall him being old. He had no home, but wandered the lands with his goats and the small boy who helped him tend to them. Sometimes he stayed in farms or villages, sometimes in caves or huddled in the shelter of trees. Everyone knew him and he never had a good word for anyone else, but he seemed to draw animals to him. Farmers hoped he would come if their cows went dry or the sheep were sick, for Goat Man understood the lore of creatures and how to heal them.

'It won't be the same without him,' Ferox said.

'Yes, it will be a lot less miserable. He never had a kind word for anyone, not that I ever heard. He's cursed me plenty of times.'

Goat Man was never happy and never grateful. He arrived at a man's house at night, took shelter and food and the place closest to the fire. He stayed as long as he wanted, then left without a word and without any thanks. Yet he was always welcome and more than a little feared.

'I've heard people say that he was a god or spirit in disguise.'

Vindex threw his head back and laughed, causing a murmur to run around the men following them. 'Humpin' good disguise if it was.' He thought for a moment. 'But he's dead as stone, and you can't kill a god.'

'I do not think they meant to kill him,' Ferox said, rubbing the thick stubble on his chin.

'That's kind of them.'

'Reckon they wanted something from him,' he continued, trying the idea out as he spoke. 'Probably wanted him to guide them, and when he refused they slapped him around and he died on them.'

'Probably just to spite 'em, knowing that miserable git.' Vindex chuckled to himself. 'What about the other one? Did he try to help?'

'No, he must be one of their band. I do not think he was from these parts. Something happened, he broke his leg and that was that. He'd only slow them down, so they killed him.'

'Nice to have friends,' Vindex said. 'Why take the head – and the hand?'

'That I do not know, but he let them.' The cut to the neck was neat and from behind. It was a hard thing to take off a head with one blow, and to do it so well suggested skill and practice. Ferox imagined the man meekly waiting, probably a couple of others helping him to kneel in spite of the agony from his leg and one of the others raising his sword, timing it carefully before the downward sweep. 'They took the hand afterwards. Maybe they have Goat Man's boy as a guide or maybe he escaped. But I think—'

Ferox broke off, brought his gelding to a halt and held up his hand to stop the others. He swung down and walked forward through the long grass. They were in another little valley, a muddy stream at the bottom, and in one patch the ground on either side was churned and marked with the tracks of horses.

'Careless,' Vindex said, but the centurion raised his hand angrily for silence. Ferox crouched, studying the ground some way from the stream.

The Brigantian took the reins of the centurion's gelding and walked his own horse forward.

'Twenty, maybe a couple of dozen,' Ferox said without looking up. 'A couple with packs and a couple more unridden. Some of the horses are big, and some carrying heavy riders.'

'As I said, but these are not the ones we followed.' Vindex and his men had found the tracks of one party the day before, following it and finding the bodies. Just before sunset they had seen another similar-sized group join the first. Now there was a third bunch, heading in the same direction and probably planning to meet, which meant a band fifty or sixty strong at least, and one that was well prepared. The bigger horses were a puzzle. The tracks looked more like army mounts than ponies.

'Looks like they came past seven or eight hours ago,' Ferox concluded as he went to his horse and grabbed the horns of the saddle. 'While it was dark.'

'Do you need help?' Vindex said nastily as the centurion hesitated.

'Mongrel,' Ferox muttered and then grunted with effort as he half jumped and half pulled himself up.

The trail headed up the side of the valley and the centurion put the horse into a canter as he followed it, the gelding bounding up the slope with obvious joy. Vindex and the others followed. The signs were clear – hoof prints and flattened grass. It meant that whoever they were they were no longer afraid of pursuit. They must be close to whatever it was they wanted.

'Get the beacon lit,' Vindex called as he caught up with the centurion.

'Not yet. I need to know more.' They came out of the valley on to a hilltop and followed the trail east. It was easy to see, and shifted direction only to avoid the patches of bog and the steepest and most rocky ravines. They went for a mile across this rolling country, riding near the top of the ridges so that all the land to the south was spread before them. Anyone looking would see them, but Ferox did not care. People in these parts knew his felt hat. It was old and battered, the sort farmers and labourers wore in the lands around the shore of the Mediterranean, and a rare sight in Britannia, let alone in the north. Locals knew it and would recognise him long before they could see his face. The raiders would see them too, at least if they were still close and watching out. Like the beacon, the sight might make them nervous or more dangerous or both. Still, if he kept to the open country then there should be warning of any threat.

They dipped down into a valley before climbing on to the next long ridge. Ferox slowed to a walk to preserve the horses, then came on to the crest and stopped as he saw something that chilled his heart. Vindex was beside him and went pale. The Brigantian tugged out a bronze wheel of Taranis, which he wore on a cord beneath his mail shirt.

'Lord of Thunder, protect us,' he murmured, pressing the wheel to his lips.

Two grey stones stood on the slope ahead of them. Men called them the Mother and Daughter or sometimes the Mare and Foal and they were old, older than memory, set up by the vanished people who left behind their mounds and their blades of flint – or perhaps by the gods themselves before time began. The Textoverdi rarely came here, and only stepped between the two stones in dire need to work some magic or make an oath unbreakable.

The Mother was the taller stone and someone had balanced a flat red brown pebble on top of it. That was a dreadful sign, one Ferox had never seen before, a warning of evil and a curse abroad. What was worse was that someone had come along afterwards, taken the pebble and thrown it to the ground so that it smashed in two. Then they had picked up one of the pieces and drawn on both the standing stones. Each picture was no more than a crude circle, turned into a face by dots for eyes and an upturned V for a mouth.

26

Ferox's voice was flat as he turned to the Brigantian. 'It appears that our fears were justified.'

'Yes.'

When he had warned of trouble the centurion had tried to explain to his seniors that Rome was seen as weak, its armies in retreat, its power ready to crumble into the dust. Especially in the far north ambitious leaders scented a chance to carve out empires of their own. Men nearer at hand spoke in whispers of war and destruction, of magicians and druids preaching hate. Vindex and his men had seen the same signs and brought word to him, but he was dismissed as over-imaginative and nervous. Yet every instinct told him that they were right, just as the hunter sensed the lurking presence of a savage beast long before he saw it.

'A druid?' Vindex said the word warily, as if the name itself had power.

'Something like that.' Only a man confident in his own power and magic would risk violating a sacred place in this way.

'Then we're humped,' the Brigantian concluded.

Ferox ignored him and beckoned to the two Roman cavalrymen.

'Crescens, who is in charge now at Vindolanda?' That was the nearest garrison, a couple of miles away to the south-east.

The curator looked flattered to be asked something, although surprised that the centurion did not know. 'The Prefect Flavius Cerialis, new commander of the Ninth Batavians.'

'They are *equitata*, aren't they?'

Crescens nodded. Cohors VIIII Batavorum was a mixed unit, with their own cavalry contingent to support the main force of infantry. The Batavians were Germans from the Rhineland, big men with reddish hair and an obvious disdain for the rest of the army – not just their fellow auxiliaries, but even the Roman citizens in the legions.

'Good. You will ride to Vindolanda and report to Cerialis – or whoever is senior if he is away. Please inform my Lord Cerialis that there is a force of at least sixty barbarians in this area. They are well armed and dangerous. They are planning an attack on the road to Coria. I would ask him to send word to the other garrisons and outposts along the road. Apologise to him that there was no time to write a report.' The army always preferred to have everything in writing.

Crescens frowned in concentration as he listened.

'Have you got all that?' Ferox said. 'Then repeat it to me.'

The curator may often have been a fussy, irritating man, but his obsession with detail was sometimes useful and he made no mistakes.

'Good man. If you hear no more from me then return to the burgus as soon as you have rested. Now ride like the wind!' Ferox turned to the other cavalryman. 'Victor, ride to the watchtower and have them light the beacon. Tell the man in charge that there are sixty raiders on the prowl, and give the warning to anyone you meet.'

As the second rider galloped away, Vindex stroked his thick moustache and smiled. 'I'm glad I brought you.'

Ferox grunted. 'We do not have much time,' he said, urging the gelding into a trot, although taking him wide of the standing stones.

'If we are right, some poor buggers have a lot less time than us,' the Brigantian said as they pressed on. 'Are you sure about the road?'

It was not truly a road. The army had only built two proper roads here in the north. The Western Road passed through Luguvallium on its way north to the few outposts left beyond, while the Eastern Road went through Coria. There were a couple of forts between those two bases, and a route had been marked out to link them, with bridges where necessary. Ferox had heard talk of plans to turn this into a proper road, but so far nothing had happened.

'Only thing that makes sense,' Ferox replied, rubbing his chin again. The centurion suspected that he sounded far more positive than he felt. 'The trail keeps on dead eastwards, not south, even though the routes that way are open. My guess is that the bands met by the end of night and will attack soon. That's if they haven't already done it. They'll do what they came to do, and scurry back north to wherever they came from. There are not enough of them to attack a garrison, so they are looking for something in the open. Perhaps a farm, but no one that important or rich lives within easy reach, so it all comes back to an ambush on the road.'

They kept to the high ground, and could see the east–west road below them, sometimes as close as half a mile, more often further away. There were a few travellers along this route, but most of the traffic was military. They passed a couple of carts going westwards at the plodding pace of draught oxen, and three score of pack mules escorted by a dozen legionaries with as many slaves to tend to the animals. The sight made Ferox think, because the convoy would have made a prime target for raiders wanting to take some heads and get some loot.

Vindex must have had the same idea. 'Perhaps they were lucky and got through before the ambush was ready?'

'Perhaps.'

Half an hour later they passed Vindolanda, its buildings a dull white in the distance, and Ferox hoped that the curator was well on his way to the fort. Victor ought to have reached the tower by now, but there was no sign of the beacon's warning smoke. Another mule convoy passed by on the road, bigger than the first, but still vulnerable to a determined band of fifty or sixty men – assuming they had not been joined by yet more warriors.

Ferox put his horse into a canter and drove the beast hard, slapping with the flat of his hand when the gelding tried to slow. They raced along, the horses' shoulders and flanks white with sweat, eating up the miles until they could no longer see the fort, but only the thin tendrils of smoke from its fires. The gelding was breathing hard and beginning to stumble, always a sign that the animal had little more to give. Ferox slowed them back to a walk.

'That's where I would do it.' He pointed ahead. The road veered a bit to the north, running along the valley side to follow a much older trackway and avoid meadows that became bogs after just a couple of days of rain. For a mile or so it was less straight, allowing wagons to negotiate a succession of little slopes and gullies. There were scattered copses and a couple of large woods, the trees big and offering plenty of cover from prying eyes. One stretch went along the bottom of a little valley and was even more secluded.

Vindex snorted with laughter. 'Trust a Silure to pick the right spot for an ambush. Bandits the lot of you.'

'They say I am a Roman.'

'So they say.'

There was a murmur from the scouts, making Vindex turn in the saddle. 'Beacon's lit,' he said.

Ferox was not really listening. Not far away was a herd of cattle being driven alongside the road, and a few travellers all going west. Passing them on the main track were ten or twelve cavalrymen followed by a mule-drawn carriage. It was not as large as many coaches, but such vehicles were rare in this part of the world, and the escort showed that it carried someone or something of importance.

The centurion touched the big wooden pommel of his sword, feeling the runnels carved into it. He wore his sword on the left as a mark of his rank, and also because it was an old-fashioned long blade and was easier to draw from that side.

'I need you to take the scouts up to the top of the ridge.' He pointed ahead, to the hilltop above the broken country. 'The sight of you may worry them if they are waiting to strike. There are too many of them for us to take, so you watch what happens. We need to know who they are and where they've come from. Follow them when it's all over. Catch one if you can, but do not take any daft risks. What you can learn is more important than anything you can do. Understand?'

Vindex nodded. 'And what will you be doing?'

'Taking a closer look.'

The Brigantian grunted and walked his horse over to his men. Ferox pulled off the felt hat and tossed it away. Twisting around in the saddle, he unfastened the helmet from where it was tied.

As usual Philo had left the woollen hat inside. He pulled it on, put the helmet on top and tied up the leather thong to hold the ends of the cheek pieces together. It had been weeks since he had last worn it, but after thirteen years with the legions the heavy helmet still felt as naturally a part of him as his hair.

Ferox walked his horse downhill towards the road. His mind felt clear and calm, though easy because the decision was made and that was that. He had left the alarm too late, and this was his region. All his warnings in the past would not help because they could not change his mistake now. There was probably someone important in the carriage, and he could not let whoever it was die without trying to warn them. Even that might not be enough, and it would be all his superiors needed to recommend his dismissal.

His head no longer throbbed, and when he drained the last of the posca from its skin his mouth felt moist and fresh. When they had forced him awake and made him ride out he had felt as if the world was about to end. The black mood of the last days engulfed him once more and he no longer cared that much if it did. Ferox rode down the hill.

'You forgot your hat,' Vindex said cheerfully, coming alongside, holding the battered old hat in his hand.

'I gave you orders.'

'No one gives orders to the Carvetii.'

The two men kept at a steady pace.

'It is important,' the centurion said. 'We will need to learn as much as we can.'

'I told Brennus to take charge. He will do what he's told.'

'I thought no one gave orders to the Carvetii?'

Vindex grinned, his face more skull-like than ever. 'Brennus' mother is from the Parisii. Anyone can order those earth-eating buggers about.'

Ferox did not laugh, but his mood lifted a little.

They rode on. The carriage and its escort were out of sight, hidden by a grove of tall oaks.

31

'Do you have a plan?' the Brigantian asked after a while.
Ferox said nothing.

'Well, that's good.' Vindex raised the wheel of Taranis to his
lips and murmured a prayer.

'No one asked you to come,' Ferox told him.

'I know. Some people are so unfriendly.'

For the first time the centurion looked his companion in the
eye. 'No shame in going back. It's not too late.'

Vindex laughed. 'Just what my uncle said to me before I took
my first wife!' The Brigantian suddenly looked grim, but then he
usually did. Only men like Ferox who knew him well also knew
his hidden sadness. Vindex had lost both his wives, the first to
fever and the second bearing a stillborn son. The sorrow was deep,
but had not dampened his enthusiasm for the pleasures of life.

Ahead of them, the escort and the little carriage emerged from
behind the trees. They were close enough now for Ferox to see
the cavalrymen's green-painted oval shields, which meant that
they were most likely Batavians out of Vindolanda. Their helmets
looked strangely dark and only the cheek pieces gleamed in the
afternoon sun. One man at the head of the little column wore
brightly polished scale armour that shimmered, and there was
an air of formality about the soldiers. Most men would not have
bothered to take the shields out of their leather covers for an
ordinary journey.

'Maybe we were wrong?' Vindex suggested, as the riders and
carriage went briskly on their way on this warm afternoon. He
reached down to swat a horse-fly settling on his mare's neck. Now
that they were lower down the insects swarmed around them,
drawn by the rich smell of horse sweat.

A horn sounded, harsh and braying, and Ferox kicked his horse
on savagely to draw on its last strength and lumber into a canter.

'Oh bugger,' Vindex said, and followed him.

II

THE BATAVIANS WERE hot and stiff and knew that they still had more than half their journey to go to reach Coria. There was an *ala* based there, one of the all-cavalry units whose troopers were better paid and better mounted than the horsemen serving with an infantry cohort. The Batavians were determined to show those arrogant Gallic and Thracian bastards just what real horse warriors looked like. Anything metal, from spear points to armour, belt buckles to helmets, and the fittings and round phalerae on the harness of their horses had been polished until it shone, and then polished again to make sure. There had been a lot of competition to get selected for this detail, and the men who were chosen had swapped equipment with the unlucky ones if their own was no longer perfect. The horses' coats gleamed almost as bright as the iron and bronze from being brushed, manes were neatly parted and tails combed. Shields were repainted, the red of the central star and the white rosettes made bright on the green field. Every man was big, even in a cohort known for the height and breadth of its soldiers, and although the horses were some of the largest available they were dwarfed by their riders. The decurion in charge wore a cuirass where alternate scales were tinned or gilded, and with his new yellow cloak looked like a god of war come to earth. He had a matching yellow plume on his silvered helmet decorated with figures of animals and hunters. The other eleven soldiers had bearskin glued to the bowls of their bronze helmets, the fur brushed so that it stood up. That was

33

a mark of a Batavian, a sign that enemy or fellow soldier alike should treat him with respect.

They kept to a slow pace, trotting only occasionally because otherwise the mules drawing the carriage could not keep up. That meant that they could not stop the flies from tormenting the horses, and holding shield and reins in one hand and spear in the other meant that there was no free hand to swat them away. So the horses suffered and pressed close behind the ones in front to let their swishing tails give some protection. It was all worth it. The job was a lot easier than doing fatigues back at Vindolanda. It was an honour to be chosen, and to guard the occupant of the coach, but more pleasant was the prospect of at least one night at Coria, which was a much bigger base, with taverns and a proper bath-house. They would drink and bathe, eat and drink some more, and if a brawl or two broke out then so much the better.

The decurion was a good-looking man, immaculately turned out, and had not been chosen because he was especially bright. Like the others he let the warmth of the sunny afternoon and the steady rhythm of horses and the jingle of harness and equipment lull his senses. Hardly anyone spoke, and they walked along as the hours passed, conscious that a dozen picked Batavians had little to fear on a road like this.

It was the coach driver who spotted the dark smoke rising away to the west and called out. That was far behind them, which meant that turning back would probably take them towards the threat.

'We keep going,' the decurion said. 'Keep your eyes open, boys.' He sent a man to ride one hundred paces ahead and another to follow a similar distance behind the coach.

Flies continued to plague them and the steady buzzing added to the warmth of the afternoon to make them sleepy. The shade of a patch of oaks was cool and very welcome, even if it did nothing to hold back the swarms of insects. The road came out into the open, before twisting to find a gentler path down into a gully and up the other side. Beyond that it wove through a long wood, the tree branches sometimes touching as they closed over the road. The decurion knew the place well and wanted to get past it as fast as they could.

The driver was good and took the coach carefully down the slope, reining the mules back when they tried to rush up the far bank. The carriage was high, not really designed for paths like this, and it would be all too easy to tip it or break a wheel.

'We need to be quick,' the decurion called back to him as the driver eased the team and coach up on to the flat. The decurion could not see the man he had sent ahead, because the track turned sharply as it went into the trees.

A flick of the whip put the four mules into a trot and they hurried on. The woods were on either side, the trees a good javelin throw away from the road at this point, but pressing nearer up ahead, where the path turned again after about forty paces. There was no sign of the leading rider.

'Bellicus!' the decurion called out. The man was not doing much good if he could not see him.

A horn blew, a harsh, high-pitched, reverberating call unlike any army trumpet. Something whipped through the air and slammed into his right thigh, driving through muscle and flesh and into the wood of the saddle. An instant later a second arrow hit his chest, piercing one of the tinned bronze plates. He was flung back hard against the horns at the rear of his saddle, gasping as the wind was knocked from him with the force of a swung hammer. A slim shaft almost three feet in length with white feathers on the end stuck out of his chest. There was a great dark stain spreading out from the arrow in his thigh, more blood welling from the wound in his chest and seeping out between the scales, and as he tried to breathe his spittle was red. The decurion slumped forward as two more arrows sliced through the air. A horse reared, screaming in agony and hoofs thrashing. The rider alongside was hit low in the throat, the long-pointed arrow spearing into the little gap between the broad cheek pieces and the top of his mail shirt, with a force so great that it lifted him up and out of the saddle. He fell, arms spread and spear and shield dropping from lifeless hands, blood

35

jetting in a high fountain. There was a rattle as sling stones struck, blinding one of the horses and striking another man's helmet with a dull thud.

An old soldier, grey-bearded and with an empty eye socket covered by a leather patch, took charge.

'Back!' he yelled at the driver. 'Get back across and get going. We'll protect you!'

The coachman nodded and pulled hard on one side of the reins, flicking his whip to turn the team.

'*Testudo!*' the old soldier shouted. 'Testudo on me!'

The rearing horse was down, an arrow in its belly and a front leg broken by a stone. Its rider was underneath, and he cried out as the animal rolled over him, limbs thrashing, and then went silent. The man hit on the helmet swayed, was hit by another stone, this time in the face, smashing his nose, and fell to the ground in a clatter of armour and weapons.

'On me!' the veteran kept yelling. He had his horse facing the woods, at an angle as if to make it a barrier, and the other six men rode to stand in a line behind him. Their long oval shields were upright, covering the rider from shoulder to below the knee and because of the angle giving some protection to their horse. It was a drill they often practised and the Batavians formed up without having to think about what they were doing.

Behind them the carriage and team were already half round and heading towards the path into the gully. Sling stones struck hard against shields. An arrow hit the old soldier's shield and punched through the leather and three layers of wood so that the tip was just inches from his body. The arrowhead was long and narrow, tapering to a point, not like the broader heads used by the army's archers. A second arrow flicked past his face, so close that he could feel the feathers brush him. He glanced back and saw the coach heading down into the gully.

'Keep together, boys!' he shouted, not because they needed the instruction but because it was good to hear a confident voice. 'Not long now. Wait for the word and then we follow.'

A man jerked his shield forward to block an arrow aimed at his horse's neck and almost spun with the savagery of the blow. Another Batavian was hit on the foot by a stone and spat curses in his own tongue until an arrow took him in the mouth.

The harsh trumpet blew, a deeper call repeated again and again. A horse turned away from the line, shaking its head from a brutal blow. The first arrow took it in the neck, making it fall forward, front legs buckling, and the second slammed into the cavalryman, bit through the rings on his mail shirt and went deep into his belly.

Twenty or more yelling men came streaming out of the woods on the other side of the track, behind the Batavians. They were tall barbarians, wild-haired and carrying the little square shields they liked so much.

'Go!' yelled the veteran. 'Back! Back!' He yanked on the reins, and the horse, its mouth in pain from the big army-issue bit, turned immediately and bounded back. The last five men were with him, all order gone as they galloped towards the gully. The old soldier saw the coach climbing the far bank; then it seemed to sway. Arrows ripped through the air and he saw the coachman pitch forward as one struck him squarely in the back, the shaft going so deep that little more than the feathers showed. The carriage juddered, then tipped and fell to the left, mules crying out as the weight dragged them back and over.

The screaming was all around them, and the hiss of javelins. Another Batavian went down, a thrown spear knocking him out of the saddle even though it did not pierce his mail. Britons surrounded the fallen man in a moment, hacking down with their long swords. The veteran turned and hurled his spear back, taking one of the warriors in the side as he raised his sword for another slash. Then his horse was at the lip of the gully, and suddenly the beast collapsed under him and he was flung forward through the air, until the ground slammed into him and there was only blackness.

*

Ferox's gelding had always been willing, and went into a stuttering run, feet pounding across the spongy grass, its breath coming in gasps. Vindex was close behind. They saw a lone cavalryman still this side of the gully, bringing up the rear, the carriage turned frantically back and the confusion as the Batavians were shot down. Someone brought a moment of order, the troopers forming a line to protect the coach as it escaped. Ferox saw arrows skimming past them and wondered at that because bowmen were not common in Britannia, let alone here in the north, and these looked to be uncommonly good ones.

The cavalryman acting as rearguard saw them just as the coach toppled and the little line split apart. He gaped, raising his spear, but then he hesitated when he recognised the crest of a centurion.

'He's with me!' Ferox shouted in case the fool mistook Vindex for an enemy. 'Come on!'

The centurion pressed on the last few yards towards the edge of the gully, waving to the man to follow. On the far side the first of the troopers came over the lip, horse slipping for a moment. A warrior was behind him, spear held low to thrust upwards.

'Kill him!' Ferox called to the Batavian left as rearguard, pointing at the Briton, and the cavalryman saw the target, reached back and threw his own spear in one smooth motion. It was a heavy weapon, designed as much for thrusting as throwing, and the distance was a good thirty paces, but the throw was good. The leaf-shaped head dug into the warrior's leg and he screamed and fell, rolling down the bank.

Ferox urged his tired gelding straight down the slope, not bothering to follow the gentler path. He drew his sword, felt the wonderful balance and the sheer joy that came from holding a good blade. The overturned carriage was close by, lying on its side, the heavy door twitching as someone tried to push it open, but that did not matter, for all he needed was enemies to kill until he had no more strength and they killed him in turn. It would soon be over.

A scream, a long and piercing cry of sheer agony, made him hesitate for it was a woman's cry. With the sound of great effort the door of the carriage was flung open and a woman pulled herself up with both hands and scrambled out, tearing her pale blue dress slightly on the edge of the doorframe. She was slim, with golden hair tied back into a bun and pendant earrings clinking as she moved. There was another scream as she reached down, pulling at something, and then she saw him, recognising the helmet.

'Help me!' she yelled. 'She's hurt.'

Vindex came over the lip, followed by the cavalryman, long sword drawn. There was one Batavian trooper in the bottom of the gully, waiting with spear ready to support the rest, and two spilling over the far edge, until the horse of one of them was killed and the rider flung down.

Ferox urged his horse over to the carriage to help the woman. It was narrower than he had thought, so that the side was not much higher than his chest. He sheathed his sword, feeling his anger deflate as he did so, and then he pushed off the front horns of the saddle and jumped on to the overturned coach. The fair-haired woman was struggling to lift another, younger and smaller than her, her black hair unpinned and hanging down on one side.

'Let me.' Ferox knelt on top of the open door as it lay flat and took the girl underneath her arms. She had delicate features, but her face was strained and as he hauled her up she hissed in agony and went limp. If she had not been so light he doubted that he could have managed it. There was a heavy gold necklace at her throat.

There were two cavalrymen still up the far bank who turned at bay and for a moment held the Britons back. The third man, and the one who had acted as rearguard, watched their flanks from the flat bottom of the gully.

'Give her to me!' Vindex had ridden to the far side of the coach and waited, arms raised to take the unconscious girl. The centurion passed her to him.

'Oh bugger,' the Brigantian said, looking back past them, the way that the two men had come.

39

Ferox followed his gaze and saw eight horsemen coming quickly towards the gully. Several had mail, a few helmets, but the leader wore only trousers, his broad chest covered in intricate tattoos, his hair washed in lime and combed up into spikes. They must have been hidden in the grove of oaks, waiting their moment.

'That way!' Ferox pointed. 'Down the gully.' He pointed southwards. 'Go!' The ground was steeper that way, turning into a little ravine, the banks above it lined with trees. They might manage to get some way down before the Britons caught them, and at least they could make it difficult for them. Apart from that, there was nowhere else to go.

'You two!' he shouted at the Batavians in the gully. 'Watch your rear!' The nearest man looked back, saw the threat and nodded. 'Give us as long as you can, then follow.' He pointed down the gully. One of the men up on the far bank tumbled down the side, his dying horse following.

The fair-haired woman screamed as a javelin stuck into the wood beside her, throwing up splinters. The gelding was done, its long tongue lolling out, and the centurion knew that it would be hard to ride far down the gully as after a while it turned into scree.

The lone Batavian up on the far bank was making his horse rear, almost dancing it back and forth as he drove at the warriors. Ferox heard him laugh, taunting them, and when one of the Britons came close he saw the trooper's long spear take him in the throat, coming back bloody as the Batavian held it poised to thrust again or throw. The other two troopers urged their horses up the other bank and with a whoop charged at the oncoming horsemen.

Ferox jumped down on the far side of the carriage, his foot catching a bronze statuette of one of the Muses on the corner of the roof, so that he landed awkwardly, rolling in the mud churned by wheels and hoofs.

'Come on, you silly girl!' He was up again, yelling at the woman to follow him. 'Come on!' He lifted his hands to catch her.

She glared at him, blue eyes angry, then crouched and sprang off. The same little bronze statue snagged the hem of her blue dress and tore it again. Ferox caught a glimpse of whitened sandals, pale green stockings and smooth calves before he caught her, slipping back a little in the mud.

'Go!' he ordered, spinning her round and shoving her down the slope. 'After your mistress, girl!' He guessed that no wealthy Roman woman would wait to help her maid, so this one must be the slave of the girl Vindex was carrying, the one with the golden necklace. A spoilt attendant with ideas above her station by the look of it, for she did not run, but looked back over her shoulder as if to argue.

'Run!' he shouted as loud as he could and slapped her hard on the rump, making her stagger forward and at last follow her mistress. Hitching up her skirts to reveal long elegant legs, she ran.

Ferox turned, drawing his sword once more. This time he did not feel the same thrill, although it was still so very natural. The sword was at least a hundred years old, a proven blade when his grandfather had taken it from a Roman to give to him. It was longer than the sort the army issued these days, but the perfect balance showed that the smith who had made it was a man of genius.

He began to walk backwards, ready to call the Batavians to follow. He could no longer see the pair who had charged the horsemen, but so far none of those barbarians had spilled over the bank. On the other side the lone cavalryman still held most of the barbarians back, wary of his deadly spear and the thrashing hoofs of his horse. Two warriors had slipped past now that there was no one left to guard the bottom of the gully. They came on in a crouch, warily, until one saw him.

The centurion kept going back, waiting for the right moment to stop. The two Britons were barefoot and bare-chested, and had their hair washed with lime to make it stiff and white so that it stood out like a wild halo. There was something dark on the foreheads, but otherwise no sign of the painted symbols worn by many tribes. Each had a small square shield with a central dome-like boss. The first had a knife at his belt and hefted a spear. The other had a long-bladed sword, without a point, but made heavy to add weight to the edge.

The two men split, so that they could take him from two sides. Ferox kept going back. The spearman was to his left and the swordsman to his right. They came slowly at first, watching him, until without visible signal both men yelled and ran at him.

Ferox charged, going to the left. He dodged when the warrior tried to punch at him with his little shield, took hold of the spear shaft with his left hand, pushing it aside, and raked the long triangular point of his *gladius* across the man's stomach, letting the shape of the blade slide in and pull free easily. Just inches away, he saw the man's snarl of anger and fear turn into one of agony, noticed that he had the lines of a horse tattooed on his forehead, and then he was past.

The swordsman came at him, blade held high ready to chop down. Ferox had no shield to block the blow, so he waited until the last moment and then dived to the side, rolling, and stabbed up into the Briton's groin, twisting the blade free. The warrior was shrieking, a high-pitched wail, doubling up with pain as Ferox pushed himself up and used the motion to thrust again, this time into the man's throat. Blood gushed out as the scream ceased and the man died. This one had the same tattoo.

Ferox pulled the blade free and let the body fall. He went back to the other man, sitting and trying to hold in his innards as they spilled out of the great gash across his stomach. The palm of the warrior's hand was tattooed as well, but with all the blood he could not be sure of the design. The centurion took careful aim and jabbed once into the back of the man's neck. With a sigh as the air left him the man slumped forward. It was unlikely that the enemy would not know where they had gone, but at least this one would not be able to tell them.

There was a great shout, and he saw that the lone Batavian had been shot in the chest with an arrow. The man's horse was bleeding from several wounds, and there were gouges on the rider's legs. Half a dozen warriors closed around him, some of them big men with long shields, and as the horse sank to its knees the Batavian was pulled down. Ferox could not see over the bank of the gully and had no idea what had happened to the other two.

He ran. The slave girl had helped Vindex lower her mistress down before he also dismounted. The Brigantian struck his horse to make the beast ride off, and then slung the still unconscious girl over his shoulder. He waved at the centurion to hurry, before lumbering on with his burden, pushing his way through a mass of brambles. The slope must have dropped sharply, because Ferox lost sight of them before he had gone a few more paces.

When he reached the brambles he stopped and looked back. There was no sign of any Batavians, but warriors on foot and horseback were swarming around the coach, yelling in their victory. One man had a tall carnyx-trumpet and raised it over his head with both hands. The tattooed rider was standing on top of the coach, waving a severed head in one hand. He was haranguing them, pointing down the gully, and then he swung his hand and let loose a cloud of powder so thick that it looked like smoke. He must be the priest, the man who had violated the sacred stones by drawing on them.

Ferox started to push his way through the brambles and bracken, unclasping the brooch and letting his cloak fall because he knew it would just keep snagging.

The carnyx sounded again and the yelling stopped. They were coming.

III

EROX CAUGHT UP with the others quickly, following the trail trampled by the tall Brigantian.

'Just us?' Vindex asked as he reached them.

'Yes.'

'Oh.' He pushed on, using his sword to beat down the clinging brambles and then stamping on them to make a path. The blonde slave girl followed him, her dress torn even more by the thorns and with patches stained green. 'Nearly through,' Vindex said. 'Then it's easier.'

The ground was getting steeper. Ferox looked back, but the crest of the slope was not far away and he could not yet see anyone closing with them. Trees reared up above the steep banks as the gully narrowed. They were thick, and at least it meant no one could ride quickly to cut them off, or even run at any speed through the woods.

Ferox's foot caught in a thick stem bent round and hidden by leaves and he stumbled, barging into the slave, who was knocked forward and nearly lost her balance.

'Who are you?' she hissed angrily.

'Quiet,' he whispered. 'Just keep going.'

'What are you?' she said in reply.

'Move!'

They pushed on, the thorns inflicting even more ruin on the pale blue dress and the darker tunic underneath, and then they were out, into rocky ground that soon turned into scree. Vindex

44

was some way ahead, slipping and sliding as much as walking, stones tumbling away ahead of him. Gusts of wind caught them, and there were more clouds in the sky, running in ever faster from the west.

Ferox wiped his sword on the skirt of his tunic. Most of the blood had gone as he had beaten the path through the brambles, but he cleaned the rest off before sheathing it. His hands were covered in scratches, his woollen trousers holed and dirty.

'What are you waiting for?' he whispered at the woman, who had watched him in obvious distaste. He set off, and as always it reminded him of childhood expeditions along the rocky shores of his homeland. The trick was not to put too much weight anywhere, and always to keep going, springing, almost dancing, from stone to stone. He was rusty, sliding and starting a minor rock fall, before his confidence grew and he went rapidly down the slope. Behind him, the slave girl picked her way more gingerly, the hem of her ragged dress held in one hand and the other arm up high for balance. The hillside was too steep for any tree cover, but the gully's sides were still high and he could not see out. Ahead of them the slope eased and opened out. There was a lake, fringed probably with soft bog, and beyond that straggling woodland. If they could make it to the shelter of the trees then they might just stand a chance. In a few hours the first patrols ought to get here from Vindolanda and begin to search. Their trail was an easy one to follow, which at the moment was not a comforting thought. There were no farms in sight, and the ones he knew were further on, in the valley of the Tyne, and too far for them to reach before they were caught.

'Come on!' he called back at the slave, already a good twenty paces behind him. 'Go faster, you'll find it a lot easier.'

The woman ignored him, her eyes searching the stones ahead of her to find the safest footing. It was all far too slow. The Britons could not be far behind, too many for him to fight, and if their archers got to the crest up there then he doubted any of them would make the cover of the wood.

'Do you want me to carry you?' he said angrily, speaking louder than was wise. Ferox started back towards the woman, but the stones slid away under his right boot and he fell, arms out just in time to stop his face slamming into the ground.

The woman laughed, a rich joyous sound, and the centurion silently hoped that her mistress gave her regular beatings.

He got up, and she was closer now so that he heard the snort when he told her to watch him and copy the way he moved, but they went quicker from then on, so perhaps she copied or had worked it out for herself.

Vindex was waiting at the bottom, crouching beside the girl, who was moaning and moving her head from side to side. One hand clutched the heavy necklace.

'Reckon something's broken,' he told them. 'And it'll be me if I go on, so you can carry her for a bit.'

'Wait.' The slave girl knelt beside her mistress, feeling her left arm. At the touch the young woman's dark eyes opened and she gasped in pain.

'Quiet now.' The slave spoke with all the tenderness of a mother. 'I know it hurts, but you must be brave.'

The young woman nodded, eyes wide and face taut as she held back her cries.

Beside her the slave had both hands around her mistress's shoulder. As she studied the injury her face was soft. It was a good face, Ferox thought, looking at her closely for the first time. A few faint lines around her eyes hinted at someone closer to thirty than twenty, although the life of a slave brought age quickly so he might be wrong. Some of her fair hair had worked loose from the pins and blew across her face until she brushed it away. She looked kind and capable, and he began to hope that the beatings were rare.

'We need to move,' he said.

'No.' Fierce anger was back and the face hardened as the slave girl looked up. 'I need to fix this and you must help. The shoulder is out of joint.'

Ferox shook his head. 'There is no time.'

'Make the time!'

Vindex rolled his eyes, but was grinning. 'Yes, your highness,' he said.

'Come next to me, be ready to move her arm as I tell you when I tell you.' She turned to her mistress. 'This will hurt, but it will make it better, so you must be brave.'

'I'll try.' The voice was weak.

'You,' she said, looking up at Ferox. 'Hold her down. She needs to be still.'

The centurion obeyed, putting one hand on the girl's good shoulder and the other across her body. There was fear in her eyes when he loomed over her, and it made him think of Hector frightening the baby because he still had his helmet on. He smiled.

'Lie still. Soon be over,' he said softly, while the slave gave short, sharp instructions to Vindex. The girl shrieked, starting to shake, and he pressed down as hard as he could.

'Good girl, good girl,' Ferox whispered, staring into her eyes, trying to reassure. A sound of grating bone almost made him flinch and loosen his grip.

'Now,' the slave girl said. 'Push!'

The scream was appalling and seemed to go on forever, the girl trying to arch her back so that it took all his strength to keep her flat and still.

Vindex let out a deep breath, and the scream faded and turned into sobs.

'Well done,' the slave said, brushing her mistress' cheek. 'Now we can go.'

Ferox eased his grip and started to lift the young woman. Vindex helped and they hauled her on to his shoulder and he set off. She was heavy for her size and he stumbled, making her yell out.

'Quiet,' he said as gently as he could and tried to shush her. The necklace was pressing hard against the cheek piece of his helmet. The yelling went on, very loud just next to his ear. He heard a slap and the girl went quiet.

'Well done, Vindex,' he said and started out across the mossy ground.

'Wasn't me,' the Brigantian said.

The slave girl strode past him, her expression blank.

'Trouble,' Vindex warned.

Shoulder already uncomfortable from the weight pressing down, Ferox struggled to look back at the little figures high on the crest above them. An arrow arched towards them, coming straight until the wind took it and it veered away.

'Run!' he said, and wondered how many times he had given the same order. The ambush had started less than an hour ago, and yet it seemed as though days had passed. He lumbered on as fast as he could, at first over spongy grass, but soon each step sank into soft mud.

'Bugger!' Vindex was looking to the west, where four horsemen galloped towards them who were not Romans. One was leading a riderless horse, and the leader carried a long red shield. There were more riders about a quarter of a mile behind them.

An arrow stuck into the soft earth just a yard or so away from Ferox, the missile going deep so that only half of its shaft and feathers were left above the mud. They were level with the lake, its dark waters still for the breeze had gone. Splashes came up with every step, boots sinking deeper and deeper.

'More of the bastards!' Vindex called. Other horsemen were coming from the south-west, and were not far off, hidden up to now by the valley. There were half a dozen, perhaps more, and Ferox could see no trace of uniform or anything else to identify them. They did not ride like Britons, but they were heading towards the main group of the enemy.

'This way!' The slave girl was pointing at a flat grey stone, the first of a line dotted towards the wood. Her feet and her once white sandals were brown from the mud, and Ferox was surprised that the clinging mire had not pulled them off.

Vindex gasped. 'Double bugger!' An arrow had grazed his right leg just above the knee, tearing his trousers and gouging a red line across his flesh. It must have had a broader head than the ones Ferox had seen before.

'Are you all right?' he asked, reaching out his free arm in an offer of support.

'Piss off!' the Brigantian said, pushing it away, and kept going. The slave girl was jumping from stone to stone, but even on that boggy ground Ferox could hear the hoof beats getting closer. They were at the first big stone.

'If you're all right then you take her. I'll try to slow them down.'

Vindex's face was grim as he took the weight of the girl, who immediately began to scream again.

A javelin whipped through the air between the two men just as they parted, missing them and the girl's legs by a whisker. The horseman who had thrown it wore a hooded cloak that streamed behind him, but was bare-chested like the two Ferox had killed. He was close, no more than ten paces away, and riding like a wild man, straight at them, his right hand reaching to draw his long sword. His horse threw up fountains of water, then one of its front feet went deeper and the animal stumbled, throwing the rider, who slid through the mire towards them.

'Stupid mongrel,' Vindex said and jumped to the second stone, which rocked under the weight.

The centurion drew his blade, splashed forward through the mud and stabbed down once. Ferox saw the same horse tattoo on the man's forehead before the long point of his gladius punched through the skull. For all his bravery, this third warrior was no more skilled than the other two. He had dropped his shield, a small one like the others, although round rather than square. Ferox picked it up.

The man with the red shield was a long spear cast away, but although he carried a slim-shafted javelin in his hand he made no move to throw it. He was a big man and yelled something at the warrior coming up alongside him, who was another of the bare-chested, animal-tattooed fighters, this time with his head shaved completely bald. A gesture confirmed that he was telling the man to stay back. The third horseman was little more than a beardless boy, fair-haired and red-cheeked, and was leading a saddled but riderless mare. There was no sign of any of the other horsemen.

Ferox bounded across the first few stones. If he must fight, then at least the mud would make it harder for anyone to come up on him from the side.

'Roman!' a deep voice shouted.

He turned and saw that the warrior with the red shield had dismounted. On foot he was huge, several inches taller than Vindex and broader across the shoulders than Ferox himself. He was bareheaded, with thick blond hair down to his shoulders and a neat beard. He wore boots and pale trousers, and had mail, with a black tunic underneath, the sleeves short and showing his powerfully muscled arms. A heavy, almost clumsy bronze bracelet was on his right wrist. His shield was hexagonal, a white star painted around the boss. He did not look like any warrior from the tribes of Britannia that Ferox had ever seen – more like a German, but that made no sense.

'Want the queen,' the man said, taking a step forward. He spoke in the language of the Celtic tribes, differing only in details among the peoples of Gaul as well as Britannia, but he did not speak it naturally. Each word took an effort to pronounce, and Ferox wondered whether he did not know the word for woman. He must be a German, perhaps an army deserter who had taken service with a chieftain?

'Why do you want her?' he asked in Latin. There was no sign of understanding, so he repeated the words in the Celtic tongue.

'An oath,' the warrior said and kept coming forward. Out of the corner of his eye, Ferox noticed that the boy was hanging back, but the bald-headed man had also dismounted and was wading through the mud. It would slow him down, but was not deep enough to stop him, let alone suck him down and smother him.

'Don't worry about him.' The voice of Vindex came from close behind. 'I'll sort him. You deal with the big bastard.'

'What about the women?'

'Oh, I tipped them in the bog.'

The big German was closer, his spear raised. 'The queen,' he bellowed, 'or I kill you both.'

'What?' Ferox glanced back, saw the Brigantian's cadaverous face broken by a toothy grin, and beyond him the blonde slave girl helping her mistress jump across the bridge of stones. They were almost at the wood.

'Look out!' Vindex yelled.

Ferox turned, saw the spear coming at him, the head glinting as it spun, and just had time to raise the shield and catch it on the boss. The blow dented the iron, rocking him back and jarring his arm. He ducked to avoid the deflected spear.

The German drew his sword, one of the long, slim *spatha*-swords issued to Roman cavalrymen.

'Come on, you eunuch, or do I have to sew your balls back on!' Ferox yelled at him in Latin.

There was no sign of understanding, and the big warrior came on. Ferox could see that this one knew what he was doing and in spite of his size was light-footed. The way the man moved reminded him of the big cats he had seen in the arena, those great lions and tigers which moved with such poise.

'Last chance,' the man said, his gaze never leaving the centurion. He jumped from the first to the second stone, water spurting up as his weight landed on it.

The bald warrior was struggling through the mud, but he had to trust Vindex to deal with the man. Ferox hefted the unfamiliar shield, keeping his sword low. He wondered whether he should have taken off the helmet, for speed might well be the key to this fight. It was too late now, with the big warrior only a couple of yards away. The man bounded forward again, and used the motion to lunge with his spatha. The blade was nearly three feet long, adding to the man's great length of arm as the point jabbed at him, faster than he expected. Ferox braced the shield, and saw the iron tip of the warrior's sword burst through the single layer of wood. He tried to keep it stuck in the wood, twisting the shield away in the hope of pulling the sword out of the warrior's hand, but the German was too quick for him. The big-bearded face broke into a smile.

Ferox jabbed low, saw the red shield blocking and pulled back, whipping the blade high for a thrust at the man's neck. The German swayed back and stopped grinning, but Ferox knew that he was in trouble. His opponent had a longer reach, and with the mud it would be hard for him to close the distance and get past his guard. The big German also looked fresh, whereas he was tired. He had one chance, and hoped that his memory was accurate. There was the sound of grunting and effort over to his left, which must be Vindex and the bald warrior trying their best to hew each other down as they struggled through the mud.

The German had his spatha held up, arm bent, ready to stab forward at eye level. Ferox watched, saw the slightest betraying flicker in the man's bright blue eyes and jumped back. His left foot landed on the next stone, the right boot squelching in mud, as the warrior jabbed at air. The centurion wrenched his foot out, feeling the leather uppers break apart as he left his boot in the clinging mud, and had his soaking sock on the stone. It was one of the larger rocks, wide and deep enough for him to stand, left foot forward and right behind, waiting. Better still, it was just a little nearer to the stone he had left than the one the German was on.

With a bellow of rage the warrior jumped, this time scything his blade in a great downward sweep. Ferox raised his shield, felt the wood cracking under the blow, and thrust, down low again, hit the edge of the red shield, went past and he felt it jar as it struck the mail rings. At least one had broken, and the long triangular tip speared through cloth and flesh. He pulled back quickly as the man slashed down again, going for his right hand.

Ferox had struck a blow, but doubted that it was enough, for there was only a little blood on his sword and he knew that the wound was not deep. The German swung again and he took the blow on the boss of his shield, feeling it dent in and the round piece of metal shudder. His own stab aimed higher than the last, only to meet his opponent's shield cleanly and be blocked.

The centurion was already tired, his breath coming in pants, while the German looked as if he was only warming up. Another downward hack and half the little shield fell away. Ferox made another attack on the same spot and it was blocked again. The sword swept down and more of the wooden board crumbled. There was little more than the boss left now. His own blade had scored the red shield, but not weakened its defence.

So this was death, the beckoning of the Otherworld. There was little for him here, but he still feared the journey to the land of shadows. He wondered whether his grandfather would speak to him or turn away in disgust. Would she be there? She had not believed in such things, but what did that matter?

Someone screamed in pain and either Vindex or his opponent must be down. The beardless youth was calling to the big warrior in a tongue he did not understand. It sounded urgent.

The German cut again and Ferox jumped to the side, slashing low as he dived into the mud and rolled. It took the warrior by surprise, and he felt his sword strike and cut the man's shin.

The boy leading the horse was shouting again. The warrior glanced down, decided not to jump into the clinging mud and finish his opponent and instead turned and bounded away from stone to stone. Ferox saw dark blood on the man's trouser leg, but knew that he would have died if the German had not run off. The warrior and the boy rode away eastwards. There were horsemen in the distance to the west, but he could not tell who they were.

'Some help would be nice,' Vindex called. The Brigantian was knee deep in mud, mail torn near the shoulder and blood seeping through it. His opponent was motionless, face down in the mire. As Ferox splashed over to help him he saw that there were figures with the women at the treeline. They were dressed in breeches, tunics and cloaks and their short hair showed them as Romans.

'Looks like we're still alive,' he said as he pulled Vindex free.

'Never doubted it for a moment,' the Brigantian said.

They made their way across the stones, covered in mud, their clothes ragged and torn.

To his surprise a tall, extremely handsome man with reddish hair was embracing the slave woman, while the little dark-haired girl stood meekly by her side, the unclasped necklace in her hands.

'I believe I owe you profound thanks,' the redhead said. He was dressed in hunting clothes, only a little stained by travel. His face was open, his hair perfectly in place and his teeth neat and very white. 'You have saved my wife and I am forever in your debt.'

'We owe you our gratitude,' the slave added. 'Although I do not know who you are – or even what you are?' There was a trace of mischief in her tone, and perhaps she saw the bafflement in his face.

'Titus Flavius Ferox, centurio regionarius, seconded from Legio II Augusta,' he said, trying not to think too much about his harsh words – or the slap on her behind. 'And this is Vindex, a noble warrior of the Carvetii and the leader of their scouts who serve with us.'

'Then I am honoured to meet you,' the man said, and shook their hands, even though they were filthy. 'I am Cerialis, Prefect of the Ninth Batavians, and may I name my wife, Sulpicia Lepidina.' She gave them a gracious smile.

Another man appeared, quite small and round-faced with thick hair that was a mottled grey even though he looked to be in his early twenties.

'Well, it looks as if you have all had quite an adventure,' he said cheerfully. 'I'm Crispinus, by the way, and equally pleased to know you. I have heard a lot about you, and I believe you know my father. In the meantime, I'm *tribunus laticlavius* with the Augusta, so I suppose that makes me your commanding officer – well, at least up in this part of the world.'

'*Omnes ad stercus*,' Ferox said under his breath.

IV

T HEY WERE A hunting party, laid on by Cerialis as entertainment for the visiting Crispinus, and even if they were only armed with boar spears, knives and a few swords, the band of twenty-eight riders and a dozen hounds had looked formidable and deterred the raiders.

'We saw the beacon,' Cerialis explained, 'so without hesitation rushed towards the road in case my wife was at risk.' He had sent a couple of riders to follow the British horsemen, while everyone else waited to see what they should do. Sulpicia Lepidina and her freedwoman, the little dark-haired girl, and a couple of slaves carrying bundles had gone off into the shelter of the wood.

'I am glad you did, sir,' Ferox told him. 'You saved us.' It was several hours after noon, with a few glimpses of blue between the slow-moving grey clouds.

'As I said before,' Cerialis said, patting him on the shoulder, 'it is I who am grateful to you for saving my most precious possession.' His smile was ready and full, yet Ferox could not help thinking that the man was acting, playing the part of the honest, brave and honourable man, and very aware of his audience. Still, educated Romans often seemed that way to Ferox, all of them soaked in rhetoric since youth so that they rarely sounded natural. It mattered to them to be seen to act in the way expected of a member of the equestrian order.

Some of that audience was less enthusiastic. Caius Claudius Super was the regionarius based at Luguvallium, the big base on the Western Road, tasked with the superversion of junior men like Ferox. He was from Legio VIIII Hispana, an equestrian directly commissioned into the army, and in Ferox's opinion had all the intelligence of a cowpat. 'If we had come any later then you would have been gutted by that big barbarian,' he said.

Ferox wondered whether the man was disappointed. Most equestrians who served in the army were like Cerialis, starting as prefect in command of an auxiliary infantry cohort and then holding a series of more important posts. Only those without the wealth or influence to follow that career joined as legionary centurions, and they always reminded their fellow officers of their superior social status. Claudius Super was worse than most, even if it was clear his family had barely scraped together the property needed to be registered as *equites* in the census. He was from Etruria, and openly disdained everyone and everything outside Italy. He did not care for any barbarians, despised the Brittunculi in general and the 'little Britons' of the north in particular as undisciplined, unreliable, untrustworthy, lazy and drunken. Ferox knew that Claudius Super considered that he was typical native of Britannia.

'It was not going well for me,' Ferox admitted.

'Indeed.' Claudius Super sounded like a schoolmaster taking delight in demolishing the arguments of one of his pupils. 'He looked a tall fellow, if not perhaps as big – or as German – as he seemed to you!' Ferox had mentioned his suspicion, only to have it dismissed. 'Damned barbarians, we shall have to go north and teach them a lesson. An iron hand' – he held his clenched fist in front of him – 'that is all these brigands understand, if only...'

Sulpicia Lepidina came out of the trees, her golden hair unpinned and hanging down around her shoulders. She wore a man's tunic, far too large so that it was loose and baggy even though she had gathered it close around her waist with a soldier's belt fastened as tight as it would go. It was a pale crimson and went down to her shins, so that only a little of the dark breeches she wore underneath were visible. She had on a man's shoes, the thongs drawn tight to keep them on as well as possible. Behind her came the freedwoman, a heavy woollen cloak pulled tight around her.

Claudius Super bowed, Crispinus smiled and Cerialis inclined his head. Ferox stood and stared. Lepidina was slim and straight, gliding more than walking. She was also beautiful, her fair skin flawless, features delicate, and her large round eyes full of life and wit. She was dressed like a man and still looked like a goddess come to earth. Ferox could not understand why he had not noticed before, wondered how he had ever mistaken her for a slave and inwardly cringed at what he had said and done.

'My lady, it is good to see you a little restored,' Cerialis said, 'but you should take my cloak as it may become cold.'

'That is kind, my lord, and I thank you.' Her voice was quite deep for a woman, yet still soft. She gestured to her servant and then called to Vindex. 'We have prepared a poultice. Bind it tightly to your leg and keep it on for three days. Keep it damp as well.'

Claudius Super looked surprised at this concern, before muttering, 'So kind,' and smiling with indulgence as the maid helped the Brigantian tie up his leg. The shoulder wound was not so serious, as most of the force had been absorbed by his mail, but they insisted on dressing it as well.

'Make sure that you keep it clean and bound up,' the lady told the scout. 'No need to coddle it. It will get stiff if you don't use it at all.'

'Thank you.' Vindex smiled, something that always looked more like a leer as he bared his prominent teeth. 'Your kindness is only matched by your beauty,' he added in his own language.

No one else had spoken while they waited. Ferox avoided meeting the lady's cold gaze.

When all was done it was she who took the initiative. 'I am ready to ride, if we are ready to depart?'

One of the huntsmen brought an unsaddled mare. The lady patted her head, spoke softly to her and then sprang up. 'It is easier like this,' Sulpicia Lepidina told them, beckoning to the freedwoman to come up behind her. She needed help, bunching her dress up so that she could sit astride, clasping her mistress as bidden. Two of the slaves were made to dismount and stay with the men in charge of the pack, so that their horses could be given to Vindex and Ferox.

They set out and soon met one of the riders that Cerialis had sent out earlier, who told them that the barbarians had fled and that there were Roman cavalry on the road coming from the east, so not Batavians from Vindolanda.

'If my lads weren't there first then I'll have words to say to the duty decurion,' Cerialis said cheerfully.

Keeping to the open fields, they climbed by a gentle route and soon encountered a patrol of cavalrymen with green shields and fur on their helmets – Batavians out from Vindolanda. Cerialis welcomed their commander by name, heard his report and then ordered them to fall in as escorts.

'You may wish to return to Vindolanda, my lady,' Cerialis said to his wife. 'I ought to take a look at the place of the ambush, but there is no need for you to see such things.'

'I was there, my lord. I have already seen much. Thank you for your concern, but it is safer if we stay together.'

'The barbarians have gone.'

'And we were assured that there was no great risk on the road,' the prefect's wife told him. Ferox wondered at the relationship between them. He guessed that Cerialis was a few years younger than his wife and perhaps that explained his willingness to defer to her. She was right to be cautious. He would expect raiders to flee once soldiers began to chase them, but this band had already done things that surprised him. On the other hand, he hoped that they would stop her from going too close. She may have seen some of the fighting, but that was not the same thing as looking in the cold light at the aftermath of a skirmish. The dead were rarely pretty.

By the time they reached the place they had met with more Batavian troopers, as well as a detachment of forty riders from the ala at Coria. Another party of legionaries with a mule convoy were at the ambush site, clearing up, so that there was little to see save rows of bodies neatly arranged, the dead Batavians covered with blankets.

'Our poor *raedula*,' Cerialis said, shaking his head at the sight of the carriage, one door hanging off and the wood scarred by arrows and from the fall. The legionaries had lifted it upright again. Two of the mules were dead and the other pair taken, but the soldiers unloaded some of their own beasts to provide a new team. Ferox found it odd to hear a grown man using a diminutive. The coach was a bit smaller than a normal four-wheeled *raeda*, but it was the sort of expression he expected from a woman trying to be charming.

One of the Batavians had escaped after charging the British horsemen. He was cut across the face, his helmet dented and cheek piece broken off, but he had ridden through them, so was able to tell his prefect what had happened. To Ferox's surprise, the man said that another of the troopers had survived. 'Longinus was thrown and knocked out cold. His horse rolled on top of him and he's badly bruised, but nothing seems to be broken, and he should be all right.'

The one-eyed, grey-bearded cavalryman was sitting up, drinking from a wineskin. Half the army was called Longinus, and it made Ferox wonder whether Batavian parents gave their sons military names because so many were destined to serve.

The man reporting to Cerialis seemed very relieved, even though two survivors from twelve was not many. Six of the bodies had been beheaded and another hacked about the head, arms and body so badly that it had not been worth taking a trophy. One of the corpses had its trousers pulled down and a dark patch of dried blood showed where the man had been castrated. Swords, armour, helmets and other weapons had all been taken, but nothing else, which suggested that the attackers had not had much time. A patrol from Coria, with the mule convoy close behind, had arrived less than half an hour after the attack, making the raiders leave in a hurry. They left behind five of their own, including the two Ferox had killed in the gully and another man also with a stallion tattooed on his forehead. Each of the three men's left hands was marked with a raven, wings folded. Ferox and Vindex exchanged glances, but said nothing. Claudius Super had already scoffed when Ferox suggested that the heavily tattooed leader of the ambush was some sort of priest or druid. According to the senior centurion, Ferox was starting at shadows, just trying to cover up his own failure.

'If only you had given the alarm earlier, none of this might have happened,' Claudius Super told Ferox.

'If my wife had not left later than planned,' Cerialis cut in, 'then it would have been a damned sight worse. There is no blame, and much praise for the centurion's quick thinking and brave actions.'

Claudius Super did not look convinced. Crispinus said nothing and just watched. As the son of a senator, and someone who would within a few years be enrolled in the Senate, he was a far more important man than anyone here and could speak or be silent as he wished. Ferox had the sense that he was watching and thinking. At the moment the centurion was too busy to worry, and too tired to work out where he had encountered the man's father, for it seemed an unlikely claim for the young man to have invented. Claudius Super was right about one thing – the alarm had been late, and men had died because of that. Women might have died too, or been raped and carried off. The fear about what had so nearly happened gnawed at him.

Ferox blamed himself for not listening to Vindex sooner, but even after that something was wrong. He had sent Victor to the tower, knowing him to be reliable and well mounted. The man should have reached the watchtower and the beacon been lit a good half-hour before the signal had gone up. Something was very wrong – yet another thing to add to the others that he did not understand.

'Fire and sword!' Claudius Super shouted the words angrily when someone told him about the castrated cavalryman. 'That's all these animals understand and it's all we should ever give them!'

Ferox let him rant, for he was busy searching for arrows and had only managed to find one, hidden in the grass and broken off six inches from the head. He felt the tip. It was not iron, or even bronze, but bone of some sort, narrow and carefully sharpened. The archers must have picked up the missiles they had used, even the damaged ones, and taken them away to repair. A legionary, seeing him looking, produced a second stump.

'Thank you.' This one was iron, similar in shape, so that all the power was behind the narrow pointed head. Ferox had never seen ones like this, and remembered the great force behind them as they had gone past or struck the carriage.

One *turma* from Coria had already gone north after the raiders. Cerialis decided to take thirty of his men to join the chase, while Crispinus and the rest escorted his wife back to Vindolanda. The prefect took Claudius Super with him, 'to make use of his experience', and Ferox doubted that it was concern for their fatigue that prevented either of them from asking or ordering Vindex to go as well. Well, let them chase. He doubted that they would catch anyone and was more concerned to ride to the watchtower and find out what why it had taken them so long to fire the beacon.

They rode west, the sun low in the sky, turning the clouds pink and gold ahead of them. Vindex had kept his hat through all the day and Ferox was glad to have it back and shade his eyes from the dazzling light. A dozen big Batavians went ahead of the carriage, with another twenty bringing up the rear. The lady rode bareback, having given the coach to the two wounded troopers and her maid – the latter briefly reluctant to be confined in the car with two soldiers, however enfeebled by injury. The legionaries had taken the loose door off rather than let it hang, so her mistress had persuaded her that it was safe. Whenever Sulpicia Lepidina passed one of the Batavians he raised hand to forehead and then touched it over his heart. Ferox could see that they were devoted to her, no doubt helped by her kindness to their comrades, especially the one-eyed veteran Longinus.

For a while she rode alongside the carriage, talking to her

maid and the injured men. Crispinus kept two lengths behind, still saying nothing to Ferox and Vindex as they followed. After a while the lady laughed, throwing her head back so that her long hair shook. Most of the soldiers grinned even though they had no idea of the source of her mirth. Soon afterwards she wheeled her horse around and came back, acknowledging Crispinus with a nod but passing him. Much to Ferox's amazement she turned the mare again to fall in alongside him.

'My lady,' he said, dipping his head and trying to avoid her gaze. He felt shabby and brutish alongside this golden woman, and deeply uncomfortable as she rode in silence next to him.

'M-my lady,' he stammered the words again. 'I must... That is to say, I wish to apologise for my conduct earlier.'

She laughed, head going back once again and hair glistening red in the light of the setting sun. Ferox looked at her, seeing a face so full of life that it was infectious.

'Am I to understand that you are apologising for saving my honour or life or both?' Her teeth were very white, her lips curling back as she chuckled. 'Is it such a source of regret? I suppose you could always hope that we are attacked again, so that you can stand aside and do nothing.'

Crispinus turned around in the saddle and winked at him.

'I did not mean—' Ferox broke off, finding her amusement infectious. 'You must forgive my clumsiness and the boorish way I treated you earlier on.'

'Oh, that,' she said. 'It was a little unusual, that is true. Not quite what I expect from a respectable army officer. You are respectable, I take it?'

'Thoroughly.'

'I thought the appearance must be a disguise.' She looked him up and down. 'It is a very good disguise. Do not worry. That is not to give you licence to maul me about or shout orders, but the occasion was unusual and we are both still alive, so it seems to have been justified. It is I who thanks you. If you had not arrived then it would surely have been unpleasant.'

Ferox thought she spoke as if they were discussing some breach of etiquette at a dinner.

'How do you know such things?' he asked, encouraged by her friendliness. 'The way you dealt with your girl's shoulder, the poultice and everything.'

'Roman nobles raise their daughters to run a household. That means that we must know about everything if we are not to make a mess of it or be cheated blind by our slaves.'

'Your husband is most fortunate,' he said and meant it. There was something overwhelming about this woman.

There was a smile now, but a thin one. An excited squeal came from the coach. 'I had better see what that silly girl is doing. She has had excitement enough today, trying on some of my jewellery. You would have thought that that and surviving a brutal ambush was enough for one day. Must she really flirt now?' she said and nudged her mare forward. He watched her go, cloak flung back, sitting as comfortably and naturally as a Numidian. Even in the plain, unflattering clothes, her hair wild and loose, she was beautiful and somehow out of place – not just here in the frontier, but anywhere in this grim, squalid world.

Vindex started to hum a tune that was as old as the hills, sung by Britons and Gauls alike, telling of the first meeting between a great hero and the queenly, magical woman who would become his wife. The names changed from place to place, but some of the lines never altered – 'I see a sweet country; I'll rest my weapon there.'

A little later Crispinus eased back and joined the centurion. 'I understand you will not come with us all the way?'

'No, my lord, I want to go to the watchtower. I sent one of my men to raise the alarm, but it took far longer than it should.'

The young tribune considered this. 'Probably nothing, but you may be right to check. When will you leave us?'

'Another mile.'

'Will it not be dark by then?'

'Yes, sir.' The tribune appeared to be expecting more, so after a moment Ferox went on. 'I'd prefer to look in daylight, but if something has happened better to know about it as soon as possible. If nothing has happened then it does not matter.'

'Well, you know best.' Crispinus grinned, looking boyish in spite of his prematurely grey hair. 'You don't know who I am, do you?'

'A noble officer, from the highest family, and of unimpeachable virtue.'

'That means you have not got a clue!' The tribune's sudden roar of laughter lacked the gentleness of the lady's. 'I fear sometimes we forget that the world does not follow the breeding habits of the upper class as avidly as we do. There are no doubt gladiators and actors more famous than half the Senate.

'Well, my father was Marcus Atilius Serranus, legate of Legio VII Claudia pia fidelis, *comes* of the late and unlamented Caesar Domitian.' He watched the centurion. 'Ah, I see that you do remember. May I add that my uncle is Sextus Julius Frontinus, former legate of Britannia and close advisor to the deified – and much lamented – Nerva and friend of our *princeps*.'

'Ah,' Ferox said in recognition and because he could not think of anything else to say. His grandfather had surrendered to Frontinus, after the legate spent four years waging savage war against the Silures of the south-west. It was the culmination of decades of struggle and 'We lost, but at least we didn't make it easy for the bastards' as the Lord of the Hills used to say. According to the terms of the capitulation, Ferox was one of several boys sent as hostages and to be part of the new order.

'Titus Flavius Ferox.' Crispinus stopped after he had said the name. He did not look much like his father, who was a bigger man, dull and unimaginative, although a better commander than many senators put in charge of a legion. Serranus had saved the life of Ferox and his men more than once.

'Let me see,' Crispinus continued after a suitably dramatic pause. 'Ferox, let me remember it all. Yes, the first Silurian made a citizen and commissioned as centurion in Legio V Alaudae,' he said, pleased to parade his knowledge. 'Renowned for his courage, picked to command the *exploratores* scouting for the expedition across the Danube, warned of the danger of ambush in vain, but when the legion was cut to ribbons he managed to lead a force that cut its way out of the disaster under Fuscus, rescued by a certain legate of VII Claudia, decorated for valour, served with distinction against Dacians and Chatti, decorated again – and I may note saved again by the same legate – then promoted into XXI Rapax and sent to the Rhineland, only to get caught up in that nasty business with Saturninus' plot against Domitian.' That was an understatement for long weeks of investigations, surrounded by informers and torturers plying their trade, all leading to dozens of suicides and executions. Only a lucky handful escaped with exile and disgrace. Ferox had been told to discover the truth and that was what he had done. It did not make it any easier to live with the consequences. Too many had died, and the only woman he had ever loved had vanished. He still did not know why, or where she had gone, because he had been posted to Britannia and not allowed to look for her.

'It is quite a career,' the tribune concluded.

'I know, I lived it,' Ferox said.

'Yes, Father always said that you had no manners. But he also said that you were a remarkably brave man, one of the ablest officers and certainly the most cunning fighter he had ever met. Uncle Frontinus just told him all that summed up the Silures – at least if you added in their cruelty. But one thing stood out all the more to him – and that was your obsession with the truth. Uncle said that was not like any Silurian he had met.'

'He did not know us well, my lord.'

'Bugger hammered you even so,' Vindex said in a low voice, 'so I reckon he knew something about you.'

Crispinus was amused and did not resent the intrusion. 'It is quite a record.'

'As I said, I know.' Ferox was remembering something else and failing to convince himself that this young aristocrat did not know. He was indebted to Frontinus as patron, but he had sworn an oath to Atilius Serranus, pledging to serve the man and his family and protect them with his life. The man had forced it out of him, as the price for sending men back to save a detachment of Ferox's exploratores who had been left behind, but that did not matter. An oath was an oath.

'Your first legion destroyed, its eagle and honour lost, your second disbanded in disgrace and the survivors mostly killed in another disaster.' Crispinus spoke as if these were minor misfortunes. 'I'm thinking the Second Augusta were none too pleased when you were posted to them!'

Vindex cackled. The noise was so loud that heads turned, including that of Lepidina, who looked puzzled. Seeing her the Brigantian started humming again, glancing at Ferox all the while.

The tribune must have noticed. 'She is something truly special, is she not?' he sighed.

'Earlier today I mistook her for a slave,' Ferox confessed. 'I may have treated her a little roughly.'

Crispinus burst out laughing once again, tears in his eyes, and could say nothing for a long time. Sulpicia Lepidina glared for a moment, a look Ferox remembered well, but then resumed her poise and ignored them.

'Well,' Crispinus said once he had mastered himself, 'there are little slave girls with all the grace of empresses – and aristocratic women who act like slaves or sluts. She is most definitely neither. She is the daughter of a consul, with ten generations of senators for ancestors, and carries herself so that even such a background seems a mean thing compared to her own dignity.'

'Well, that makes me feel better,' Ferox said, making the tribune relapse back into uncontrollable laughter.

The sun was setting when Ferox and Vindex peeled away from the road. Sulpicia gave them a smile and nod, Crispinus a hearty wave.

'Always search for the truth,' he called after them.

The truth proved to be grim as they rode up to the tower, lit by a red glow from the dying embers of the beacon. Victor stood on the high balcony that went all around the tower just beneath its shingle roof. He had lit torches and placed one at each corner, but kept back in the shadows until he saw them. His horse was tethered to a post inside the circular ditch surrounding the tower. The outpost had no stockade, for it was felt unlikely that anyone would ever attack it.

'Thank the gods you're here, centurion!' he shouted down. They could already guess some of the story from the body lying just a few feet outside the tower's single door. It took a while for Victor to come down, for he had pulled the ladder up on to the highest floor so that no one could get to him.

Seven men were serving at the tower this week, their names written on the wax tablet hanging from a nail inside the door. There were a couple of legionaries, and five auxiliary infantrymen from three different cohorts. Now there were six corpses and no sign of the last man. By torchlight Ferox examined the scene as Victor told his story. The cavalryman had made good time, but when he reached the tower there was no one on guard, the body outside and the rest on the ground floor. The door had not been forced, and there was little sign of a struggle. There was a lot of blood, long dried but still stinking. Only one of the men was in armour, and someone had grabbed him from behind and slit his throat. Ferox could see the blood on the neckerchief and all down the scales of his cuirass. The rest were half dressed and had been hacked down before they had much chance to fight. Ferox leaned down and saw that two of the men had deep cuts to their arms. Another had his left arm sliced off just below the elbow. He imagined the desperate, terrified men crouching, arms held up for protection as the blades slashed again and again.

From what Victor said they must have been killed early in the day – perhaps at dawn or soon afterwards. Even if he had sent warning as soon as Vindex arrived at Syracuse he could not have saved them.

Victor had done well. The beacon was prepared, but someone had taken the flints and kindling, and shattered the pot of oil kept to light it. A little had survived in one shard, and he had found a tiny piece of old flint among the rubbish piled in the ditch behind the tower. Somehow he had got a fire lit and then set the piled timbers aflame. It had taken most of an hour, but he had done it. Then he had climbed to the top of the tower, pulling up the ladder, and waited through the long day, surrounded by the stench of blood and butchered flesh.

Ferox asked if he wanted to ride straight back to Syracuse, but the man said that he would wait until they left, or would stay if the centurion felt that the tower needed to be manned. In fact Ferox planned to leave soon, just wanting to look one more time. Once he had done that, he helped them drag the corpse from outside back into the lower chamber of the wooden tower.

Ferox had found a lock and used it to fasten the door from the outside. After that they left, riding through the still night to Syracuse. They rode in silence apart from the breathing of the horses and the jingle of harness. Ferox wondered whether he had the energy to write the reports he knew needed to be sent. Most of all he wondered about the names on the duty roster, for one of them was British. The man might be among the corpses, but he might not, and that was worrying. Crispinus had told him to search for the truth. As so often in the past, Ferox feared where it would lead.

V

FEROX HEFTED THE shield again, holding the cross-grip tight enough to be secure without becoming rigid. His sword was high, arm back and elbow bent almost double ready to jab the blade forward at eye level, striking for the face, or lunging over the top of his opponent's shield if he saw a gap open. It was not his own gladius and felt heavy and cumbersome in his hand.

Both men were breathing hard, watching for their chance. Ferox's arms and legs ached, and his right shoulder was sore from a slamming cut that he had not seen in time. He suspected that the blow had driven some of the rings of his mail through the padded jerkin to bruise the skin. The centurion stamped forward with his left foot and punched with the boss of his shield, the weight of his body behind the blow. His opponent lifted his own shield to block as he sprang back, landing well and cutting down with his longer sword, catching Ferox on the helmet. It was a weak blow with no real force in it and did not bother him.

Ferox panted as they both went back to watching and waiting. This one was good, old in war and dark in cunning, and the centurion was weary with not much more to give. The greaves on his shins were heavy and uncomfortable. He was sure the top of the left one had cut into his skin. If he did not win soon then he was finished. He let his shield drop a little before raising it with visible effort, wanting the man to think that he was even more tired.

The Thracian shouted, the first cry in an otherwise silent

fight, and came at him, slamming his lighter oval shield high and jabbing with the point of his sword. Ferox went back, step by step, giving ground and not getting a chance to reply to the flurry of blows from left and right. He was near the post now, the ditch only a couple more paces behind him. One jab punched through the wickerwork near the top of his curved rectangular shield and he tried to twist it to trap the blade, but the Thracian was too quick and while Ferox's guard was down scythed his long sword through the air and struck his left shoulder. The centurion staggered, hissing with pain, and lost his hold on the shield's handgrip so that it fell to the ground. The Thracian grinned wickedly as the centurion crouched.

Ferox sprang up, flinging himself against the cavalryman, hurling them both sideways. His hand grabbed the Thracian's right wrist, pushing it so that his long spatha was driven against the heavy wooden post. Ferox cut at it, not with much of a swing but with all his force, and there was a sharp crack as the wooden training spatha broke. Half the blade was hanging down loose and the Thracian was so surprised that Ferox was able to hook one foot around his leg and trip him up.

The watching soldiers sighed in disappointment, until someone started laughing and the rest joined in. The Textoverdi who had started to come to watch just stayed wrapped tight in the cloaks, their faces expressionless, after the manner of the clan.

'Time!' called the man on sentry duty in the gate-tower of Syracuse.

'Nearly, but not quite,' Ferox said, reaching his left hand down to pull the Thracian up. He had promised any man five denarii and an amphora of good wine if they could put him on his back. This was the fourth day, and so far he had not had to pay, although Victor had come close more than once, as had this Thracian. They were the pick of the bunch, the rest solid enough and stubborn, but too tied to the drill book to be really good. It was good training for them, and even better for him. Ferox was worried and drove himself hard to prepare for whatever was coming. He spent an hour each day working at the fencing post outside Syracuse, using the regulation wooden swords and wickerwork practice shields to go through the fighting drills the army had copied from the gladiatorial schools. Sword and shield were heavier than the real things, to strengthen the arms and make it easier when a man was given proper equipment. For the same reason he wore helmet and mail, and strapped iron greaves on to his lower legs. He had never liked greaves, clumsy things that made a man slow, and rarely wore them even in battle, but the weight made every drill harder and that helped. Once that was done he let three of the stationarii challenge him, each bout lasting a tenth of an hour measured by the water clock. Nothing matched facing a real opponent, and they had landed quite a few good blows and surprised him plenty of times. It reminded him of how rusty he had become, letting himself become lazy because things were quiet and no one believed him when he claimed that trouble was brewing.

When there was time he ran – at least three miles a day, choosing routes that forced him to drive himself up steep hillsides. There was no need to look for opportunities to get on a horse, for each day he rode many miles. He went to Vindolanda several times and to Magna, the next garrison to the west, up to the watchtower again, and all the while did his own job of going to villages and farms and meetings with chieftains. He spent most of his time listening to the usual grievances. With harvest done, taxes were due and the procurator's men were out collecting the empire's share of grain, livestock or hides, and sometimes money, although few in this part of the world paid levies in coin.

Ferox drove himself hard and, as always when he was kept busy, had no urge to drink more than was needed to slake a thirst. Her face still came to him, hazier now after all these years, but still with the dark eyes, olive skin and raven-black hair. The memories made him sad, but sometimes he pictured another woman, blonde, fair-skinned and blue-eyed, and there was little similarity in looks but something akin in their essence, that sense of life and joy.

Sulpicia Lepidina puzzled him, not least because if all Crispinus had said was true then it was odd to find so distinguished a lady married to a mere equestrian.

That was one mystery, but not the foremost in his mind. Cerialis had chased the raiders for two days before losing their trail altogether. By then his Batavians were running short of hard tack and salted bacon for the men and barley for the horses, so they returned to Vindolanda with nothing to show for their pains. The detachment from Coria was better prepared to take the field and had gone further, pushing well north into the lands of the Selgovae and Votadini. Even so they had not caught up with any of the raiders and had ended up coming back down the Eastern Road with nothing to show for all their hard riding. No word had yet come from the Brigantian scouts, although Vindex had ridden after them in spite of his injuries.

'Go on then and kill yourself,' Ferox told him as he left. 'At least it will save me the trouble.' The Brigantian had kept the poultice damp and tied on tightly and claimed that he felt fine.

The raiders had got away, avoiding roads and outstripping the pursuit. They were well mounted – even bringing spare horses – and well prepared. They had also taken nothing that might slow them down. All they had looted was some weapons, some horses and a few heads as trophies. It was not much of a haul, and Claudius Super was hailing the raid's repulse as a great victory, ignoring the dead Batavians – and the men at the tower.

By the time Ferox had returned to the tower in daylight a party had come to clear up and the ground was even more disturbed. Even so he was sure that there were no tracks from a group like the raiders they had followed on the day of the ambush. There were prints from half a dozen or so army horses, heavily burdened with their riders and gear. Whoever had killed the little garrison had not had to force their way in. Everything pointed to the killers being soldiers – or looking the part of soldiers – and being let inside to unleash sudden violence. The seventh man from the tower was still missing. Four of the corpses had been recognised, and the

Briton was not among them, nor was he thought likely to be either of the remaining corpses, given that they were dark-skinned and stocky. They should know soon when men came from his unit to look at the remains.

Ferox had not been able to find the track made by the horsemen as they left the tower because there were too many trails from the frequent patrols passing this place. In spite of a careful search he could see no sign that they had gone east to join the raiders. Yet a coincidence was hard to accept. Someone had slaughtered the men at the beacon on the very day that the raiders struck. Only Victor's quick thinking and some luck had allowed the alarm to be raised at all.

It all looked very deliberate and well planned, for these were not normal raiders. They had disguised their numbers coming south, moving stealthily past the garrisons, and would have escaped notice altogether if it had not been for Vindex and his men finding their trail and then coming across the two corpses. From the beginning the aim was surely to attack the road at that one spot between Vindolanda and Coria. Ferox could not believe that the raiders were trusting to luck, relying on something worth attacking to come along at the right moment. They were waiting for Sulpicia Lepidina and her escort, waiting just for her. He thought of the big warrior demanding that they hand over the queen.

Raiders liked to take women. Seizing a woman from an enemy and forcing her gave a warrior power, strengthening his spirit and proving his might, as much or even more than killing a man and taking his head as trophy. Yet rape of an officer's wife and her maid hardly justified the scale of the attack. They could be sold as slaves, it was true, or ransomed, although this was likely to provoke a major response by the army rather than payment. Perhaps whoever was behind this wanted war, but again it seemed an unnecessarily complicated way to go about it.

Ferox had not yet spoken again about the tattooed priest who had led the raiders, for Romans tended to become hysterical when they heard words like priest or druid, and Claudius Super would once again dismiss him as alarmist and certainly would not understand. Lots of men and some women called themselves druids these days, and most were wandering healers and magicians of no importance, preying on the superstitious, but without real power or any reputation. This one was bold, daring to break the sign at the Mother and Daughter and scratch the images on to the stones. Then there were warriors, each tattooed on forehead and left hand. They were not marks he had seen or heard of before among the tribes – and neither had Vindex, who knew the peoples to the north well. Warriors liked to look different, not the same, and he had never heard of any people marking themselves with such prominent and identical symbols. That meant that they must mean something, and he wondered about oaths to gods or to follow their servant on earth. Yet alongside these fierce but inexperienced followers there had been other warriors, not marked in the same way, as well as the big man. Ferox was still convinced that the giant was a German, and was equally sure that he was not a deserter. That begged many questions that he could not answer.

On the fifth morning Ferox attacked the post with unusual savagery. He found that he thought best during this exercise, going through the proper guards, cuts and thrusts and quite a few moves of his own. He was not aching as much as in the first few days, but his mind was weary. He had been roused before dawn by a farmer claiming that thieves were taking his cows. Hastily dressed and accompanied by Victor, he had given chase. The trail was easy to follow and stretched no more than five miles to a farm in another valley. The head of that household was muddy and travel-stained and did not bother to deny the charge, insisting instead that he had only taken back what was his. There was much shouting, swearing of oaths and a few threats, the noise fuelled as neighbours wandered over to see what was happening. Ferox was still not sure of the truth of the matter, but suspected villainy on both sides. The men agreed to be judged by two chieftains, one to speak for each man, with the centurion to arbitrate and give the casting vote. It would almost certainly come to that, since he would be surprised if the chiefs did not simply back their dependant whatever the truth of the matter.

Back at Syracuse, Ferox read a new report that added nothing to their knowledge of the raid, but took a long time to say it. He dealt with Crescens, who had brought a number of trivial matters to him. The man seemed to have lost a lot of his bluster and was looking for guidance on more and more matters. Ferox kept hoping that he would take up the challenge to fight him, even though he realised that putting the curator down would probably not be good for discipline. The stationarii were a very mixed bunch, with a few eager volunteers among men sent here because their units did not want them.

Ferox lunged at the post, then stepped back before coming in again and cutting at head height, his shield all the while held up over his body. The German warrior bothered him. During one of his visits to Vindolanda he had asked to see the two survivors from the escort. The man cut across the face was in hospital, head bandaged.

'Ask whatever you like,' the orderly told him. 'But his wits are in and out at the moment. Woke up screaming last night and said that there were horses chasing him and wanting to trample him beneath their hoofs.'

The man seemed well enough, sitting on the side of a cot and playing dice with another convalescent. If anything he enjoyed telling his story, which did not tell Ferox anything new.

Longinus was in the barrack block occupied by his turma and Ferox got the impression that the Batavians were not keen on letting him visit. They were a strange, clannish bunch, the closed expressions of the soldiers stopping just short of insubordination, and he had to insist for some time before a soldier led him to the right part of the fort. Men working on tack and equipment under the shelter of the colonnade running the length of the building watched him with cold eyes.

For all that, Longinus was welcoming when Ferox knocked on the open door of the room at the far end of the block. He was the only man there, and there were no blankets on either of the other two low beds. As he perched on the side of one, Ferox wondered if they belonged to men killed in the ambush. The old Batavian sat on his bed running a whetstone along the edge of his long spatha. When he tried to get up, obviously with some discomfort, Ferox gestured to him to sit. 'No need to stand on ceremony,' he said. 'But if you are not too tired I'd like to draw on your experience.'

'Sir.' An old soldier could make that short word do so many things.

The floor was covered in straw and rushes, fresh layers piled on the old and all giving off a musty odour. There were sounds from beyond the back wall. Cavalry barracks were built with a line of ten rooms backing on to ten horse boxes. Up above was an attic for storage and the army felt that it was convenient for troopers to be near their horses. It also meant that the rich scents of manure, horse sweat and old leather were everywhere, and there were always flies crawling on the walls or buzzing through the air.

'You have been with the cohort a long time, I understand.'

'Sir.'

Ferox had been surprised to learn that the man had served over forty *stipendia* – fifteen years more than the normal enlistment. It was not his business to ask why, and Longinus did not seem inclined to talk about it. He must be nearly sixty, and yet still remarkably hale.

Instead the centurion asked the man to tell him about the ambush. 'All that you can remember – no matter how trivial it seems.'

The man's single eye glinted in the dim room. Ferox felt that the veteran was studying him, amusement mingled with curiosity. His account was precise and matter-of-fact. The decurion was dozy, led them into it, letting the scout get out of sight so that he did them no good. Then the arrows had come.

'Have you faced archers like that before?'

'No.' The eye never left his face. There was a steady grating sound as the old soldier honed the edge of his sword.

Then the sling stones hit them, more arrows, and the screaming charge. Longinus told him about the testudo, the brief respite, of the carriage nearly escaping, until the driver was killed and it tipped over. 'Got a bit hot then,' he said. Ferox knew from his own experience how hard it was to remember a fight after it was over, and how it was even harder to recount it. Men who told long detailed stories of battles and heroism were usually making it up.

'Did you get a good look at the Britons?' he asked.

Longinus snorted. 'Too damned good – the buggers were swarming all over us.'

'Notice anything odd about them?'

The eye was still fixed on him. Longinus stopped sharpening his sword and reached up to scratch his empty eye socket.

'How did you lose that?' Ferox asked, letting curiosity get the better of him.

'Cut myself shaving. Now what did you ask before?' The man's Latin was good, for all his slang. He had a Rhineland accent, but did not clip the ends of words or roll his vowels like most of them.

'You have been in Britannia a while.'

'Sir.'

'Well, what did you think about the attackers? Were they like other Britons you have seen?'

There was the slightest nod. 'Some of them. Not seen those daft ones with the painted heads before. Not much skill in them, but they came on well enough. A couple were wearing tunics without breeches. Don't see that much hereabouts.'

Ferox had not noticed that little detail. Thinking back he thought the men he had fought had all been in trousers, but it was so hard to remember everything. At the time he had worried more about not getting killed. 'And the others?'

'Ah, you noticed.'

'Big men, one of them really big, heavier set than Caledonians, if just as fair.'

'Germans,' Longinus said, 'or I'm a Syrian.'

'Germans?'

'That's right. Don't tell me you had not thought the same thing.'

'I wondered, but they told me I was a fool,' Ferox said, half to himself.

'Can't say one way or the other about that, sir. But they were Germans. They did not have time to say much, but the words were in German. I met one of the Gotones once who talked like that. At least, people said that he was one of them and he certainly wasn't from any tribe we knew well. These ones sounded the same. They're from far away – the east, or maybe from the north, but enough akin to the closer races to recognise.'

'Thank you, trooper, that is very helpful.'

A horse whinnied loudly from the next room, then started to kick hard against something wooden. 'Excuse me, sir.' Longinus looked up and yelled through the trapdoor into the attic. 'You there, Felix?' There was the sound of panicked movement and then stillness in response. 'I know you're there, boy!' There was a low acknowledgement. 'Do your job, you little bugger!' Longinus shouted. 'They want feeding, so get on with it!' The one eye fixed on the centurion again. 'Good enough lad, but you have to chase him or he'll dream the day away.'

Ferox got up.

'Sir?'

'Yes, trooper?'

'Bad business at the watchtower.'

'Yes.'

Longinus winked – or since he had just the one eye perhaps it was a blink, although Ferox did not think that it was involuntary. 'Something is rotten, sir. And there is something in the air that isn't good. Smelled it before, or something much like, and that ended in a lot of killing.'

'Thank you once again, trooper.'

Ferox wondered what the old soldier had meant, but did not doubt the conviction or the shrewd mind in that battered, one-eyed face. He also wondered why the man had not been promoted after all these years. Drink perhaps, or insubordination, or perhaps for all his sharp mind Longinus could not read and write well enough.

Yet others sensed something similar. It had been growing for a while, but since the raid he noticed a dark mood among the Textoverdi. 'Bad times,' men said to him over and over again. 'There's a storm coming and a cruel winter.' People were worried and they would not tell him why, or perhaps they could not explain, something they sniffed in the wind like the one-eyed Batavian. 'Bad times.'

Ferox launched a fresh assault on the post, hacking with more fury than skill until he was pouring with sweat. He had seen horsemen coming down the valley, but knew he could not hurry them so kept at his exercises.

'I'll give you five to four on the post,' Vindex announced as he reined in.

Ferox nodded, breathing heavily. 'Well, it is a very good post.'

'Got good news and bad,' the Brigantian continued, his skull-like face serious even by his standards.

'Let's have the bad news.'

'No, let's have a drink and then all the news.' Vindex sprang down and walked with him into the outpost.

'We found the Goat Man's boy,' he said, staring down into his flagon of beer, sitting on a three-legged stool in the centurion's quarters. The room still showed the damage from the struggle to rouse him all those days ago, in spite of Philo's best efforts. Ferox was sticking to well-watered posca but was thirsty after his exercise and glad to have it.

'He is dead?'

Vindex nodded and there were tears in his eyes. 'The bastards buried him.' He could see that the centurion did not understand. 'He wasn't dead. They just trussed him up and buried him on a mound beside a stream.'

He drank for a while, brooding and angry, and Ferox thought it better to let him. He knew that his own rage would grow. People did not come and do this on his patch.

'We caught one,' Vindex said after a long wait, the silence only broken by the crackling of the fire. 'One of the mad buggers with the horse on his head. He was Hibernian, came across the water to follow the Stallion, the seer blessed by Cocidius and the Morrigan to lead the peoples in the war that will end the world. Reckon that's the lad we saw at the ambush, waving them on. This boy swore that this Stallion has powerful medicine, and is blessed by the gods, who want him to purge the whole island of the corruption of Rome.'

'Nice names and nice ambition,' Ferox said. 'But you said "was"?'

'We didn't do it – not that we didn't want to after finding the boy. He strayed from the rest. Told us a dream told him to look for a sacred oak and cut a branch from it. He left a track a blind man could follow and we took him by surprise. Knocked him around a bit to get answers, though in truth he talked readily, boasting almost, so knocking him about was more for fun.

'The next day we had him with hands tied behind his back and a man leading his horse, when he just starts chanting. On and on he went in a nasty, high-pitched voice. Then all of a sudden his horse gallops off and he flings himself down. Head hit a stone, lights out forever. Think it was deliberate, but can't be sure.'

'That is a pity.'

'Aye. Still, he told us a lot. The Stallion and his men set out from the far north-east, sent by a high king of the Vacomagi. Said he didn't know his name.'

Ferox whistled through his teeth. 'Didn't know the Vacomagi had a high king.'

'Well, that's what he said, and from the way they were going they were heading that way. The lad claimed this king realised the truth of the gods' purpose for this great Stallion or horse's arse or whatever he's called and gave him warriors and horses to help in his quest. Some of the warriors were from deep beneath the sea, summoned to help by the great druid.'

'Not horse's arse?' Ferox asked.

'No, this one is different, much more powerful. The lad said something about the Stallion being a great storm to sweep the land clean, while this great druid is part of the land itself. Old and wise, he is able to change his shape and work even greater magic. They say he walks among the Romans when he wants and they do not see him. That he can make them turn their swords on each other. He wasn't with the raiders, but they saw him now and again, shaped like a raven and flying above them.'

Ferox listened as the Brigantian continued, telling everything he had learned about the Stallion and this carefully planned raid. .

'What did they want to do?'

When Vindex told him the room turned cold, even on this bright day and with a good fire burning.

'Bad times,' he muttered.

'Aye.'

VI

I T WAS THE sixth day after the Ides of September and the
birthday of the new Caesar, Marcus Ulpius Trajan, adopted
son of the deified Caesar Nerva who had ascended to the
imperial purple on the same day. It was also raining steadily, had
been raining since before dawn and showed every sign of raining
for the rest of the long day. Ferox hoped it was not an omen,
although if every drab, dank and windy morning in these parts
were a bad omen, then the world would be a grim place indeed.

Bad times. A storm coming. The phrases kept going through
his head.

Vindex was unhappy, although not for that reason. 'Do I have
to go?'

'Yes.'

Both men wore hooded Gallic cloaks, drawn tight around them.
The hood shadowed the Brigantian's face and made his expression
especially bleak and sinister.

'I do not like crowds,' he said, in the tone of a man announcing
that he did not care to have his feet roasted over an open fire, but
was resigned to the ordeal. They were riding to Vindolanda to
witness the sacrifices to mark the occasion and the festivities to
follow. There was also to be a meeting of senior officers on the
following day and Ferox was required to be present to explain
what he had learned about the ambush and report on the mood
in his region. He wanted the Brigantian to be there if this was
permitted, or at least be on hand in case he needed to ask him

82

about anything. For all that Ferox remained unsure how much he would reveal. He feared treachery, probably by someone of high rank, and knew none of the men well enough to trust.

Behind the two horsemen trailed an unhappy Philo, riding a borrowed army mule. The Alexandrian had insisted on accompanying his master to make sure that Ferox was turned out respectably. No doubt the boy had long since begun regretting his persistence.

'There it is.' Ferox did not bother to point as the fort was barely a quarter of a mile in front of them. On a clear day they would have seen it long ago, not least when they crossed the ridge to the north, but today the mist and rain had hidden the base until the last minute.

'Too big,' Vindex muttered. 'They must live like rats down there.'

There were dozens of buildings in front of the fort – houses, shops and bars. Wherever the army stopped, such settlements or *canabae* grew up, filled with people wishing to take on contracts for the army or sell things to the soldiers. It was a safer place to live in wilder country, governed by law – if a law that usually favoured the state and the army.

'You have been to Eboracum.'

'Aye,' Vindex admitted. 'Once.' He thought for a while. 'It stank.'

Eboracum was the depot for Legio IX Hispana – or VIIII as the legionaries usually insisted just to show that they were different. The Batavians here at Vindolanda had campaigned alongside the legion when they were first formed and had picked up this affectation.

Vindolanda was built to house the double-strength Batavian cohort, over a thousand men with a fifth of them cavalry when at full strength – which of course, like the rest of the army, they rarely were. It also had space for detachments, some of them large, from other units, and like any base individuals and small parties regularly passed through. Eboracum was ten times bigger than Vindolanda, and Ferox would be the first to admit that it did

83

stink. The military mind was keen on cleanliness. Every base was provided with latrine blocks flushed by a flow of water and sewers to carry the waste away. Yet once it was outside the walls they tended to lose interest. At Eboracum the excrement of thousands emptied into the river and it reeked to high heaven, especially in summer when the water was low. It was the same at most bases. Here at Vindolanda the sewer pipes drained into the pretty little valley on the eastern side beyond the fort. No one complained, and would not have got far if they had tried, and all the while vegetables grew very well on that slope.

'Too big,' Vindex said. 'Just too big.' Most Brigantes lived on farms or in small villages, with only a few of the more important chieftains maintaining larger holdings. In the old days of the kings and queens it had been different, although even then there were few big towns compared to the tribes of the south. Ferox wondered whether he could ever convince Vindex of how small this was compared to the many great cities in Gaul and how plenty of people liked to live in them – let alone explain that vast, teeming, beautiful and filthy anthill that was Rome. He had only spent a few months there and after all these years the memory had an unreal, dream-like quality. He had no great desire to go back.

They followed the road running just north of the fort, the land gently sloping down. A couple of buildings stood apart from the rest of the canabae. There was a cluster of beggars by the roadside. They tended to get driven away from the houses, so there were usually a few here, even in bad weather. Some were familiar, such as the hunchback with the drooling lip, the one with both hands gone, and the two old women who went everywhere together, one of them blind and the other deaf. All started to call out for money or food, but one voice cut above the others.

'Alms for a blessing!' It came from a hunched man standing a little apart, leaning on a stick. His long white hair was plastered against a dark and ragged cloak. Both hair and the garment were filthy, as was the toe poking out from a hole in the front of one shoe. He had a straggling white beard and a face lined with age, suffering and dirt, but kept his eyes down, staring at their horses' feet. A little mongrel, almost as filthy as its master and with several bald patches, was curled up by his heels. The two old women shrieked and spat at him, but he ignored them.

Vindex reached into his pouch and tossed him a bronze coin, which the beggar caught without looking up.

'Generous?' Ferox said as they rode on.

'Bit of luck never did anyone any harm,' Vindex told him.

'Only if it's good luck.' He blinked as heavy drops of water fell from the edge of his hood and blew into his eyes.

The Brigantian was not listening. 'Look familiar?' he said.

There was a tall building just on their right beyond where the road forked and a branch led down to the main gateway of the fort. A square central tower topped with a pyramid-shaped roof of red tiles was surrounded by covered galleries on all sides, although these had large windows open to all weathers. It was the Temple of Silvanus – or Vinotonus as the Brigantes knew him, god of the hunt and of fertility – and outside the entrance waited the four-wheeled carriage. Ferox felt sorry for the driver, sitting in front, hair drenched and cloak sodden. Still, at least his luck was better than that of his predecessor.

They took the track towards Vindolanda, and as they came level with the temple's entrance saw a short woman standing in the shelter, dark hair carefully arranged. It was the lady's maid and Vindex gave a grin and big wink. She looked around to see whether anyone else was watching, realised that she was safe and stuck her tongue out at him. Shifting slightly and twitching her arm, the girl let her cloak part to show a bright white dress, cut rather low in front.

'Making friends?' Ferox said, wondering just how much time the Brigantian and the freedwoman had spent together on the day of the ambush, given her injuries. She looked well enough – and lively enough – a week later.

'She's a grateful lass. Hope so, any road.' Losing two wives had done nothing to dampen the Brigantian's enthusiasm for women.

Ferox was tempted to linger in spite of a fresh deluge of rain driving into their backs, but did not have to, as a moment later the lady appeared. She was in pale blue again and it suited her, so that he rather regretted the maid handing her mistress a heavy cloak in a grey wool even darker than the skies.

He clambered down, limbs stiff after a couple of damp hours spent in the saddle, and opened the door of the carriage. The repairs had been done well, and apart from one deep gouge made by an arrow he could see no sign of damage.

Sulpicia Lepidina smiled and then she and her maid dashed for the shelter of the carriage, each of them holding their hooded cloaks tight with one hand and using the other to lift their hems.

'It appears I am in your debt once again,' the lady said after clambering inside, followed by her servant. The curtain to the carriage window was clipped back so that she could see out.

Ferox bowed his head. 'Happy to be of service, my lady.'

'Are you well?' She looked over him to Vindex.

'Thank you, lady. I am much restored. Your treatment has worked wonders.'

The centurion pulled himself back into the saddle and they rode beside the carriage as it went back to the fort.

'It is an indulgence to travel this way on so short a journey,' Lepidina told him, 'but on a day like this...'

'Do you go there often?' Ferox took pleasure in talking to her, seeing the life in her face, although he wondered whether he ought to suggest that she close the curtain and travel the rest of the way in more comfort.

'I go most days. There is much to be said for silence and seclusion. Have I said something amusing?'

'My apologies, it is just that someone else said something very similar to me earlier on.' Ferox heard Vindex chuckle.

'Today there was a greater reason. I made an offering for the recovery of young Flavius. He has a bad stomach and a fever and it has not improved after two days. I am not sure the camp *seplasiarius* is that skilled in preparing his potions. Apart from his back, he is a strong child, and may recover even without aid, but there is no harm in seeking help from the heavens.'

'You should visit the Spring of Covventina, lady,' he said automatically, without giving it sufficient thought, for the sacred spring and grove lay to the east, along the road past where she had been ambushed. 'The waters have a potency, they say, against many evils, but then men say many things that are false.'

Sulpicia Lepidina gave a gentle laugh. 'Yes, *men* do.' Her deep blue eyes sparkled. She wore her hair simply, tied back in a bun by a deep blue ribbon. 'But thank you for your concern.'

'It is nothing. I can only imagine the dreadful worry of a mother for a sick child.'

'Flavius is not my son,' she said, the laughter gone. 'He and his little sister and brother are the children of my husband. His first wife died giving birth to the second boy. I have no children, so I suppose that I have failed in the duties the divine Augustus and most of the other Caesars have encouraged, but my husband is father of three and has all the benefits and respect that entails.'

'I am sorry,' Ferox said, flustered and then realising that it would not be clear just what he was sorry for. 'And I am sure that there is plenty of time.'

'Perhaps, but I doubt it. I shall be twenty-eight next year, so time – and other things – are not on my side.' When he made no reply, she leaned out of the window, lowering her head so that her eyes stared up at him. 'That was the moment when a well-mannered young officer was supposed to look shocked and assure me that I have all the bloom of a virgin bride and that I could not possibly be so old.'

'If you have ever glanced at your reflection in a mirror, then you would have no need to seek such praise because no words would be adequate to describe your perfection.'

Vindex started humming again, the same song as before.

'That is a pretty tune, and those were pretty words and bold – perhaps too bold?'

Ferox had not come to play games. 'I am a soldier, lady. The emperor pays me to be bold.'

They were passing the last building to stand apart from the others, a big two-storey house built in stone, the plastered walls painted a white that was bright even on this dull day. It was owned by Flora, once a dancer, slave and prostitute, who ran the most expensive brothel north of Eboracum, but there was nothing on the outside of the building to show what it was. Ferox wondered whether the commander's wife knew about it.

'I have offended you,' she said. 'For that I apologise.'

'You have caused no offence,' he said, feeling clumsy and brutish again.

'When I say that you are offended, you will be offended.' The words were sharp, spoken as if to admonish a slave by someone with the assurance of many generations of aristocratic blood. Then she pulled back in through the window, threw her head back and laughed. 'You are an odd fellow, Flavius Ferox, Prince of the Silures and centurion of Rome,' she said after a while. He assumed that she must have spoken to Crispinus. 'Your wife is a fortunate woman.'

'I am not married.'

'A woman?'

'There was once, but no longer.' He was surprised to find himself telling her.

'Did she die, poor thing?'

'I do not know. She vanished many years ago.' The words came out, but for once to his surprise the sorrow did not engulf him, neither was there much of the shame at his failure to devote his life to searching for her.

'Then I am sorry, I did not mean to open old wounds or to pry.' He could see no trace of regret in her voice or expression, neither did he believe that the questions were idle ones. 'We all have our sorrows and disappointments, and may not always find it easy to live the life given to us. Things are not always as we imagined they would be, and yet the world goes on and on, whatever we feel.' She glanced away, looking through the other window of the carriage at Flora's place. 'Close the curtain,' she said to her maid.

Time was running out and they would soon reach the gate where it would be harder to hover around the carriage without inviting comment. 'On the day of the attack,' he began, deciding that he must be blunt, 'you were going to Coria, I understand?'

'Yes, sir, very good, sir, straightaway, sir.' She mimicked the tone of an obedient soldier. mocking him. 'Yes, I was. I was to attend the birthday party of Claudia Severa, wife of Aelius Brocchus, whose ala is stationed there. It ought to have been a pleasant excursion, and yet I found myself under assault from barbarians – then yelled at and slapped on the behind by a friendly barbarian!'

'Once again, my sincere apologies.'

'And my insincere acceptance.'

'How long ago did you receive the invitation?'

'Do you want the hour and the day – and a signed chit from my commanding officer? Well, I don't know, but several weeks at least. It is not as easy as calling on a friend back home. I dare say the letter inviting me is in the house somewhere. I can look if it would interest you and clear my good name?'

Ferox tried to stick to the point. 'Your departure was delayed?'

She made a face like a guilty child. 'Yes. One of the mules got kicked and the poor thing broke its leg. After that I was all ready and then *some silly girl*' – she nodded towards her maid and was grinning broadly – 'spilled half a bottle of scent on me. I could not go reeking like a whore, so had to change. I suppose you know well what a whore smells like?'

'I have little knowledge of such things.'

'Huh.' She raised her eyes to the sky. 'Well, of course I must believe you.' She stared at him straight-faced, and then laughed that rich, musical laugh. 'Nearly home,' she said, a moment later. 'So I had better become the great lady once more.' Sulpicia Lepidina gave him a stern look, lips pursed in exaggerated distaste as she glanced down at his mud-stained cloak, and then with a jerk she pulled the curtain closed.

They were through the canabae and approaching the main entrance to the fort. Compared to Syracuse it was massive, with double gates each high enough for a horseman not to have to lower his spear and wide enough to let a big wagon – let alone the raedula – through, or a rank of men pass four abreast. The rampart of the turf wall with its palisade on top was fifteen feet high and the wide tower over the gateways was as high again, although it was not roofed. Ferox could see a pair of sentries standing miserably on the platform on top. Vindolanda was in the process of being rebuilt for the second time in less than a decade, mainly because the previous fort had been thrown up too quickly for it to last.

A file of sentries straightened up, spears held perfectly straight to salute the passing carriage. One of the men stepped forward in a less welcoming manner as Ferox, Vindex and Philo walked their mounts forward, coming level with the deep ditch on either side of the road through the gates.

'Flavius Ferox, centurio regionarius.'

'Sorry, sir. Didn't recognise you, sir.' The man stiffened to attention, without quite matching the respect shown to the commander's wife. 'And your party, sir?'

'Vindex, son of the high chief of the Carvetii and commander of the scouts that serve alongside us, and Philo, scholar, philosopher, doctor and teacher from the great city of Alexandria.'

The senior soldier knew when an officer was having his little joke. 'Yes, sir. Very good, sir. I'm sure you know best, sir. Officer and two others to pass!' he shouted up to the sentries in the tower. 'Use the right-hand passage if you please, sirs,' he added.

Ferox also knew the signs and could see the big puddle and churned mud in the middle of the road behind the open gate. 'Let the horses walk two paces then canter through,' he whispered. Vindex followed his lead, kicking his horse so that it surged forward. Philo was confused, and when he kicked the mule the animal bucked and threw him. The other two just made it through before a jet of water shot down from the underside of the rampart. Ferox guessed that there was a gutter leading from the open platform to funnel the rain downwards and that the men on top had opened a little sluice.

'Sorry about that, sir,' the sentry called. 'Nearly a nasty accident there.' Philo was grubby and even more miserable than before, but otherwise unhurt. He led the mule behind them as they walked their horses along the *via principalis*, the main road through the centre of the fort. On either side were rows of long buildings, wattle and daub rendered over the top and whitewashed. Ahead of them the road met the *via praetoria*, the second road of the fort, which lay at right angles to it, running between the side gates in the middle of the long walls. Neither were paved and both were rapidly turning into mud as rainwater flowed down the gentle slope.

Where the two roads met was the *principia*, a square courtyard complex with an assembly hall, offices, storerooms and the shrine where the cohort's standards were kept. To the right was another building, the *praetorium*, which was almost as big, but this time a house for Cerialis and his family.

Vindex sniffed. 'Doesn't look very cosy,' he decided. 'Bet it's cold too.'

'Doesn't worry us,' Ferox said, before dismounting and going through the high archway into the principia to report his presence. He was soon back. Men came to take the horses, and another to show them to a couple of rooms at the end of a barrack block. The rest of the block was empty at the moment.

'It's allocated to part of the vexillation away at Coria,' the soldier explained. They were given a pair of rooms in the apartment at the end of the block, which accommodated the centurion and provided some office space for the administration of the century. No one had used the rooms for months, and layers of dust were heavy, even if Philo was too cold, wet and tired to register his horror. The soldier got a fire going, provided a pair of lamps and some oil for light, and then left them to it.

Two hours later, at noon, the parade was held to honour the emperor. The rain had slackened, becoming no more than a fine drizzle, and this had no doubt encouraged someone – presumably Cerialis – to hold the ceremony on the drill-ground as planned. About four hundred men from cohors VIIII Batavorum stood in three ranks, forming one side and the base of a U-shape. The other long side was composed of one hundred and seventy men of cohors I Tungrorum and a mixed bag of individuals from other units who were at the fort at the moment. None of the men carried shields or spears and they stood with their hands straight down at their sides. They were permitted to have cloaks – Ferox noticed that the Batavians' were uniform in colour, with the infantry in dark green and the cavalry troopers in dark blue, whereas the Tungrians, let alone the detachments, were in a broad rainbow of colours. He suspected that someone was making a point. All the men wore armour and helmets and had belts around the waist and over the shoulder supporting the scabbards of their swords. There was little to choose between the two cohorts in the state of their equipment, everything polished as brightly as possible.

Cerialis stood with the officers of his cohort in front of the standards. Ferox and the others present, including the staff of the Tungrians, stood to the side, watching as the prefect covered his head with a fold of his white cloak and poured a libation on a stone altar inscribed to Jupiter Optimus Maximus. He prayed aloud to Rome's great god and to the other gods of the city for the health and success of their beloved Caesar. A round cake, specially baked from flour of the finest wheat, was offered and another long prayer recited. The rain was getting heavier all the time. Ferox could almost hear the equipment of nearly six hundred men tarnishing and rusting as they stood and watched. The hours spent preparing for this parade would be nothing compared to the days spent restoring everything to order.

Ferox let the words roll past him without paying much attention. Trajan had become emperor when the elderly Nerva had fallen ill and died. A brass image of his face mounted on a silver disc replaced that of Nerva on the *imago*, the image of the emperor carried with the other standards. It was the first time Ferox had seen a picture of the man, although past experience suggested that it would not look too much like him. Trajan came from the city of Italica in Baetican Spain, and his family had done well by backing the Emperor Domitian's family in the civil war thirty years ago.

A garlanded bull was led forward. This last part of the ceremony was probably the only good reason for holding it outside rather than in the covered hall in the principia. The bull was docile, no doubt drugged, and stood dumbly waiting in front of the altar. Most legions had professional priests and assistants and some auxiliary units copied them, but the Batavians did things their own way, in this as in so many other matters. A massive soldier, almost as big as the warrior Ferox had faced, stood in just his tunic, the wool plastered to his skin. He carried a *dolabra*, the army's pickaxe, but this was a special one, carefully forged, sharpened to a razor's edge and with a longer wooden shaft. The man waited, his great chest and heavily muscled arms tensed, and then swung once just where the bull's head met its spine. The animal grunted and dropped on to its knees, tongue lolling out. Blood was pouring from the wound, great pools forming around the beast as it fell over on its side.

'Good luck for the cohort, he did it in one.' Ferox heard a standard-bearer whisper the words to the man next to him.

Cerialis uncovered his head and called on the men to salute the emperor.

'Long life and good fortune to the Lord Trajan!' the men shouted, raising their right arms up straight in salute and holding them rigid as they repeated the phrase twice.

'Tomorrow you shall parade to receive the gift he promised you on his proclamation – a donative of three *aurei* per man!' Cerialis' voice carried well in spite of the wind and rain. 'The parade will be at noon in the principia!'

'Long life and good fortune to the Lord Trajan!' The cheers were more enthusiastic this time, whether at the money – a quarter of a year's pay – or the prospect of being in the dry.

Cerialis let them repeat the chant three times.

'Tomorrow is also the anniversary of our great victory at Mons Graupius.' He paused, looking along the lines of soldiers. 'This will be commemorated in the usual way!'

The cheers and chants were almost ecstatic in their enthusiasm. Ferox had heard that the anniversary was the time for eating and drinking to excess.

As the units were marched back to the fort to be dismissed, Cerialis passed him.

'Centurion, my wife the Lady Sulpicia Lepidina and I are entertaining friends to dinner this evening. I do hope that you will join us.'

'Thank you, my lord. That is most kind.' A hope from a senior officer was an order in all but name, though this one surprised him, as he would have thought that he was beneath their social circle.

'Wonderful. At the start of the second hour of the night watch. We shall look forward to seeing you there. It will not be anything special, I am afraid, but at least it will be warm and dry!' Cerialis grinned and patted the centurion on the shoulder.

VII

FEROX STRUGGLED TO keep pace. It was an hour into the dinner and he felt bloated and his elbow ached from supporting his weight. The borrowed toga was stiff and uncomfortable, and every time he shifted on the couch there was tightly bunched-up wool underneath him. He hoped that Philo had not lied when he assured him that the garment was on loan from the slave of one of the centurions in the garrison, and that everything had been properly arranged. The little Alexandrian had been delighted when he heard of the invitation. In moments it revived him from a bedraggled wreck into a whirlwind of excited activity. 'A pity it is not a symposium,' he kept saying, but that disappointment aside, the slave was happier than he had seen him for years. Much to Ferox's surprise, he produced the centurion's best tunic, cleaned to an almost dazzling whiteness, and his best shoes, free of any speck of dirt. 'I had hoped for some invitation of this kind,' Philo confessed, as if he were going to the meal, but had worried that the senior officers would fail to realise the true importance of his master. The lack of a toga caused panic, and the slave vanished for nearly two hours before returning in triumph, then fussed until the centurion was ready. Philo inspected him, walking all around, with less of an air of disappointment than usual.

'No scent,' Ferox told him firmly when the lad produced a small bottle of blue-green glass.

'Very well, my lord,' the Alexandrian replied, meaning nothing of the sort. 'But do you not think, my lord, that a slight touch would be beneficial after the rigours of the last days?'

'You mean to cover the foul reek of filthy centurion?'

Philo said no more, lifting the bottle and reaching for the stopper, convinced of the correctness of his judgement.

'No.'

'My lord, please?' The voice was imploring, tinged with regret.

'No.' Ferox sighed. 'Do you know that the Emperor Vespasian once gave a promotion to a man recommended to him, but when the fellow turned up, in he walked in a cloud of scents and perfumes. Then the emperor – the very wise emperor – rescinded the commission and sent the man packing. Said he'd rather he smelled of garlic if he had to reek of anything.'

'I see, master, but the Emperor Vespasian is long dead' – and good riddance to bad rubbish was the implication – 'while I am sure the other gentlemen will be properly turned out. And there will be great ladies present...' The boy pulled the stopper from the bottle.

'No.' Ferox wondered where the lad had got the stuff, and thought it might be best not to ask. It was obviously expensive and unless the boy had raided his purse he could not have bought it. In the past he had wondered whether Philo had a flexible approach to the concept of property, hence his concern about the 'borrowed' toga.

He was glad that Vindex was not there, for the Brigantian would no doubt have found all this very funny. He was out somewhere in the fort, probably at one of the small taverns inside the walls. Ferox had warned him not to go out to the canabae in case the guards were reluctant to let him back in.

'It must be time by now?' he asked, rubbing his chin.

'Almost, my lord. Although if you wish it there would be time for another shave.'

'It's fine.' Ferox ignored the doubting look. He had been shaved this morning and again a few hours ago, so that even his dark stubble ought not to be showing again so soon.

'As you will, my lord,' Philo said, bearing another of life's disappointments with dignity. 'The rain has stopped and it is a clear night,' he added with satisfaction. Ferox wondered whether the boy had done some deal with his Jewish god. At least it made the walk to the praetorium more pleasant, following the walkway of laid planks running alongside the buildings. Vindolanda was a damp place and after the rain the roads were muddy. Philo yelped in horror when the centurion stepped in a puddle and dirty water lightly spattered his shoes and legs.

The prefect's house was large, grander than some of the aristocrats' houses he remembered from his schooldays in Lugdunum. Only a few cracked patches on the rendering of the outside wall betrayed its construction in timber rather than stone. When he was ushered into the porch it proved to be a large room, with polished plank floorboards rather than the straw-covered earth of the barrack blocks. The walls were plastered and painted in panels showing simple rural scenes. Cerialis was there to greet him with warmth, and the other male guests were also waiting. Philo gave his master a reproving look, before being taken off to wherever he and the other servants accompanying the visitors would wait until the end of the night.

The host and guests walked through a corridor opening on one side to the little square ornamental garden and Ferox caught the scent of flowers on what was now a pleasantly warm evening for the time of year. It always amused him that the Romans insisted on building their houses this way, so perfect for giving shade from the hot Mediterranean sun – something less of a worry here in the north. Flavius Cerialis and his family lived like the gentry of an Italian town, even though they were thousands of miles away and the prefect had not a drop of Italian blood in him. He was a Batavian, like the soldiers he commanded, for the old treaty with the tribe stated that they should serve in units commanded by their own aristocrats.

Crispinus was the only real Roman in this Italian house as they gathered for a quintessentially Roman dinner party. Aelius

Brocchus, prefect of the ala stationed at Coria, was slim, hawk-nosed, with thick black hair and piercing dark eyes, and was a long way from his home at Gades in Baetica. It would not have surprised Ferox to learn that the man had Carthaginian as well as Iberian ancestors. Neither could he help wondering whether either he or Cerialis had ever visited Rome. Claudius Super had been there, and liked telling people about it, as had Ferox and the remaining guest, Titus Flavius Vegetus, a very short, very fat Bithynian who had been a slave of the imperial household until given his freedom a few years earlier. Then and now he worked for the procurator, and had clearly done well out of it, with large rings on each of his stubby fingers.

All six men were Roman citizens, including Ferox of the Silures, and each wore a toga carefully draped over his left arm, except Crispinus, the most Roman of them all, who had a light Greek cloak instead. Three of the six were named Flavius, which meant no more than that they or their family had received citizenship from one of the Flavian dynasty, founded by Vespasian, victor in the civil war after Nero's death thirty years before. Ferox guessed that, like him, Cerialis had become a Roman through a grant of the founder of the dynasty. During the civil war the Rhineland had erupted into rebellion led by Batavian aristocrats backed by Batavian and other auxiliary cohorts. The most important was Julius Civilis, an equestrian prefect just like Cerialis. Up until then he had had a distinguished record, and had been wounded several times and lost an eye fighting for Rome. At first Civilis and his men claimed to be fighting for Vespasian against his Roman rival, but then it all became messier and there was talk of an Empire of the Gauls. That made them rebels, not Romans, and Vespasian had to eradicate the revolt, but some Batavians stayed loyal and others surrendered quickly. In the end the rest were defeated by a cousin of the new emperor, a man named Petilius Cerialis. No doubt the prefect's father had stayed loyal or switched sides at an opportune moment, and got citizenship and preferment as a reward, taking the emperor's name and that of the victorious commander.

The ladies were waiting for them in the dining room, standing in front of the *triclinia*, the three couches surrounding the low table. The room was big, the ceiling above of carved beams, but the walls painted and painted quite well, for they had brought a man up from Corinium in the south. There were scenes of hunting and of stories. In one Hades in his chariot charged towards a mildly shocked – and blonde-haired – Persephone, who did not appear to be making much effort to escape. Others showed a half-naked Leda kneeling by the side of a lake as the swan approached, and Europa astride a great black bull.

'It does make one wonder about everyday life for aristocratic young ladies in those far-off days,' Sulpicia Lepidina said softly, having noticed him inspecting the paintings. 'I have a pair of cats, but they are pets and no more.'

'I am sure they know their place,' Crispinus added. 'Neither would your husband nor any of us wish you to be carried off.'

Cerialis was not paying attention, instead listening with pleasure as Claudius Super and the imperial freedman Vegetus praised the splendour of his house and this room in particular. Their comments were fulsome, but justified, and even Ferox was surprised to find that the floor consisted of well-laid and evenly cut flagstones.

'I got the idea from Julius Caesar,' Cerialis explained. 'He used to carry stones to use as a floor for his tent.'

'They may become a bit chilly when the winter comes,' Sulpicia Lepidina added, gently grasping each guest by the hand in more formal greeting. 'But it does make the place feel more like it is ours.' She was in a dark blue dress, the shoulders fastened by finely cast brooches, and her hair in its usual bun, this time tied back by a ribbon studded with white gems. She had pearl droplets hanging from each ear and a delicate gold necklace stood out against her fair skin. Her slippers were in pale leather, a single thong between her toes and the soles built up to the heel making her a couple of inches taller. Her husband's shoes were almost as expensive, the uppers a lattice pattern allowing glimpses of his dark red socks.

Introductions were made. Claudia Severa was dark-eyed and dark-haired like her husband Brocchus, although her skin was fashionably white, and lightened further by make-up that seemed strong in comparison with Lepidina's. Her hair was also tied back, but a servant had teased the fringe into a row of curls and combed up the top to make it look very thick. It made her already round face look rounder, but that drew attention to her big eyes, giving her a gentle, doe-like appearance. She was in dark pink, with gold bracelets, earrings, necklace and brooches, and pale shoes, the tops of whitened calfskin. She greeted Crispinus with a peck on the cheek, standing on the balls of her feet to reach him for she was very small. Claudius received a similar welcome, perhaps a little less sincere, and it was obvious both men were known to her. Ferox and the former slave had to make do with a warm smile and a gentle press of the hand.

Vegetus' wife Fortunata was different, her dress expensive red silk that shimmered in the lamplight, barely concealing her full figure. Ferox thought that she might be a Gaul, from somewhere in the far north-west by the shape of her face and her green eyes. She was quite tall and a little plump, but much of her weight was carried on breast and hips and she walked with grace. Her hair was so fair that it was almost white, arranged in an ornate confection of curls and combs rising into a dome. If it was not a wig, then a small army of servants had spent hours creating such a monument. With each movement heavy bangles clinked together on her arms. Her sandals were similar in style to the ones worn by Lepidina, save that the soles were built up much higher. Fortunata welcomed all of the men with a kiss – her lips soft and moist, lingering a little too long for courtesy on Ferox's cheek. Her manner as much as her name proclaimed that she had been a slave, like her husband, although probably not one working as an administrator's assistant.

Crispinus joined the host and hostess on the main couch. To their right were Brocchus and Claudia with Claudius Super beside them. In each case the lady reclined between the two men. The couches were large and well cushioned so that there was plenty of room, save perhaps on the third one, which Ferox shared with Vegetus and Fortunata. Both were smothered in enough scent to make even Philo's eyes water. The freedman also spread across the cushions, taking up almost half the space. Ferox had the uncomfortable sense that he was about to fall off, the back of the freedwoman so close that he felt the thin silk of her dress brush against him whenever she moved. The guests lay on their sides so that they could see the main couch.

It had been years since Ferox had attended a formal dinner and he realised that he no longer had the stamina of the past. Food kept arriving, dish after dish of well-presented and finely cooked food. Cerialis was fond of poultry. They had small chickens, one for each diner, and two large geese carved for them by the slaves. A supervisor was always in the room, and another grey-haired slave who cut portions and served as necessary. Other slaves wafted in and out, moving silently, taking old dishes and replacing them with new, or serving wine.

'Falernian,' Cerialis announced when the first cups were poured. 'I can never resist it even though there are other vintages. And after all "cups were meant for joy".' He beamed happily. '"Cease this impious row, my friends, and rest as you are, propped on your elbow, or would you not wish me to drink my share of dry Falernian?"'

'I do love Horace,' Claudius Super declared. 'Quite my favourite of the great poets.' The generous condescension in his voice suggested that composing verses was something he could do in his sleep.

'I am fonder of Virgil,' Aelius Brocchus said. 'And I should be loyal to Martial of course, if we include more modern singers of songs.' Crispinus smiled in understanding.

'Oh, because he is from Iberia, like you,' Claudius Super said after a moment, obviously pleased with his deduction. The man was flushed, making Ferox wonder whether he had begun drinking before he had arrived. For himself it had been a long while since the vintage mattered. Drink was something to provide occasional oblivion, and strength had come to matter more than taste. Tonight, he drank slowly and made sure that each cup held far more water than wine. His knowledge of literature was modest, not because he disliked reading but because books were expensive and bulky, very hard to obtain in this part of the world and even harder for a man to carry around. He let the conversation flow around him and said nothing. Even he could sense that Claudius Super was not well read, but believed that he was. Cerialis' knowledge tended towards famous passages, almost as if he had studied to masquerade as an educated man.

Ferox had half forgotten how much he hated reclining to eat. In spite of his schooling in Gaul, the spell in Rome after that and the formal dinners in the army since then, it did not seem natural. A man should sit at the table – something Romans only did as a sign of deliberate denial of comfort. He felt far more at home visiting the houses of local chieftains, sitting on stools or cross-legged around a fire, or eating alone in his quarters at Syracuse, without fuss or making a great pantomime of it all.

A slave girl with long brown hair offered him fish stew. She was a pretty girl, as were all the female slaves serving them, neat and tidy in simple buff-coloured dresses and slippers. He smiled in thanks, but declined.

'It is good,' Aelius Brocchus said encouragingly, spooning up the contents of his own dish with evident pleasure. Ferox saw a bowl filled with oysters being carried in and felt his usual revulsion at the sight of this delicacy.

'I am not fond of food from river or sea,' he said, for the man's goodwill was genuine. 'My people believe it is bad for the soul.'

Sulpicia Lepidina chuckled gently, mistaking his words for a pun, but the sound was covered by a guffaw of laughter from Claudius Super. No one joined in – not even Fortunata who giggled whenever she thought that a joke had been told – and he fell into embarrassed silence.

'Do you believe in the soul?' Crispinus asked. The young tribune spent more time listening that talking, but when he spoke tended to be direct. Everyone's face turned to stare at Ferox, apart from Vegetus, who continued to eat. Fortunata frowned as she looked at him, her face barely a foot away.

'Yes. When you see a dead man all you see is flesh and bone.' He tried to shrug, a difficult thing to do in this posture, and made do with moving his head gently from side to side. 'I must apologise to the ladies.' He glanced at each in turn. 'I had not meant to speak of such grim things, but it does explain my sense. Our bodies are no more than meat. The spirit, the spark, the life itself leaves at death. That is the soul and that is eternal.'

Crispinus was interested. 'Yet can it be seen?'

'It is the life and light in a man or woman,' Ferox said, 'how can it not be seen? Without it we are no more than statues.' He was not comfortable talking about such things, so hoped to end their interest. 'You wonder whether you can see it. Well, my people say that the rattle in a man's throat as a blade takes his life is the soul leaving. At least you can hear it.' He did not apologise this time, largely because Fortunata screwed up her face in obvious distaste. Another slave girl, this time with black hair and golden-brown skin, appeared, offering freshly baked white bread, so he took some.

Cerialis began to talk of philosophy and the different schools' ideas of the nature of life and whether or not men had souls. Brocchus joined him, Crispinus added a little, Sulpicia Lepidina made a joke about Cynics, and the conversation moved on. When the slave girl served Vegetus the top of her dress sagged a little and the fat man leered. Fortunata noticed, and when she turned back to face the main couch she shifted so that her body was pressed up against Ferox. She did not appear to have much on under the silk dress.

Philosophy exercised their interest for some time, and Ferox was left to listen and try to guess how much of the food he was obliged to eat for courtesy's sake, and whether this amount would still cause his stomach to burst. The others picked at things, taking a little from each dish and leaving more. He had never acquired the knack of eating so lightly. To him it was a waste, and with meat, good bread or broth he felt a man should devour it all. As a strategy it was not comfortable.

Only for a moment did the conversation require anything from him, when Crispinus asked about druids and their teachings.

'They have gone now,' Ferox explained. 'The real ones at least. We' – this was the Roman 'we', but they all instinctively understood – 'have suppressed the cult. It used to be organised, the senior druids standing outside the tribes, schooled by twenty years of training. All that is long gone. Some claim to be druids now, but they are little more than magicians and medicine men wandering the lands. Only a few are dangerous.'

'Here you go again.' Claudius Super spoke louder than was necessary. 'Our friend Ferox sees trouble and druids under every bed. They're gone, as you say, and good riddance to the murderous bastards.'

Claudia Severa's lips twitched in restrained disapproval, and Ferox noticed Lepidina glare at the man.

'That sounds like business and this is not the time for that,' Cerialis told them, before steering the conversation to less sensitive subjects, asking whether there were natural philosophers and if true learning had all begun in the East.

Ferox found it hard to listen, in part because he did not care, but mainly because Fortunata had begun to shift back and forth on the couch, rubbing her round bottom against him. It was difficult to ignore, and even if he found her foolish and vulgar, she was an attractive woman. His body began to respond in spite of his distaste for her. She moved slowly at first, but as time passed the rhythm little by little became faster. All the while she whispered in her husband's ear, chiding him lightly when he eyed up another slave girl. Still she moved, the silk smooth, almost like a second skin, as her body slid up and down against his.

'And what do you think about it, centurion?' Sulpicia Lepidina asked and the room went silent as they turned to look him. Fortunata went still.

Ferox had not the remotest idea of what she meant. 'I am not a learned man,' he said, 'so I would not dare to offer an opinion.'

'Indeed,' she said with a knowing expression. Beside her Crispinus looked amused.

'Well, one learned man is our new consular,' Vegetus put in, speaking with force for the first time in the dinner. He had the assurance of a man with private information, which he planned to make public. 'Our *Legatus Augusti*, Lucius Neratius Marcellus, should arrive in the province before the year is out.' The imperial freedman spoke with the satisfaction of a man who had just rolled Venus on the dice.

Britannia was one of the major military commands in the empire, given only to senior senators and former consuls to command as provincial legate. The last governor had fallen sick and died in office almost a year ago. Nerva had been too ill to choose a replacement, and it had taken months before his successor made the appointment. The new provincial legate did not appear to be in any hurry to get here.

'Well, centurion, you must have an opinion on our new governor,' Sulpicia Lepidina asked. 'Or are you not sufficiently learned for that either?'

Fortunata began to rub against him once more, and Ferox did his best to ignore her. 'I would not presume to judge a former consul and my commander.' The other officers nodded in agreement, even Claudius Super joining in.

'However, I will say this. It will be a good thing to have a governor again. Many in the tribes see us as weak, and who can blame them.' He warmed quickly to his theme and shifted in his seat so that he knocked Fortunata. 'I am sorry, lady,' he lied as she was forced to move away from him a little.

'They live in mud huts, and yet they see us as weak?' Crispinus spoke, eyes fixed on him, looking very alert and not like a man who had been eating and drinking for hours.

'Why should they not? Tomorrow the cohorts celebrate Mons Graupius. When Agricola was legate we overran all the lands to the far north. A few years later we abandon them and withdraw more than a hundred miles. In the last decade a legion and many auxiliaries have been posted away. Most of the units we have left here are short of recruits and scattered in detachments here, there and everywhere. The tribes do not see a great army any more, but they do see tax collectors. The last governor died, the one before that was summoned home in disgrace by Domitian and executed.'

'We do not speak that man's name here,' Cerialis cut in. Ferox assumed he meant the Emperor Domitian, whose name had been formally damned by the Senate and chiselled off every monument in the empire. On the other hand he might have meant Lucullus, the legate killed for letting a new lance be named after him. 'And while this is very interesting, my friend,' he continued, 'it is once again business and not suitable for this gathering. So since I believe we have finished, I shall tell the slaves to clear away. Then, may I beg my lady wife will play and sing for us?'

A modest refusal, persistence from the husband, supported by the growing pleas from Crispinus, Brocchus and Claudius Super – the last almost shouting and clearly half drunk – and once the things were cleared away a stool was brought and with it a small lyre.

'I am not sure this has travelled well,' the lady said, picking up the instrument, 'and setting up house has not given me much time to practise. That is apart from such minor interruptions as barbarian attacks!' They laughed, Claudius Super red-faced and loud.

After some tuning and plucking a few chords, Sulpicia Lepidina began to play. The room went quiet, not simply from courtesy but because she was well trained and gifted. The tune was soft and mournful. Claudia Severa's eyes soon were glassy in the flickering lamplight.

Sulpicia Lepidina began to sing, the words in Greek. Ferox did not have much call for the language these days, and it took him a while to understand that she sang of love, passion and loss. It was from Sappho, set to music, and her voice was deeper than that of many women, powerful and resonant so that the room filled with the song and with music. Claudia Severa wept, her husband touching her cheek fondly. Fortunata began to move closer to him again, so he stood up, wandering a few paces away to listen with more concentration. After a few minutes, the Tribune Crispinus joined him.

When the song ended there was silence for a long while before they all applauded – Claudius Super with violent force, and Fortunata with surprising enthusiasm. Ferox wondered whether she had been an entertainer and listened with the educated ear of a professional.

The next song Sulpicia Lepidina sang was an ancient folk song from Achaea. Ferox recognised the tune, but not the words, which told the story of a shepherd boy and a nymph. After that the lady turned to Latin, and sang verses by Horace and Ovid, the last a frivolous tale. Her voice had grown richer.

'I have rarely heard better,' Crispinus said quietly as Sulpicia Lepidina paused and took a drink. 'She is a truly remarkable woman.'

'"Abundantly favoured by fortune,"' Ferox quoted from distant memory, '"well read in Greek and Latin literature, able to sing and play the lyre more skilfully than an honest woman need..." At least I think that is it, and I mean no offence.'

Crispinus smiled. 'Sallust always took a jaundiced view, though our hostess might have softened even his cold heart and won true praise. Although if I recall the lady in question danced rather than sang. Like that one, I suspect.' He spoke quietly and gave a nod and smile towards Fortunata, whose elaborate hair remained in order.

'Conversation in the audience is not considered a compliment,' Sulpicia Lepidina told them, one eyebrow arched in mock disapproval. 'Now perhaps something fitting for this place and this land.'

The tune was very familiar, but Ferox was paying no attention and watching her fingers as they moved and plucked the strings of the lyre. Someone gasped in surprise when the lady began to sing, but he was intent on her playing. It was one of many regrets that he had not learned an instrument.

To his amazement he realised that she sang not in Latin or Greek, but in the Celtic tongue of the Gauls and Britons, and the tune was a favourite of Vindex.

'And the Hound caught sight of the girl's full breasts over the top of her dress,' the lady sang, and he realised that she was watching him. '"I see a sweet country," he said, "I could rest my weapon there."'

Ferox glanced around, but saw no sign that anyone else understood the words. He wondered whether Lepidina knew what they meant. She certainly sang as if she did. The heroine in the tale kept telling the hero that no one would travel 'that country' until they had performed a series of impossible feats. Each time he answered, 'In that sweet country, I'll rest my weapon,' and the story told of how he undertook all the tasks and won his bride. The lady sang it through, her eyes never leaving him.

The applause was long and sincere.

'You could almost civilise the barbarians,' Claudius Super told her. Vegetus announced that next time his wife should entertain them with her dancing, and perhaps the lady would consent to play for her.

'Perhaps,' Sulpicia Lepidina said, and her husband regretted that it was time to bid their guests good night for tomorrow would be another busy day.

'You have a friend there,' Crispinus whispered to Ferox, catching him watching their hostess.

VIII

THE ARMY'S DAY began at Vindolanda much as it did at Syracuse or Eboracum or anywhere else, and this morning Ferox was glad of such familiar routine after the strangeness of the night before. Dawn found him in the principia of the fort, standing with the row of officers from cohors VIIII Batavorum milliaria equitata in front of the *aedes*, where the standards stood securely in the slots made for them in the plank floor. There were ten *signa*, one for each of the centuries composing the infantry of the cohort, each with a number of large silvered discs mounted on the pole, topped by a wreathed ornamental spearhead. The eight *turmae* of cavalry had their own smaller standards, with a single symbol and cross bar trailing weighted ribbons beneath the elaborate heads. Almost half of the cohort was currently absent on detached service, but the most important standards all remained here unless the unit as a whole marched out. Any big detachment carried a *vexillum*, a square red flag hanging from a crossbar on an otherwise plain pole, the banner bearing the name of the cohort in gold lettering. Empty slots in the floor alongside the single flag suggested that two important vexillations were away. In the centre of the mass of decorated poles was the *imago* of Trajan. In spite of yesterday's wet parade, even the tiniest metal fitting on each standard gleamed, while the shafts were freshly oiled and polished. Ferox had heard some men say that soldiers worshipped their standards. That was a lie, but in any half-decent unit they worshipped the idea that the standards represented.

Flavius Cerialis was in armour this morning, even though he sat on a stool behind a desk, reviewing a succession of wax writing tablets presented to him by his personal clerk, the *cornicularius* of the prefect. They listed the current strength of the cohort, recent acquisitions and losses, and detailed every individual and group away from the base. Ferox wondered whether at this very moment the legate of II Augusta – or whichever senior officer was present – was glancing down a list without paying much attention to the entry stating that one centurion was absent serving as regionarius. The legion had its main depot at Isca Silurum, there on the riverbank in his homeland. He wondered whether he would ever see the legion or his own people again. It was doubtful either would welcome him with open arms.

Hobnailed boots stamped on wooden floorboards as the *optio* of the day marched across the room, halting with a final shattering crash in front of the prefect and saluting.

'Good morning, sir!' The greeting was more like a battle cry and echoed around the high hall. An optio was second-in-command to a centurion, responsible for much day-to-day administration of the century and commanding in the officer's absence. This one was short by Batavian standards, but immaculately turned out. He had the accent of his people, as well as the typical yellow moustache and beard glimpsed between the broad bronze cheek pieces of his helmet. On either side of the fur-covered top of the helmet was a tall feather dyed yellow and standing straight up to mark his rank. His scale armour shone, as did the fittings on his belt and scabbard, and the ornate top of the staff of office in his left hand.

'Good morning, Arcuttius,' Cerialis replied, his voice clear and quiet. The prefect's iron helmet with its high plume and enamel decoration was on the desk beside him. The other officers, four centurions and five decurions present at the base, stood in a row, in armour, carrying their helmets in the crook of their left arms. That was the tradition for the Batavians, and Ferox had got Philo to find out so that he was properly attired. The

110

Alexandrian enjoyed such details, and revelled in preparing his master for yet another formal occasion. He was also very happy, filled to the brim with gossip picked up from the other slaves and servants at the prefect's house.

'Thank you, sir!' The optio bellowed the words, lowering his arm from the salute. He reached into a pouch at his belt and produced one of the thin wooden tablets used for routine documents. 'Seventh day after the Ides of September. Report of the Ninth Cohort of Batavians. All who should be are at duty stations, as is the baggage. The *optiones* and *curatores* made the report. Arcuttius, optio of the century of Crescens, delivered it.' The optio recited from memory – apart from the names and dates it was the same thing said every morning.

'Thank you, Arcuttius.' Cerialis stood. 'The watchword for today is "Fortuna". Pay parade at the second hour.'

'Sir!' The optio saluted again, turned about and marched noisily away. Ferox wondered whether the password was just coincidence, or a little joke of the prefect. Philo swore that the kitchen staff and other slaves in the praetorium had told him that their master and mistress had not shared the same bed since they arrived at Vindolanda six weeks ago, and rarely before that. It was not that the master lacked interest. He covered many of the slave girls at every opportunity and had visited Flora's establishment. He just did not seem that interested in his wife, which the servants found odd for they liked her and anyone could see that she was beautiful, if a little old at twenty-seven.

'They think he does not want the expense of more children,' Philo said with great assurance. 'He is a gifted man, and going places.'

The boy's tone reflected the obvious pride shared by Cerialis' household in their young master. Ferox certainly did not doubt the man's ambition. Marriage into a senatorial family, let alone such a well-established one, was rare for any equestrian, and surely unprecedented for a Batavian aristocrat, son of the first in his family to become a Roman citizen. There was no sign now that it was so unlikely a thing as a love match, which meant that something had persuaded a former consul to give his daughter in marriage to an upstart from the Rhineland.

Cerialis obviously planned to 'go places' and was working hard to that end, cultivating the acquaintance of Crispinus, the other equestrians, and even the imperial freedman. Former slaves of the emperor sometimes climbed very high indeed, reaching the top of the imperial administration and having an influence behind the scenes greater than many a senator. The days of the Emperor Claudius were gone, and Domitian, of damned memory but prudent rule, had replaced some of the freedmen in his staff with equestrians. Even so, there was no knowing how important Vegetus might one day become, for all his humble start in life. Ferox had asked his boy about the freedman and his wife.

'The Lord Vegetus and his lady' – Philo was grudging in his use of both titles – 'stayed at the praetorium rather than returning to the *mansio*.' There was a way-station for those travelling on official business in the canabae. 'They did not receive the best of the guest rooms, but were comfortably accommodated in separate rooms. The Lord Vegetus was feeling ill,' the Alexandrian added with a knowing look, 'and sleeps soundly and snores loudly, they say.'

The morning reports complete, Flavius Cerialis picked up his helmet and led the assembled officers out. He was in a bright mood, and perhaps the man was revelling in his good fortune after an energetic night. Slaves knew a lot about their owners – more than the latter cared to admit – but they were inclined to embellish and invent like anyone else.

In the central courtyard of the headquarters building they saw a travel-stained cavalryman walking towards them. He had an oval red shield with the Capricorn symbol of II Augusta, which meant that he was one of the small contingent of horsemen in that legion to serve as escorts to senior officers or as messengers. In his right hand he held a spear with a feather tied just below the head, which showed that he was the latter. Tradition older than anyone could remember and certainly older than they could explain made this the mark of a despatch rider, although it was something of an affectation to carry the symbol when not on the battlefield or at least campaign. The cornicularius took a wooden tablet from the man. It was tied up and sealed.

'Ah, it looks as if everything is starting sooner than expected,' Cerialis said, taking it from his cornicularius before the man had a chance to break the seal. Ferox must have missed something, for he had not heard that any major operation was planned. 'It is probably for the best. I leave you to your duties, fellow soldiers. My dear Ferox, if you would be good enough to come with me?'

A little later they were in one of the side rooms off the courtyard. Crispinus, Brocchus and Claudius Super were there, as was a tired-looking officer with the narrow dark red band of a *tribunus angusticlavius,* one of the five junior equestrian tribunes in a legion, and another officer who, from his uniform, looked like an equestrian too. There was also a leathery-faced centurion, whom he recognised as Titus Annius, the acting commander of cohors I Tungrorum.

Introductions were soon made and kept brief. The junior tribune was one Julius Flaccus from VIIII Hispana, who had accompanied the despatch rider, and the other man was Rufinus, commander of the auxiliary cohort stationed at Magna to the west, a unit of Vardulli from Spain. Crispinus was senior to the others in status and rank, if not years or experience, but let Cerialis begin the conference by summarising all that was known of the raid earlier in the month and the murder of the soldiers at the tower. It was certain that the missing soldier was the Briton.

'May I ask from what tribe, my lord?' Ferox asked.

'What does it matter? They're all the same,' Claudius Super muttered. Ferox suspected that the man had a bad hangover and enjoyed his obvious discomfort.

Cerialis nodded to his cornicularius who fished out a wax tablet from the file. 'Trinovantes from down south, although enlisted with the Tungrians.'

113

'Good record up to now,' Annius told them, 'seven years' service.' He paused to stare at each of them. 'I should like to state on record that the man has disappeared and there is no direct evidence of complicity in the attack. It is perfectly possible that he was taken as a prisoner, poor devil.' Annius was junior to all the equestrians, but he spoke with force and his pride in his own soldiers was obvious.

'You cannot trust Britons,' Claudius Super told them, unimpressed by this display of loyalty. 'Lies and treachery come too naturally to them.' Ferox ignored the insult, suspecting that the man had forgotten he was there, but worried that the sentiment was a common one. When he had returned to his quarters after the dinner last night he had found a bruised and battered Vindex.

'Some of the Batavian lads held Britons responsible for the men killed at the tower and in the ambush,' he explained. 'I told them that I was Carvetii and a Brigantian, not a Briton, but that didn't seem to matter. They wanted to show their annoyance and I was there, drinking quietly and talking to a few of their women. All harmless,' he assured Ferox. 'Just being friendly, but then it turned nasty, and might have got a lot nastier if that one-eyed old bugger hadn't turned up and knocked a few of them down. He stopped it all, told 'em I had saved their lady and then they all bought me drinks. They're mad, the lot of them.'

'Trinovantes, though,' Rufinus said as if thinking aloud, and Ferox's mind returned to the present. The prefect had dark skin and curly black hair, the accent of Africa Proconsularis and an air of competence. 'That lot were out with Boudicca.'

Cerialis did not sound convinced. 'That is ancient history, surely. All forgotten after nearly forty years.'

'People remember, especially down south,' Rufinus assured them. 'My father was in the province then and saw what those bastards did. Women impaled, mutilated.' The Trinovantes had joined the Iceni and other rebels, sacking three cities and massacring everyone they caught, whether Roman or just from another tribe.

'Well, a one-man rebellion by a soldier sounds unlikely,' Cerialis concluded. 'We must hope to find him or at least discover what happened. However, there are concerning signs of priests and magicians stirring up the tribes here in the north.'

Ferox explained what he had seen and heard, speaking of the shadowy figure of the druid, and his guess that the priest known as the Stallion had led the ambush. He did his best to make them understand the difference between the two holy men, and how the tribes feared men of power and magic even if they did not like them. Claudius Super kept interrupting, scoffing at his fears, and Ferox suspected that even the more sympathetic ones in the room did not understand. He pressed on, but kept back his suspicion of treachery in high places. If for the moment they wanted to believe that it was the raiders who had wiped out the men at the tower then let them. He had one surprise, and waited until the end in the hope of shocking them and at least making them cautious. 'The ambush of the Lady Sulpicia Lepidina was no accident, but part of a deliberate plan, of that I am sure.'

Claudius Super made a scoffing sound and several of the others looked doubtful. These were wild barbarians on the prowl for prey, any prey, not some organised army capable of planning.

'I have no doubt at all,' Ferox went on. 'The captive taken by the Brigantes told them that they wanted to take the noble lady alive, lead her back north and burn her in the fire.'

The room went so quiet that Ferox could hear the sound of the lesson going on in the next room, even though there was no adjoining door. A group of soldiers were being taught to read and write, and were reciting lines of the *Aeneid* with the foot-dragging, lifeless tones of schoolboys. Flavius Cerialis had gone pale. The rest, even the senior regionarius, gaped in sheer horror.

'Bastards,' muttered Annius.

'Animals,' Rufinus said. 'Just animals.'

Cerialis recovered quickly. 'Well, that merely reinforces my gratitude for the centurion's arrival at the vital moment. I shall make another offering to thank the gods that my wife is safe. But all this talk of druids, magicians and kings in the far north must be left for another time, as we have more urgent matters and new orders.'

Crispinus took over, telling them that the provincial legate was on his way to govern the province, but that he might not arrive until the winter was well under way. In the meantime the governor had sent word authorising the acting governor, the Legate Julius Quadratus, commander of II Augusta, to carry out active operations here in the north before the weather rendered them too difficult. Quadratus was at Luguvallium, ready to take the field in person with a column drawn from the forces concentrated there over the summer, including detachments from his own and other legions as well as auxiliaries. They would advance along the Western Road as far as it took them. A second column was to advance from Coria along the Eastern Road.

'We shall form a third, smaller column, staying between the two to ensure that they can communicate, and acting boldly on our own if the opportunity permits. I shall command this force – although I shall of course readily take advice from more experienced men. There is no need to remind you that the emperor will look with great kindness and generosity on those who serve him well in the field, and that a victory, even a small one, will resound to our credit.'

They took that in, all looking eager. There had been few chances for senior officers to make names for themselves in Britannia in the last few years. Yet Ferox was puzzled that no one had asked the obvious question.

'Where are we going, sir?'

Crispinus smiled. 'Of course, I am remiss. Several chieftains of the Selgovae need to be reminded of the power of Rome. Claudius Super can give more details.'

The senior centurio regionarius battled with his headache to explain the situation. He mentioned several leaders and clans who had failed to deliver the cattle and grain due to the empire.

Ferox got the impression that Claudius Super was one of the main advocates of an aggressive response.

'Give them time,' Ferox argued. 'I am sure that they will pay eventually.' None of the leaders mentioned struck him as especially militant. 'If we get it by the end of this month then that will be soon enough.'

'They are late.' Claudius Super implied that this alone demanded retribution.

'It gives us a pretext at least for a display of power,' Crispinus told them. 'And it may well be that no harm is meant and they will deliver what is owed to us without the need for any unpleasantness. If so then all to the good. The campaign is intended to be short and to show that we will strike hard if we are provoked in any way. Now, let us attend to the details.'

Ferox said little as they planned. The contingents to form the column were agreed upon, equipment, baggage and supplies stipulated, all to be ready to leave in three days' time. Arrangements were as thorough as was possible in the time, reminding him of something once told to him by a veteran centurion in Legio V Alaudae, one of those rare old sweats who had risen from the ranks through sheer talent. 'It doesn't matter whether or not it's a good idea,' the man had said. 'Our job is to make sure that it's done well.' Ferox doubted the wisdom of this plan, but when he tried to speak Claudius Super ordered him to be silent. There was an awkward pause, and Crispinus looked intently at him for a while, but was not moved to speak. Claudius Super was senior to Ferox and supposed to know more than the men who reported to him.

Yet when the meeting ended and they began to disperse Crispinus tugged at Ferox's arm. 'I shall want you by my side,' the young aristocrat told him. 'And your Brigantian scouts will be invaluable, of course.'

IX

T HE RIDER SAT motionless, watching them, as the cool
wind gusted along the valley, hissing and rippling through
the long grass. It must have been stronger and colder up
on the hilltop, yet the man was bare from the waist up, his chest
covered in a curving web of blue tattoos, his face painted red from
the nose down and black above, his dirty brown hair plaited into
a pigtail reaching halfway down his back. He carried a thick-
shafted spear and a little rectangular shield, the face covered in
dark leather and with studs around the iron boss.

'They know we are coming then,' Crispinus said, squinting as
he stared up at the man. It was the first time he had seen a Briton
since they had set out – at least one who might well prove an enemy.
The sight was as unsettling as it was exciting.

'They have known we were coming since we set out,' Ferox
told him. 'Probably earlier than that.' He hoped the words did
not hint at British spies and traitors in their ranks, but he judged
the tribune to be a fair man and he needed to learn how quickly
news travelled and how difficult it was to achieve surprise. The
Roman army was not made for stealth and since you could not
hide the movement of any sizeable force, the best to be hoped for
was to move so fast that the enemy did not have enough time to
prepare. Ferox did not want to think of the clans of the Selgovae
as enemies – at least not until he was forced to do so – but in
the field it was always wise to expect the worst and look for the
slightest sign of danger.

They were four days out and almost fifty miles as the raven flew from Vindolanda, making good progress in spite of the country, which had added some distance to the march. Smaller forces always moved faster than big armies, and Crispinus' first independent command consisted of scarcely one thousand fighting men, marching *expedita*, with only the bare essentials of baggage and supplies, which still meant one hundred and thirty pack animals and some eighty slaves and other followers. They had food for another eight days, although good fodder for the horses and pack mules and ponies for only half that time. At worst the animals could eat grass, and for a few days that should not do too much harm to their condition. Otherwise they would demand more supplies from the clans as proof of their loyalty or as a mark of submission, depending on how things went.

Ferox was sure that given a little more time the chieftains would have handed over all that was owed without the need for threats. As he saw it, the procurator's men had changed the rules by demanding payment earlier than usual. The chieftains were bound to resent that, for they had a strong sense of what was fair – especially when it came to their obligation to others. They would pay in time, but only after showing that they could not be pushed around. It could all have been tactfully managed with faces saved on all sides, but that would have required tact, something lacking in Claudius Super's soul. None of this was necessary, but Quadratus, as acting governor, wanted to mount a display of Roman military might, and the real provincial legate had given permission, and so the army marched. Nobody seemed bothered that they were putting on a show of force for a people who had had nothing to do with the ambush on the road.

For all that, there was excitement in being with a column in the field, especially since it had been several years since he had last taken part in a campaign. Idleness did not suit Ferox, for it gave him too much time to brood and to sink into black moods, when drink seemed the only shelter. It was always better to be busy and to feel that each moment and each decision he made mattered, not least because mistakes and misjudgements could kill him and plenty of others. His life had purpose again, at least for the next few days.

The campaign began with pageantry, as they marched from Vindolanda at dawn amid the ceremony that the army could never resist. At the head of the column were the massed standards of the Batavians and Tungrians, guarded by an immaculately turned-out honour guard from the troops who were to remain in the garrison, their brightly painted shields uncovered. These marched up the via principalis, through the gate and over the causeway between the ditches, before parting to parade on each side of the road.

Crispinus and Cerialis waited until the standards were in position before mounting. They were at the head of the column, and after the trumpets sounded three times Cerialis raised his voice and shouted words Ferox did not recognise, even though he knew what they meant. The prefect was asking his soldiers in their own language whether they were ready to fight.

'Huh!' The Batavians bellowed a sound, half animal grunt and half shout of rage. Behind them the centurion Annius called out in Celtic asking his Tungrians whether they were ready, prompting an answering shout of 'Yes!' Three times he shouted and three times the cry was returned. That was the normal way, but the Batavians boasted that they only needed to be asked once if they were ready for war. At the rear because they were setting out from the base of other units, Aelius Brocchus spoke in Latin to his cavalrymen and received a whooping reply from his men.

'Expect we'll leave eventually,' Vindex said to his men as they waited at the very rear, behind the baggage train. Some of the Brigantes grinned. Others, who never seen even such a small Roman force muster, just stared in wonder.

At the head Crispinus drew his sword and pointed towards the gates.

'Forward, march!' Cerialis shouted and they set off. The men were ready for the field, wearing dark cloaks, shields protected by drab calfskin covers, and armour and other metalwork well greased and oiled to fend off rust. Three turmae of Batavians followed the senior officers, each decurion leading two dozen men in three files so that they could get through the gate without having to slow down. They went in silence apart from the clink of harness and the dull thump of shields swinging gently against the horses' left shoulders. Decurions had high yellow plumes running down the centre of the helmets, as well as the animal fur sported by their men. Behind came the infantry, helmets with deeper, broader neck guards and uncovered ears so that they could hear commands better. Apart from the officers and one or two men who liked to dress up, their helmets were covered with moss, which looked like fur from any distance. There were seventy-five Batavian cavalry and two hundred infantry divided into three centuries, one of them led by the optio Arcuttius as acting commander because only a pair of centurions were available. The last remaining vexillum was carried by one of the standard-bearers at the head of the infantry.

Ferox stood beside his horse watching them pass. The road was lined with well-wishers, other soldiers off duty, and scores of women and children from the camp watching their menfolk march away and not knowing whether they would ever see them again. The law said that soldiers could not marry, but many of them ignored the rule and the army turned a blind eye, content as long as they did not expect extra rations or pay. The women were a tough bunch, some from home, many more picked up wherever the unit served. If their man survived his twenty-five years of service and was honourably discharged, then as an auxiliary he would gain citizenship for himself, his wife and their children, which was fine as long as he did survive. In the meantime they lived in the barracks, making love and giving birth in the little rooms shared with the man's comrades. The children grew up knowing the army as their only world. The boys usually enlisted when they were old enough, while many of the girls would marry soldiers. There was a tall boy of eleven or twelve not far from Ferox, standing to attention with a ferocious determination, obviously yearning to be marching with the men. Alongside was his mother, a thin pale woman with long brown hair streaked grey and moist eyes that made it clear she wished her man was not going and that they had sent someone else instead.

The families did not cheer, watching in silence as the men filed past, looking straight to the front, and yet the scene moved Ferox as it did every time he saw an army marching off. Sulpicia Lepidina was next to him, wrapped up in a heavy deep blue cloak against the chilly morning air.

'You must stay with me and explain what is happening,' she had told him and he had obeyed, although there was little to explain and he had not said much. The lady was silent, watching her husband as he rode at the head of the column, dressed in martial finery. Her maid was with her, as were two male slaves and the two centurions left in command of the rest of the Batavians.

The Tungrians followed the Batavians, with two of their double-sized centuries mustering a total of one hundred and eighty men. Their helmets were bare bronze, polished to a dull sheen. Titus Annius rode at their head, his transverse crest a wide spray of tall white feathers tipped red. He nodded respectfully to Sulpicia Lepidina as he passed, for he was a commander and granted more licence than the parading soldiers. Ferox noticed that the second century was also led by an optio.

Aelius Brocchus came next, with seven turmae comprising some two hundred men, so that each was close to its full strength. The ala Gallorum Petriana – until a few years ago with the additional name Domitiana, now quietly forgotten – saw themselves as the best horsemen of the army in Britain and took every opportunity to show it. Another part of the ala was serving with the column marching up the Eastern Road from Coria, and Ferox wondered whether they were as splendidly equipped and mounted as these men. The horses were excellent, bigger than those provided for the Batavians, well groomed and grouped by colour, so that there were two turmae on greys, two more on chestnuts and the rest on bays. It was an affectation only possible when active campaigning was rare. Each man carried a strong-shafted spear upright and had three lighter javelins in a long quiver hanging from the right rear horn of his saddle. They wore their long spathae on their right hips in the Gallic fashion, the weapons hanging low so that it was easier to draw them while mounted. Their helmets were iron, with brass decoration, most of them shaped to look as if the bowls were covered with locks of thick hair. Each man had a shirt of mail, split at the sides on the hips for comfort. A third of each turma, the men who would form the front rank, also had laminated guards of iron sections on their right arms, protecting them from shoulder to wrist.

After the glorious cavalry came the pack train: mules and ponies supervised by a few soldiers and around eighty personal servants and *galearii*, slaves owned by the army, given boots, uniform tunic and cloak, knives and old patterned helmets to wear. Behind them, at the very rear of the column, walking their horses through quite a few piles of fresh dung, came Vindex and his scouts, their numbers raised to nearly thirty by some fresh men sent by his chieftain, They sauntered along, chattering or ogling the women in the crowd. Vindex winked at the maid as he passed, prompting a burst of giggling and feigned modesty until her mistress glared at her.

'Lady, I had better go,' Ferox said. 'I do hope that the boy's condition continues to improve. After all, we Flavii should stick together!' He had brought her water from Covventina's Spring to add to the sick child's broth, and whether by this or something else, Cerialis' son's fever had broken.

'Thank you. You have been very kind.' Sulpicia Lepidina stood close to him, and, unseen because of her heavy wool cloak, her hand clasped his for just a moment. 'Good fortune,' she added, her blue eyes staring up into his.

'I'm sure your husband will return in glory,' he said.

'I am sure he will.' For the first time since he had met her she looked fragile. 'Good fortune,' she said again, before dropping her voice to a faint whisper. 'Come back.'

'I will.' As he mouthed the words he wondered what he was doing. Her song at the feast still echoed in his mind, as did her good humour and signs of pleasure in his company whenever they met. He was drawn to her, but then surely any man with blood in his veins would be drawn to such a woman. What he did not understand was why she seemed interested in him, and he could not quite make up his mind whether she was singling him out or was simply always so full of charm. He tried to stop them, but in the last days wild, absurd and dangerous dreams kept bubbling up in his mind, feeding his good spirits as much as the activity.

Philo waited with his horse.

'You should stay here,' he told the boy for the tenth time.

'My place is with you.'

'You won't enjoy it,' Ferox said.

'That is the lot of a slave.'

They rode after the column, and Ferox forced himself not to look back. It was ridiculous and dangerous to them both – and maybe it was all in his imagination, and he mistook natural charm and understandable gratitude for real interest. He made himself stare at the fort buildings as they went along the road and out under the gate. The serried ranks of standards were in place, although the escort had stood at ease now that there were only native scouts ambling past. More people had gathered to watch the column, standing in the fronts of shops and bars or in the alleys leading off the main route through the canabae. They lived here because the army was here and were part of it even if they were not soldiers. Batavians and Tungrians were customers, friends, drinking partners and lovers and some made signs to bring good luck as the ranks of soldiers went past. At the far edge of the crowd were beggars, with all the ones he had seen the day before and a few more. The old man to whom Vindex had given a coin was a little apart as usual, leaning on his crooked staff, his filthy beard and hair down to his waist, and his scruffy dog beside him. The man stared at the soldiers' boots, never looking anyone in the eye, and all the while he muttered words that made no sense.

'Chin up, Father,' Vindex called to him, but the beggar did not react. Ferox wondered whether his appearance was a bad omen and then tried and failed to dismiss the thought. By this time he was riding alongside the cemetery with its rows of wooden pillars. It did not depress him and instead he thought of a woman with golden hair and big blue eyes and wondered.

Two hours later they met the vexillation brought by the Prefect Rufinus to complete the column. Cohors I fida Vardullorum equitata was a mixed unit like the Batavians, and had sent fifty horsemen in two turmae and two hundred and fifty infantrymen in four centuries. They were small men in the main, dark-haired and clean-shaven, recruited from the highlands in Iberia, and they marched with a jaunty confidence. They were new to this northern frontier and to Britannia itself, but looked to be good soldiers, confident in themselves and their leaders. They wore black tunics, a rare sight in the army, and Ferox suspected that some would see this as unlucky. The Vardulli just said that it was unlucky for whoever met them.

A third of Crispinus' column consisted of horsemen, but if they wanted to stay together they could go no faster than a man or mule could walk. By day the cavalry from the cohorts provided scouts ahead, on the flanks and to the rear of the main force. Brocchus' men were split into two, as vanguard and rearguard; they were kept formed up and ready to fight. The Batavian infantry led, the Tungrians protected the baggage and the Spanish infantry were in the rear. Vindex and his men rode far ahead to scout, and often Ferox went with them, wearing his battered old floppy hat so that the tribesmen would know him from afar. At night the cavalry provided pickets while the infantrymen did the digging, making a ditch and throwing up a low rampart of cut turves and piled earth and stones when the ground was too hard. It was rarely more than waist high, but would slow an assault if one came. Tents were pitched inside, although they had carried as few as possible so each one was packed fuller than usual. Men on guard during the night watches came back to climb under blankets left warm by the men who had relieved them.

They dug in each night because it made them a little safer and because that was the army's way, but because they pushed on and marched as far as they could there was never time to do the job properly. Cavalrymen always hated to dig, and the infantry did their best, and men from both arms formed the outposts beyond the ditch and rampart with the job of dying noisily if an attack came.

For three days there was no sign of any enemy – indeed little trace of people at all.

'They're wary of us, sir,' Ferox explained when Crispinus expressed surprise to find another farm empty of humans and animals alike. There were four huts, a raised grain store, and dry stone walls to form animal pens. Some of the dung in these was no more than five or six hours old.

'Why?' the tribune demanded. 'These are not from one of the clans we are sent to chastise.'

'They don't know that – at least, not for certain, and would you take a risk?'

Ferox was pleased when a Batavian cavalryman asked whether they should burn the houses and Crispinus was aghast at the thought. 'Of course not.'

The soldier looked disappointed, but resigned to the vagaries of senior officers.

The tribune brought a dozen troopers with him whenever he joined Ferox and some of the scouting parties, something he did more often as the days passed. Now, at long last, on the fourth morning when they reached the lands of one of the chieftains who had not yet paid his tax, Crispinus saw his first warrior. The Briton with his painted face sat on his pony, watching them as they watched him.

'Do they always paint their faces?' he asked. Crispinus talked a lot and asked many questions, so that his early long silences were no more than a blessed memory of a better world.

'Means the bugger's taken a vow,' Vindex explained when the centurion said nothing. 'He will either vanquish an enemy and take a trophy before returning home or he will die in the attempt.

They're queer folk, the Selgovae. Good hosts, though, and fairly honest if you don't trust them too much.'

Crispinus was puzzled. 'So he really will not go back to his home unless he kills an enemy?'

'Pity we haven't got any archers, we could solve his problem for him now,' Ferox suggested, making the tribune stare at him.

'I thought you wanted to talk to him?'

'Well, I'll try.' Ferox urged his horse into a trot up the slope towards the lone warrior. He raised his empty right hand high to show that he was coming in peace. The man watched him, letting him come close, until the centurion was twenty paces away. The Briton raised his spear and Ferox reined in. He shouted out that they did not want to fight unless they had to and wanted to speak to the chieftains. The man rode away.

'Get anywhere?' Crispinus asked Ferox when he returned.

'We shall soon see, sir.'

They pushed on, down one valley that opened into another, steeper sided with high hills on either side. Ferox did not like this country. If they had had a bigger force and plenty of time then he would have wanted them to advance covered by pickets on top of the ridges. As it was even the main force did not have the manpower to do it, so relied on mounted patrols to see any threat long before it appeared. He hoped that he was right and that the Selgovae did not want to fight. All the while Crispinus kept chattering away. Some of it was nerves, but there was also a genuine curiosity and desire to learn so that he could do his job better. With just a few months of military service, the young aristocrat was now in charge of over a thousand men, their lives at risk if he made a mistake. He was nervous but eager, and the man gabbled away almost as much as Vindex and his Brigantians.

'You do not paint your face?' Crispinus asked the head of the scouts.

'No, my lord, I'm pretty enough as it is.' Vindex leered at him to demonstrate, his teeth more than usually horse-like. 'Not many do, apart from these people.'

'Yet you are kin to them.'

'Me! No, not to this lot.' Vindex shook his head at such ignorance. He was polite to the tribune, but no more than he would be to a chieftain of his own people, and among the Brigantes blunt speech was admired. 'Some of the Textoverdi marry among the southern Selgovae. Not many of my folk – the Carvetii – though. Leastways only if we took their women as captives, but that doesn't count. That was in the old days, of course.'

'You sound wistful.'

'Not me. Long live Rome and long live the emperor! By the way, who is the emperor again?'

Crispinus laughed at the time. Later, when he had followed Ferox away from the others and was out of earshot, he showed more concern.

'This is a dangerous time,' he said. 'Our Lord Trajan is not well known, can boast of no real victories and proved embarrassingly loyal to Domitian just a few short years ago. There are far too many people, like our friend, who have no idea what sort of man the emperor is and struggle even to remember his name.'

'He is princeps,' Ferox said, as if that settled the matter.

Crispinus waited for a while, before realising that the centurion had nothing more to say.

'Our Lord Trajan is princeps, first citizen, first in the Senate, and many other titles. For the moment at least. It would be good for the state if he remains so.' Once again, the tribune stopped and looked at the centurion.

'I have no objections,' Ferox said eventually.

'He is a good ruler.' Crispinus' voice contained a hint of irritation. 'But others do not consider such things and instead look only for personal power. I am sure that you heard the rumours about the army in Syria.'

Ferox nodded. A year ago the provincial legate commanding the main army in the east had tried to win over his men to back him in a bid for the throne. 'It came to nothing, though.'

'It was handled with delicacy,' Crispinus told him. 'Retirement to private life because of ill health, postings to distant frontiers, that sort of thing.'

'Is that why you're here, my lord?' Ferox said before he could stop himself.

The tribune glared at him, anger in his eyes, until his aristocratic calm restored itself.

'Why are you telling me this, my lord?' Ferox asked.

'Because this campaign matters, even though it is a small and local affair. Our Lord Trajan is new to power, comes from Spain of all places, and is not that well connected at Rome. There are plenty of senators who feel themselves more suited to the supreme office. They must be shown that they are wrong, that he is wise and under his rule the empire will flourish and the armies win victory after victory, so that the Pax Augusta will reign supreme. That being so, there can be no defeats – not even small ones on distant frontiers like this.'

'Would anyone care?'

Crispinus pinched the bridge of his nose. 'I fear that I have a cold. Does it ever get warm in this benighted place?' He sniffed hard to clear his nostrils. It was a Roman habit Ferox still found strange. 'People will care,' he said. 'Not for the right reasons, but because they will scent weakness. Our Lord Trajan is on the Rhine, and the armies of the two Germanies will most likely stay loyal, but the legions in other provinces do not know him and might be willing to follow someone who promised them wealth to raise him to the purple. It happened when Nero died and that was only thirty years ago, and tens of thousands died in the chaos. It could happen again, very, very easily.'

'Is that why Trajan – my apologies, our Lord Trajan – is loitering on the German frontier rather than going to Rome to be welcomed by his adoring people? Or is that an impolite question?' Ferox's expression gave no hint of repentance.

Crispinus stared at the centurion, who stared back impassively until the tribune gave up and looked away, pretending to follow the flight of a bird. 'My father was right,' he said. 'You have an imaginative and suspicious mind. He said that you did not trust anyone else, but that you followed the scent of the truth like a hound sniffing a trail. Well, he also believed that you can be trusted because of your oath to serve him – and his family, if I am not mistaken.'

Ferox nodded. He had been waiting for Crispinus to remind him of the oath, taken all those years ago on the Danube as the price for convincing the man's father to march and save some of Ferox's men.

'I swore to aid him as long as it did not conflict with my *sacramentum*, my pledge to Rome and the princeps,' Ferox said, his voice flat. 'I am sworn to Trajan and as long as he remains princeps I will keep my word, whatever may happen.'

'Others may not be so diligent in keeping that same sacred promise of a soldier. There are some who would be happy to make mischief and let our armies be defeated and our soldiers killed simply to discredit the Lord Trajan. They are distinguished men – or friends and dependants of distinguished men – and they may well be in positions of authority. We cannot let them betray the empire and us by engineering defeat.'

They had reached the top of a low rise, and Ferox stopped to stare along the valley ahead of them. He could see pairs of Vindex's scouts some way ahead and watched as two of the Brigantians paused. Crispinus glanced over his shoulder as Vindex trotted up to join them.

'Be vigilant and trust no one,' he whispered to Ferox. 'If we learn the truth in time then we can stop them.'

From noon onwards they saw more riders shadowing them. Ferox tried once again to meet them, but these proved even more skittish and rode away before he was close enough to call to them. They did not go far and kept watching. From the heights he looked down on the scouting force of a dozen troopers and about the same number of Brigantes. Vindex and his men took turns to go ahead and he could see some of them, lone warriors or pairs of them on the slopes of the valley for some way ahead.

Back down the valley were the Batavian patrols. They were about a mile back, and he could see the main force as a dark patch on the green another half-mile beyond them. From up here, the column looked tiny. He stayed up on the crest for a while, keeping pace with them as they trotted along down in the valley. Half an hour later he saw another darker patch on a hillock ahead of where the ground rose to join another glen. It looked as if someone was waiting, but whether to fight or speak was hard to tell. The force was a good size, so it could be either.

Crispinus was still talking when he returned.

'I had assumed you Britons would all be much alike,' the tribune declared, 'but in fact you vary a great deal, far more than the tribes of Gaul.'

'You've studied a lot then,' Vindex said sarcastically, as if the young aristocrat had just announced that rain comes from the skies.

Crispinus darted him an angry look and was ignored. He smiled. 'I do remember my uncle telling me that the Silures were different from everyone, perhaps from every nation on earth.'

'Oh well, everyone knows that,' Vindex agreed. 'Odd people. Funny customs. Don't talk much. Don't swear much either and you cannot say that is natural.'

'Is it true?' Crispinus asked. 'Now that you mention it I have not heard you swear.'

'Waste of good anger,' Ferox said without looking at him. It was something his grandfather had often said. Do not waste rage. Nurture it, cherish it and use the strength it gives. Hot anger gets a man killed. Cold anger will put the other man in the earth.

'Silures like killing.' Vindex was enjoying stirring things up. 'They like it more than food or drink – even women.'

Ferox said nothing. For the first time in years he wished he was back with his own people, men of sense who enjoyed silence for its own sake. He was tempted to say that his people most liked winning, but saw no point in the conversation. Things were as they were, and the tribune was marching into the lands of the Selgovae, not the Silures.

'My uncle Frontinus,' Crispinus went on, 'the man who conquered your people, did say that the Silures were cruel and cunning, that they killed without remorse and tortured without mercy. He said that they despise everyone and have no honour. According to him half of what a Silure told you was a lie and the other half wasn't true.'

Vindex roared with laughter, then explained in their own tongue to his warriors who found it just as hilarious. Ferox shrugged, half his mind wondering about what the tribune had said earlier. Some of what Crispinus said was more than idle talk. 'But Uncle also said that if one did give you his word, then he would keep it until the end of the world.'

Ferox would keep his pledge to Crispinus and his father as long as it did not interfere with his oath of allegiance to the emperor. The question was which side was the tribune really on – apart from his own, like any other ambitious aristocrat. Ferox said nothing, but heard his grandfather's deep voice telling him that a solemn oath could never be broken, that a faithless man was lower than the dust, doomed to grim punishment in the Otherworld. He also remembered standing in the hall of a principia thirteen years ago and swearing loyalty to Rome and emperor. At the time he had been young enough to thrill at the grandeur of the big parade where the oath was taken. These days the sense was one of habit as much as anything else. It was simply part of him, but that oath held him forever in a vice, and in life he could not be free of it unless the empire crumbled into ruin and was no more.

'There's someone waiting to meet us up ahead,' he told Crispinus after the man had finally relapsed into silence, broken only by occasional guffaws from Vindex and his men. 'We will see them soon, when we crest that rise.'

A Brigantian scout appeared, riding back with the same news.

'Should we wait for the column?' Crispinus asked.

'Let's take a look, sir. Walk the horses on the way so that we can run if needs be. They'll know the main force is coming, and this way we look as if we have no doubt that they will do what we ask and not give trouble.'

The tribune looked pale, but nodded assent.

There were several hundred Selgovae standing or sitting on the hillock. They wore dark trousers with faded patterns of tartan, and some had striped or checked tunics and long cloaks. One or two in the front wore helmets and armour and carried swords. Most of the rest had a spear or javelin and a little round or square shield. Ahead of them were forty or so warriors sitting on their ponies, and a chariot, the wooden frame brightly painted in red and blue. It was drawn by one black and one grey pony, and carried a charioteer, naked from the waist up and covered with tattoos, and a short, stocky warrior in mail, an old legionary helmet clasped under one arm and his long red hair falling down his back. As they approached the driver twitched the reins and the chariot came towards them. The warrior spread his arms high, waving the helmet in one, but apart from the long sword on his right hip he carried no weapon.

'He wants to talk, sir,' Ferox told the tribune. 'It would be wise for us to meet him so that he can see your face and decide whether or not to trust you. And by the way, I'll lay good odds that he is letting us see no more than half his warriors at best. The rest are in the trees on either side of us.'

'Are you sure?' Crispinus glanced around. 'I don't see anything.'

'That's why you know they are there,' the centurion assured him, and then the chariot came round in a wide arc and slewed to a halt in front of them.

The chieftain was named Egus and he did not want to fight unless the Romans gave him no other choice. Ferox had met him before, although he did not know him well as it was less than a year since the man had succeeded his brother as leader. His reputation was as a good lord to his people, and the clan had always paid what was due to the empire on time, or near enough. This Egus was willing to do, but he resented the levy being demanded early.

'It takes time to gather and sort the grain, and even longer to kill the animals and prepare the hides,' he told Ferox, who interpreted. In ten days they would have everything as usual.

'You should accept, sir,' Ferox told the tribune. 'He is offering his own son as hostage until everything is delivered.'

Crispinus was unsure what to do. 'Do you trust him?'

'Don't look at me,' Ferox said in a low voice. 'Keep your eyes on his and do not smile. He needs to know that you are a serious man and one he can trust.' He switched back into the language of the tribes and spoke to the chieftain in short, clipped sentences, getting similar replies. At last Egus held out his right hand to the tribune.

'I have agreed to the terms,' Ferox told the young officer.

'You take a lot on yourself, centurion,' Crispinus whispered, but took the outstretched hand and shook it firmly. 'I agree,' he told the chieftain, hoping that the man either knew a little Latin or would sense the meaning from his tone.

The boy was brought, and all the while more and more warriors appeared on the edges of the woodland. Egus' son looked to be about nine or ten, skinny and with a drooping lip. The warrior attending him was the man with the painted face they had seen earlier in the day. By the time they all went back to join the rest of the party, there were hundreds more tribesmen watching them from the hillsides.

'You were right,' Crispinus conceded. 'There are a lot more of them than we saw. A fight would have been harder than I thought. Yet I believe that I command. As I said, you presume a great deal to decide without consulting me.'

'It's my job,' Ferox said. 'Usually there is no time to seek approval. I am here to keep Rome's peace, if I can. Once the main body came up we could have beaten this lot – probably. But we would have lost men, they would have lost a lot more and the rest of them would hate us. This way everyone is alive and we have a loyal ally.'

It started to rain, which made the wait for the column to arrive seem even longer. They pitched camp on the fairly level ground in front of the hillock where Egus and his band had waited. By now there were probably over a thousand Britons watching the soldiers as they went through the routine of entrenching and laying out the tent-lines.

'They don't get a lot of entertainment up here,' Vindex said.

The hostage, lank hair plastered flat by the rain and huddled in his cloak, was sent to Crispinus' tent as soon as this was erected, at the junction where the line of the two main roads in the camp met, just as if this was a proper fort.

'Pity we could not get up into the next valley,' Ferox said, half thinking aloud.

Crispinus scanned the hillsides in the fading light, watching the Selgovae as they watched the Romans. 'We are with allies, so you tell me. And we have their leader's son at our mercy.'

'If that's who he is, and assuming his father actually likes him.'

For the first time Crispinus appeared shocked.

'It will probably be all right,' Ferox said. 'Probably.'

X

I T WAS A nervous night in a cold camp, the rain turning into a downpour that doused fires and made it hard to see very far or hear any movement until it was close. Crispinus and the other senior officers slept very little, all of them visiting the sentries in each of the four watches. Early in the third watch there was a scare from the picket in front of the northern entrance to the camp.

'There's something out there, sir.' The Tungrian in charge of the six-man picket was certain. 'Something moving towards us.'

Crispinus and the other equestrian officers had heard the call and run to see what was happening. They squinted as they tried to see in spite of the driving rain.

'There are a lot of them.' Cerialis had almost to shout into the tribune's ear to be heard above the howling wind. 'Look, up there!' He pointed. 'We should sound the alarm.'

Crispinus hesitated, and then jumped when a hooded and cloaked figure slid out of the darkness and came up beside him. He fumbled as he tried to grab the wet handgrip of his sword.

'I'm on your side, tribune,' Ferox said, throwing back the hood and grinning.

'Have you been out there?' Crispinus was breathing hard, his face so battered by the rain that it felt numb.

'Just took a little walk.'

'They're coming closer!' Cerialis shouted again, but by some chance the wind slackened and his voice sounded terribly loud.

136

'It's cows,' Ferox said. 'The warriors have all gone to shelter and I don't blame 'em. It's just a herd of cows.' He was feeling happy, after testing himself to see whether he could still move quietly in the darkness. Silurian boys were taught stealth and concealment from infancy, to help them hunt game and enemies alike, but he knew that he was out of practice. In truth the main danger on a night like this was stumbling into someone else rather than being spotted from a distance.

The rain stopped late in the night, and in a grey, sunless dawn the column prepared to move. There was no sign of the Selgovae, apart from a thin tendril of smoke rising from one of the hearths in a farm half a mile away, but there was also no sign of a horse and mule, taken from inside the camp. The animals had simply vanished, and no one seemed convinced when Ferox assured them that the creatures had been stolen.

'But how did they do it?' Crispinus demanded, since all his sentries swore that they had seen nothing.

'Why is as big a question,' Brocchus suggested. 'Do they mean to break the agreement?'

'They did it because they could,' Ferox said, 'and to show you that they could and so are men to be treated with respect. They could do it because men get tired and sleepy on guard, and if you take the time and know what you are about you can get past them.' He had to keep reminding himself that none of these men had spent long in this part of the world, apart from Titus Annius, who did not ask foolish questions. 'They're not breaking the treaty. If they were doing that we'd be counting slit throats, not a couple of animals gone.'

'Allies aren't supposed to rob each other.' Cerialis sounded genuinely offended.

'They see it as up to us to look after our property. If we're daft enough to let ourselves be robbed then that's not their fault.'

Crispinus frowned. 'This is a strange place,' he said.

The column moved out in the usual order, save for the addition of twenty more Batavians to add to the tribune's escort when he joined Ferox and the scouts. They headed westwards, as far as the land allowed, which at first was not much, so that they kept going north into the teeth of a cold wind. The aim was to move closer to the bigger force coming up the Western Road under the legate of II Augusta, and at noon they dropped into another valley taking them in that direction. They were sheltered from the wind, but the sky remained a resolute and unbroken field of grey.

In spite of the agreement with Egus and his people, there was little more sign of life. Farms were empty when they arrived, although now and again they saw flocks of sheep and clusters of brown cows in the far distance. Warriors riding ponies watched them, sometimes letting Vindex's men come close enough to exchange greetings or joking insults.

Just before noon they left the territory of Egus' people and entered the lands of another chief, a man named Venutius, who never looked anyone in the eye and was renowned as a great cattle thief.

'You make that sound like a compliment,' Crispinus said when Ferox described the man.

'It is in these parts.'

'Well, at least he ought to have enough hides to pay his tax.'

The valley was just as empty, but the sides were dotted with clusters of pine trees, straggling groups of alder, and thick heather.

Crispinus was beginning to learn. 'I presume that we are being watched.' Ferox just nodded.

An hour later they saw a dozen riders some way ahead. Half an hour after that there were other horsemen high on the hills behind them, watching the main force march along the bottom of the valley. One of Vindex's scouts came back, clutching at his side. His tunic was dark with a spreading patch of blood, which oozed between his fingers as he pressed them against the wound. He had been one of a pair of men sent along the valley side to the left. The other warrior did not return.

Ferox and Crispinus reached the wounded man as Vindex and two others were lowering him to the ground.

'Bastards with horses marked on their heads,' Vindex told them, looking grim even by his standards. 'Shouldn't have happened, though. The lad he was with rushed after the first one he saw. He's one of the new boys.' He shook his head. 'Brigus here went after him and three of the buggers jumped him.'

'What does it mean?' Crispinus asked.

Ferox was scanning the trees on either side. 'That we need to be more careful. And that we are probably in for a fight.'

Vindex kept his scouts closer from then on, and let the Batavian horsemen leading the main force come close before he pressed on. More and more little groups of warriors on horseback and on foot moved on the heights above them. A rider came from Brocchus to say that there were others closing in behind them.

They pressed on, fighting a sense that the valley was about to close in over them. The land sloped down and a little brook meandered along, finding the easiest path downhill. They had to cross the water again and again, following a track used by cattle. Up ahead there was the blackened trunk of an oak tree, struck by lightning and long since hollowed out, yet still standing.

'I see it,' Ferox said when he saw Vindex turn round. Crispinus strained, shading his eyes against the pale glare from the clouds, but shook his head because he could not make it out, until they got closer. Then he blanched.

The severed head of the lost scout was nailed to the wood. Whoever had done it had used an army nail, one of the long heavy iron pieces used to fasten great beams of timber. They had also cut off the man's genitals and stuffed them into his mouth. Above the head, impaled on another long nail, was a straw effigy of a man, dressed in a tunic with red wool for hair and grey to show a breastplate and helmet. There was something wrapped around one of its arms and tied into place.

'Do not touch it!' one of the Brigantes shouted as Ferox jumped down and walked towards the ghastly warnings. Vindex did not speak, but looked as worried.

'It's not meant for me,' the centurion told then, 'so it cannot harm me.' He hoped that he was right. 'Get me a sack.'

The red-headed doll must be Cerialis, and that would fit with the attack on his wife, even though Ferox could not understand why the couple were singled out. He pulled the little figure off, ripping it to get it past the broad head of the nail. On the arm was a tiny scroll of papyrus, covered on both sides with writing in Greek characters, although many of the words did not make sense. 'Barbaso Barbasoch Barbasoch,' it began and looked a lot like magic, some spell or curse presumably meant to strike the prefect of the Batavians.

'I thought they did not read and write up here,' Crispinus said, his face almost as grey as his hair.

'They don't.' Ferox tore the doll to pieces and flung them in the air, and then spun around his arms held high. 'The spell is broken!' he yelled. Vindex touched the wheel of Taranis to his lips. The centurion used his knife to prise the second nail loose. Vindex helped him and they freed the head and put it in the sack so that they could treat the remains with honour when the force stopped for the night.

The main column would not have to see this grim message, but Ferox had little doubt that word would spread like wildfire and worry the men. He was known to be a strange man and a Briton, so perhaps his little charade of dispelling the curse would help.

Late in the afternoon the cloud thinned and they saw the sun for the first time that day as it set in magnificent splendour. Mounted Selgovae hovered around them, keeping well away as the column closed up and laid out the camp. They had stopped an hour earlier than usual and did their best to dig in the stony soil; in the end they had to be content with a ditch not much more than a foot deep. The wall was better, with a base of turves, some piled earth, built up with stones pulled out of the soil, gathered off the ground and ripped from the cattle pens around a cluster of round houses. They built just three entrances, for the fourth wall lay alongside the stream, and in each of the openings the left-hand wall curved out in front of the gateway. It meant any attacker would have to swerve to come in, all the while exposing their unshielded right side.

No tents were pitched, so that the perimeter was as small as possible while still enclosing all the men and the animals. Crispinus detailed double the normal number of men to stand guard, and told the rest to sleep rolled up in their cloaks and with their arms to hand. At least it was dry so that fires could be lit and a hot meal prepared. Oddly, for all the rumours of severed heads and curses, the mood was brighter than the previous night. Ferox ate quickly and slept during the last hours of daylight. He had given the scroll to Philo to decipher and the task cheered the young slave, making him feel useful and important. After a moment's glance he told his master that the language was a mix of Greek, Aramaic, Old Hebrew and Egyptian, but that much of it was gibberish or secret words of power. Yet one theme was repeated in all the tongues. 'Blood of king, blood of queen, blood of power and blood of woe,' it said again and again. 'It will take longer to work it all out,' the slave said. 'I'll keep at it.'

'Good lad,' Ferox told him. 'It may be important.'

Halfway through the first watch Ferox slipped over the wall beside the stream. His face was smeared with ash so that his skin did not shine. He wore his boots and trousers but no tunic and was glad of the heavy hooded cloak because the air was chill. His only weapon was his army-issue dagger, unsheathed and tucked into the back of the simple rope belt he wore. Vindex had wanted to come, but the Brigantian was not used to this sort of work, and Ferox was happier on his own. He did not tell anyone else of his plan, including Crispinus and the other officers. If nothing happened then they would be none the wiser.

At first it was easier than expected. A stallion, one of many ridden by the ala Petriana, sniffed a mare on heat and began to whinny and pull at the stake to which he was tethered. Men gathered, there was shouting, and the guards on the wall by the stream turned to see, giving him all the time in the world to vault the rampart, jump to the far bank of the stream, run ten paces and then fall flat and lie still. Lying still was a big part of the game, and that was why the elders taught Silurian boys to love silence and stillness. Covered in the long cloak he would be hard to see. He waited until he was sure that no one had spotted him, then made himself wait even longer before he began to crawl slowly forward, wondered why whenever a man did this it took him straight over a cowpat, and then stopped, watching and listening.

It was another hour or more – time was hard to judge because the cloud covered the stars and there was no moon – before he sensed and then saw figures ahead of him. By now he was some five or six hundred paces away from the outlying pickets, having swung around the camp in a big arc, helped by a series of gullies deep enough to jog along if he kept low and was careful.

There were Britons out on the slope and the fools were talking. He expected that of Roman soldiers, men who had stood guard so many times than even on campaign it came to feel routine and safe. More than once he had heard chatter and laughter from the camp, the sound carrying clearly in the still air. Now there were two men whispering as they crouched behind some boulders some way in front of him. They were tribesmen, but the accents did not sound local and neither was easy to understand.

Ferox lay flat on the earth, watching them. He spotted another pair about a hundred paces to the men's right, and searched until he found two more a little further away to the left and better hidden. After a while he crawled back into the gully and crept along it, stopping as always to wait and listen as he worked his way gradually up the slope.

He sensed the man before he saw or heard him, and could not have explained to anyone how he knew. The centurion lay on his chest, head raised to scan the darkness. At last he saw him, a monstrously tall man standing straight and still, looking down into the valley. He did not move or speak, and Ferox did not sense that he knew the centurion was there. He told himself that he was getting old and sloppy to go so close before spotting the man.

There were shouts from the Roman camp. Probably another false alarm because soon there was silence again. All the while the huge man stood like a statue. He looked to be seven or eight feet tall, but then the cloud parted for a moment and in the bright starlight Ferox saw that the man wore a stag's head, antlers and all, as a headdress. He was tall enough, his bare chest lean and muscled, but he was no giant or being from the Otherworld, just a man who could be killed. The cloud closed and the centurion waited for his eyes to adapt again to the dark.

Ferox began to inch forward.

More shapes came out of the shadows towards the man wearing antlers.

'Are you ready?' The voice was a strong one, used to command, and Ferox guessed that it was from the tall man. Two others appeared beside him.

'Soon. The lot took longer than I thought, but the ones are chosen and have taken their draughts.'

'Good. Strike at the ones on this side. There are ten or twelve. Tell them to pay no heed to the enemy's shouts or blades. Each of them will be given the strength of a hundred. They must kill and burn until there are none left to kill and burn or they fall and receive their reward.'

'Yes, lord.' None of the men sounded like Selgovae, but this one spoke like a southerner, maybe even like the Trinovantes. Ferox wondered about the soldier missing from the tower. Had he really slaughtered his comrades and deserted to join these fanatics?

'Good, then go to them and tell them that I will invoke the pleasure of Cernunnos to guide their hands and uplift their hearts. I will be here watching their glory.'

That's nice, Ferox thought, and a good excuse if anyone was fool enough to swallow it.

'Follow the raven! Follow the stag! Follow the stallion!' the tall man called, lifting his arms and no longer caring about quiet.

The shout seemed to echo across the valley and Ferox was sure that the Romans would hear it. Maybe that was what the man wanted.

'Go my friends, go!'

The two other men slipped away, going towards a darker shade in the night that was a long patch of woodland. Ferox wondered whether to follow and try to catch the southerner, but doubted that it was possible. Instead he let them go and then resumed his snail-paced crawl.

In the end it was easy. The tall man began to chant, dancing round and round in a circle.

'O Morrigan! O Cernunnos! O Vinotonus!' he screamed, and drew a long sword, waving it in the air. 'O Isis! O Hades! O unnamed gods and demons of darkness!'

Ferox was close now, reaching back to pull out his *pugio*. The man was chanting, calling on gods from many lands, and as he spun again, facing away, the centurion pushed himself up.

'*Barbaso Barbasoch Barbasoch!*' The man turned. Spittle flew into Ferox's face as his left hand seized the man's throat, grabbing a heavy torc, and the right hand punched the knife under the man's ribs. The priest gasped and choked as the centurion drove the dagger further in, twisting the blade, his hand warm with fresh blood.

The night came alive with shrieks from down in the valley and as Ferox held the dying man up he saw a band of warriors charging at the picket outside the camp. He saw them because the men waved torches in the air and in the flickering red light forty or fifty men charged, bare flesh shining and bright weapons in their hands. Trumpets sounded the alarm, but glints along the rampart showed that it was already lined with waiting men.

The tall man struggled violently and then went limp and heavy so that Ferox almost fell over with the corpse as it slumped down. He lowered the body to the ground and crouched beside it. No one was moving nearby or seemed to have noticed what he had done. In the valley there was a confused whirl of fighting around the picket and more of the torch-carrying warriors streaming past at the entrance to the camp. Some of them dropped, hit by javelins he could not see in the darkness. The rest kept going, swinging to the right to go through the gate. More of them fell to missiles, and the score or so of survivors met a line of waiting soldiers, shields raised. Blades glinted in the light of the last few torches.

Ferox could see no sign of other attackers, and there was nothing he could do to help. This looked like a diversion, something to distract the men on the far ramparts before a heavier wave of warriors swarmed out of the night to overwhelm them. Yet there was no sign of anyone approaching from another direction, and what he had heard the dead man and the other warriors say suggested that this was it, and the warriors were being sacrificed in a doomed attack whose only purpose was to kill as many enemies as possible. He looked down at the body and even in this light saw a chest covered in tattoos like ivy on an old stone wall. He pulled back the headdress and there was the mark of the horse. Pressing hard at the torc he prised it open and lifted the man's head so that he could take it off.

Below him in the valley the fight was dying as swiftly as the attackers. A few of the dropped torches smouldered on the ground, but the only one flung across the rampart had failed to set fire to anything for there was not much in the camp to burn, given that the tents had not been set up. The fallen torches gave a little light to see the heap of naked corpses piled in the entrance. There was still a fierce struggle around the picket, a cluster of Romans standing back to back.

Ferox picked up the man's sword and ran his finger along the edge, finding it distressingly blunt. No doubt that was fine for a man who liked to stand back and send his warriors off to fight. It was all he had, for the knife was no good for such work, so the centurion raised it and sliced down with all the force he could muster. The blade buried itself in the man's neck, without severing the bone. It took three more blows, using all his might and grunting with the effort, before the head came off. He drove the blunt-tipped sword as deeply into the earth as he could and balanced the headdress on top of it. It tilted to one side, but would do to mark the corpse of their priest or druid or whatever this man had claimed to be. Ferox took the head, glad that the man had hair because it was hard to carry the head of a bald man, tucked the torc into his belt and jogged at a low crouch towards the nearest gully.

Trumpets sounded and he guessed that horsemen were charging from the entrances not attacked to go to the aid of the picket. Peering over the edge of the gully he saw the pairs of warriors still squatting along the slope and watching the last of their comrades die. He bundled the head up in his cloak, keeping his dagger low in his left hand, and set off towards them, walking down the slope, hoping that with his bare chest they would mistake him for one of their own.

A shriek of pure horror came from behind him. It sounded like a woman and he guessed that she had discovered the headless corpse of their leader. Pale faces turned to look back, hissing questions.

'I don't know,' Ferox called. 'What's happening?'

He stopped. The warriors were getting up, coming up the slope.

'Something is wrong,' he said as the closest pair came towards him. Ferox dropped the torc, which rolled along the ground. 'What's that?' he asked the nearest man.

The Briton followed the necklace, bending down to pick it up. His companion stared at the centurion.

'Who are you?' he asked and Ferox whipped up the knife and slashed across the man's throat, dark blood jetting out over his pale skin. He swung the bundled head like a weapon on to the back of the bending warrior's head and knocked him down.

Flavius Ferox ran. The time for hiding and caution was over and he sprinted down the slope towards the camp. Men shouted, but the Britons were still confused. The woman howled again and a man's voice bellowed in anger, recognising the torc.

Ferox did not look back or slow, but drove himself to flee, wrapped head in one hand and knife in the other. Horsemen appeared ahead of him. 'I'm Roman,' he yelled in Latin. 'I'm Roman!' One of the riders came at him, raised his spear and threw. Ferox flung himself to the side, hitting the ground hard. 'I'm a centurion, you stupid mongrel!'

The other rider held the man's hand as he drew his sword. 'I know him,' he said. 'He's one of us.' It was Crispinus, and his teeth looked white as he grinned. 'Although the gods only know what he's been up to! Deserting, eh?'

'With all due respect, my lord,' Ferox said, getting to his feet, 'you should not be outside the ramparts during an attack. You are the commander of the whole column.'

'Well, I am sure that is the voice of wisdom,' he said. 'The voice of something at any rate. Now would you care to tell the commander of the column just what in the name of all reason you have been doing?'

XI

'I AM GUESSING that they want to fight this time,' the tribune said, looking up at the masses of warriors on the spur above them, and the shields lining the rampart of an old fort. Hardly anyone lived up there these days, and the rampart was covered in grass and the ditch half filled with rubbish. Yet several hundred warriors had gathered there and it would not be easy to storm. Many more of the Selgovae formed a rough line across the saddle to the north of the fort, the warriors sitting or standing in loose masses. They had standards topped by bronze figures of gods or animals and men blasting out calls on their tall carnyxes, each trumpet's mouth shaped like the head of a boar. The sound reminded Ferox of the ambush on the road. A picture of Sulpicia Lepidina came to mind and he shuddered at the thought of what they had planned to do to her.

The ground sloped up steeply to the saddle, which on the far side went down into a bigger, longer glen. If the campaign was going to plan, then the western column should be advancing up that valley towards them. Yet if they were to meet up, Crispinus' men must force their way through this pass. The column was concentrated now, formed at the foot of the slope apart from half of the infantry of the Vardulli from Spain and all their cavalry who protected the baggage animals and watched the rear.

'Despatch coming.' Titus Annius pointed to the ridge behind them. Half a dozen cavalry were cantering down the smooth slope, led by a man with a luxuriously plumed helmet and a trooper holding his spear aloft, something flickering just below the head. As they came closer Ferox saw that it was a feather, as the commander of the Tungrians had guessed, and realised that the plumed officer was Flaccus, the junior tribune from VIIII Hispana. One of the cavalrymen in his escort had a freshly tied bandage round his thigh. They must have come from the Legate Quadratus and the main column.

'We had a time of it getting through,' the tribune said to Crispinus, before the two men moved to the side and spoke for some time.

It was an hour before noon on the morning after the attack on their camp. There were seven wounded men back with the baggage train to add to the eight given hasty burials before they set out. All but one of the dead were from the picket, for the attackers had hacked to pieces anyone who fell. The four survivors were all wounded, but had managed to stay on their feet and close together so that they were back to back. The attackers left forty-seven corpses on the ground and few if any of them had fled. There were no prisoners.

All of the dead bore the tattoos on forehead and hand and had fought with the same wild aggression as if they did not care whether they lived or died. None were skilful, and some carried woodsman's or carpenter's axes or just clubs rather than proper weapons. Yet they came on very fast and slashed or bludgeoned at anything within reach, keeping on striking even if they were covered with wounds. Soldiers spoke of men crawling towards them leaving the ground slick with blood, but still brandishing weapons. One of the Romans had been stabbed repeatedly when he went to check what he was sure was a corpse, given the horrible injuries to the Briton's face, arms and chest.

As far as Ferox could tell, few of the dead appeared to be Selgovae, and instead were from many different tribes and much further afield. Quite a few looked half starved, with little trace of the muscles on arms and legs built up by warriors who practised for war. He had told Crispinus and the other senior officers about this, but was not sure how much they understood. Romans were apt to see all barbarians as much the same.

The man Ferox had killed was more of a puzzle. His forehead was marked with a stag, rather than a horse, and underneath were traces of an older tattoo: *ten e q a ugi*. It was a Roman mark in Latin, not something put on by the tribes, and Ferox's best guess was something like *tene me quia fugi* – 'Arrest me, for I have run away'. The antler-wearing priest rallying the tribes against Rome was a former slave, a man who had fled from his owner and been recaptured, then escaped again. He was a runaway slave, a *fugitivus* from the empire, perhaps from Britannia, although the man with the southern accent made Ferox wonder whether there were more runaways from far afield among this strange band. It helped to explain a man who used magical words of power and called on Isis and Hades and other gods not widely known among the tribes.

Crispinus read the despatch, spoke for a while with Flaccus and then summoned his officers to a *consilium* to explain what they were to do. 'The Legate Quadratus is attacking from the south, driving up the valley towards us. There are strong forces facing him, but the enemy have placed these bands here to stop us from fighting our way in behind their main force.' He saw Ferox's questioning expression. 'The enemy are two chieftains. Venutius, as we expected, and his neighbour Tagax.'

That was a surprise, since the second man had a reputation for mildness and was a frequent victim of his neighbour's cattle rustling. 'The legate has advanced, putting farms and villages to the torch if the people did not welcome him.' That explained the resistance of the chieftains – push the mildest man too far and he will push back, especially if he was as proud as the leaders of the Selgovae. Ferox suspected that the clumsy hand of Claudius Super was behind the needless aggression of the Roman approach.

'Our job is to storm the pass, then move through and block anyone from retreating up the valley.' Crispinus sounded calm and confident, although Ferox noticed that he kept drumming the fingers of his right hand against his thigh. His plan was simple, but so was the problem and there was little opportunity for subtlety.

'Flavius Cerialis and his Batavians will lead.' The tribune smiled at the prefect. 'You had better order your troopers to dismount and form with the infantry. I know that they will not like it, but the pass is not good ground for cavalry.' Now he was looking at Brocchus, who gave an almost imperceptible nod.

'Titus Annius?'

'Sir.'

'Your Tungrians will be to the left of the Batavians, held back a little. You will face the fort, but your job at first will be to guard the flank of Cerialis' men against any charge. Once they have driven off the warriors in the pass, you will mount a combined assault on the ramparts. I shall give the order when it is time.'

'Sir.'

'The remainder of the infantry of the Vardulli along with Aelius Brocchus and the ala Petriana will act as a formed reserve, following at two hundred paces behind the main line. If we can sweep them out of this pass, then there ought to be good hunting for the cavalry. However, unless the enemy come down from their position you are not to attempt a charge without my express orders. Everyone clear about the part they are to play?' The tribune's fingers kept drumming against his thigh as the officers assured him that they understood. 'Ferox, you will stay by my side as I may need you.'

'Yes, sir.'

'Good. The Tribune Flaccus informs me that the main column will be driving up the valley, forcing the enemy towards us. That may mean that we will face very large numbers for a while, but we will be relieved.'

'I must also urge haste,' Flaccus cut in, prompting a brief flash of anger from Crispinus. 'I fear it took me much longer to reach you than we expected. I do trust that you will attack quickly.'

'We shall obey our orders and do the thing properly.' Crispinus spoke in a clipped and dismissive tone. 'If things have worked out, the eastern column from Coria is already further north and closing in on the enemy from that direction.'

Ferox was dubious, and thought that the chances of the three columns meeting up on time and as planned were slim. Best to forget the eastern column. That larger force would have moved at reasonable speed along the road for some distance, but as soon as they left it to march cross-country he suspected that they would crawl along, even if there was little or no opposition. Give them another day or two and they might be coming down behind the enemy, but he doubted that they would be there any earlier. They should count themselves fortunate that Crispinus' small force was approaching Quadratus and the main column in the west. Now all they had to do was to fight their way through to join up.

The Batavian infantry formed up in four ranks, the three centuries abreast with only a slight gap between them. That gave a frontage of fifty men, with the vexillum carried proudly in the centre of the formation, their green shields uncovered because they were to fight. Cerialis put the cavalry on the right in a block eight men wide and eight deep. Covering their flank, Titus Annius placed his Tungrians with their yellow shields, one century behind the other, each drawn up in six ranks, apart from twenty men who carried leather slings as well as their normal weapons who formed a thin line of skirmishers.

A bowshot behind the front line the Vardulli were stationed in a dense column, with the turmae of ala Petriana to their rear.

'Some archers really would be nice,' Crispinus said to Aelius Brocchus, as the prefect arrived to inform him that everyone was ready. 'Soften them up a bit before we go in.'

'Yes, and some scorpions.' Light bolt-shooters or *scorpiones* were often taken by the legions on campaign and had the ability to pick off enemies at a range far beyond a sling or bow, but auxiliaries were rarely given them in the field.

'Ah well, no use lamenting what we do not have. We shall just have to do it at close quarters.' Crispinus was deliberately ignoring Flaccus, who kept making hints that time was passing. It had taken a good half-hour to get the units into position. Men had taken last gulps of posca, or something stronger if they had it, as the clouds blew away and a bright sun beamed down on them. Now, stripped down to their fighting gear, they carried no canteens, although some of the galearii were posted behind each formation with waterskins.

'With your permission, sir,' Ferox asked. Seeing the nod, he waved to Vindex who raised aloft a long spear topped with the head of the priest. The pair of them cantered up behind the Batavians and then walked their horses along in front of the Roman line, giving the tribesmen a good look.

There was a roar from up the slope, turning into shouts of anger and promises of vengeance. The warriors jeered and taunted, although he was not sure whether anyone recognised the man or they simply guessed that he was one of their own. When they came in front of the fort, Vindex dipped the spear and Ferox pulled the head free. He waved it around up in the air and then flung it forward. Warriors howled at him from the fort, and he heard them assure him that soon his own head would roll in the grass and get pissed on by their women.

'Time to go,' he told Vindex. 'You had better join the scouts with the rearguard.'

'And miss the fun?'

The Batavians clashed the shafts of their spears against their shields three times, the pounding sound sending echoes back down the valley. Ahead of them the Britons blew their trumpets and screamed defiance. The tall auxiliaries then raised their shields over their faces and set up a low murmur.

Vindex's horse flinched at the unearthly sound, tugging hard on the reins and turning full circle. 'Think he wants to change sides.'

The murmuring slowly grew louder, the Batavians letting the sound reverberate against the boards of their green-painted shields. It built up like a tide washing ashore, the crests of the waves rising.

'What is it?' Vindex asked.

'They call it the *barritus*,' Ferox told him. 'It's a German thing. They say you can tell who will win the battle from its sound.'

The steadily rising chant began to drown the challenging cries of the Selgovae. Warriors faltered, puzzled by a war cry that had no words, but kept getting louder.

'If those boys had any sense they'd charge,' Ferox said, looking up the hill as he and Vindex went back behind the Batavian line.

The Selgovae did not charge as the Batavian shout reached a crescendo, but the warriors had sunk into sullen, browbeaten silence. When the auxiliaries stopped the silence was oppressive. To Ferox it looked as if the lines of warriors up on the slope were quivering. He saw a few men at the rear walking away over the saddle. He was just about to urge Cerialis to move when the prefect drew his sword.

'The Ninth Cohort will advance. Forward!'

The Batavians stepped out, left leg first so that the shield remained closest to the enemy. They were silent, eerily so, with only the clink of armour and equipment as they went at regulation pace up the slope. Cerialis rode just behind the flag in the middle of the line, a pair of picked veterans walking on either side of his horse.

The Selgovae started to shout again, jeering at the enemies, but somehow it did not sound as if their hearts were in it. A few ran out in front of the mass, javelins ready in the hands. More were drifting away to the rear across the saddle and out of sight.

Ferox joined Crispinus as he followed some twenty paces behind the Batavians. The Britons kept yelling as the Romans marched forward in silence. The first javelins were thrown. One struck a Batavian's shield and bounced off, its force already spent. The others did not even come close. A few of the Britons out ahead of the mass became bolder and scampered nearer. The next missiles were better aimed. A Batavian was hit on the shin, the broad head of the javelin gouging flesh. He stumbled and fell flat on his face, hissing with pain.

'Leave him!' an optio yelled from his station behind the rear rank.

Another soldier cursed as the point of a thrown spear burst through the board of his shield. 'Bastards!' he screamed up the slope, shaking his own spear at them.

'Silence!' the optio bellowed. 'Keep quiet and stay in your place!'

The Tungrians were moving as well, their slingers dropping stones on the rampart of the fort. It was awkward for the auxiliaries with the large flat oval shields to put a stone in the sling and swing it properly, so the Tungrians worked in pairs. One man covered his comrade with his shield while the other laid his shield down and lobbed missiles at the enemy. There were a few slingers among the Selgovae and stones whizzed through the air in response. They were harder to see than an arrow, let alone a javelin, which made it more difficult to dodge them. A Tungrian was down, kneecap badly bruised or broken by a stone.

'Hey, reckon the legion is busy.' Vindex was pointing past the enemy at a dark smear rising from the valley beyond. 'There's another,' he added a moment later. The Legate Quadratus and his troops must be further forward than expected, already putting houses to the torch.

'They're breaking,' Crispinus said, the words almost a question because he did not believe what he was seeing.

The Batavians were still fifty paces from the main line of Selgovae, but that line was dissolving as more and more men streamed back across the saddle.

The tribune slammed his spurs into the side of his horse, drawing blood and sending it shooting forward. 'Charge, Cerialis! Charge!'

Flavius Cerialis obviously had the same thought. 'Charge!' he yelled, pushed his horse through the line of his own men. 'Charge!' The Batavians started to yell, raising a great angry howl as they broke ranks and sprinted up the slope, spears raised ready to throw, but their targets were fleeing ahead of them. The trumpeters did their best to sound their curved *cornu*-horns, but the notes were ragged and thin as the men ran to keep up.

'Wait,' Ferox told Vindex. 'If they have the men and the wits to use them, they'd have a thousand warriors crouching just beyond that crest ready to hit us.'

Aelius Brocchus had not followed the tribune and gaped at the suggestion.

'Trust a Silure to think like that,' Vindex said.

'They're just barbarians,' Flaccus said, but there was doubt in his eyes along with the excitement of the moment.

They watched as the Batavians surged up the last few yards on to the crest, led by Cerialis and with Crispinus now amongst them. They did not halt, but kept going, disappearing from view.

Aelius Brocchus let out a long breath and grinned. 'Good job we are not still fighting the Silures. I'll bring up my men.' He headed down the slope.

There was a cheer as the Tungrians charged up the slope towards the old fort, their slingers tagging along with the main column. Its defenders were running like the other warriors, but going out through another entrance and fleeing along the heights.

Crispinus appeared back on top of the crest, beckoning to them.

Up close Ferox saw that the young aristocrat was flushed with excitement and finding it hard to keep still, so that he kept waving his sword and twitching on the reins with his other hand. His horse fidgeted almost as much as its rider. Down in the big valley there were farms burning and strong formations of Roman soldiers advancing. Ahead of them thousands of warriors retreated, most seeking the safety of the heights, and keeping well ahead of their pursuers. There were a couple of dead warriors lying on the grass around them, men who had stumbled as they tried to escape. 'We need Brocchus and his cavalry!' Crispinus was shouting in his enthusiasm. 'If he moves quickly then we will have them.'

The side of the valley was steep, rocky and broken by plenty of little rivulets and gullies. This was the Selgovae's own land, and the lightly clad unarmoured warriors bounded across it at great speed and were gaining ground quickly. The Batavians were already flagging, weighed down by their armour and equipment, and by that strange feeling of emptiness when a man had geared himself up to fight only to find that there was no battle. Some of the keenest were still running as fast as they could after the fleeing enemy. More were slackening pace and giving up. There was no trace of formation, just a couple of hundred panting men scattered across a hillside.

Ferox was just about to suggest sounding the recall when Cerialis found a *cornicen* and ordered the man to blow the signal on his trumpet. Crispinus started in surprise, frightening his horse, so that the animal bucked and kicked out violently. The tribune's face was angry until he mastered himself.

'Yes, of course. Order is vital,' he said, more to himself than those around him. The same sapping disappointment mingled with relief began to do its work and his shoulders sagged. He took a deep breath. 'Ferox. Ride to my Lord Brocchus and tell him to pursue the enemy as well as he is able, but to make sure that he does it in good order and takes no risks.'

The ala Petriana was already climbing towards the saddle, each turma in column one behind the other, so it did not take long to deliver the order.

'We shall do our best,' Brocchus said, and took his men forward. By the time Ferox rejoined the tribune, Titus Annius was there. Crispinus ordered the Tungrians to hold the fort and guard the pass. He expected that the whole column would cross and join up with the main force in the next valley, but would ride to find out the legate's intentions. Nothing was said, but it was clear everyone expected the combined force to march back to its bases before their supplies ran out.

'Ferox, come with me.' Crispinus went to see Cerialis and told him to form his infantry on the slope and remount his cavalry. They were to wait for the rest of the column to catch up and then be ready to move at short notice. In the meantime, he was to send a messenger to Rufinus to bring the baggage and rearguard up.

Ferox was again told to follow – something Vindex did without being asked – and Crispinus headed down into the big valley to search for the Legate Quadratus and further instructions.

'I cannot help being disappointed in the courage of our opponents,' the aristocrat said. 'They had the advantage of ground and could have put up a stern fight.'

'And been slaughtered when they were trapped by the legate's column?' Ferox spoke bluntly. 'They did what anyone would do. It's not about courage, but sense.'

Crispinus did not appear to be listening. 'Even so it was victory, albeit unfashionably bloodless.'

'Shame we did not attack sooner,' Flaccus said.

When they found him, the Legate Julius Quadratus evidently felt the same way. 'You were late,' he said. He was a squat man with a creased forehead and the belligerent expression of a caged bear. 'You should have come through that pass three or four hours ago.'

'We would,' Crispinus said, as a senator's son able to speak freely to a man even of such high rank. 'We would indeed, had we received orders to do so in time.'

Quadratus turned to the tribune from VIIII Hispana and glared at him, his little eyes red-rimmed and angry. 'What do you have to say, Flaccus? Was it your fault?'

'I carried the message as fast as was possible. We lost one dead and another trooper wounded getting past the Brittunculi. I cannot carry the responsibility for other delays.'

The legate looked at each man in turn, wondering which was most at fault. 'Well, then. No matter. What is done is done and the world moves on. We have taught the clans not to despise our power.' He swept his arm along the valley, showing the burning houses. 'We will press on for another couple of miles, kill or take any we can find and then camp for the night. You, Crispinus, will bring your men to join us. Tomorrow we can start home happy with what we have achieved.'

Ferox wondered whether the senator was already composing in his mind a heroic – perhaps even a poetic – account of the campaign. The truth was less impressive. They had burned farms, but not fought a major action, so on balance they had given the Selgovae plenty of good reasons to hate Romans and little reason to fear them. Few of the warriors had been taken or killed, and their families were safe as were their livestock. Homes could be rebuilt before the winter arrived. It would be a hard time for the clans, which would only make the tribesmen's hatred deeper and provide fertile ground for druids preaching vengeance.

Claudius Super was delighted with the operation, and that was yet another reason to doubt that they had achieved very much good.

'They'll not despise us again!' he declared, his mood so ebullient that he was friendly even to Ferox. 'My dear fellow, it is so good to see you. We must have a drink to celebrate the triumph once the camp is pitched. This is a glorious day!' From what he said it was clear that the legate's force had begun laying waste to the farms several days ago. 'They did not pay their tax so have only themselves to blame. This is justice!'

Ferox was glad to leave him when Crispinus asked him to take Vindex and his men and patrol the lands behind the column to make sure that no one tried to harass their rear as they went through the pass. For the next few hours they covered a wide area and saw plenty of warriors, all keeping their distance and tending to gather on the high ground. In the meantime the Vardulli escorted the baggage train over the saddle and down into the valley. The sun was low in the sky when they followed, so that he was all the more surprised to see the Tungrians still behind the ramparts of the old fort. Looking down from the top of the pass he could see no other Roman troops closer than a mile and a half. The camp was another mile beyond that, a dark rectangle of tents lit by lines of fires.

'Something's wrong,' Ferox said and trotted over to the old rampart.

Titus Annius hailed him from the gateway. 'Do you have new orders for me, centurion?'

Elderly gateposts stood on either side of the entrance, but the gates themselves had gone long ago. There were cattle pens inside the walls, and the daily movement of the herds to get water and food left the entrance way churned into a mire.

'Afraid not, sir. To be honest we did not expect to see anyone still up here.' Ferox was just outside the entrance to the fort, able to lower his voice.

Titus Annius had served for many years, but for most of that time had acted under the orders of someone else. Ferox could see the doubt in his face. 'We were told to hold up here until we were relieved or got the order to rejoin the column.'

'I fear that there has been some oversight. Our own troops have joined the main army and are some way north, setting up camp. I suspect the order to recall you has been lost or forgotten.'

It was obvious that Annius' instincts told him the same thing. He had one century of his own men, for the other had been sent to help guide the baggage train over the pass and had left with them. There were also thirty legionaries with a couple of pack mules, who had come up to set fire to the houses in the fort. There were only half a dozen still with thatch on them, and the straw was damp, so that it had taken them a while to set the first one alight. After that it was easier, lighting torches from the blaze and holding them against the lowest parts of the roofs. As they spoke the last of the round houses caught fire, the strengthening wind blowing dense clouds of black smoke towards them.

Ferox blinked and coughed; the heat was strong even at this distance. Little pieces of smouldering straw floated through the air. 'How long ago did you get your last order, sir?'

'Must be three or four hours ago by now. The Tribune Flaccus came up in person with orders from the legate.' The long habit of obedience fought against Titus Annius' instincts until his mind found a happy compromise. 'Would you be kind enough to ride down into the valley and remind them of our presence?'

'If you wish, but I do think it would be wise for you to pull out now, before it gets dark.'

Titus Annius undid the tie on his helmet's cheek pieces and rubbed his chin. There was a young centurion with the legionaries and he now wandered over to report.

'Buildings destroyed, sir,' he said, and then broke into a fit of coughing as he swallowed a bit of ash. The man noticed the plumed helmet slung behind his saddle, so gave an affable nod to Ferox, probably trying to work out his seniority and unit. Many officers from the legions disdained centurions from the *auxilia*. Titus Annius was very senior, but if he had not been a former centurion in a legion then he doubted that the man would have paid him so much respect. 'Do we have fresh orders, sir?'

Titus Annius shook his head. 'Not yet.'

Ferox swung down to the ground, boots sinking into the deep mud. 'Sir,' he said, 'this is certainly a mistake and you have not been left behind for a reason. There will be no blame.' The words were out before he had thought properly and he knew that they were a mistake.

Titus Annius' eyes widened and he clenched his teeth for a moment. 'Blame?' he muttered. 'I have orders, regionarius, and until I have new ones I shall obey them. No one will ever question the discipline of the First Cohort while I am in charge.' A few of the auxiliaries nearby nodded with approval.

'They're coming!' Vindex had galloped over and yelled out the warning.

XII

THERE WERE EIGHTY-NINE men in the century from cohors Tungrorum, along with an optio as acting commander, supported by a *signifer* and *tesserarius*. That was little more than half of the full complement for in theory the cohort had an unusual organisation, with six centuries of one hundred and forty men apiece. A decade ago they had often mustered something close to that total, before the army's priorities changed and few recruits were sent to Britannia. The young legionary centurion had thirty men from Legio II Augusta, with carefully painted Capricorns on either side of the bosses on their rectangular red shields. Stretched all along the rampart, without keeping any reserve, that would still have meant no more than a man every three or four paces.

Ferox grabbed Titus Annius by the arm. 'We should go, sir!'

The commander of the cohort shook him off. 'I cannot,' he said. He looked tired, the lines on his face harsh in the light from the burning houses. 'If you can get new orders for me, then that would be different.'

'I'll do my best.' Ferox walked a few paces away and then stopped as he made up his mind. 'Go down to the main force,' he shouted to Vindex. 'Tell them what is happening and that we shall need help!' The Brigantian waved and rode away to rejoin the other scouts.

Ferox watched, wishing that he had gone with him and not quite sure why he had chosen to stay. 'Hold this, lad,' he told one of the auxiliaries, passing over the reins. Ferox stuffed his hat into a pouch on his belt and put on his helmet. At least the silhouette would mark him out as a Roman and a centurion. He checked that his gladius and his dagger slid easily from their scabbards and ran to follow Titus Annius, wondering whether he was staying simply because he liked the Tungrians' commander.

There were tumbled circles of stone clustered inside the ramparts, the remains of old houses, making it hard to move quickly, while the dark smoke drifted slowly across the fort and it was impossible to see very much. Two of the burning huts were at the far end, upwind in a fitful breeze that fanned the flames without being strong enough to blow the clouds away quickly. Ferox gave up trying to thread his way through the ruined huts and instead bounded on to the rampart. There were fifty or sixty warriors in a mass down the slope from him. Far more were on the top of the next peak on this long ridge. Closer still, men with slings and javelins were edging nearer to the fort.

Ferox ran along the grassy top of the rampart. Here and there were the stumps of posts showing that there had once been a palisade to protect men on the walls. A pebble from a sling flicked through the grass just ahead of him as he ran. Another whipped past inches from his face. There was no protection for a man on the rampart any more, and the Tungrians were wisely waiting behind the wall rather than be targets on top of it. For the moment the Selgovae were only probing, unsure how many Romans were in the smoke-filled ruin, but soon they would see the defenders' weakness.

He ran on. There were two old gateways in the rampart. The one he had come through faced the approach to the pass, while the second was at the far end, looking towards the rest of the ridge. The wind veered and gusted, letting him glimpse the high plumes of Annius and the legionary centurion near the far gateway. Ferox hurried towards them, running down the inside slope of the rampart and scrambling over the dry stone walls of a cattle pen.

Titus Annius saw him and looked angry. 'Thought you had gone for orders.'

'I have sent my men, but reckoned that you might need an additional officer.'

The cohort commander shrugged, and went back to telling the legionary centurion to form his men to block the open gateway. Earlier in the day the Selgovae had pulled a cart across the gap, but when they abandoned the fort they had dragged it away and pushed it down one of the slopes. It lay there now, both wheels shattered so that they could not recover it.

'You hold here, Rufus,' Titus Annius told the centurion from II Augusta. 'I'll put a detachment on the other gate, and keep the rest formed up in groups of twenty ready to take anyone who comes over the walls.'

Rufus nodded. His face was dark with patches of soot. 'What about the other gap in the wall?'

Titus Annius slapped his hand against his leg in annoyance. 'I'd forgotten. I'll put men there.'

'I did not know that there was another way in,' Ferox said.

'It's not a real gate,' Rufus told him. 'Just a bit of a gap on the far side where they bring sheep in and out. We came through with the mules.'

The smoke was getting denser and Ferox realised that sparks from burning thatch must have set the bracken and heather alight. It was mainly on the slope of the big valley, but the wind had veered more westerly and was driving the banks of smoke back over the fort.

'Shields up!' Rufus' men braced their big curved shields as javelins hissed through the air towards them. There were dull thumps as the heads struck hard against the leather-coated wood and bounced back, and a high-pitched ping as another deflected off the domed iron boss in the centre of one shield. The legionaries stood three abreast and three deep in the gateway. Each man carried a *pilum*, the heavy javelin used by the legions and no one else, with a small pyramid-shaped iron head at the end of a slim two-foot-long iron shank attached to a four-foot-long wooden shaft. Its weight gave the pilum a short range, but was concentrated behind that small point to drive through shield or armour as if it were soft butter.

'Wait for the order!' Rufus burst into another fit of coughing, but the young centurion sounded calm and confident. The carnyxes were blowing outside, gathering the warriors together and lifting their spirits. With a sudden shout dozens of warriors surged forward at the men in the gateway. They were led by a tall man with a bronze helmet and white horsehair plume waving behind him. He had a long sword and large round shield painted with the symbol of a boar in white. Behind him came others in tunics and trousers, with little shields and javelins or blunt-tipped slashing swords.

'Wait!' Rufus stood to the right of the nine legionaries holding the gateway, his unshielded side to the enemy but sheltered by the rampart. Five more soldiers waited just behind him and the rest were formed in ranks ready to support both groups. The piled stone ruins of a house stood on the other side of the gateway, which would make it hard for anyone to come across the rampart there. Even so, Ferox drew his sword and stood ready. Titus Annius was beside him, a shield as well as sword in his hand, and the two auxiliaries from his personal escort on either side of him. Ferox had not seen anyone bring the commander his shield.

'Throw!' Rufus shouted to his men and the three legionaries in the first rank took two paces forward, right arms swiftly back before they hurled the heavy *pila* forward. As they threw the second rank followed them and loosed their own pila. The three men in the rear allowed the same slight pause before they followed. Pila were big and bulky and the slight delay reduced the chances of weapons hitting each other and being wasted.

'Charge!' Rufus screamed, for legionaries were taught to be aggressive. The yelling men surged out of the gateway, reaching down with their right hands to draw swords as they ran. Ferox, Annius and the others followed them. Clear of the gateway, he saw that the enemy leader was down, a pilum having punched through his shield and pinned it to his body. Another man was wailing in high-pitched agony with the long javelin driven into his groin. He sat on the grass, blood bubbling from his mouth. Beside him a warrior was dead, the pilum still stuck in his head, and a fourth man had the slim shank sticking out for a good six inches from the back of his impaled thigh.

The rest had halted, confused and shocked, as the legionaries ran forward ten paces into them. The Romans punched with their heavy shields – Ferox saw one of the Selgovae lifted off his feet by the blow – and followed up with jabs of their swords. It was over almost as soon as it began. Three more warriors were down, the wounded finished off with economical thrusts, and the rest fleeing back.

Neither Ferox nor Annius had got close enough to cross blades with the enemy. Rufus had blood on his sword and a spatter of enemy's blood across his face. The legionaries were chattering excitedly, some of them trying to recover their pila and having little luck. One of the ones to hit the ground had broken when it had hit a stone. Two more were intact and usable, but the ones that had found victims were stuck fast, designed to penetrate rather than to slide out with ease.

'Given us some time anyway,' Titus Annius said.

A legionary grunted as a javelin came at him from his unshielded right side. It hit one of the plates of his segmented cuirass, the force knocking him over even though it did not pierce the soft iron.

'Get back!' Titus Annius called. 'Re-form in the gate.'

Warriors were beginning to close on them. Another javelin arced down, not sticking when it hit the ground, but sliding forward through the grass to stop just in front of Ferox. One of his comrades helped the man knocked down as the legionaries walked backwards, using their shields to stop the missiles. Stones from slings smacked against them, and one went low, cracking on a man's shin, breaking bone. The legionary dropped, and as the man beside him leaned down to help a javelin hit him in the right arm. He hissed, dropping his sword.

'Run!' Ferox shouted. The gate was close and it was better to dash back to the protection of the ramparts rather than try to block missiles coming from all around. He ran to the fallen man, grabbing his arm and dragging him across the grass. Someone else took the legionary's other arm and to his surprise he saw Titus Annius, sword back in its sheath and trying to use his shield to protect them all. The cohort commander grinned.

'Nearly there,' Annius said, and then a stone grazed the bridge of his nose and slammed into his right eye, turning it into bloody pulp. He staggered, letting go of the man's arm and raising his hand to his face.

Ferox dragged the legionary another pace, to where one of his comrades was waiting. The two Tungrians escorting the cohort commander were at his side, one leading him away and the other doing his best to cover them. More legionaries came out of the gate to help.

A long ululating scream and a naked warrior came bounding towards them, spear in one hand and a little axe in the other. He was covered in tattoos and for the first time today Ferox saw the mark of the horse on his forehead. The warrior threw his spear at the Tungrian auxiliary who caught it on his shield, the point bursting through a couple of inches, but not enough to reach him. A pilum would have pierced the wood and slid through to hit the man behind. The auxiliary swayed back from the blow and the warrior ran past him, ducking the thrust spear and raising his axe to cut down at Ferox, who caught the man by his wrist and stabbed him in the throat. No more warriors followed him and instead they hung back, content for the moment to lob missiles.

'Come on!' he said to the Tungrian, turning to run. A sling stone brushed the doubled-up mail armour on his shoulder, stinging a little, but doing no damage. They were through the gate, the last to retreat, and Rufus shouted at his men to re-form in the gap. Titus Annius was sitting propped up against the wall of the collapsed hut beside the gate. His helmet was off and his escort and another Tungrian were cleaning and bandaging the wound as best they could. It looked bad, an eye destroyed at least, and the centurion was clearly in no state to command.

Ferox strode over to Rufus. 'I am Flavius Ferox, centurio regionarius, and I am senior here.' That was probably true and he hoped that the man would accept it without debate. 'I'm also from the Second, albeit on detached service.'

'Oh,' Rufus said in surprise. 'That Ferox.' Ferox thought he caught a low '*omnes ad stercus*' from one of the soldiers nearby. He guessed that they had heard about the disasters on the Danube, and maybe they thought him unlucky to be around.

The young centurion checked himself and stiffened to attention. 'Of course, sir, you can rely on the Capricorns.' Ferox had not heard the nickname before, but then since he had spent no time with the legion that was not surprising. 'Sir?'

'Yes.'

'Why are they holding back? They could swarm all over these walls and there isn't much we could do about it.'

'My guess is that they're waiting for dark. If they come now, we will take a lot of them with us.' He spoke loudly so that the men could hear as well. 'A hell of a lot of them if I know Second Augusta.' The legionaries looked pleased. 'And these Tungrian boys can handle themselves as well. They won't get in easily and they might not get in at all. So they'll wait for night and try to overwhelm us. What they don't know is that we won't hang around for that.'

'Sir?'

'We're pulling out back to the column, but we have to be smart. Hold here with your lads while I sort out the others. We will pull back from the walls into the centre of the fort before we bring back the men from the gates. We also need to get all the wounded away. Your mules, too. I don't want anybody to have their pay docked for losing army property!' A few of the men grinned.

Before he left he had the Tungrians rig up a stretcher from a couple of spears and some cloaks to carry the now unconscious

Titus Annius. He got the legionaries to make something similar for their own man wounded in the leg. The heather was burning for a long way along the slope behind them. He looked at the little gap in the rampart that Rufus had mentioned, but saw that the hillside beneath it was ablaze so that they could not use it. That meant the other main entrance, the one near the saddle and in plain view of the Selgovae. The optio of the Tungrians had taken charge of the gateway and had a line of men occupying it. So far no warriors had tried an attack, but a few were skirmishing with javelins and slings, so he had sent his own slingers out to hold them in check and even drive them back some distance. One auxiliary had an injured knee and another man had had his nose smashed, leaving his face swollen and bloody, and there were several bundles of rags down the slope – tribesmen who had not spotted the cast lead bullets used by the auxiliaries. They were harder to see than pebbles and flew straighter because of their even shape, but by now the Tungrians were running low and using whatever stones they could pick up. So far the Selgovae had not noticed and were keeping their distance.

It was getting darker, and not just because of the fires that kept the air thick with ash and unpleasantly hot. Ferox looked for the tesserarius, a quiet veteran with face and arms the colour of teak.

'Pick a dozen good men and come with me.' As the man gathered his detachment, Ferox told the optio to keep the men at the gate, but to form the rest up in a deep column inside the fort. The wounded commander arrived, carried by four men. 'Detail ten men to stay with him at all times.'

Ferox hurried back to the far end of the fort, the tesserarius jogging alongside. 'What's your name?'

'Gambax, my lord.'

'You and your men wait here, but keep off the path.' There was a narrow track winding through the centre of the old settlement. Over to their right, the thatch of a burning house collapsed, sending up a flurry of sparks. 'I'll be back to take charge, but your job is to cover the retreat of the legionaries, so once they go by, you form a line across the path and hold. Someone else will be waiting to cover us. Understand?'

'Yes, sir.'

'Good. I'll be back.'

The legionaries had two more wounded, both in the foot or shin where missiles had gone under their shields. Four more corpses in front of the gateway showed that they had thrown back another little attack. Three men too injured to walk, four to carry each of them, and another man with a wounded arm left fourteen fit men to stand with the centurion. Ferox sent the wounded and the carriers back and got Rufus to divide the others into two groups. Seven men went back along the path to where it turned the first corner.

'Count to fifty and then bring the rest back. If no one is following then get everyone back. I have a covering party waiting to protect you.' He snatched up a shield left by one of the wounded men, feeling the weight, but glad of the hours he had spent using a heavier practice shield.

Ferox counted in his head and was past fifty before he reached the Tungrians. Turning, he saw the first legionaries come into sight, coughing from the smoke. Rufus and the others appeared a moment later. He beckoned them on, and told the auxiliaries to open out and let them through. Sweat poured down his face from the heat, leaving pale rivulets in the grime from the smoke.

He repeated the count and reached fifty again. 'Go. Form on the back of the column. I'll be right behind you.'

The Tungrians doubled away and he stared down the path. The shout came from his left, and he saw a warrior crouching on top of the rampart, calling back to the others that the Romans were fleeing. Ferox followed the auxiliaries.

'Sound the charge!' he shouted at the cornicen. 'Now!' The man was standing next to the dense column of Tungrians, with the signifer carrying the vexillum. Both had bearskins over their helmets, the paws crossed and pinned into place on their chests.

The cornicen licked his lips and played the three rising notes of the charge, the last one drawn out.

'Go!' Ferox yelled.

'Charge!' That was the optio at the head of the century. The Tungrians guarding the gate dashed forward and down the slope towards the Selgovae. The warriors skirmishing scampered away, not sure how far the Romans were going. Behind the optio and his men, the main column jogged out of the gate, shields and equipment thumping, and then wheeled to head up to the saddle. Ferox panted as he ran to catch up, for he needed to be there if he was to make this work. Behind the Tungrians came the wounded and the legionaries' mules, with Rufus and his fourteen men and Gambax's party at the rear.

The Selgovae were chanting war cries, blowing their tall trumpets, the noise growing louder all the time, but were still unsure what was happening. It would not last. The optio halted his men. Ferox was near the top of the pass and yelled at the Tungrians to split into two halves. The front of the column kept going, vanishing over the crest, while the others turned about as the wounded were carried or limped past them.

Ferox stopped on the crest beside the waiting auxiliaries. He looked down into the valley and saw the front half of the column going rapidly downhill. For a moment he worried that they were panicking and had forgotten their orders, but then they halted and faced about. A bigger worry was that there was no sign of any troops from the main force coming back for them. For over a mile the valley side was empty. Back nearer the fort there was only flames and masses of dense smoke, which should at least make it harder for the Selgovae to follow them that way. A great howl of rage and excitement surged up as the tribesmen realised that their enemy was not only in the open but running.

Rufus and the rearguard struggled up to the crest, the legionaries burdened with their bulky red shields, the Tungrians loping up the slope with more ease. 'Stop fifty paces down the slope,' Ferox told him, pointing down towards the main valley.

The optio and his men were turning now, running back as he had ordered, but the closest warriors sprang forward very fast. Javelins flashed as they went through the air. An auxiliary fell, a spearhead driven deep into his thigh, and beside him another man slipped or tripped. Two Britons were on him before he could push up again. They jabbed with their spears, piercing his mail, and the man writhed, back arching from the pain. Another warrior reached the soldier hit in the leg and slashed down with his long sword, easily beating aside the wounded man's feeble attempts to block the blows. Scores more Selgovae were bounding up the slope. Hundreds more were surging around from the heights at the far end of the old fort, racing to join the hunt.

Ferox saw the optio in the middle of his men, the two upright feathers on his helmet making him seem taller than the rest, but then the man fell, perhaps hit by a stone. Two of the Tungrians went back for him only to be engulfed by the tide of warriors streaming up the slope. Ferox heard a long piercing scream, saw flashes of swords hacking and the three auxiliaries were gone. The optio's remaining men sprinted away, some dropping shields and spears in a desperate quest for speed.

'We are going forward,' Ferox announced to the thirty or so Tungrians formed in three ranks at the top of the pass. 'When I give the order, I want you to cheer harder than you ever have in your life. Then we march forward ten paces and keep banging your spears against your shields. Front rank will throw spears and the rest keep theirs ready. But we halt!' He turned to stare at the faces, the usual mixture of young and old, all of them nervous, but some hiding it better than others. 'Once we are done, you wait for the order and then we go back at the double the way we came and down the other side. Understand?'

Men nodded.

'I can't hear you.'

'Sir!' they shouted.

'Good.' He took a deep breath. 'Forward, march!' Ferox banged the blade of his gladius against the brass edging of his borrowed shield. The auxiliaries cheered and beat the shafts of their spears against their own shields as they went down the slope.

'Come on!' he shouted. 'Make these scum hear you!'

The Selgovae looked up, surprised to see the Romans come on. Many hesitated, slowing down or stopping. A few chased after the fleeing remnants of the optio's men.

'Go to the side!' Ferox yelled angrily at the fugitives and pointed with his sword. He was counting the paces in his head.

'Halt! Front rank, throw!'

Moving gave force to a thrown spear, but these men had all trained to throw from the halt as well and the slope was in their favour. Eleven broad-shafted spears spun through the air, leaf-shaped heads glinting. One lucky throw hit a charging warrior squarely in the chest and burst out through the man's back, flinging him over. Two more warriors were hit and the rest ran back a short way.

'Back! Back!' Ferox yelled. The Tungrians needed no urging and turned and fled, equipment banging as they jogged up the slope, barging into each other. Ferox followed. There were fresh shouts of triumph from the Selgovae and the trumpets blared again.

'Keep going!' The Tungrians spilled over the crest and Ferox saw that the other half-century was waiting there, with the legionaries formed up alongside them. Rufus was in front, his white crest standing out, his sword raised high. That was not the order he had given, but perhaps the man was right to reinforce this first surprise for the enemy. Ferox glanced back over his shoulder, saw a sea of tribesmen rushing up the hill, the nearest no more than twenty paces behind. He felt the draught as a javelin hissed through the air just beside him, then was running down the far side of the crest and safe for at least a few moments.

'Form up there! Form up down the slope!' he yelled at the Tungrians, trying to make sure that they remembered his orders. Each group was to do a bound of one hundred paces and then turn about to face the enemy and protect the other units as they went back. He was about to join the covering party when Rufus grinned and gestured with his sword down the hillside.

'We'll be fine!' he called. 'You're needed there.'

Ferox smiled back and kept going, his back slick with sweat from the weight of his armour and from all this running.

'Halt!' he yelled at the Tungrians. 'About turn!' The auxiliaries obeyed, even though they did not know him. For the moment it was working, but it would not take much for panic to break out and then there would just be a stream of fugitives running down the valley side, and the slow, the weak, the clumsy and the unlucky would die. Perhaps none of them would get away, for he still saw no sign of supports coming to aid them. He wondered whether Vindex had found someone senior yet, and whether they would have the sense to take the word of a Briton even though he was one of their scouts.

A warrior appeared on the crest, and in a moment there were dozens more alongside him. Rufus' men cheered, and the Tungrians and little detachment of legionaries charged up towards them. That was always tiring, even for a short distance, but the men pounded up the hill. Ferox could not hear the order, and a shift in the wind wafted a mist of smoke over the charging Romans so that it was hard to see. There was no mistaking the ripple in the formation as the first rank threw spears or pila, then the second and then the third. Warriors fell all along the crest and then the legionaries and Tungrians ran into them, and even if they were panting, they charged with spirit.

'Don't wait too long,' Ferox said softly, worrying that the young centurion would get carried away with his success. 'Come back, back.'

He realised that he was holding his breath, so let it out and saw the ragged line of Romans turn about and march back down this side of the crest. The top of the pass was covered in bodies, and Rufus' men had inflicted heavy losses on the boldest of their enemies. There were also two Tungrians and a legionary wounded so that they had to be carried, taking more men away from the fighting.

'Ready, lads. Our turn next!' Ferox told the auxiliaries. Once they were safely behind the crest, Rufus ordered his men to double down the slope. It was hard to keep at a steady pace going downhill, especially burdened with bulky shields and wearing armour and helmets, and by the time they passed Ferox and his men the legionaries and auxiliaries were half running, half stumbling along, formation ragged.

A lone warrior appeared on the crest. He was slim and tall, with mail armour, a red-and-white-striped cloak and a bronze helmet. Everything about the man seemed to glow, apart from his shield, which was drab and plain.

'Step back five paces, slowly now.' The Tungrians obeyed Ferox's quiet order. 'When the time comes, second rank to throw their spears. If I say charge we go ten paces and then stop. If I say hold we hold, and if I say run you follow me and run as if the demons of hell are behind you.' He saw surprise on the auxiliaries' faces, and was pleased that there were a few grins.

Britons appeared all along the crest, stepping up around the lone warrior. Tall carnyxes began to blare out their challenge.

'Step back,' Ferox ordered. 'And another pace.' He glanced behind and saw that Rufus had turned and re-formed his men, but they had gone much further than he had wanted and were a good hundred and fifty paces away. That was always the problem with a withdrawal. Men hurried back, going faster and running for longer than they were supposed to until the officers managed to stop them.

The Selgovae were walking down the slope, most of them coming in ranks, side by side, banging weapons on their little shields and chanting something that might have been a word and might have been a grunt over and over again. The warrior in the striped cloak was in the middle, and beside him was another, bare-chested man, taller and broader, with streaks of grey in his long brown hair. He carried a big rectangular shield, its battered and scarred surface still showing the thunderbolt symbols of Legio XX, but painted over with a charging boar. Just behind them someone carried a standard with a bronze cockerel at the top.

'Steady, lads, back another step.'

A couple of Britons ran out from the front of the formation, javelins poised to throw.

'Keep it steady, lads. Shields braced, back another pace.' One of the auxiliaries in the third rank slipped and fell with a loud curse. Javelins thumped into the shields of the men in front, one driving through the board of the shield and sending a splinter to graze the man's face.

Ferox glanced back. The shape of the valley side was less even than he had thought and rose behind him in a low spur, so that he could no longer see the Roman camp. He had no idea whether or not help was coming. The wounded men were being carried across a little gully just in front of the low spur. The Selgovae kept up their chant, the noise getting louder and louder, so that it almost seemed to punch at them. Ferox was about to turn back to judge whether he had time to run faster before re-forming again when there was a flicker of movement on the spur. A man appeared, almost doubled up in a crouch, spear and shield held low as he came on to the low rise. It was too far away to see, but Ferox could sense the man smile as he stood up. The warrior was naked save for a cloak, his body scored with lines and circles of blue woad, and as he brandished his spear in the air dozens and then scores of men answered his shout and poured over the spur.

'Orb!' Ferox shouted. 'Form an orb, two ranks deep! Move!' It was not the order they were expecting, but long practice or instinct took over and the Tungrians in the rear rank faced about and stepped forward, the men in the middle going faster. The front ranks bent back on the flank and in a moment they formed a very rough circle. Ferox was in the middle, pulling men from the second rank to strengthen the sides and rear, shouting and shoving to get them into place. One of the auxiliaries grunted as a javelin came over the top of his shield and drove through the reinforced mail on his shoulder. Ferox pulled the man back into the middle of the formation.

The Selgovae were closer now, more and more missiles thumping into the Tungrians' shields. One of the soldiers was hit square in the face with such force that his helmeted head snapped back as he was flung to the ground. Ferox looked down the slope and saw Rufus and his men running downhill, charging back to protect the wounded against the new threat, but more and more warriors streamed over the spur. They must have gathered there out of sight, waiting for the moment. The Romans charged in a loose swarm, all order gone, and he saw the young centurion at their head, but doubted that they could break through against such numbers. Well, there was nothing he could do to help and each group must fight its own little battle and see who lasted the longest.

Ferox pushed his way into the middle of the front rank, in time to feel his borrowed shield shudder with the strike of a javelin. 'Right, lads. Let's show 'em how the best soldiers in the world fight,' he called. 'The poor bastards don't know who they're facing yet!'

'Poor buggers,' someone said.

'Don't feel sorry for them, just kill 'em,' he told the auxiliaries.

The Selgovae charged. They threw more javelins first, and Ferox felt his shield rock with another blow. The man next to him folded as a heavier spear smashed through the layers of wood and stuck fast in his belt. He was pulled back and another soldier stepped into his place just in time to meet the warriors.

Ferox's world became small, for there were no more orders to give and all that mattered were the men standing alongside him and the wild-eyed men coming at him. The first was young, only a boy and eager to prove himself in battle, rushing at the enemy, his terror turning to rage. He flung himself forward, shield thrust out as Ferox raised the boss of his own big legionary *scutum* and put his weight behind it. A bigger man might have knocked him over, but Ferox was solid, heavy in all his armour, and he was just pushed back, boots sliding a foot down the gentle slope. He saw the boy raising his long sword to slash down and jabbed forward with his gladius, the long triangular point sliding into his armpit.

177

The boy's mouth opened wide although Ferox did not hear any cry amid the shouting and clash of arms, and he turned the blade to help free it as he pulled back and jabbed again, straight into the throat. Blood jetted over his shield and sprayed on to his face and he had to blink to see, but already his gladius was back, poised to strike again.

When Ferox opened his eyes the boy had fallen and an older man jumped over him, thrusting with his spear at his head. He ducked his head out of the way, felt a heavy blow against the cheek piece of his helmet, stabbed forward, but was blocked by the man's square shield. The soldier on his right was hit by a low slash, coming under the shield and slicing into his leg beneath the knee. He swayed, lowering his guard, and the warrior behind the one he was fighting thrust a long spear through the Tungrian's eye. The dying auxiliary was pulled forward into the mass of the enemy, and his adversary stepped on to him. Ferox twisted a little to the left, punched hard with the boss of his shield and managed to knock the man back, but felt a hammer blow to his right chest as the warrior facing him slammed his spear forward. The tip caught on the fastening of the shoulder piece and broke off. If not for that fluke then he suspected that he would be down.

An auxiliary from the second rank pushed his way into the space and let Ferox concentrate on his own opponent. The man had a lined face and the look of someone who had fought many times. His eyes never left the Roman, and there was no warning when he flung his spear at the centurion's face. Ferox raised his shield, saw the now blunt head punch through the wood and leather, and felt the clumsiness that came from the long-shafted spear stuck into it. He slashed down at the wood, managed to push the spear free, and by that time the warrior had drawn his long slim sword, the blade notched in several places.

Ferox brought his gladius up, elbow bent, blade at eye level ready to strike and waited for the warrior to slash at him. He was only dimly aware of men squaring off all around him. The warrior feinted a cut to the left of his head, once, twice, and then scythed the blade down. Ferox leaned down, lifting his shield, and saw the iron blade slice into the brass edging. His own gladius shot forward at the man's face, was pushed aside by his shield and did no more than graze the warrior's cheek. His shoulder and chest ached, and he was panting with sheer effort.

The warrior punched with his shield, but it was so much smaller than the scutum that it did not unbalance Ferox. His gladius shot forward again as the man's head bowed a little, his right arm swinging down, and the point went through his mouth with such force that Ferox felt teeth smash and bone crack.

The Tungrians cheered, a thin, exhausted sound, but one of triumph none the less because the Selgovae were going back. They did not go far, the warriors stepping away a few paces to be out of reach of spear thrusts. Ferox lowered the dead warrior to the ground, and had to put a boot on his neck to drag his sword free. Two of the auxiliaries were dead, four more too badly wounded to stand and most of the rest were hurt, but able to fight on. All were red-faced, breathing heavily, dripping with sweat from armour and helmets that now felt as heavy as lead.

'Well done, lads.' Ferox gasped the words and had to make a real effort to raise his voice. 'We're showing them. We've got them worried now.'

'Yeah, bet they're terrified,' one of the Tungrians said. 'Pissing in their boots.' The men laughed and it was a wonderful sound that made Ferox feel close to all these men he had known for just an hour or two. He glanced behind. There were dead and wounded strewn all over the grass down the slope. There were two knots of Romans surrounded by hundreds of Selgovae and he saw that the Romans were trying to push their way forward.

'Shields up!' he shouted, for javelins and spears were coming at them. Surely they must run out of things to throw soon. One of the auxiliaries threw his own spear up the slope, and shouted in triumph as a warrior was pitched back. A moment later he was struck on the foot and squealed like a pig until one of his comrades yelled at him to stop.

'Shit,' someone said. The warriors were coming forward again, slower this time, but with determination and not bothering to chant.

'Steady, lads. We'll show 'em!' The fight was much like the first, men grunting like tired labourers as they thrust and hacked at each other from just a foot or two away. Ferox took a glancing cut just below the knee and was lucky that it did not do any real damage. His helmet crest took another blow, sheering almost half of it away, and he was struck twice on the shoulders and knew that he was bruised even if the blades had not penetrated. He cut his first opponent across the face and when that man slipped back and another replaced him, he unbalanced the second warrior with a strike of his shield and thrust into his belly.

The Tungrians did not cheer the second time that the enemy pulled away, going further back up the slope to rest and gather themselves for the last great effort. Instead the auxiliaries gulped for breath like men surfacing after time under water. Only a dozen were still on their legs and they formed a single rank, spaced wider apart than was safe and still only just managing to shelter the thirteen wounded. The rest had been dragged out of the formation by the Britons and slaughtered if they were not already dead. Several of the Selgovae waved aloft heads cut from the corpses. There were more warriors dead or crippled than Romans, but it did not matter. Ferox doubted that they would stand against another attack. Down the slope one of the groups of Romans had vanished, and the other had shrunk and was beset on all sides. He wondered what had happened to Vindex and the message and why no help had come, but it no longer really mattered, for unless they came very soon there would only be corpses to find.

Ferox sighed, breathed deeply, and stepped out of the ring of soldiers. There was one last gamble, and he might as well roll the dice, because if it did not work then they were all dead men. He raised his heavy shield and his gladius high.

'Does any dare to fight me?' He glared at the mass of warriors just a couple of spear lengths away. 'I am Flavius Ferox, centurion of Rome and Lord of the Silures.' The last was not true, but what did that matter in a man's last moments? 'I am a warrior and spit on you cowards who do not dare to meet me man to man.' He spoke slowly because the local accent was so strong and he wanted them to understand. In their place, he would have lobbed a couple of spears at such a boastful idiot, but they were not Silures and Ferox relied on the tribesmen's sense of pride and their love of a gesture fit for song.

The man carrying the Roman shield stepped forward and then turned to face the warriors, raising his spear high and roaring at them. The Selgovae cheered him, while Ferox fought back the temptation to run forward and stab the man in the back. He needed time, and that meant playing by the rules.

'Come on, then, or do you need the shouts of others to make you brave?' Ferox said.

The warrior ignored him, still with his bare back towards the Roman, before turning round very slowly. 'You sound like a sparrow chirping,' he said. He looked to be about forty, a fraction shorter than Ferox, but just as broad and with arms that looked even thicker. There was a silver torc around his neck, slim bracelets on his wrist, and a long sword at his belt. He wore plain shoes and trousers made from wool dyed in a blue, green and grey tartan. Old scars criss-crossed a chest that was free of any paint or tattoo. Patches of the red-painted shield showed wood where the leather surface was torn. The man must have kept it that way deliberately, no doubt to show that he had taken it from its owner in a fierce fight.

'You are the Silure who is a slave for the Romans.' The man had the palest eyes Ferox had ever seen, their gaze as bright and cold as winter sun, and it was that which sparked the memory. This was Venutius himself and as well as a great thief he was known as a deadly fighter. 'I'll give your head to my dogs,' he said. Close behind was the warrior in the red and white cloak, and now that he was nearer Ferox could see that he was no more than fifteen or sixteen, the few sparse hairs on his upper lip a weak attempt at a moustache. Next to him was the standard.

'If they are like you, they'll yap more than they bite!'

Venutius, the lord of these valleys, chuckled as if amused, then threw his spear with all his might. At this distance it would pierce the board of any shield and Ferox punched at it with the boss, felt the iron dent so hard that it pressed against his knuckles, and he slid back through the grass, struggling for balance. The chieftain had his sword out, the slim blade three feet in length, shaped into a point as well as sharpened on the edges. He surged forward at the Roman and his people cheered him on.

Ferox's left hand stung and his arm felt numb. He raised his scutum again as the Briton slammed his own shield into it, and again Ferox went back. The long sword slashed down and the centurion felt the blow slam on to the top of his shield, bursting through the binding and cutting a slice through the three layers of wood. He jabbed forward with his gladius, but the chieftain jumped back, surprisingly nimble for so big a man, and the iron point struck only into empty air.

It was hard to breathe and he felt the strength draining from his body. He had not seen Venutius or the youngster in the fighting, and they looked fresh and strong while he was close to exhaustion. He was too tired to be afraid.

Venutius came forward, dancing as much as walking, his legs bent. He thrust with his sword and Ferox blocked it, but his own swift jab forward went over the man's shield and broke the skin in a slash across the chieftain's shoulder. Venutius punched with his shield, but was too close for it to have much force, and Ferox swerved out of the way, making the man turn so that now they were on the same level. The chieftain jumped back again.

Ferox made sure that his breathing was even more laboured than it needed to be. It was unnerving having his right side to rows of enemies just a few paces away, but he had to ignore them and fix his mind and spirit on his opponent.

The chieftain came on again, his sword raised high this time, ready for a great downward slash. It was the way the Britons fought, and always a risk for it left much of his body unprotected by shield. Ferox had his sword high, ready to stab at eye level, but he guessed that Venutius' guard was a feint and so was his. The Briton wanted to draw his eyes up to the sword.

Venutius twitched his right hand as if to hack down, but checked it as the centurion raised his own blade high to parry, and instead put his weight behind his shield and punched it forward. Ferox stepped into the blow, weight behind his own scutum, feeling the terrible slam that knocked the breath from both men. It brought him close to the chieftain and he kept his gladius up, but slammed the carved wooden pommel into the man's face. It was shaped like a globe and had a small bronze nipple on the end.

The chieftain reeled from the unexpected blow, and Ferox followed it with a second, even harder, and felt the man's nose break. He struck again and again, aiming at the forehead, and Venutius swayed, face bloodied and cold eyes suddenly empty. Then he sank to his knees. Ferox jumped back and let the man fall.

The young warrior in the striped cloak yelled, a sound without words, and rushed at him, sword high. Ferox barely had time to raise his shield before the blade carved through the air. It hit the top of his scutum, widening the great rent torn in it by Venutius, and Ferox let it drop to the ground, because the boy's sword was stuck in the wood. He darted his gladius at the boy, the point going between the top of his mail and the cheek pieces of his bronze helmet, the crest a raven hinged so that the wings flapped.

'You have a lot to learn, boy, but may not get a chance.' Ferox held the sword there, pressing hard enough so that the lad would feel it and know that only a little more force would open his throat to the bone. The young warrior gulped, and although his green eyes stared wide in terror, he did his best to look brave.

Trumpets sounded. Not the vibrating call of the carnyx, but the rasp of the army's brass cornu-horns and iron trumpets. The Selgovae were chattering, men pointing past the centurion, but Ferox did not take his eyes from the boy.

'You are brave,' he said, 'and it is no disgrace to lose to an older fighter.'

'Get it over with.' The lad did not sound like one of the Selgovae and had more of the lilting tone of the Caledonians of the far north. The warriors were going back up the slope, turning to run.

Ferox pressed just a little harder. The boy closed his eyes, but did not flinch. The centurion held the sword there before pulling it back.

The boy opened one eye and then the other.

'Go!' Ferox told him. 'Take him with you.' He pointed with his sword at the groaning Venutius. 'Get away if you can and go with honour as brave men who met other brave men. Let us hope that next time we meet in friendship.' The boy was gaping, so he thought one of Vindex's favourite expressions might help. 'Piss off!' he told him.

The young warrior laughed and leaned down to help the chieftain up. Venutius was bruised, his nose smashed, but he looked at the centurion and gave a gentle nod of his head.

Ferox turned away from them to look at the battered remnants of the Tungrians as they stood, leaning on their shields and panting, struggling to understand that they had survived. Down the slope he saw Cerialis and Brocchus leading turmae of their horsemen over the low spur. They cut some of the Britons down, but the rest were running and most would get away because the horses could not go fast on this ground. There were legionaries behind them, but he doubted that the heavily laden soldiers would catch many of the nimble warriors.

'Well done, lads,' he said to the Tungrians, but could find neither the words nor the energy to say more.

XIII

'THE LEGATE IS delighted, truly delighted.' Crispinus leaned forward to scratch his horse's ears. 'And he is especially pleased with your conduct. Claudius Super assures him that you are one of his best men – at least when you are sober.'

Ferox did not share the tribune's enthusiasm and made no reply. Twenty-nine Tungrians and fourteen legionaries had died during the retreat from the old fort, and almost as many were badly wounded. The few survivors left on their feet at the end were all grazed or bruised. Ferox's right shoulder ached and was stiff, but he knew that he had got off lightly. Rufus was dead, his head taken by the enemy, and Titus Annius had been stabbed as he lay on his stretcher and the surgeons held out little hope for him. The four auxiliaries carrying him had all died defending their commander. They and many of the other corpses had been mutilated after they had fallen. Men spoke of warriors tattooed with animals on their foreheads as the most vicious of the enemy, and there had been a lot of them as well as ordinary Selgovae in the group that overran the party carrying the injured.

'I have spoken to Vindex the Brigantian and he is even more fulsome in his praise.'

Ferox stared at him sceptically.

'Well, what he actually said was, "He's a hard, clever bastard, and one you want on your side." I am pretty sure those were his words, although sometimes his accent baffles me – as does his directness. It's as if the man has no manners, but perhaps that is just the way among his people.'

The centurion shrugged, but said nothing.

'He also told me a lot about you. From all that I have heard I do not believe that you are truly the drunken fool described by Claudius Super. You are sober most of the time, but now and again you brood and feel sorry for yourself and drink yourself senseless. Vindex reckons that you are so fond of being miserable because it makes you feel important. I suspect that he is right.'

'I cannot help what you believe, my lord.'

'Well, believe this at the very least. This is a victory,' Crispinus assured him, letting go of the reins and spreading his arms wide. His weight did not shift in the saddle and the horse did not stir and just plodded on. The centurion had to concede that the aristocrat knew how to ride.

'Some might not call it that,' Ferox replied.

'Perhaps.' Crispinus sniffed his fingers and wrinkled his nose at the strong scent of horse. 'But the only thing that matters is the report Quadratus is writing, which will say that we won a great victory and punished the tribes for refusing to pay their taxes and daring to oppose the might of Rome.'

Ferox said nothing. If the reinforcements had not arrived when they had, then he doubted that anyone would have survived. Vindex had reached the main force quickly, but had trouble finding a senior officer or anyone who knew where the legate or Crispinus were. In the end he met the junior tribune Flaccus, who told him to wait while he reported to Quadratus. The Brigantian waited a long time, until Crispinus appeared and expressed surprise at his presence. By that time Ferox had started to retreat, and it was only the urgent demands of the tribune that gathered enough men and got them moving in time to save the survivors.

'I shall take your silence as agreement with my fine argument,' the tribune said. 'The story will be told of success and we shall all share in the rewards of victory. I do not think that I am breaking any great confidence if I tell you that your name is on the list of those recommended for *dona*.'

'I already have plenty of decorations.' The day after the fight the two chieftains had sent messengers to say that they were willing to make their peace. There was too little food left for the columns to remain in the field, and on top of that the Legate Quadratus wanted to declare victory in the neat little campaign he had been so keen to fight. In the afternoon he met with Tagax and Venutius. The latter was badly bruised and had a bandage tied around his face, but greeted Ferox with great warmth.

'We met yesterday as enemies, let us talk now as friends,' the old horse thief declared. 'I come now because you fought as a man and I can trust you as one brave warrior to another.' The chieftain's voice boomed out as he spoke, and Ferox suspected that the words were intended as much for his own warriors as anyone else. This was a good, honourable way to end the fighting. Both chieftains promised to pay all their taxes within ten days, including an additional levy of grain and cattle demanded as the price for peace, and to give hostages from their families as a pledge of their firm alliance with Rome.

'Be a lean winter for their people,' Vindex had muttered when the terms were agreed by both sides.

'Even tougher for Venutius' neighbours. That rogue will rob them blind to find the cattle he is supposed to give us. I'll bet Tagax's folk will lose more than a few over the next few nights.'

It was over, and Ferox wondered whether Crispinus, let alone the legate, realised that the Selgovae would not feel beaten. They had stood up like men to the great empire and had inflicted some losses and proved their courage. The tribesmen would remember the burning farms, and they would also remember cutting up the Tungrians and legionaries as they retreated and a few other sharp skirmishes where they had taken heads. Their courage was proved by the plain facts that the Romans had withdrawn from their lands, and had had to talk to them to end the fighting. The soldiers of the emperor had gone and they were still the Selgovae, 'the brave ones' as they called themselves, warriors to be feared and respected by all their neighbours, including the Romans.

Ferox still felt that the campaign was a foolish waste of everyone's time and too many lives. He remembered reading that the Emperor Augustus described fighting a needless war as like a man fishing with a golden hook, where no possible gain justified the risk.

'Our luck held,' Crispinus said. 'Only just, but it held. If over a hundred men had been massacred then the story would no doubt have grown with the telling and brought delight to the emperor's rivals. But that did not happen and Trajan has a victory. Some of you survived, which means that the fallen are heroes who helped us to win.'

Ferox did not bother to comment, but was reassured that the young aristocrat had some sense of the folly of it all. It had been very, very close. Luck mattered, but too many mistakes had been made by the senior officers. Crispinus' column ought to have moved sooner to drive into the main valley and cut off the Selgovae's retreat, and Titus Annius ought to have withdrawn much sooner. Flaccus claimed that his orders had allowed the centurion to make his own decision when to pull back to the main force, and blamed him for hesitating. So far Annius was in no state to reply.

Flaccus always seemed to be around when mistakes occurred and the man might be no more than a fool. There were always plenty of them serving in the higher ranks, and most had the knack of being just where they could cause the most harm. Yet the tribune might also be a friend or a relative of someone of greater importance, the sort of man Crispinus claimed wanted the emperor to fail.

'You should trust me, Flavius Ferox,' Crispinus said, as if reading his thoughts. 'You really should.' They were riding ahead of the main column as it marched back south, and far enough ahead of their escort to be able to speak freely.

Ferox hesitated, balancing the risk, and then decided that at

188

most he would be fishing with a brass hook, and Crispinus might just be honest and able to help. If someone did not do something, then there was the risk of war and ruin here in the north and spreading afield. This was his patch, and it was his job to keep the peace. He told the young aristocrat of his suspicions of Flaccus and perhaps others working to start a war and wanting failure and defeat. The tribune listened, occasionally asking questions that were precise and to the point. Ferox talked for a long time, speaking of the priests and the tattooed warriors, many of whom came from far afield and some from inside the empire, and of the great druid who was able to change shape and make Roman fight Roman, and the men murdered at the tower back on the day of the ambush.

'The tribes always know a lot about us, but lately they know too much,' he said. 'It all points to someone helping them, and someone senior enough to know the big things as well as the small.'

Crispinus let out a long breath. 'That is a lot to think about.' He stared at the centurion. 'You do not strike me as the sort of man who starts at shadows. Still, I doubt that Flaccus would be working on his own. He was recommended for his first post by the legate of Syria whose resignation came as such a surprise to us all,' he added drily.

'Then why is he still here, and promoted to legionary tribune?'

'Any senator of importance, let alone a former consul and provincial governor, recommends scores of men every year – hundreds probably. It would be hard to dismiss them all and not worth the effort. Flaccus is not a clever man, or very important – or ever likely to be. He might just be covering up his mistakes, or one of those people convinced that every mistake they make must be bad luck or someone else's fault.'

'Typical senior officer.'

Crispinus ignored the sarcasm. 'Yet I suspect you are right and he is acting deliberately. But what matters is who is giving him his orders. Someone much more imaginative, I suspect. Do you have any suspicions?'

'Plenty, my lord, but I have learned that it is prudent to treat everyone as a fool or an enemy until their deeds show them to be something else.'

Crispinus grinned. 'If your friend Vindex were here he would no doubt make some comment about Silures. I do hope that your present company is not included in your suspicions – or have I shown myself to be trustworthy?'

'Early days, sir, early days. And I have been wondering just what you and the prefect were doing on the day when his wife was ambushed.'

The tribune frowned for a moment, then slapped his thigh and threw back his head to laugh. 'The truth really does matter to you, doesn't it? Well, in this case it is mundane. We were hunting, as you well know.'

'That was a strange place to choose, especially if you were after boar, as you claim.' Ferox paused before adding, 'Sir.'

'You must seek that answer from the Prefect Cerialis. I was merely the guest. As far as I know it was all just coincidence – a fortunate one for you, let alone the Lady Sulpicia.'

'As you say.' Ferox did not care for too many coincidences, and at that moment a rider came with orders summoning the tribune to a conference with the legate.

'I meant what I said about trusting me,' he said in parting.

'My lord, I am sure that you did.' It was far too early for that, but it would be interesting to see what the young aristocrat did.

Crispinus sniffed and kicked his heels to put his horse into a canter.

That was the last day of good weather, and from then on driving winds brought in rainstorm after rainstorm. The track was churned into mud by marching boots and the ruts left by carts, and the better road connecting the forts was not much better. It took a week to return to Luguvallium, and then a long day for the Batavians and Tungrians to reach Vindolanda. Titus Annius clung to life, and Ferox could only imagine the agonies the man must have endured in the back of a lurching army wagon.

'He's a tough one,' Vindex said, when he went with Ferox to pay their respects. The centurion seemed to recognise them, and gave a weak smile. His face was pale, tinged with yellow, and there was a bandage strapped over his ruined eye. The *medicus* told them that most of the time he was unconscious, taking only a little thin broth prepared under the orders of the seplasiarius.

The centurion was in a fever when they reached Vindolanda, babbling nonsense and now and again shouting commands or giving orders to an imagined parade. They kept him in his house rather than the hospital, and off-duty soldiers clustered around the side entrance hoping to hear news of their commander for he was well respected by all and liked by most. Perhaps the realisation that he was in his home helped for he revived a little, enough to eat several meals. For a while his doctor dared to hope.

Crispinus brought the news, stopping at Syracuse accompanied by a patrol of twenty cavalrymen from II Augusta, meant to exercise the horses and keep the men in trim more than to gain useful information. It was strange to find so senior an officer joining so small and routine an activity, and Ferox could tell that it made the decurion in charge very nervous. The tribune did not appear to care.

'I ought to learn as much as I can about how the army does things,' he said. 'And I cannot do that sitting in the principia reading endless lists and reports.'

'Endless lists and reports are what the army does best,' Ferox told him.

'Why Syracuse?' The tribune swept an arm to encompass the little courtyard of the wooden outpost. 'I cannot say that I see a resemblance.' His horse was drinking from the trough, while the tribune was drinking posca from a dark, locally made cup. He grimaced at the taste, but drained it and held his cup out for more. Philo, immaculate as ever, took great pleasure in tending to such an important visitor.

'Why not Syracuse?' Ferox replied mildly.

Crispinus shook his head, but let the matter drop. 'We were told that some deserters had been seen in the area. It would be good to find that Briton – the one from the tower.'

'As long as he is in a state to talk.'

'Have you heard anything in the last few days?' The tribune lowered his voice.

'Not much,' Ferox said. 'Venutius' men are lifting herds from far and wide, so we should get paid in full. Apart from that people are talking more about the Stallion and his great power. It seems he was up a mountain in a trance receiving messages from the gods while the fighting was going on.'

'He must have been so disappointed when he heard.'

'Gutted, I'm sure. But they are saying that one of his foals went in his place, so that must be the one in the headdress, the one I killed. But people aren't telling it that way. They are saying that he died along with all his band after falling on the Romans at night and slaying ten times their number. He is supposed to have broken his sword from hewing through Roman necks. The last he killed was the Roman commander. With his sword gone, the pupil of the great priest rent the Roman apart with his bare hands.'

Crispinus looked down at himself and then used his free hand to pat his other arm and his chest. 'Seems to have worn off. So this was the fellow skulking in the darkness who had the misfortune to run into you?'

'The same, but people will believe anything else quicker than the truth.' When Crispinus raised an eyebrow, Ferox explained. 'That is a saying of my people.'

'Of the Silures, you mean – you are a Roman after all.'

Ferox let that pass. 'It's taken a while to learn, and come in whispers and hints, but it seems that the Great Stallion has six foals – well, five now: followers who learn from him and are mighty in their own right.'

'Do the people you meet like him and his men?'

The centurion had forgotten for a moment that the tribune knew so little of these lands and the folk who lived there. 'That does not matter – they fear them. Men who can work magic and have one foot in the Otherworld are dangerous. As long as they have power then people will do what they want whether they want to or not. We need to do something about them.'

'You are probably right, and I will see what I can do. For the moment keep your eyes and ears open.' Crispinus tossed the cup to Philo, who fumbled, but managed to catch it before it dropped. 'Nearly caught you there!' the aristocrat told the slave. 'Time to go. I think it might be a good idea if you went to Vindolanda. If he is well enough, ask Titus Annius about the orders given to him by Flaccus. We won't be able to prove anything, but it gives us more to go on.'

The tribune leaped into the saddle and clicked with his tongue to make the horse walk on. He had almost reached the gate when he turned and came back. He snapped his fingers and then pointed at the centurion.

'Augustus,' he said. 'I am right, aren't I? The divine Augustus used to go to a special room in the palace when he wanted peace and quiet and to get away from it all. He called it Syracuse, and I dare say you would struggle to find anywhere better than this for getting away from it all.' His horse tried to pull towards the water in the trough, but the tribune held the rein firmly.

Ferox nodded. 'You are a learned man, my lord.'

'And you are full of surprises. Farewell for the moment, Flavius Ferox, centurio regionarius.'

The wind picked up overnight, coming from the east with the bitter hint of the coming winter. It ripped half a dozen tiles from the roof of the gate-tower, and a few more from the buildings inside the fort.

Ferox rode to Vindolanda the next morning, swathed up to stay warm and dry in the saddle as best he could, but it was not long before his face felt numb from the battering of the wind. He passed a young birch tree snapped almost in half and an older tree pulled from the ground by its roots. When he reached the fort he was not surprised to learn that Titus Annius had died.

This was the sort of day a good man's soul would leave its body. The centurion had seemed to be at peace, but then had cried out during the night and when the slaves ran to his room they found that he was dead. Ferox thought it odd that no slave was with him all the time, although the centurion was well known for his frugal lifestyle and for his fixed ideas of how things should be done.

His will was a case in point. He had no wife or children, and no other family members to whom he wished to bequeath his estate. No one at Vindolanda knew much about Titus Annius' background. Every detail of his funeral was set down. The centurion wanted no hired mourners and only the simplest procession to a spot near the road outside the *porta praetoria*, the main gates of the fort. 'Let whoever come who chooses, and let a dozen of my boys see me off. Burn me, drink to cohors I Tungrorum and to the emperor, and tell my lads that I'll be watching them and they had better never disgrace me by their turnout or conduct or I'll come back and haunt them.'

A copy of the will was posted up outside the small praetorium where he had lived – a far more modest building that the one housing Cerialis. All day there were Tungrians gathered around it, half weeping and half laughing, those who were able reading the words out to the others. Titus Annius' estate was considerable, and he left most of it as a fund to give a year's pay to each widow or child left behind when one of his auxiliaries died going about his duty or from sickness. The recent losses meant that there would soon be plenty of calls on the legacy. One thousand denarii were set aside by special arrangement with Flora, who for the three days after the centurion's death was to welcome without charge any Tungrian who knocked on her door. 'Give the lads whatever they want. I want to hear humping as I make my way to the Elysian Fields.'

As Ferox watched the wrapped corpse burn, he wondered whether Titus Annius had got his wish. Cerialis was there, as was Crispinus, Aelius Brocchus, and Rufinus, the prefect of the Spaniards. The twelve picked Tungrians sparkled even on this drab, rainy morning, with every piece of metalwork polished like a mirror. Two of the men wore bandages from wounds taken on the day the centurion fell, and one of them limped as he carried the couch on which the body was laid. Around them, forty or fifty more men from the cohort watched. No one gave orders, but they stood in ranks and files, and all had found a reason to appear in their best uniforms. Quite a few Batavians had come as well, and there were civilians from the canabae. The centurion had said that no women were to attend, and this was obeyed, although several cloaked and hooded figures watched from a distance.

No one cried openly, for that was another rule, but plenty of eyes were moist, not least because a fitful wind stirred the smoke and blew it around. The Tungrians had done their job well, though, and Ferox could feel the heat from twenty paces away, even though the only wood available was damp, so that its smoke was thick and black. Now and again the wind carried the smell of burning flesh, the scent lingering even after the skin and fat must have burned away. It was the smell of death, and he had never cared for the Roman custom of watching a man being cremated. The smoke reminded him of the burning thatch in the old fort and not for the first time he wondered whether or not he had done the right thing in ordering the retreat. Had he killed Annius and all those men or saved the survivors from being surrounded and slaughtered inside the ramparts? Instinct and reason told him that they had had to leave, and that the supports should have come much sooner. He wondered about Flaccus – and about the plausible Crispinus, standing just a few feet away in a black cloak.

With a great flare of sparks, the piled wood collapsed, letting the remnants of the body fall, and soon the remains of Titus Annius, centurion of Legio XX Valeria Victrix and lately commander of cohors I Tungrorum, would mingle with the rest of the ash. When it cooled they would gather some of the ash in an urn and bury it, letting the rest blow on the four winds. The tombstone was already being carved and would be erected in nine days' time.

It was almost time for the funeral banquet, although thankfully Titus Annius' will had stated that he wanted this to be simple, a soldier's meal and not some great feast. They had brown bread and a stew made with salted bacon and hard tack biscuit, all to be washed down with posca, and not just his own men, but any soldier who passed was welcome to join. It ought not to take long, once a libation had been poured, and Ferox was glad. He had never understood the way the Romans would laugh and joke so soon after burning the remains of a friend. Titus Annius had gone on his own journey to the Otherworld or wherever it was that Romans went. Did the man truly believe in the Elysian Fields? Ferox met so many Romans who did not seem to believe in the soul and thought the whole essence of a man ended with death, or slowly faded away into nothingness.

The sun came out as they were eating and drinking, and this seemed to make the mourners merry. Ferox stayed as long as courtesy and respect to the departed required, but let himself gradually drift away to the edge of the crowd. No one noticed as he strode away up the slope to the parade ground. He wanted open space and quiet, and the prospect to the west was a good one.

There were a few cavalrymen exercising horses at the far end, beyond the rostra from which the officer commanding could address a parade. Otherwise it was empty, and he went to the far side and looked to the west. The clouds had closed in again and he looked in vain for a break in the hope of glimpsing the setting sun. He was surprised at how moved he was by the centurion's death, for he had not known the man at all well.

After a while he heard voices behind him, but the wind was strong, driving into him, and he could not pick out any words. He pulled his cloak tighter and did not turn, making it clear that he was not looking for company. There were steps in the grass and the sound of horses, but he ignored them.

'I like this view.' Sulpicia Lepidina stood beside him. 'It seems to stretch on and on, the hills rolling into the distance.'

'My lady.' He took off his helmet as he faced her, and the wind ruffled his dark hair. 'I am sorry, I did not know that it was you.'

There were a couple of male slaves with her, as well as her maid, the girl looking cold and miserable in spite of a heavy tartan cloak. There was also Longinus, the one-eyed veteran, and another soldier leading a couple of horses. On one sat a boy, his hair flame red and his face so like Cerialis' that it was obviously his son. Ferox guessed that he was about six, but tall for his age. The boy sat awkwardly, hunched forward and legs dangling low, shifting back and forth. Then he remembered that the lad had been born with a crooked back, the deformity slight, but obvious as soon as he remembered.

'His father insists that Flavius rides every day. I do wonder whether he is still a bit young, but the prefect insists that if he learns now he will sit more naturally.'

'The Lord Cerialis is right,' Ferox said. 'I was younger than he is when my grandfather first sat me on a pony. I confess that I was terrified.'

She smiled, the warm smile that lit up her face, even when the wind blew hard and her skin was cold and pale. 'I find it hard to imagine anything terrifying you, centurion. Your grandfather sounds quite a character. Tell me about him?'

Ferox was surprised at how readily he answered, talking about the Lord of the Hills and his own youth among his people. She listened, asking question after question with no hint of disdain at any of his answers, and when she mocked it was gentle. In the meantime the cavalrymen began to take the boy through some basic riding exercises.

'None of my family have served in Britannia,' she said after a while. 'Indeed I am the first to invade!'

'And the only one we could never resist, lady.'

The boy was cantering in a circle, and in spite of his back he was shaping up well, better balanced now if still ungainly to the eye.

'I do not understand why,' she said, 'but he wears out shoes faster than any child I have ever known.' Her tone was fond. 'His father drives him, wanting him to grow up as a true aristocrat, and the boy is eager to please. Sometimes I wish—' She stopped, and turned back to look over the hills.

'Do you like Vindolanda?' he asked, as much for something to say because she seemed uncomfortable. Then he realised that he had forgotten to address her properly. 'I do not mean to pry, my lady. Please forgive me.'

She looked up at him, wisps of her golden hair blowing loose across her face. 'Forgive you?' She smiled, trying to push the strands out of her eyes and failing. She had on the same drab cloak she had worn to visit the temple. Her eyes looked very blue as she stared at him in silence for what seemed like an age.

'Well,' she said at last, 'there are many ways of answering that. The house is adequate, the household learning my ways – those who did not come with us in the first place. Claudia Severa is a dear thing, her husband a decent man, and there are others whose society is not unpleasant. It is something of a bore to have everyone looking up to me, but I do not suppose there is another woman of my rank closer than Eboracum. Would it shock you to hear that I do not miss the company of my own class?'

Ferox was not sure how to respond. He wondered whether there was opportunity for a compliment, but could not think of one.

'I do not believe that anything you could say would shock me, my lady,' he said in the end, feeling that honesty was the simplest response.

'Really. Then it seems I have grown dull in a very short time.'

'M-my lady,' he stammered. 'I did not mean... That is I did not imply...'

'For such a bold warrior you tease very easily!' Sulpicia Lepidina laughed softly. They were standing close together, and after a glance to see that the troopers and her stepson were some way away, she took his hand. 'This time you must forgive me for being cruel. You are a soldier under discipline, and not free to act or say what you wish to me.'

'Duty and discipline, my lady.' He thought that he ought to pull his hand free, but did not and instead pressed hers. 'There is little left for me in this life.'

'The soldier's life,' she said sadly. 'That of the noblewoman is not so different. We marry as we have to, live as we have to, and try to avoid disgrace. Duty and discipline in another guise, its hold on us just as tight.' The lady slid her hand away back under the cover of her cloak.

She turned away, looking out across the hills. 'I like it here. Duty commands me to come and assist my husband. Discipline makes me run the house well and try my best to raise his children – our children, I should say. I serve my husband and my own family as best I can. It is not perhaps what I expected. Children have such dreams. When your grandfather put you on that pony did you ever think that your path would lead you here?'

'No. It is hard to remember what I expected from life, but this was not it.'

'Loss is a terrible thing, and yet the gods seem to have placed it at the heart of our lives. Little turns out as you expect. Loss of dreams and loss of hope are almost as sad as the loss of people. I liked Titus Annius, even if I do not think he had much time for me or even for my husband.'

'He was a good man,' Ferox said, and hoped that did not imply an insult to her or the prefect.

'Duty and discipline.' She looked up at him again. 'It is not all bad. At least it has brought me to places that I might only have read about. Life at home can be very dull. To return to the question you have no doubt forgotten. Yes, I like Vindolanda. I like it because it is near the edge of the world. That does not release me from duty and discipline, but at least now and then I can glimpse freedom.

'I had better go. Flavius tries very hard and I do not believe his father gives him sufficient praise, so I try to make up for that.'

Sulpicia Lepidina walked away, and Ferox forced himself to stare at the hills and not watch her go.

XIV

THREE HOURS LATER he passed a couple of drunken Tungrians staggering happily out of Flora's place.

'Only us today, centurion,' one of them said, grinning to show broken and yellowed teeth. 'You'll have to wait. Unless you want to take that old bitch herself!' The man found his own wit hysterically funny and doubled up with laughter.

'Sorry, sir. He don't mean anything,' his companion said, looking down with glazed fondness at him. 'You were with us, weren't you?' Ferox nodded. 'Then I don't think "Old Iron" would grudge you your turn.'

Ferox had not heard the nickname before, and nodded amicably to the man as he passed. He was going to Flora's, but not for the usual reason.

'I would like to see the mistress,' he told the thickset slave standing in front of the open back door. 'I am expected.' He had sent a note earlier in the day and been told to call at this hour.

'Of course, centurion, you are always welcome,' purred the oily voice of Flora's clerk, who was sitting at a desk inside the porch. This was the entrance used by the more important clients and led to the luxurious rooms as well as Flora's office and her apartment. Everyone else climbed the wooden steps at the front to the second floor, where matters were dealt with efficiently, if with less style. 'You know the way, do you not, sir?' The man was small and had eyes that only focused on the page in front of him.

200

As Ferox went down the corridor, the one-eyed Batavian cavalryman appeared from the main office.

'Centurion,' Longinus said, nodding respectfully and moving out of the way to let the officer pass. The walls were plastered and painted, less gaudily than the upper storey, and by the look of it the same artist who had worked on the main rooms of the praetorium had done these.

'The terms are the same as usual,' Flora said as the centurion went into her office, a simple room equipped with several cabinets, a marble-topped table and three well-upholstered chairs. The wall panels showed pastoral scenes with plenty of nymphs, each with the face of a girl who worked or had worked here.

Flora was a short woman, so slightly built as to be almost boyish, and still slim and strong even though she must be well past her fiftieth year. There were deep lines on her face – at least on those rare occasions like this when she appeared without heavy make-up. He was also surprised that she was dressed simply, and that there was a little tear at the neck of her plain brown robe. Beside her stood a slave boy in a brightly bleached tunic. She wrote something more on a wooden tablet, and then looked up, noticing his gaze.

'I thought a lot of Titus Annius,' she said, and one hand fingered the torn linen. Ferox guessed that this must be the way her people mourned. He had never been quite sure where Flora came from. She had olive skin, dark eyes and long thick hair – these days dyed a bright henna red. No doubt there were many stories from her rise from slave to prosperous businesswoman, but she hardly ever spoke of her past and he did not pry. Crispinus talked a lot about trust, and that was something Ferox did not give readily. Yet he trusted this little whore mistress and she had always been fair with him.

'Here is the contract.' She held out the sheet of thin wood, its surface carefully rubbed with beeswax so that the ink would not spread. 'You have the money?' For the moment she was all business.

Ferox took a bag from his pouch and poured the contents on to the table. 'Sixty denarii, including the tax.' The coins were the pooled resources of the men stationed at Syracuse. Every year or so they put together the cost of hiring a girl for a month. Ever since he returned, their spokesman, the Thracian, had pressed for him to arrange matters with Flora.

'You will see their entitlements laid out in order. I'm letting you have Procla. She – and only she – will keep the tally and charge whatever is necessary.' The initial lease would only cover so much, and once that allowance had gone the soldiers would have to pay each time just like any other customers.

'She can come up next week when the cart brings our supplies.'

'Good.' Flora turned to the slave. 'Wine.' She looked questioningly at Ferox.

'Thank you, but plenty of water.'

Flora nodded as the slave left on his errand. 'Good. Glad to see that you are being sensible. Sometimes I worry about you.'

'I'll get by.'

She smiled, the creases around her eyes and mouth becoming deeper. 'You have so far. Are you stopping for a while or just here on business?' A burst of singing came from above them. The ceiling was made from thick beams, and normally kept out any noise from above, but a group of merry Tungrians were bawling out an obscene song about a centurion and an army mule. 'That's an old one,' she continued. 'It's not a peaceful night, but I've kept the twins out of it, and young Cytheris.'

The twins, two women unrelated and utterly different in appearance, but of equally great skill in their trade, were the most expensive girls at the place. Cytheris was fairly new, not yet up to such a robust evening.

'Thank you for the offer, but I shall say no.'

'It will not cost, you know that. Not with everything I owe you.'

Ferox shook his head. 'You've long since paid me back.'

'You cannot pay back a friend – though that cheeky sod Vindex reckons I ought to keep trying!' Her laugh was deep and earthy, a laugh that should have come from someone fat and drunk.

'I reckon friendship with Vindex costs everyone a lot.' Flora laughed again, a bubbling sound. She drank a lot, but Ferox had never seen her the worse for wine. 'I'll pass today, all the same – unless you have changed your mind!' He grinned, a rare gesture that always made him look younger.

'You're as bad as he is!' Flora flushed with pleasure. 'You know I'm retired – and old enough to be your mother.'

'Would you talk to me a while?' he asked.

'Still business, eh? Well, you know you don't have to ask.'

'Was Titus Annius a guest here?'

That surprised her and she raised her thin, well-plucked eyebrows. The slave appeared and placed two blue-green cups on the table. A slim girl aged about twelve with thick, mousy hair appeared with a flagon each of wine and water. Flora poured her glass unmixed, and waited for the slaves to leave. 'Good kid, that one. She'll have to decide soon which way she goes. Her mother raised enough to buy her freedom, but where would she go if she doesn't work here? Not easy for a girl on her own and there's a lot of bastard men out there.' She drained the glass and poured herself another.

'Well, that's as maybe,' she said after a moment. 'And if you were another man we'd talk about that and the struggles of life and move on. But you're not like that, and never give up. I guess it's not my business why you want to know, and there's no need to tell me.

'Yes, the centurion came here, regular as clockwork every third month. Didn't favour one girl over another, didn't talk much, but they said he was kind enough – no trouble, he just got on with it. Not like you, singing to them for hours before getting down to business!' She laughed again. That was another old joke. Ferox had not come here for years except to talk to the mistress, but she swore than when he used to visit he had always got drunk and started to sing. 'They quite liked it, tell the truth. You've a nice voice.' Ferox could not remember anything about those times and still wondered whether this was Flora's little joke.

'How about Flavius Cerialis?'

203

'Huh! Trying to be clever again.' She waved her glass at him, and it must already have been almost empty because nothing spilled out. 'Well, don't bother with me because I've seen it all and don't get shocked, and you should know that I'll tell you what I wouldn't tell most.

'Yes, he was here within a few days of arriving, and then a couple of times each week after that. Only stays away when that ponce of a freedman is about, along with his wife.'

'Fortunata?'

'That's the one. Knew her in Londinium when she worked for a friend. She was a dancer, and not a bad one, although reckon she's out of shape now.' Flora frowned. 'Poor lass, I doubt she'll ever learn, but she's one of those who tries to please every man she meets. Probably thinks that will make her safe. The more important the man, the harder and quicker she flings herself at him.'

Ferox remembered the freedwoman rubbing against him and the servants' gossip passed on by Philo. 'What does make you safe?' he mused.

'Nothing.' Flora's tone was brutal. 'Not any damned thing. Money helps, and influence, and luck, quick wit and real friends, but it can all go in a minute. Doesn't matter if you're an emperor or a slave, it can all end just like that.' She tried to snap her fingers, but no noise came until she did it for the fourth time. 'See, can't even rely on that. It's just the world, and the world doesn't care and it ain't always kind and it ain't always nice.'

'You always cheer me up.'

The dirty laugh came back again. 'And you always get me talking and preaching.'

'Cerialis?'

'Oh, still nosy. Well, he's always the same. Wants the twins, both of them together. They say he's keen and energetic – I can draw you a picture if you like, but I didn't think you were the sort who likes that sort of thing. Talks a lot and likes to tell them things, though – quotes poets and books. They swear he's the wisest man they've ever met.' Flora was dismissive. 'What do those silly things know except what to do in bed or out of it? Now I'm thinking that if he was really so clever then he'd be discussing such things with his lady wife and not a couple of tarts. So I reckon he likes to feel big in every way – not just the same way as all the other men.'

'What do you know of his wife?'

'Hmmm. Sniffing around, are we?' she said and laughed again. She offered him the wine, but he shook his head.

Ferox looked down at his cup. He had always been drawn to the delicacy of fine glass – so beautiful and yet so fragile. It was a wonder of the empire, smaller and less important than many, but never failed to make him marvel at the skill of its craftsmen.

'I like her,' Flora said after a moment. 'She came here once – no, not in that way! You should be ashamed of yourself, you little beast.' She drained her glass and wagged it at him reprovingly. 'Not that there's not some who would, but not that one. No, she sent a slave to ask for an appointment, then came and bid me good day and took my hand as courteous as you like.' The brothel owner, former slave and whore, preened at the memory. 'They were making a little bathing pool in the praetorium and the workmen were telling her that it couldn't be done the way she wanted, so she wanted to see mine and ask whether I was happy with it.

'Venus alone knows how she had heard about it,' Flora continued. 'Husband's been in there often enough, but doubt he tells her!' She sniggered for a moment, before resuming a dignified posture, her free hand in the air, fingers outstretched like a statue. 'Took her there, and she didn't bat an eyelid at the pictures.'

Ferox had not been in the bath here for some time, but could dimly remember walls covered in paintings of nudes and couples, of a whole wide and sometimes baffling array of lovemaking, some accurate, some mythical and some surely downright impossible.

'Well, she asks precise questions, and I got the clerk who arranged it to answer. He turned to jelly under her gaze, but spoke up well enough. From what I hear she lectured the work party and now the prefect and his wife reckon they have almost as good a bath as mine.'

'Perhaps without the pictures.'

Flora chuckled. 'Perhaps without the pictures.' She thought for a moment. 'Might warm her up though, poor thing. Not a lot of joy in her life. As I say – emperor or slave, it doesn't matter.'

'Do you know much about her?'

'You don't give in, do you?' She stared at him, glancing at the flagon of wine and then changing her mind. 'If you weren't a friend I'd let you wonder. Still, truth is that I don't know that much, just bits and pieces I hear from the girls or when I keep my ears open. A blind man could see that the marriage is not founded on love, but then how many really are, especially with the rich?'

'Keeps you in business.'

'Cheeky lad, aren't we?' Flora glared at him and then tilted her head from side to side. 'You know enough of the world to know that the likes of me will never be short of business. There are some, you know, who are happy, really happy. Take Aelius Brocchus and his wife. Not the brightest, either of them, but they're well matched and content.' Her admiration was mixed with wonder at such good fortune.

'Do you know everyone, Flora?'

'You know the old joke about the most famous whore in Antioch. They asked her whether she knew every man in the city, and she said no, but there was one part of all of them she knew about.'

'They don't usually tell it that way.'

'Just because I grew up in a sewer doesn't mean I have to live there whether I want to or not. Now, do you want to know what I can tell you or not? No skin off my nose either way, you're the one who asked. Good, then shut up for a moment and let me speak. The Lady Sulpicia had to marry him. She's got a brother in exile and a father up to his neck in debt. Cerialis has money, lots of it, although no one is quite sure how he got it. He's also got the favour of the emperor – the new emperor – so might help with influence, and he's a kind man even if he's only marrying her for her name and her ancestry. He's a fool, if you ask me, and I speak as a professional, because that's a beautiful woman, so if I were him I wouldn't be wasting so much time with whores who don't really give a curse about him.'

'Brother in exile?'

'Thought you'd pick on that. Seems it's the second time. Was a young officer on the fringes when they caught Saturninus. Might even be one of your victims?' When the Legate Saturninus rebelled against the Emperor Domitian it had not lasted long before his plans fell apart and he was deserted. The investigations ordered by the vengeful ruler had gone on a long time, and Ferox had spent months examining charges. He had done his best to blot out the memories of those dark days, but some of the faces returned in his nightmares.

Ferox shook his head and hoped that he had had nothing to do with her brother. He did not remember anyone called Sulpicius, and most of the men he had been sent to find had ended up dead. He wanted to say that he had only found out the truth, but knew full well that even men he had shown to be innocent were still executed.

'Well, perhaps, perhaps not. He gets recalled by Nerva and a couple of months later is posted to Syria and gets caught up in a new conspiracy led by the provincial legate. Not the smartest boy, by the sound of it, but then the father doesn't sound much either. Reckon the lady must take after her mother.'

Ferox stood up and walked over to the little woman, putting a hand affectionately on her shoulder. It was the closest to intimacy they ever got, and a rare privilege, but he felt her shudder. Too many men had touched her too many times.

'You never cease to amaze me, Flora. I thought you said that you didn't know much.' He took his hand away and she relaxed. 'Sorry, but I haven't really got much family any more, and somehow you make me feel as if I have.'

She looked up at him, and perhaps it was the light, but he thought he saw a moistness in her eyes.

'Piss off!' she said and then sighed. 'Why do you always pull me back towards the sewer? If I didn't like you I'd pay someone to kick your teeth in. Not that I'd probably have to pay, if I asked in the right places. You're not good at making friends, are you?'

'Then all the more lucky that I have you as one.'

'You won't if you don't look after Procla! Any of your lads hurt her or not pay and it'll be your bollocks along with theirs that they'll be feeding to the pigs.'

A door opened and there was a burst of shrieking followed by a man's bellow. Two women were pushed into the room. One was pale with chestnut hair and the other dark-skinned and black-haired. Their hair was wild, and they wore fine slippers in whitened leather and nothing else. It was the twins, and they were rowing as they often did, so that a big broad-chested man, one of Flora's slaves, had to hold them apart. Ferox had seen neither woman for a long while, and certainly not like this.

'Quiet!' Flora screamed, the sound echoing in the room and probably audible upstairs even above the din. The two women froze and went silent. 'Are you still here?' she asked Ferox. 'Thought you came on business?'

Ferox did his best to look only at the mistress of the house and failed, his eyes flicking over towards the naked slaves. 'One last question. I saw Longinus as I came in. Do you know him?'

'I know everyone, don't I – at least by one thing.' She leaned her head so that she was peering at him. 'You'd better not be up to any mischief. Yes, I know him. He's a friend, and has been for years – much longer than you. We've been through a lot together, and sometimes we like to sit and talk about the old days and how glad we are that we're not living them any more.'

'Do you trust him?'

'With my life. Yours too, not that that counts for much! Now clear off and let me get on, you idle soldier – before you start enjoying yourself and shock us all.'

'Thank you.'

'Just go!'

XV

O N THE NONES of October Ferox returned to Vindolanda.
The weather was better than it had been for weeks, but
there was something in the air that hinted at the coming of
colder and shorter days. Leaves were turning brown and beginning
to fall, and for days the sentries on duty in the tower at Syracuse
had watched as swallows flocked and wheeled across the valley
in front of the burgus. They would leave soon, before the frost
began to bite and the trees were stripped bare.

All this was what happened each year, a sign that the world
moved on, whatever anyone felt about it. When Ferox rode out
he found people nervous and secretive, and the mood was even
darker than it had been at the end of summer. Fewer than usual
came to him with requests, and there was less theft and raiding
than in the past at this time of year. It might have been because
the Roman expedition had reminded everyone of the empire's
willingness to punish, but he doubted that. Vindex was even
more scornful.

'Don't think that scared anyone. They're frightened of what's
on its way, not what's happened already.'

Ferox did not blame them. There had not been much news of
the Stallion and his tattooed followers, although it was whispered
that many were going to join them, journeying from distant lands
to pledge their lives to the cause of flame and purging. It made
it hard not to look with suspicion at any travellers. Philo had
deciphered more of the curse they had found wrapped around the

effigy. Most of it was meaningless incantation, but there were lines that made sense, and he showed them to Crispinus and Cerialis when he met them at the fort.

'"Three times nine years and three, and the house of Jupiter will burn and with it all of Rome. The wolf cubs will bite each other unto death; all will die and all will burn. Fire will cleanse the world, and leave behind a better land for those worthy to inherit."'

'All cheerful stuff,' Crispinus said when he had read the boy's translation. 'If I remember rightly the Temple of Jupiter Optimus Maximus on the Capitol was struck by lightning and caught fire, back at the time of the Civil War, thirty years ago.'

'Yes, and there was trouble in Gaul then, with men claiming to be druids foretelling the destruction of the empire.' Ferox remembered studying in Gaul, and how no one openly spoke about druids, and yet all knew they were there and paid great heed to what they said. If there were runaway slaves from the empire at the heart of this movement, perhaps some came from the Gallic provinces. All that Philo said added to the picture of a mishmash of beliefs from all over the world, twisted into one message of hate and destruction.

'"Filled with the strength of the gods,"' Crispinus read aloud, '"no blade will pierce the pure and brave." Sounds a good trick. Presumably the ones we killed when they attacked the camp were not sufficiently pure. What does this mean? "When the dead walk among the living and the two worlds join for a night, and when new life begins, these are the times appointed. Blood of king, blood of queen, all shall burn as offerings to please the gods and feed the cleansing fire."'

'The souls of the dead walk the land at Samhain, as do creatures from the Otherworld,' Ferox said, and he believed it, for that was a strange night. Yet somehow to say such a thing here, in a room off the courtyard of the principia, made it seem unreal. 'It is the night before the Kalends of November. My guess is that new life beginning means Imbolc, the feast around the time lambing begins. It is a guess, and hard to tell when they have plucked ideas from all over the place. To me it seems to promise a sacrifice of important captives at one of the festivals, working a great magic that will give power and victory to this Stallion and his bands.'

'I still find it hard to believe that this nonsense will be taken seriously.' It was Aelius Brocchus who voiced the opinion, but Rufinus nodded in support and Ferox sensed that none of the Romans – perhaps not even Crispinus – suspected the real danger. Fortunately Claudius Super was sick, and unable to attend the consilium, which at least removed the most sceptical of them all.

'If you will forgive my frankness, my lords, whether or not we believe it is not the point. Enough people out there *will* believe – or feel afraid and so go along with it just in case it is true. If enough leaders decide to back them then that will give them armies big enough to pose a real problem. We have already heard that there is a high king among the Vacomagi who shelters and aids this Stallion and his allies, and has the support of the great druid. Other leaders might decide to do the same.'

They took him seriously, and at least that was something. All were only too aware that the garrison of the province was not big enough to fight a major war with confidence of victory.

'The centurion raises many important matters,' Crispinus said after a long pause. 'And one is most relevant to our purpose today. An ambassador has come from Tincommius, High King of the Venicones and Vacomagi, seeking the friendship of Rome. Anyone ever heard of the man before?' The question was general, but the tribune was looking at Ferox.

'No, sir. Never heard of the two tribes under one ruler either.'

'Then it may all be boasting, but either way the Legate Quadratus feels it prudent to send a delegation to meet the man. The purpose is to talk rather than fight, so they will take an escort of no more than thirty.'

Rufinus let out a low whistle, making the others turn. 'Sorry,' he said. 'But that is a long way from any rescue. If this high king isn't friendly, or anyone else goes for them – this Stallion or whatever he's called – then there won't be much hope. Has the legate chosen some poor devil to go?'

'I am going,' Crispinus said, his expression wooden.

'Oh, well, look...' Rufinus glanced around the room for aid, but then gave up. 'No, I cannot think of a way to make what I said sound any different, so might as well stand by it. It is a big risk. Haven't we just been talking about this mad priest wanting to sacrifice an important captive? You'll be there in plenty of time for the whathisname festival.'

'Samhain,' Ferox said, and already sensed an inevitability about the course of the meeting.

Crispinus turned to him with a smile.

'Your local knowledge will be invaluable as usual, Flavius Ferox.'

'Ah. Of course, sir.' Orders were orders, and there was also the oath binding him to the tribune's family.

Rufinus gave a mirthless laugh. 'Talked your way into that one, boy,' he said. At most he was a year or so older than Ferox, but he was an equestrian and so the air of superiority came easily.

'I shall take a decurion and twenty-four of your Batavians, prefect, if that is acceptable to you.' Cerialis nodded assent. 'Good. We will also want Vindex and four or five of his scouts. Our job is to talk, see if this man can be dealt with, and most of all to find out as much as we can about him and these priests. If all goes well we shall be back in time to celebrate this Samhain.'

'I shall lay on the best food we can find,' Cerialis said, 'although Batavians have their own festival that begins at dawn.'

'We shall look forward to it with keen interest, and experience of your table leaves me with no doubt that it will be a dinner to remember.'

'If you like eggs,' Rufinus said under his breath. 'Just hope friend Cerialis won't be eating it all on his own.'

They were all invited to dinner at the praetorium that evening, and with Claudia Severa visiting along with her husband, there was a determined effort to avoid serious talk. Sulpicia Lepidina wore a dark dress and Ferox hoped that this was not a bad omen for their journey. Yet the sight of her lifted his spirits, as did the ease with which she helped steer the conversation and involve him in it to a degree appropriate to his status without ever making him feel awkward. In the lamplight she seemed to glow, enriching them all merely by her presence, and he thought how strange it was that fully clothed she was far more arousing than the naked twins, for all their smooth beauty. He was disappointed that Cerialis did not ask his wife to play and sing for them. Instead, the prefect invited the men to bathe, apologising for the poor facilities.

'My predecessor did not consider a proper bath necessary, and there was a limit to what could be done in the house.' The timber praetorium did not lend itself to the underfloor and flue heating possible in a stone house, so the prefect had had a work party of his soldiers dig a circular pool reinforced with stone and lined with concrete, a deep shelf raised up from the floor so that bathers could sit and soak. A broad pipe brought heated water from a collection of big coppers hanging over open fires, and another pipe could be opened to let it drain. Ten people could cram into the pool, and with just five it was comfortable. Steam filled the air, but did not make the first shock of the hot water any less and Ferox let out a hiss and blew out. The others stared at him in amusement – the barbarian centurion reverting to type.

Once he was used to it, Ferox sat, arms outstretched on the lip of the pool, and let the warmth seep into him. He had last had a bath at Flora's, and he could see that this was very similar, apart from inoffensive paintings of dolphins and other sea creatures on the plastered walls and ceiling. There were three slaves, and Cerialis insisted that they wait to be oiled and scraped clear rather than doing it for themselves.

'There is a cold shower in the next room, for afterwards,' he told them, but Ferox did not plan to use it. He felt drowsy and content and had forgotten how refreshing so simple a thing could be.

Two nights later they were at Coria, and were given several hours when the big bath-house outside the fort's ramparts was set aside for their exclusive use.

'I'll be so glad when we finish building our one at Vindolanda,' Cerialis said as they went into the raging heat of the *caldarium*. There was plenty of building going at his garrison, but Ferox could tell that the greatest enthusiasm and effort was being lavished on the long stone bath-house outside the rampart and down the slope.

'It is less convenient having to take our turn,' Aelius Brocchus replied. 'I wish the pool in our house were as fine as yours.'

This was the full experience, throwing leather balls to each other and exercising in the high, echoing hall, before going from warm to raging hot, then to a plunge into the cold pool, and repeating the circuit several times. It was invigorating, although for Ferox could not compete with the ease and comfort of a long soak in decently hot water.

They set out along the Eastern Road an hour before dawn on the next day. There were twenty-four Batavian horsemen under the command of a decurion named Masclus, a quiet, steady man. Each rider had a heavy cloak and a blanket rolled up and tied behind his saddle, and a pair of sacks filled with barley grain slung over the horse's back. Two galearii rode mules and each led a string of four more with provisions and tents. Vindex had brought four of his best men, including the stolid and reliable Brennus, and the scouts watched the heavily laden troopers with curiosity and a hint of disdain.

'What do they want all that lot for?' the gaunt Brigantian asked Ferox. 'Thought we were just going to talk to the man?'

'An ambassador of Rome needs to look the part. And these Batavians are handy lads, so we'll be glad of them if it comes to a fight.'

'If it comes to a fight we're humped, and they won't make any difference.' They were speaking in the language of the tribes, waiting as the escort checked their harness and equipment. Cerialis and another forty horsemen watched. He was not coming any further and would return to Vindolanda later today.

'So we're going to talk to this Tincommius, which means that you're doing the talking. Why is the dandy coming along?' He smiled at Crispinus who gave an affable nod in return.

Ferox did not know the answer. *Regionarii* like him usually dealt with negotiations of this sort, even with the kings of major tribes, and it was odd for a young aristocrat to be sent. It seemed a needless risk, and he was not sure whether Crispinus had lobbied to go or been picked for the task. He would make a valuable hostage – perhaps a great sacrifice – and the thought that there might well be senior men trying to engineer disaster on the frontier made him afraid that they were walking into a trap.

'Reckon he fancied an adventure,' he said.

'Oh, good.' Vindex sniffed and wrinkled his long nose. 'You smell funny.'

'It's called being clean.'

A trumpet sounded, harsh and brazen in the still air. Masclus gave orders for his men to mount up.

'Bet they don't even crap unless they're told,' Vindex said.

Ferox ignored him and walked his horse over beside Crispinus. The decurion saluted the tribune and then went to his prefect and saluted again.

'Third day after the Nones of October. Report of the detachment of the Ninth Cohort of Batavians. All who should be are at their duty stations, as is the baggage. Masclus and his men are ready to depart, and ask permission from his king and lord to set out.'

'Permission granted.' Cerialis was wearing his high plumed helmet. 'Ride to good fortune and a successful return.'

'My lord!' Masclus saluted again and went back to the head of the little column. 'Prepare to march!' he bellowed. 'Forward at a walk.'

Crispinus nudged his mare to follow. Ferox stayed back with Vindex, ready to send his scouts ahead once they were properly clear of the fort and canabae. The civilian settlement at Coria, including a number of official buildings, spread far wider than at Vindolanda so that soon it would earn the more formal status of a *vicus*, but it was early and the few people up and about were not inclined to pay them much attention. On the edge of the village, he heard shouts and saw three small boys lobbing stones at the white-haired beggar as he walked down a lane on to the road. Their aim was not good, but the sight annoyed Vindex.

'Piss off, you little buggers!' he shouted, and his savage face was enough to send them scampering back around a corner. The boldest peeked back to look at him, but fled again when the Brigantian snarled.

'Alms for a blessing.' The man seemed even more hunched than usual, staring down at the road as he held out his hand. His dog growled at them.

'Here you are, Father,' Vindex said, throwing down a couple of coins. 'We won't need it where we are going,' he explained. 'And I reckon we need all the blessings we can get.'

'Strange how he seems to follow us around,' Ferox said. 'Or it would be if you didn't keep paying him! Wonder why he's here?'

Vindex frowned. 'Everyone's got to be somewhere. Just wish we weren't going where we are going.'

'A man cannot avoid his destiny. We go where we are meant to go.'

'You saying all this is our fault?' Vindex gave his leering grin.

'Not mine – I reckon it's all your fault. Usually is.'

Crispinus turned and stared at them when he heard the roar of laughter.

They went north along the road, making good progress on a day of clear sunshine. A thought nagged at Ferox as he rode, just in the back of his mind and too vague to pin down. Someone had just done or said something strange when they set out, but he had not really been paying attention and could not remember what. When the horses had warmed up they trotted for some time, but even the jogging motion failed to help his thoughts. After an hour they dismounted and marched. They halted twice to rest and water the animals, and to eat a meal of biscuit and salted bacon. Masclus was a quiet man who never seemed to need to shout, and although no more than twenty-five had the authority of a much older officer. Ferox felt that the decurion was a good choice to command the escort.

Even Vindex expressed grudging approval. He and his men spent most of the day riding ahead and behind the column. Not that there should be any danger yet, but Masclus had suggested without prompting that it was wise to get into good habits from the start. When Vindex came back to report that the road was clear and that they would reach Bremenium before sunset, the decurion beckoned to one of the slaves who had food to give to the scout and more bundles of biscuit and meat waiting for his men when they returned.

They reached the fort at Bremenium as the sun began to set and the western skies were ablaze with colour. Vindex and his men had closed with the column, and he reported to the three officers. Progress had been good, the day a pleasant one, and if they were tired all were united in a determination not to show it to the garrison of this base.

'Good lad, that one,' Vindex said as they watched Masclus and Crispinus ride forward to report to the commander of the guard at the towering porta praetoria. 'Even if he is a bit oily.'

'You like anyone who feeds you. Why oily?'

'Well, smarmy then. Bit of a crawler. Remember how he called the prefect his king?'

'*Omnes ad stercus!*' Ferox spat the words with such violence that his horse shied. The troopers looked at him in surprise. That was it – that was what he had been trying to remember. Dark fear grew within him as he remembered the big German warrior demanding that he hand over the 'queen'. He had a vague memory of something he had heard about the Batavians, but he needed to find a way to raise the subject with delicacy and wondered how to do it.

'So is Prefect Cerialis your king or what?' Vindex asked the decurion as they rode up the main street of the camp. Ferox sighed.

'He could be,' Masclus replied without any hint of awkwardness. 'The prefect is from the royal house of our people. We are soldiers

217

of the Ninth Cohort, sworn to Rome and to our emperor and we will die to keep that oath. He commands us because he is the prefect, but he also has our loyalty because we are Batavi and he is our lord. Do you not also have a king?'

'Aye, several of 'em.'

'And you obey them as well as serving the emperor.'

'It's my chief who sends me, and he does that because his king tells him.'

It was not until late in the evening that Ferox had a chance to talk to Crispinus privately. '"Blood of king, blood of queen,"' he said. 'I have been blind. Cerialis is the king they want and the Lady Sulpicia his queen. It's their blood they want to make the priest's miracle.' He went through all that he had learned about the ambush, once again telling the tribune about the attack and how the raiders had ignored better targets and only seemed to want the lady.

Crispinus was unsure. 'He's not really a king. Just an aristocrat of one tribe.'

'You are thinking like a Roman, and not like an ambitious priest wanting to proclaim a great magic through the shedding of special blood. How many kings of any sort can be found among the Romans in this part of the world? No emperor has come to Britannia since Claudius.'

The tribune made up his mind. 'I'll write a letter and send one of the troopers back to Vindolanda. We cannot do much, but at least we can remind Flavius Cerialis to take every precaution for his own and his wife's safety. Doubt they can do more than they are already doing, but it will do no harm.'

'The greatest danger will come as Samhain approaches.'

'Hopefully we shall be back by then.' Crispinus patted him on the shoulder. 'Good work. It would never have occurred to me. The more we understand these murderous bastards the more chance we have of stopping them. Get some rest. It's another long ride tomorrow. And don't worry. I'll send the letter.'

XVI

TRIMONTIUM TOOK ITS name from the three peaks on the ridgeline above the fort. It was twice the size of Vindolanda and these days the northernmost garrison in all Britannia. Lying in the circle of the river, the brown waters high from last month's rain, it looked like a town, the neat rows of buildings rendered and whitewashed, roofs either red tile or dark shingle. Apart from the rectangular fort with its curved corners, other ramparts extended out on three sides to enclose the canabae, with numbers of thatched round houses dotted among the Roman-style buildings. There was a village within bowshot of the ditch, several more out on the plains to the west, and an earth-walled hill fort up on the high ground. This was the very edge of the empire, and the end of the Eastern Road, but on the whole the Romans and the allied Votadini tribe got on well with each other.

It was a long ride from Bremenium on a drab day with a sea of brooding grey clouds overhead, but Crispinus was determined to make the trip in one stage and not to stop at the smaller fort that lay in between the two. All twenty-four Batavian troopers rode with them, and the tribune explained to Ferox that he had sent his letter to Cerialis with the regular courier who had left in the early hours.

'He's well mounted, will get a fresh horse every time he stops at a garrison, and will do the trip much faster. Besides, we may need every man we can get.'

'Sir.'

The tribune scented scepticism. 'Hercules' balls, you really should trust, man!' There was anger in his voice.

'Of course, my lord,' Ferox said and remembered something his grandfather was fond of saying. 'A man who keeps asking you to trust him is always hiding something.'

As they approached Trimontium the setting sun appeared beneath the clouds and shone a reddish light across the fort, casting long shadows, and they were all cheered by the sight.

'Wonder if a man can get a drink there,' Vindex said, for once willing to set aside his dislike of crowded places.

Accommodation in the barracks and stabling for the horses and mules was waiting for them, all supervised by a cheerful tribune from Legio XX Valeria Victrix, who was in overall command of the mixed garrison of legionaries and auxiliaries at the base. His name was Attius Secundus and he entertained Crispinus and Ferox to a lavish meal before he and some slaves led them to a private bath-house.

'The lads have a bigger one on the far side of the fort,' he told them, 'but someone had the nice idea of building this one for the senior staff and for any officials who pass through. We'll probably meet a couple of them.'

It lay in one of the enclosed areas of civilian occupation, and was itself isolated from the rest by its own rampart on which sentries stood watch. 'Nice to have a bit of privacy,' Secundus said happily as he gave a casual wave to a saluting legionary. 'Evening, Longus.'

A paved path took them to the main entrance of a long stone building, the walls left bare rather than rendered, perhaps to show off the fact that they were stone rather than wattle and daub. They found three occupants being massaged by slaves after completing their bath. One was the plump imperial freedman Vegetus, along with a colleague, a little taller and even fatter, who also worked for the procurator of the province and supervised the collection of taxes and the private contractors hired by the state. With them was a *negotiator*, a businessman who undertook some contracts to supply clothing and mounts to the army, as well as carrying out plenty of trade on his own account. He was a Treviran with the accent of the Rhineland, but had been in this part of the world for years, spending a lot of time in the far north. Ferox thought that there was something familiar about the man, but could not remember where they had met. There was something about his thin hands, the long fingers engrained with dirt even after washing that sparked a memory.

'Similis is a splendid fellow,' Vegetus assured them, patting the merchant with one plump paw. 'Must be ten years since we first met and I do not regret a day of it.' The freedman's wife was not with him on this trip. 'It's a bit bleak up here, and she has picked up a cold. The Lady Sulpicia Lepidina' – the man glowed with pride as he mentioned so eminent an acquaintance – 'graciously offered an invitation for my dear wife to stay in her house until I return.'

No doubt Cerialis was all in favour of such generosity.

Ferox asked Similis whether he knew anything about Tincommius, and could sense the man balancing whether he would gain or lose from answering the question, and giving up each snippet of information as if it caused him physical pain. Yes, he had met the new high king, but could not claim to know him well. His rise was recent, a mixture of brute force and considerable effort in winning friends and allies. 'He's got three wives, has daughters married off to other chieftains in his tribe and further afield, and sons out to fosterage. He also welcomes exiles and their followers, so that he has more warriors at his beck and call than any chief anyone can remember.'

'What about priests?' Crispinus cut in. Ferox saw the man's eyes close as if curtains were shut across a window and wished that the aristocrat had left the matter to him.

'Wouldn't know about that. I've only been to his dun once, to buy hounds and some bears to sell to the circuses down south. Only really dealt with one of his men. He was tough but fair and we both did well out of it.'

'It's just that we have heard stories of druids,' the tribune insisted.

'There're always stories, but in my line you don't pry,' the merchant said.

'Pity. It would have been most useful for us to learn more.' The young aristocrat had just been shaved by a slave and was rubbing his smooth chin with considerable pleasure. 'Well-informed men can be so helpful, which of course obliges us to be helpful in return.'

'Sorry, my lord, I cannot tell what I do not know.'

Liar, thought Ferox, and suspected that the man judged friendship with the two financial officials more valuable in the long run than the fleeting gains to come from helping a young officer who would only be in the province for a year or so. Presumably the procurator's men would prefer to keep his friendship something only they enjoyed.

'I truly am sorry, my lord. If there is any other way that I can help, you have only to ask, for the gratitude of so great a man as yourself is a prize above all others. Perhaps there is something you cannot get here in the wilds. There are few things I cannot obtain in time, and would happily give them as a gift.'

'What did they want in trade?' Ferox asked softly.

A brief chink of light showed from behind the curtain before it was tied closed again.

'Tincommius, I mean,' the centurion went on. 'I doubt you paid him in coin.'

'Oh, this and that, you know – the usual trinkets, some silver vessels and plenty of wine. The Britons like their wine, although quantity matters more than the quality. They are just barbarians.'

'Flavius Ferox is a Briton from the south,' Crispinus said with smooth and courteous malice.

'I meant no offence,' the Treviran replied. Ferox could sense the man's relief at the change of subject, and was sure that he had been up to no good, selling something that he ought not to the ambitious tribal leader. Weapons perhaps, or the iron to forge blades – or just information.

'Slippery fellow, that,' Secundus said when the trader and the two officials left some time later. 'Cannot say I really trust the others either.'

'Taking more than is due in tax?' Crispinus asked.

'Well, obviously that. I mean, they all do, don't they? Just afraid they're taking more than most and enough to drive the poor devils paying it into penury. No sense in making the locals more desperate than they already are, is there?' Attius Secundus could tell them little more about the tribes to the north and the high king. 'Patrols don't go so far these days, not without good reason,' he explained. 'We don't have enough men, so keep our distance unless someone asks for our help. If you ask me that's half the reason why the other tribes and clans are turning to this Tincommius. Heard rumours about your druids more than once, but nothing definite. We certainly have not seen any of these bloodthirsty tattooed fiends you were telling me about. No, I'm afraid that it's you who will have to tell me what is going on and not the other way around.'

A guide was waiting for them at Trimontium, as had been arranged. 'Looks a rogue to me, but I can't offer anyone better,' Secundus said as he bade them farewell. 'Good luck. Hope to see you back before the end of the month – and of course to avoid the inconvenience of having to avenge your horrible deaths!' He grinned happily.

They left an hour before dawn, without trumpets or ceremony. 'Be on your guard, lads,' Masclus said to his men as they left the fort behind them.

Their guide was a thin man with leathery skin who looked ancient in years, but still appeared to be vigorous and untiring. He was simply dressed, in shoes, long-sleeved tunic, trousers and a heavy cloak fastened with a simple brooch. He rode a shaggy little pony, his legs trailing down and brushing the long grass, for he did not ride on the fading remains of the Roman road, but kept to the far side of the ditch beside it. The man gave them no name, and spoke only when he could not avoid it, but Vindex knew who he was.

'I've heard of him, and I think we are honoured. He is known as the Traveller, and that is what he does. They say he came from one of the islands in the far north-west – Thule or even further away – and that he never stays in one place very long, before he gets up and walks or rides away. Knows all the paths, even the ones you cannot see, and all the places, knows the spirits and the gods of every valley and lake. I've even heard tell that he sails the seas to lands far away, following the whales and the great demons of the deep.' Vindex touched the wheel of Taranis to his lips. 'Who knows, but what I do know is that the chiefs use him to take messages to each other. They cannot force him – no one can – and he will only agree if he wishes to do it and thinks it is important. As I said, we're honoured.'

The Traveller carried a staff that had leaves and berries tied to its top.

'That is the mark of an envoy,' Ferox told the tribune.

'Is not mistletoe a mark of the druids?'

'It can be. It can also just be mistletoe.'

The road north had been built by the army twenty years ago and was meant as a temporary route, but no one had got around to laying it down properly before the bases it reached were abandoned. Since then many stones had been pulled up by the locals wanting material for cattle pens or house walls, and weeds and grass had sprung up in the gaps between the ones the thieves had left. Much of the time they followed their guide and rode beside the track rather than on it, but the line of the old road was easy to follow.

'Not sure we really need him yet,' Crispinus remarked. 'Guess it will be different further on, but he could have waited for us there.'

'We need him for the things we cannot see,' Ferox said. 'And if you will forgive me, I would like to ride out to see how Vindex and his scouts are doing.' He galloped off before the tribune could reply. From the very start of the journey Crispinus had resumed his questioning and discussion, and the centurion once again found the endless chatter oppressive.

Some things he did not mind explaining. 'Whenever we pass a village or any big cluster of houses – let alone a walled place – we must swing round to the left,' he had told the tribune on the first day.

Crispinus waited for more and finally forced the issue. 'Why?'

'Because it means that they will be on our right.' Ferox said, his tone suggesting that it was obvious, and there was another long pause before he realised that he still needed to explain. 'Our shields are on our left side, so the right is unprotected. It shows them that we come in peace and so willingly offer our exposed sides to them. Enemies would not take such a chance.'

'Unless it was a trick,' Crispinus mused. 'But these people are Votadini, so allies of ours.'

'Then no harm in reminding them of that, my lord. The Selgovae are allies and we attacked them just a few weeks ago.'

Each night they made camp, but they were too few to entrench the position even if the cavalrymen had been willing. There were three big tents made of panels of calfskin stitched together for the Batavians and the army slaves, and a slightly smaller one shared by the three officers. The horses and mules were tethered in lines, beside the stacked shields and spears of the soldiers. Five of the troopers were always on guard, with one standing fifteen paces out on each side of the camp and the other man watching the horses.

'We are under the king's protection,' Crispinus said. 'Surely no one will risk his anger by molesting us?'

Ferox was insistent. 'There are outlaws in every land, men who do not care much for the word of kings, chiefs or even emperors. And there are quite enough folk who might be tempted if the risks looked slight. Best not to tempt them in the first place,' he said and was backed up by Masclus. The tribune deferred to their experience, but Ferox still worried. A really skilled thief might take animals from under the sentry's nose. He arranged with Vindex that one of the scouts would patrol the darkness each night and took a turn himself to spread the load.

Yet if there were such men in the neighbourhood, they held their hand. The camp went undisturbed each night, save for the persistent calling of a wildcat. On the second morning they woke to frost on the leather tents and grass that was white and crunched underfoot. It vanished quickly once the sun rose, with only a few patches left where valley sides kept the land in shadow.

The following night they pitched tents beside a brook, overlooked by a cluster of round houses perched on a hillock. The headman invited the officers to share his meal. Masclus remained with his troopers, and the tribune and centurion took a couple of Batavians with them. Crispinus squatted uncomfortably by the fire, blinking and coughing in the smoky atmosphere inside, for like most local houses it had no chimney and let the smoke seep into the thatch. Yet Ferox was surprised and pleased with the way the young aristocrat conducted himself, drinking and eating all that was offered, and treating his host with the greatest respect.

'Good manners are important,' was all that he said afterwards, although that may have been because he was feeling a little the worse for wear after downing several wooden cups of beer. The Batavians had sucked the liquid down like sponges and after initial suspicion had greatly enjoyed being chosen.

The next day the tribune had a green pallor and Ferox was spared questions for the first few hours. The respite was temporary. 'Why do the houses have doors facing south-east?' 'Why no chimneys?' 'Were those people from a certain clan and how can you tell?' On and on, until the centurion set off to visit the scouts. Crispinus was only prevented from going with him when Masclus insisted that as commander of the escort it was his job to ensure the tribune's safety and that would not be easy if he started gadding about away from the column.

Two more cold nights were followed by bright days with only gentle winds and the tribune talked about how everyone exaggerated the savagery of northern climes. They passed the great trading post of the Votadini, a walled stronghold and market on a great hill that rose above miles and miles of gently rolling pastures. Ferox had been there a couple of times and often seen the place from afar. It always reminded him of a painting he had once seen of the pyramids in Egypt. They did not go close, for it was out of their way, but he could see that even Crispinus was impressed.

'Never expected to see so many people up here,' he said, shaking his head. 'There are farms everywhere, villages, well-tilled fields and fat cattle and sheep.'

'What were you expecting, my lord?'

'More of a wilderness – marsh and dark woods.'

'Well, there's some of that, to be sure, but hopefully we won't need to go through it.'

They kept going, until the crest of a rise gave them a view of the estuary of the great river opening out into the sea. The water sparkled in the morning sun, white-capped in places for the wind was blowing strong and bitter cold from the east.

'"Thalassa! Thalassa!"' Crispinus proclaimed at the sight. Ferox felt his heart lift, but he was thinking of his own homeland more than Xenophon and his Ten Thousand mercenaries glimpsing the sea that led them home to Greece. The water up here was a clear blue like glass, not like the muddy brown of the channel near his homeland, and yet its moods were the same. He caught the faint hint of salt on the air and it made him yearn for the simplicity of his childhood when no oaths bound him tight. Here he was, several days' ride beyond the furthest outpost of the empire, and he still felt confined. More than once in the last days the tribune had asked him why he stayed in his out-of-the-way post.

'No one else wants me,' he said the first few times, but Crispinus persisted.

'There is always a need for able men.'

'I like it at Syracuse,' Ferox confessed at last. 'No one breathes down my neck – at least until now. I'm on the edge of the empire, almost the edge of the world, if you like. I can see where it ends.'

That appeared to satisfy the tribune's curiosity. Ferox was not sure whether or not it was the truth. After so many years serving

Rome and the emperors, he could not really imagine any other life. Like it or not, it seemed to be his fate.

They had to go west for some distance before they were able to cross the river, ferried across four at a time, men and horses together on a raft. No payment was demanded and the sight of their guide seemed enough to make the locals help them.

Within hours of crossing the water the skies darkened and the rain started to fall. It rained all night, defying their best efforts to light a fire, and kept raining throughout the next day. It was warmer, but the wet seeped into their clothes and their souls and they did not feel any benefit. The next night they were glad of the hospitality of the chieftain whose people lived in a small walled enclosure beside a mere. There was a hot meal of stew and plenty of beer, so that they went to their tents content. The chieftain belonged to the Venicones, and told them that he had known to expect them today.

Crispinus was pleased with this proof of power and goodwill on the part of the high king. They made quick progress the next day in spite of driving wind and heavy showers of rain. The route followed the line of another road built by the army. Outlines of old ditches and ramparts showed in the grass, little squares like Syracuse and more circles or smaller rectangles that would each have protected a watchtower. It was not until they went past a bigger rectangular enclosure than Crispinus recognised what they were.

'This was a garrison? It looks almost as old as the land itself.'

'Ten years, maybe twelve since it was abandoned,' Ferox said. 'The army likes to be thorough so they knock down the buildings, rip up the posts, pile the wattles and burn them.' He pointed to patches in the grass that were a different shade to the rest from the heat of the fires. 'There'll be thousands and thousands of nails buried in pits around here, and plenty of other stuff that was useless or too heavy to be worth carting away.'

'Why don't the locals dig it up? The iron would be useful if nothing else.'

'They probably do if they know where to look.'

They were heading north-east, and whenever the rain stopped and the cloud lifted a little they could see the line of mountains to their left. On the next day they followed a ridge, passing a succession of old outposts.

'Amazing how fast the grass covers everything,' Crispinus said.

Ferox shrugged. 'Ten years is a long time.'

Some farmers used the old ramparts as cattle pens. People were wary of them, but not unfriendly. When they stopped in the day to rest their horses, men would come and stare at them. The children were less bashful, and wandered into the little camp. They kept away from Vindex, at least until he began doling out pieces of biscuit, and seemed most fascinated by Crispinus, trying to touch him as he passed.

Ferox listened to their chatter and could not help chuckling. 'They think you're the Emperor of Rome and that it's good luck to touch you because gold flows in your veins instead of blood.'

'I've been trying to persuade women of that truth for years,' the tribune joked, but seemed pleased with the attention.

The rain stopped the next day, but it was grey and cold, so that their breath steamed and at the end of each ride Ferox found his feet numb and painful when he dismounted. They kept passing abandoned outposts of Rome and finally came to a vast enclosure bigger than anything they had seen before.

'The Twentieth Legion built this, although they never quite finished it,' Ferox said. He could see the tribune gazing in astonishment at the vast remains of the base. 'Now do you understand?'

'I think so,' the young aristocrat said, and for once he lacked his usual confidence and poise. 'We were once strong for all to see and then we left. Why should they fear us now? Why should they deal with us?'

'We – that is you – need to tell them why,' the centurion said, gripping the tribune by the arm.

XVII

TINCOMMIUS DWELLED AT present within the ramparts of an old army base about the size of Vindolanda, and from a distance it did not look so different. Instead of the half-filled ditch and grassy rampart, men had toiled to rebuild the defences. There were timber towers over new gates, more towers at the corners, and a wooden parapet protecting the walkway. Sentries paced the walls or watched from the towers, and if few had helmets, even fewer armour, and their clothes and shields were of every colour, they still appeared vigilant.

Horns blew as the little column approached, and the gates swung open. That was one difference, because during the day camp gates were wide open unless there was an immediate threat of enemy attack. When they went under the tower into the fort the impression of an army base vanished altogether. There were no streets, no ordered rows of barracks and granaries, and instead dozens of round houses with conical thatched roofs stood in no sort of pattern, some clustered tightly together and others scattered. There were wide-open spaces, even a few young trees, and animals and people wandering around. As they came inside Crispinus wrinkled his nose at the sight and smell of a couple of men squatting down and relieving themselves out in the open. Roman cities and big bases stank, but this was different, and had the feel of a great farm.

The high king lived in one of two great houses in the far corner of the old fort. The buildings were fenced off from the rest and guarded by tall warriors in mail coats and bronze helmets, carrying long oval shields painted half red and half black and spear shafts well oiled so that they shone. Each one had a sword on his right hip, almost all of them army issue. Large dogs were chained to posts near the entrance, and loud barking came from a pen behind the house.

Crispinus, Ferox and a single Batavian carrying a wooden chest were ushered towards the higher of the two houses. Their guide had vanished, and instead they were led by a little man with a crooked leg, who leaned on a staff. He wore a thin circlet of gold around his neck, and had on a white tunic trimmed with green and trousers checked in blue, grey and green. The top of his head was bald, the skin mottled and creased, and the fringe of hair around it was rough and thick like horsehair and stuck up at odd angles. The pupil of one eye was a lifeless off-white, and the other peered at them as if struggling to focus. Two warriors stood beside him, not as tall as the other guards but as splendidly equipped. One had raven-black hair and a smooth-shaven face and the other was red-haired and had a long moustache.

'This is the hall of Tincommius, High King of the Vacomagi and Venicones, Overlord of the Caledonians.' The small man had a surprisingly deep voice and even more surprisingly spoke near perfect Latin. 'He is the Red Branch and the Tall Tree, the Great Bull of Camulos, the Mountain that stands alone in the storm, the Bloody Sword and the Unpierced Shield, the Black Cloak.'

One of the guard dogs was looking at Ferox and snarling. He had never cared much for dogs, except as a meal for the desperate. Somehow the creatures always seemed to know how he felt and to return his dislike.

'He is the Lord of the valleys and mountains,' the little man continued just when they thought that he had finished. 'The Horn sounding on the hilltop, the Blade that flashes in the dawn, the Spear that flies true and strong, the Sky that covers the lands and brings rain, the Ram that brings plenty, and the Wise Judge of deep matters.'

Crispinus let out a long breath once he realised that the list was done. The little man limped over to the porch of the house. The door was low, so that even he was forced to duck as he went in. Ferox had almost to bend double, as did the trooper and the two warriors who followed.

It was brighter inside than he had expected, for a fire raged in a long trench in the middle of a wide floor and torches burned, mounted on iron holders or attached to the circle of posts near the edge of the great hall. Crispinus gasped in surprise at the sheer size of the place, the high ceiling dark with shadows and smoke, and the almost empty circle of floor around the fire. There was a single chair, high-backed and richly carved, and on it sat a boy of eight or nine, his hair the colour of pale gold tinged with red by the firelight.

The deep voice began again. 'Welcome to the Hall of Tincommius, High King of the Vacomagi and Venicones, Overlord of the Caledonians, the Red Branch and the Tall Tree, the Great Bull of Camulos, the Mountain that stands alone in the storm, the Bloody Sword and the Unpierced Shield—'

'I think that is enough for now.' The clean-shaven warrior stepped in front of them, and he also spoke in Latin, though with a lilting accent than made ordinary speech almost like verse. He had given his spear and shield to the other man, and now took off his helmet and ran a hand through his well-oiled black hair. 'I am Tincommius, and I cannot remember all the rest of that stuff, nor do I care to listen to it all again. The gods alone know how he does. That's if he really does. Often I wonder whether he makes half of it up. Haven't a clue where some of those titles come from. Do I look like a ram to you?'

He did not wait for an answer. Without his helmet he was not much taller than Crispinus. His face was young, but there were faint creases around his eyes and they had the hardness born from experience that usually came with age or suffering. 'Welcome, Tribune Marcus Atilius Crispinus, son of Marcus, former consul of Rome. Welcome Flavius Ferox, centurion, descended from the Lord of the Hills and prince of his people.' A woman appeared

232

beside him, carrying a wooden platter with a round loaf and a cup of red Samian ware. She was taller than the man, paler skinned, but with long hair almost as black as his, though it reached down to her waist. Her dress was of bleached white linen that clung to her full figure and was gathered at the waist by a belt of silver rings.

'Come, eat from my table.' The king broke off a piece of bread and passed it to Crispinus, and then did the same for Ferox. He raised the cup to his own lips, sipped and then passed it to each in turn, this time including the Batavian who had stood woodenly to attention throughout all this. 'You are guests of the king and under his protection.'

The tribune gestured to the soldier, who opened the chest to show the silver platters and cup held within it. He bent down to lay it on the ground and then stepped back, resuming his stiff, parade-ground posture.

'Thank you. I bring greetings and this token of friendship from the Legate—' Crispinus began, but was cut short.

'We shall talk together later, and discuss high matters tomorrow. First, you must be tired. They will show you to your bowers. Rest, eat and refresh yourselves. Tonight we shall feast, and tomorrow we shall talk. You must forgive me my little subterfuge – is that the right word? It is? Good. I try to do everything as well as I can and it is better to be corrected than to continue in ignorance, don't you think? Farewell. We shall speak again.'

The high king tossed the cup away and put his arm around the waist of the woman. He pulled her towards him, making her drop the platter, and reached up to kiss her. She responded with enthusiasm. Ferox nudged the tribune with his foot and they left, ducking to get out of the low door. Men waited to escort them, but a few paces away another three men knelt on the ground, hands tied behind their backs. A big warrior with a long sword paced up and down in front of them. It took a moment for Ferox's eyes to adjust back to full daylight before he recognised the man he had fought on the day of the ambush. If anything he looked even bigger.

The sword swung, the first head rolled and a fountain of blood only just missed the warrior's legs.

'Who are they?' Crispinus asked.

Their escorts did not seem to speak Latin, so Ferox spoke to them in their own tongue.

'Thieves who stole from the high king,' he told the tribune. 'And I dare say this is a demonstration for our benefit – like everything else.' The blade fell for a second time, another head dropped and the dead man slumped forward. Tincommius was parading his involvement with the ambush of Sulpicia Lepidina, no doubt to remind them that he could be a dangerous enemy, so that it was better for the Romans to persuade the king to become their friend.

'Better to be corrected than to continue in ignorance,' Crispinus said. 'What message is he trying to send? That he is a barbarian of great power and ruthlessness?'

'That he's strong and clever, more like. He wants us off balance.'

'Sounds like a strategem. Uncle Frontinus is obsessed with them. He's even writing a book about them. But all the ones he goes on about had a purpose. What do you think that is?'

'Isn't that the answer we have come to find?'

They were taken to an area of the fort away from other buildings. There was a corral for the horses, and the animals were already being fed and groomed. One large hut was provided for the troopers, scouts and slaves, and two smaller ones for the officers. Ferox was happy to share with Masclus and let the tribune rest on his own – at least he would be spared the constant talk. There were servants waiting in each house, and he heard the decurion swearing that he would castrate any man who mistreated them. 'We're a long way from home, boys, and if you want to see home you won't do anything daft.'

With a lot of units Ferox would have worried that some of the men would see the chance to desert, now that they were so far from the nearest garrison, but he doubted that there was much risk with these Batavians, who were a clannish bunch and stuck close to their comrades.

234

It was dark by the time they were summoned, and men came with torches to lead them to the great feast. Masclus was included in the invitation, but they had decided that a tactful fatigue and illness was prudent in his case, so the three of them, Crispinus, Ferox and Vindex, went on their own. The tribune had abandoned uniform and was resplendent in white tunic and toga, a garment Ferox had never truly mastered, for he tended to wave his arms around when he talked and that spelt ruin to its drape.

The tribune walked with elegance, but seemed perplexed.

'Do you feel well?' Ferox asked.

'Yes, yes. Indeed I suppose I ought to say better than well. Did, um, I mean to say, were you also…?' The young aristocrat trailed off. 'I am not quite sure how to put this, but did women come to you while you were waiting?'

'No,' the centurion said. Vindex was sniggering. 'But you are our leader and the guest of honour and hospitality in these parts demands certain courtesies.'

'She just came in,' he said in a tone of disbelief. 'Smiled as if I was an old friend and undid the brooches on her shoulders so that her dress fell to the ground. Pretty thing, and without the falseness of your usual whore, but very direct. Walks over and starts…' Again he seemed lost for words.

'It is courtesy. And she will not be some tart, but one of the King's household. A wife perhaps, or a daughter.'

'His daughter?' The aristocrat was shocked at the thought. 'You cannot mean that. Who would send his own daughter to…'

'Hump a stranger in welcome,' Vindex suggested. 'Begging your pardon, my lord, but you're a lucky sod.'

They walked on in silence, and were soon near the hall.

'Wish I'd known,' Crispinus said wistfully. 'I might have enjoyed it all the more.'

They entered to a great roar of noise, and Ferox was glad that he had gone in first because the shout of greeting made the tribune flinch in surprise. He hoped that no one noticed this as he raised his arms and bellowed in reply.

There were low tables forming a circle with the fireplace in the middle. There was one gap in the circle to allow the servants to come and go, and opposite it Tincommius sat on the carved chair. Men stood beside the table, arms lifted high in welcome. All were splendidly dressed in brightly coloured clothes, and most wore gold or silver torcs and bracelets and had jewelled brooches pinning their cloaks into place. Ferox guessed that they were chiefs and kings for behind them stood more plainly garbed warriors, resting long shields on the ground. These were men sworn to the high king, or ones he wished to win over, and it could not be coincidence that they gathered for this feast. Tincommius was showing his influence.

There were two gaps, and the bald-headed steward led them to the wider of the two. Crispinus took his place between them, with Ferox on his right and Vindex on his left. The big warrior who had beheaded the thieves glared at the centurion before moving to make room.

'You should have attendants,' the German rumbled in his guttural, thick-accented voice.

'We have no need,' Ferox replied and hoped that he was right. Batavians were fine soldiers, but apt to be aggressive, especially if drink was freely available, and he did not regret leaving them behind.

The big warrior boomed out something the centurion did not understand, and the dark-haired woman appeared, her white dress almost luminous in its brightness. She whispered to the high king who gave swift orders to three of the warriors standing in the shadows behind his chair. The men wore mail that glistened a dull red and had rich fur cloaks that must have been almost insufferably hot in this hall with its blazing fires. In silence they walked to stand behind the three Roman envoys, and in silence they stood there, faces wooden.

Crispinus glanced back and up at them, for they were all taller than him by a good six inches. 'Are they here to guard us?' he whispered. 'Or worse?'

236

'They're here to carry us home when we can no longer walk,' Vindex replied before Ferox had a chance.

The tribune laughed and then saw that he was serious. He looked at Ferox who nodded in confirmation.

'Better,' the German rumbled.

They waited for a short while, until the high king looked at the last remaining empty space at his table, his calm expression unchanged, and then beckoned with his arms for his guests to sit. Ferox and Vindex readily sat down cross-legged like the others. The tribune took a little longer, the act awkward for a man in a toga. As he spread his legs his tunic bunched up over his thighs.

'Glad that table is in front otherwise this might not look too elegant for an envoy of Rome,' he whispered.

Sitting next to Vindex was a lanky warrior who must have been fifty if he was a day, his long white hair hanging down on to his shoulders and his moustache bristly. From his speech he sounded a local man, and was affable enough, although he talked mainly to his neighbour on the other side. Most of the men wore tunics and trousers, the wool in a wide range of intricate tartan patterns. There were also several bare-legged wearing long tunics, a habit most common among the Hibernians, and Ferox wondered whether they had come from that island to the west.

They began with wine, Gallic by the taste of it, poured out unmixed and strong into cups placed in front of them.

Vindex glanced at Ferox, and Crispinus' face was concerned. 'Will you manage?' he asked.

'We shall see.' Ferox nodded towards the far side of the ring of tables, not far from the king's seat. 'More surprised to see that one.' Venutius, face still mottled with bruises, saw that they were looking at him and raised his cup affably. Behind him stood the young warrior Ferox had beaten and allowed to go.

'He's not hiding anything from us, is he?' Crispinus whispered. 'He's letting us see his power and connections that include some of our allies.'

'Don't assume it's everything.' Ferox doubted that the people close enough to hear could understand Latin, but could not be sure and wished the tribune would not chatter. He sensed Crispinus' nervousness and knew it must be difficult for him sitting there, unable to speak the language and follow what was happening. He remembered the first Roman dinner he had attended and how alien it all seemed. 'We are seeing only what he is letting us see,' he added after a moment.

The food started to arrive, beginning with a thick stew of beef and vegetable. Beer came with it, and more wine, and, after a dip in the noise as men ate with great enthusiasm, the hubbub of conversation grew louder. The big warrior next to Ferox spooned up his stew as if he had not seen food for a month, spilling the liquid as he shovelled it into his mouth. He called for a second bowl when a serving girl passed, and dealt with that as speedily. His moustache and beard dripped so he wiped his sleeve across them. 'Good,' he grunted to Ferox, but did not seem a man given to much talk.

Roasted venison came next, a generous cut for each of the guests. Ferox noticed that the high king ate little and spent most of his time watching and listening. Occasionally he laughed loudly at something someone said. Crispinus struggled manfully with the unfamiliar feast.

'Wish I'd brought a fork to hold it steady while I cut.' Ferox had told the tribune to bring a knife and spoon to help him eat.

'Use your hand.'

Crispinus grimaced, but followed the advice. The big German simply tore the meat apart with his fingers, licking off the gravy once he had finished.

A bard stepped into the circle around the fire and began to sing unaccompanied. He was thin-faced and young, but with prematurely white hair and a livid dark blemish across his right cheek – marks that would surely have been seen as a curse if he had not possessed a rare talent with verse and song. He sang slowly, in the low nasal whine the peoples of the north loved so much. Most

Silures had higher-pitched, sweeter voices, and Ferox wished that it was one of their bards who sang because the best of them had a beauty that helped a man's soul to soar up to the heavens. Yet he had to admit that this man was good, and for a while the talk faded to nothing as everyone listened, and it was almost as if he conjured pictures in the flickering firelight.

Crispinus could not understand a word and swiftly tired of the monotonous tune. 'How long do we have to put up with this?'

'A while yet.' Ferox did not want to worry the man by saying that it would probably last for hours. 'He is singing praises of the high king, of the man born to lead his people and to unite the tribes. Of his keen eye and strong arm...' He stopped because he could see that the tribune was not interested and also because he wanted to listen.

The bard told a story, most of which was wholly new to Ferox and helped to give him a better sense of Tincommius and how the high king wanted men to see him. It was a remarkable tale of a boy who survived the murder of his father and older brothers at the hands of a neighbouring chief. They were all burned alive, trapped in a hut set on fire by an enemy who had pretended to welcome them as friends. The young Tincommius had somehow scrabbled his way through the mud wall of the house before the smoke and flames reached him, helped by one of the enemy who rejected the treachery of his leader. The bard sang of the hunters chasing the boy, of the warrior giving his life to save him, and of how he went to an island far in the north and trained to fight. Grown to manhood, he came back to exact vengeance and there was much about this, of enemies killed in battle as the blood ran red off the wheels of Tincommius' chariot, and of others taken by surprise and slaughtered like pigs.

'Hercules' balls, when will he stop,' Crispinus muttered, until a young woman appeared and offered him more wine. The aristocrat hung his head and may have blushed, although it was hard to tell in the red light and smoky atmosphere of the hall. The woman looked to be about sixteen or seventeen, and had her thick auburn hair plaited and coiled up in a tower on the top of her head. She was pretty, and her checked dress was held at the shoulders by a pair of bronze brooches.

Vindex laughed and nudged the tribune with his elbow. 'Lucky bastard.'

Ferox did not pay much attention, although he felt a flash of envy. The bard paced slowly around the circle of tables as he sang, and apart from drawing breath he did not pause in the tale. Tincommius' own people welcomed the returned exile and rallied to him. His clan were not numerous, but were brave and proud-hearted and stout fighters. The gods led him to a hoard of weapons and fine swords, crafted with cunning and magic to bite through bone and armour as easily as butter. His men armed and armoured, and with Tincommius, the bravest of all, at their head, they fought and beat each of the neighbouring clans in turn, even when three joined forces to face him. Yet he was wise and merciful. Only the men who had wronged him were killed, their families enslaved or slaughtered by their sides. The rest had only to take an oath to him and serve him loyally and then share in the glory and spoils to come. His power grew, chieftain after chieftain and clan after clan swearing to serve him. The great druid – Ferox's attention doubled at his appearance – had watched the contest for power, not taking sides, until the gods spoke to him and he came to Tincommius and guided his steps. It was the great druid who proclaimed him high king in front of all the leaders of the people. Soon clans from other tribes pledged allegiance: Venicones, Caledonians, Selgovae, even the strange Epidii of the far west. Warriors came from across the oceans to serve him. Great chieftains begged to foster his sons and offered their daughters as brides to the high king.

For a while the bard turned to praise of the men gathered around the table. He would gesture towards a man, then sing of his fame and lineage, of his great deeds and his staunch faithfulness. Some men leaped up or punched the air when they were named, while others sat impassively. There was mockery within the praise, for this was the high king's hall and no one could be praised more than him. When the bard reached Venutius he made verses about his beautiful face and how much it had improved from the beating he had received. The chieftain of the Selgovae laughed and pointed at Ferox. Then the bard told of how the young Venutius had been walking out on the moors when a beautiful woman appeared to him, her eyes huge and brown, her naked breasts vast and milky white. She told him that she was the goddess of cows and that she loved him with a passion. Ever since all the cows of the world rushed to be at his side out of an unquenchable love. The whole gathering guffawed and Venutius took it all in good spirit and laughed with them.

Not everyone was so mild in their response. Crispinus gasped in surprise when the first fight broke out. Two of the chieftains stood up and bounded across the table towards each other. They screamed abuse, then threw punches, and only when one had a split lip and the other a swiftly blackening eye did other men pull them apart. The next argument went no further than yelling, but in the third blades were drawn and sparked as they clashed. One of the chiefs was a Hibernian, and he took a graze on the cheek and a deeper gash on his bare thigh, but then tipped his opponent off balance so that he fell into the fire in a flurry of sparks. The man rolled out, and then rolled again to quench his burning shirt. All the while the Hibernian held his sword aloft and screamed in victory.

Then the door of the hall was opened to let in a gust of wind so strong that the great fire rippled like a field of corn. Heads snapped round to see what was happening. The Hibernian went silent and walked back to his place.

A tall man strode across the rush floor towards the gap in the circle of tables. He was covered in a cloak made from a bearskin, his face shadowed by the animal's mask. Ferox noticed that his feet were bare and dirty.

The man stopped and then flung his cloak down and stretched his arms high into the air. The skin of each arm was a network of long scars left by cuts from a sharp knife, cuts that he had surely given to himself. He was naked apart from a heavy gold torc and a grubby loincloth of the sort worn by slaves labouring to tend the furnaces in a bath-house. All of his body was covered in blue tattoos, images of animals and horned gods mingling with curving patterns and shapes. Both his hair and moustache were washed with lime so that they stood out stiffly.

Ferox saw Vindex's lips move and could guess the words he mouthed. 'We're humped.'

It was the priest who had led the ambush all those weeks ago. The one they called the Stallion.

XVIII

'YOU ARE LATE,' said the high king, one leg hooked casually over the arm of his chair. There was no emotion in his voice, and only the slightest hint of reproof as he waited a moment before adding, 'But you are welcome as always. Sit, eat and drink with us.'

The priest did not bow or say anything in reply. He looked around at the faces behind the table until he fixed on the Romans. For a long time he stared at them. Ferox stared back, and hoped that neither of the others would do anything foolish. The priest rubbed his hands together and then spat on the floor and at last turned away and went to his place at the table.

Ferox heard Crispinus breathe out. 'Are we in danger?'

'We have been from the start,' he whispered back. 'But we are guests of the high king and this is his hall. We should be safe here.'

The bard resumed his song, but the mood had shifted and become uneasy. It took a while for talk to grow again. Most of the guests drank heavily, saying little, and for a while there were no more arguments.

'I do not like that priest,' the German growled. 'He is...' He struggled to find the right word and said something in his own language first. 'He is a bad man. He likes to kill.'

Ferox thought back to the beheadings earlier in the day, and the calm skill with which this big man had performed them. 'Sometimes it is necessary. We are warriors.'

'To kill enemy, yes. To kill when our lord tells us to kill his enemy, yes. To kill for pleasure, no.' The big man grinned at him, his beard still stained with food. 'If your friends had not come, I kill you that day.'

'Yes.' Ferox did not see any point pretending otherwise.

'Now we are friends, until the king say different.' It sounded as if this was the most he had said all year. 'You are brave and know how to fight. Share a drink.' He offered his cup. Ferox took it, drank what he guessed to be half and handed it back.

'I like you,' the German rumbled and clapped the centurion hard on the shoulder, the friendly blow feeling as if it would drive him a foot into the floor.

'I like you,' Ferox replied, a little surprised to find that he meant it.

The German bellowed for more drink.

It was always hard to judge time at a feast like this. The beer and wine kept coming, as did the food. Crispinus was struggling, but Ferox admired the way the man persisted and could not help being impressed by his capacity for drink. Vindex was already slumped forward on the table, head on his folded arms and snoring away in satisfied contentment. The Brigantian was not a great drinker, but neither was he the only one, and a good quarter of the chiefs had also fallen either forward or back and no longer moved.

The German showed no signs of diminished hunger or thirst, and probably always spoke and thought slowly. Opposite them the priest drank little and spent most of his time watching them, his spiked hair and the harsh shadows of the fire making him seem like a creature from the Otherworld. The bard still sang, but now he told old tales of love and hate, of raids and battles, and most people were too drunk or too concerned with their own talk to pay much heed.

Ferox happened to glance at the high king just as Tincommius gave orders to some of his servants. They returned bearing a roast boar and carried it into the circle of tables before laying it in front of the royal chair. Silence returned, broken only by the crackling of fresh logs put on to the fire.

'Who is worthy of the first cut?' Tincommius did not raise his voice or shout and yet it carried along the tables.

The Hibernian who had flung his opponent into the fire was the first to stand. His neighbour and fellow countryman joined him a moment later. Three others got to their feet. Tincommius pointed to the first Hibernian and one of the others and the pair sprang across the table into the open space by the fire. Servants hastily moved out of the way to clear space for them.

'Are they going to fight?' Crispinus was frowning and his speech was a little slurred.

'Yes. For the right to receive the first portion – the champion's portion.'

The chiefs drew their swords and waited while their attendants walked around to the gap between the tables and came to them, handing over their shields. They bowed and left the circle to the challengers.

'Sweet Mother Isis,' the tribune muttered. 'It's like something out of Homer. Is the fight to the death?'

'Sometimes.'

The two men launched themselves at each other and there was the dull beat of blade on wooden shield. The Hibernian was good and fast, hacking his opponent's shield to pieces in spite of his wounded leg.

'Enough!' Once again the high king did not shout, but the two men at once drew apart. Tincommius pointed at the Hibernian to show that he was the victor. The other chieftain bowed to him and to the king as the other guests roared approval and banged the table with the palms of their hands.

The other Hibernian took on one of the local men, a gaunt redhead, and the Hibernian lost, his right cheek gashed open so that it flapped, and blood mingled with spittle sprayed out whenever he tried to speak. Next the victorious redhead fought the last remaining challenger and this turned into a bitter and prolonged struggle. Each man's shield was hacked to pieces, and soon they were landing blows on each other's arms, heads and shoulders.

245

Ferox wondered whether an old grudge was being settled for the king let the fight go on longer than he expected and the two fighters were gasping for breath as they slashed and cut. The priest showed little interest, and when Ferox managed to tear his eyes away from the struggle he noticed that the bard was beside the Stallion and that the two men were deep in conversation.

Crispinus started to gag, and then threw up noisily and messily on to the table. As Ferox turned to see how he was, there was a great shout and a harsh rattle as the redhead opened the other's man's chest with a terrific slash that cut through mail, flesh and bone.

'I'm fine,' the tribune said, and he smiled weakly.

The redhead ought to have been tired, for he had just fought two combats and the last had been arduous. Yet when the victorious Hibernian faced him there no sign of fatigue. The man was fast and strong and if anything his opponent seemed the tired one. Ferox had seen it before and sometimes felt it – that strange mood of battle when a man became one with his sword, when he knew that he could do anything, defeat anyone and those around him were slow and weak. Perhaps this was what the bards sang about when they told the tales of great heroes, of men who no longer knew fear or doubt and wanted only to kill, so that they did not feel the wounds dealt to them. If the redhead lived he would collapse once it was over, as the love of battle left him.

Not bothering to call for another shield, he wielded his sword two-handed. That was awkward, but gave dreadful power to the blows. He cleft the Hibernian's shield in two, breaking the man's arm, and did not seem to notice the wild slice that cut off a piece of his scalp and took the top off his ear.

'Enough!' This time the high king shouted, sensing that the red-headed warrior was so lost in fury that he would not hear. 'Enough!'

The Hibernian gave ground as the man came at him, blood pouring down the side of his face. He swung again, sweeping the long sword down, and the Hibernian jumped back only just in time.

'Enough!'

Ferox pushed himself up and leaped over the table, spilling a flagon of beer and sending a plate clattering away. The Hibernian dodged another blow, but lost his balance and fell, managing to roll away from the fire, but losing his sword in the process. The redhead raised his sword above his head.

'Stop him!' Tincommius shouted, and Ferox did not know whether the high king meant him or the frenzied warrior. He ran at the man, crouching low, as the redhead turned and snarled at him, spraying drops of blood from the side of his head. The warrior checked his blow, and slashed one-handed at the centurion.

Ferox dived, arms outstretched. He felt the sword strike his back, but the angle was poor and he was moving fast so that the blade did not cut into his mail. He locked his hands around the man's knees, hitting him with all his weight, and the warrior buckled and fell. Ferox felt the fierce heat of the fire as they landed with the man's head and shoulders in the flames. His hair flared and burned and the man started to scream. The centurion rolled back, pulling at the man with all his might, and then someone was beside him and rolled the redhead in a cloak. It was the big German.

'This is an outrage!' The voice was shrill, almost as high as a woman's, as the Stallion stood and screamed at them. 'See how the Romans mock our customs! How they humiliate us in the king's own hall! They are filth and must be swept from the land.'

Ferox pushed himself up. The priest was not looking at him, but sweeping his gaze around the chieftains. He was wilder than the warrior at the height of his battle madness, yet cold, almost lifeless, and whether or not it was an act Ferox could understand men believing that the man was no more than a mouthpiece for a god.

Tincommius said nothing, but the big German patted the centurion on the shoulder and grinned. The gesture outraged the Stallion.

'They are not of us!' The priest shrieked. 'Neither of them.

The one has forgotten and the other was not born in these isles blessed by the love of the gods. They pollute us by their presence, but soon it will be gone.' He jumped up on to the table, and Ferox could see that he was not as tall as he had thought.

'Rome is weak!' he yelled. 'Every day it withers and if we strike hard enough it will die. They fled from these lands, and they will flee from the rest if we have the courage to defy them. Now is the time, for if we let them they will grow again like weeds in a field and choke us once again. Kill them! Kill them all! Kill them now!'

A few of the chieftains cheered, but only a few and Ferox wondered whether they shouted just because they were drunk and would cheer anything. The rest said little, but their faces were scared. There was a force in the priest, an unearthly force that cowed bold men.

'Kill them!' The Stallion drew a long knife, the only weapon on him, and jumped down into the circle. He ran at the fire and leaped through the flames and men gasped because he did not seem touched.

Ferox gripped the handle of his sword, but the German stepped in front of him and grabbed the priest's thin arms, holding them tight.

'Enough!' Tincommius shouted and held up one hand. 'Enough,' he repeated, calmly this time. 'This is my hall and you are all guests. Let him go, Gannascus.' The German did so with obvious reluctance. The priest stood still, his whole body quivering.

'Keep your blade in its sheath, centurion,' the high king said. 'Your deed was an honourable one and it seems that you now have best claim.' He pointed to the boar. 'Take the portion of the champion and eat it with pride.'

The Stallion's eyes had rolled up so that only the whites could be seen. He was still shaking, froth at his lips. 'They will die,' he said, quieter now, but in a voice suddenly deeper even than the big German's. 'All will burn and all will die.' He sagged, shoulders slumping, and then he fell flat on the floor, his limbs twitching as he writhed. Some men touched wheels of Taranis like the one

'The free tribes of the Britons. The Romans have tried to crush our spirit and take our lands, but they have failed here in the north. For the first time they have failed and the tide has turned so that we will sweep them from the whole island and go back to the old ways.

'Rome is finished, its gods fading away. Thirty years ago the Temple of Jupiter on Rome's Capitol burned. Within nine times three years it will be struck again by the fire of the gods, and this time it will burn into ashes and nothing will be left. That time is fast approaching. Thirty years ago the seers in Gaul prophesied the end of Rome. They were premature, and had not read the signs properly for they no longer had the true knowledge. I have that knowledge. I saw the groves on Mona before they fell, and I was taught secrets no longer known to anyone. The fire will come and the end will come if only we listen to the gods and obey them.'

Ferox pushed his mail shirt down comfortably over his hips. 'You sound like that fool in there.'

'He is a child – a gifted child certainly, but no more than that. He seeks only to kill. I too would sweep Rome away, but we must build something better. Will you help me?'

It was hard to remember the hunched beggar muttering to himself. This man looked hale in body and sharp in his mind. He also seemed genuinely eager to persuade.

'I am sworn man to the emperor and to Rome.'

'Which emperor? No one had heard of Trajan until a few years ago.' The voice was reasonable, the knowledge obvious. This was a man who spoke of the Capitoline Hill in Rome and of emperors and understood what he was saying. Ferox knew without having to be told that this was the great druid, although he could not guess how the man came to understand such things.

'Civil war is coming again, and this time the empire will not survive. They will turn on each other like rats and rush down the road to their utter ruin. Leave them, boy. Leave the people who disdain you and leave you to rot and drown your sorrows in drink. What have they ever done to earn your faith?'

251

Acco knew too much, and at that moment if he had brought up her name and promised to lead Ferox to her, he might just have gone with the man.

'I am sworn. If you truly knew my grandfather you would not expect me to break an oath.'

'An oath to them? What does that matter? Do you know that even now some of them send us arms and information, that they even kill their own when we ask? They are filth, worthless in every way. Rome is a poison killing the whole world and the world will die if it is not stopped now.' The man was getting wilder, his voice louder, and the first spell was broken. 'Be free of them, boy. Leave them and be free of oaths to the unworthy.'

Ferox did not love Rome, but neither did he put much store in prophecies and predictions of doom. There was much about the empire that was rotten and much that sickened him. Honesty forced him to admit that there was also much he hated about the way the tribes lived and preyed on each other and he had known plenty of chieftains as ruthless, cruel and treacherous as the worst emperors. He suspected that Tincommius was one of them, otherwise he doubted that the man would have proved so successful. The same was doubtless true of this druid.

'There was an old man and boy,' Ferox said, not wanting to discuss the evils of Rome. 'Men called him the Goat Man. I never knew the boy's name. You must have met them or heard of them.'

'What of it?' Acco frowned. 'They are gone now and do not matter.'

'Yes, they are dead. The Stallion's men buried the boy alive.'

'I was not there,' the druid said. 'But I lived with your kin and stood with them as they fought Rome. Your grandfather fought with all the cruelty of your people. Evil things must be done in war.'

Ferox sighed. There was no point in trying to explain to a man like this. The druid's hatred burned less brightly than the Stallion's, but it had the strong deep heat of iron worked in a forge. The old man could see nothing beyond his own path, and that was paved with blood and ruin.

'I am a centurion of Rome, sworn to serve the city and the emperor,' Ferox said.

'Then I cannot save you.' The beggar or great druid or whoever this was sounded disappointed and sad. 'And you could have served us so well. You are Flavius Ferox indeed and no longer anyone else. I am sorry. Soon all will be blood and fire and you will perish. I have failed your grandfather.' The old man stalked off into the night.

For a moment Ferox nearly followed. He did not remember his father, for he had been a babe in arms when he was killed, and part of him wanted to learn more about what sort of man he had been. Yet he knew that it would not change anything.

He went back to the feast and drank beside the German. Eventually they both passed out.

XIX

EROX WOKE WITH hair in his mouth. For a while he just lay on his back and felt the wiry strands on his lips. There was a weight resting against him and something over him, but he was comfortable and did not mind. Above was the high thatched roof and there was a dull light, which made him suspect that the morning was well advanced. The fire had died away to nothing sometime during the night and his eyes did not want to do any hard work, so he let them close and only now and again looked up at the roof. There was movement there, probably the usual roaches or other vermin in the thatch, but the more he stared up the more he became convinced that this was not the hut he had occupied with Vindex and Masclus. It was smaller, for one thing, and the gentle sighing breath beside him did not sound much like either man.

The centurion blew the hair out of his mouth. It was long and raven black. He licked his lips and squinted to see the long slim arm draped over his chest and outside the warmth of the furs covering them. Turning as gently as he could, he twisted his head to see the mass of long raven-dark hair sprayed out like a great fan. Most of the owner's face was covered as she rested, but he could see the outline of a pale cheek and full lips that seemed very red in contrast. It was the woman embraced by the high king at their first meeting – a day, and what seemed like months ago. She was naked, for he could feel her bare skin on his under the coverings. The woman stirred slightly, murmured something, and hooked one long leg over his.

There were worse ways to wake up, far worse, but he could not remember anything after the feast. This was surely the hut given to Crispinus and the woman here to offer the hospitality of the royal house to the honoured guest. Was it all a mistake, and he had been carried here instead of the young tribune? That seemed unlikely, for the high king struck him as a deliberate man, which meant that there must be a reason why he was here, lying with this woman. He doubted that anything had happened, for he had drunk far more than he had done since the ambush over a month ago. Yet someone had undressed him, and as he lay he felt the warmth of his companion. She was a royal favourite, and the way that Tincommius had embraced her made it obvious she was his lover, whether mistress or one of his wives.

The dark-haired woman stirred again, leaning her body back to rest more on her side than over him. He could feel her breasts brushing against his skin. She smelled very faintly of flowers, a hint of a perfume which could only have come from the lands far to the east of the empire. Fortunata had worn something similar, but the former slave had daubed it on, perhaps revelling in the sheer cost, whereas this woman had no more than a drop of two on her. How a bottle of Indian scent had come to the north was a mystery.

Ferox was tempted to lie there in peace and enjoy so comfortable a bed and such beautiful company. Yet there must be a reason why she was here. The obvious seemed unlikely, but his clouded mind and throbbing forehead did not offer better explanation. Moving his hand with care, he slipped it under the furs piled over them and began to stroke the woman's skin. It was smooth, her flesh soft and yielding.

The woman moaned, shifting a little. Ferox kissed her on the forehead, still running his fingers across her skin, and she stirred, turning to lie on her back. He kissed her on the lips, fighting the powerful urge to swing himself on top of her. His hand cupped one of her breasts. Her eyes opened, pale grey and flecked with spots of green. There was a flicker of surprise, then realisation and she kissed him back. It was no longer easy for him to think about anything apart from their closeness.

Then the woman pulled her mouth away and the arm that had rested over him instead pushed him back. Ferox lay on his side, head propped up on his left hand while the fingers of his right continued to stroke her. She did not stop him or move any further away.

'Good morning, centurion,' the woman said. At least that removed any last thought that he was here by chance.

'Good morning,' he replied, for what else was there to say? The woman spoke in the language of the tribes, although there was a strange brusqueness to her speech. If she did not know Latin then that might be the reason why he shared her bed rather than Crispinus.

'I am called Galla.' It was not a name he had ever heard before and did not sound local. Her eyes were big and intelligent, the lashes on her eyelids long and dark like her hair. 'I am the king's and I am sent by him.'

'I am honoured,' he said. 'And I am also not the leader of our embassy – as you must surely know.' His hand was still on her, exploring and caressing. Ferox was not sure whether this was more of a distraction to him or to Galla.

'The tribune is young and inexperienced. Tincommius judges him to be clever and if that is so he will listen to an older and wiser man like you.' She gasped as his finger drew a circle on her breast, and for the moment said nothing, running her tongue over her lips. Her hand slipped down under the covers and smoothed his chest.

'Tincommius does not want to fight Rome unless he has no choice,' she said at long last. 'He is strong, and has done much in the last ten years to become a great leader, but there is still much to do. There is little for him to gain and much to lose if he makes war on you.'

'The tribune will be pleased to hear that. We want only peace with the high king.'

'Others think differently.' Her eyes looked straight into his and showed no emotion, even when his fondling became more vigorous, instead responding in the same way, running her fingers across his skin. 'They hate the Romans and believe them to be rotten and weak, like a tree decayed from the inside. They cannot wait to set an axe to the trunk and topple it over.'

Ferox thought of the ranting Stallion and of the calm persuasiveness of the druid. It was odd that so many people wanted to talk to him and to enlist his aid.

'Tincommius cannot be seen to be cowed by Rome or to show any fear. Great kings are never afraid, never forced to do anything. Many of his people yearn to take their spears against the Romans and dream of slaughter and spoils. There are chiefs who tolerate his overlordship only because they are afraid of his power. He is like a bear fighting hounds. They fear him, but it will only take one or two to attack and bite and slowly he will weaken.' She moaned in pleasure, eyes staring up past him.

'I did not tell you to stop,' she told him when he thought that he might have gone too far, so Ferox resumed. For a while she panted, her hand back on her own body.

'The Stallion preaches war, and he is a guest of the high king?' Ferox said.

'He has been useful – a way to win over men who would have been more reluctant without the promise of help from the heavens. He wants war and Tincommius does not. The high king will not be ordered about by any man, least of all such as him.

'The king's only wish is to rule here, far from your province. He does not seek to challenge, but neither can he be seen as a suppliant.' Galla – or Tincommius if the words were solely his – understood a good deal about Roman diplomacy. 'There can be no surrender or subservience. What he wants...' She lost her thread for the moment and Ferox kissed her again on the forehead, on the neck and then on the lips. Their mouths parted and tongues met, until she pushed him away.

'This is important,' she said breathily. 'It must appear as a friendship between great chieftains. Gifts would help.'

'What sort?'

'Gifts fit for a high king. Silver is good, weapons even better. He must be strong if he is to be a useful friend to you. There will be much to gain for you.'

'"And your friendly thighs,"' he joked, quoting an old poem about a queen promising everything if a warrior would swear loyalty to her, with her own virtue as well as her daughter in marriage.

Galla shook her head. 'I am the king's.'

'His queen?'

'We are not man and wife, but he is my love and I am his. I cannot be queen, but he has several of those and none matter beyond the alliance they bring with their father or brother. He needs me and I guide him.'

'You are not from these shores?' Ferox was curious about this tall, slim woman.

'My people come from far away, across the Grey Sea. There was a war, and my father lost it to another man who stole his throne. My brothers saved me and led our loyal folk away. We were chased and at last took to boats. There were twelve when we rowed away from the shore. Five only reached this land. I saw three of the others sink, the heads vanishing in an instant under the rolling waves. One brother died, and only Gannascus was left to lead.' Ferox realised why her manner of speech was familiar, for it was a softer, more fluent echo of the big German. 'Although I was young he needed my help – he is not a thinker, but he is a brave and good man.

'We had barely a hundred of us left and did not know where we were. Seventy were warriors, bold men and big, and so we did not fear too much, but the weavers of fate were with us. The local chieftain was wary, and – better still for us – when we did not attack him and just camped peacefully on his shore living off the fish we caught, he sent word to Tincommius. He came to us, just the king, and I saw him and loved him and visions came. Since then we have been one and I have led him as he walks the path to greatness. It was meant to be, and in after years he has welcomed others from other lands. All serve him because he is faithful and generous as a lord should be.'

Ferox remembered the Hibernians at the feast. Broken lords and chieftains beaten in their homelands, they too had fled here and found safety and success and a measure of wealth fighting for Tincommius. If their numbers were few, such men and their followers were likely better warriors than most and had little left to lose. He tried to imagine a dreadful voyage in little boats on the open sea and shuddered at the thought, so that she looked at him in surprise. He leaned over to kiss her again.

'No.'

'I am a guest; there is no shame,' he said, not believing a word of it, but reluctant to let her move.

'I am the king's. I have delivered our message and shown you that I am serious. There will be no more.' She must have thought that there was anger in his face rather than mere disappointment. 'If you force me Tincommius will cut it off before he cuts your throat.' A glance downwards was enough to show what she meant.

Ferox lay back, folding his hands underneath his head. Galla stood up, the furs and other coverings sliding away so that she stood tall and completely bare. He watched her and she did not appear to resent him looking. Her white dress was draped over a stool and his eyes stayed on her as she dressed, neither of them saying anything. In the end the woman drew a heavy brown cloak around her and the dim light in the house became even dimmer.

'Tincommius has a high opinion of you and believes that you are a man who can be trusted,' she said, breaking the long silence. 'He is fond of the son you spared, very fond, even if the boy is from a lesser wife and unlikely ever to become king.'

'What son?' Ferox had no idea what she meant. None of the men who fought for the champion's portion were young enough to be the king's son, and it stretched even the most generous praise to say that he had saved one of them, even the man he had wrestled to the floor.

'Epaticcus,' she said. 'You really do not know, do you?'

He shook his head.

'Epaticcus is foster son to Venutius of the Selgovae. Both are here now, and the boy stood behind the chieftain at the feast. That was his first battle, and all say that he fought with courage and also that he was at your mercy, but that you spared him and told him to go with honour. Since he proved his courage he is at last fit to appear in his father's presence. Tincommius sent him away seven years ago.'

Ferox struggled to remember the fight at the fort and the scrambling retreat down the valley side, but like most battles it had faded into a few memories of fear and exultation. 'I think I told him to piss off.' He laughed at the thought. 'But he did fight well and that is why I preferred not to kill him. I honestly did not know who he was, so cannot boast of it as a favour.'

'That is what we thought, which only makes the obligation to you all the deeper. Tincommius is grateful and thinks that you are a man to trust. I believe that he is right, and I am glad that we have met and spoken.'

'And I am glad that you sleep so deeply,' he replied and his mischief was rewarded with a moment of uncertainty and doubt in this confident young woman. It did not last.

'Farewell, centurion. We shall never be alone again.'

'Farewell, Galla.'

She left, crouching down to go through the low doorway and closing the door behind her. He let out a long breath and just lay, staring up at the roof. To his surprise his head felt clear and calm and he had no desire for any drink other than spring water or some posca.

After a while the door opened and a man came through, bent almost double. It was Vindex. It would have to be Vindex.

'Good night?' the Brigantian said, baring his big teeth.

XX

THE HIGH KING went hunting that day and the Romans were not invited.

'Is it a snub?' Crispinus asked as they ate the food brought to them by servants. It was early afternoon, with a bitter wind, and they were all glad to sit inside the house that the tribune had reclaimed for his own use.

'In other words, no poaching,' Vindex muttered when Ferox told him. As they took their meal, Ferox told the others what had happened from the moment the Brigantian had passed out at the feast. He spoke of the priest's rage, and of the great druid disguised as a beggar.

'Bugger me,' Vindex cut in at this point. 'Suppose at least the blessing ought to be worth something given all the money I gave the old liar. I ought to be the luckiest man in the world.'

Ferox did not hide the druid's attempt to win him over to their cause, and then he came to Galla and he talked at length about her message, while skimming over everything else. It was clear that Vindex's imagination readily filled in the rest, no doubt in the most lurid way. Even Crispinus was jealous.

'From all you tell me, by rights it should have been me greeting so fair and important a visitor.'

Ferox shrugged. 'She could not speak your language, and you cannot speak hers.'

'Curse my parents for neglecting my education so shamefully. Well, that is past remedy – at least for the moment. What matters is that she claims Tincommius wants peace. Do you believe her?'

Ferox weighed his answer. 'Yes he does, because the stakes are too high for him to want to risk war with Rome. He wants recognition, friendship and help.'

Crispinus was pleased. 'Not too high a price for removing the most powerful of our enemies, since you say that the Stallion and his followers are set on war.'

'He is, and there are bound to be a good number who follow him. If he wins even a few little victories that number will grow rapidly.'

'Then all the more reason for us to befriend Tincommius and tilt the balance more in our favour.' The tribune frowned. 'I do not understand your caution.'

'We make Tincommius stronger, then in a few years he may not be so friendly.'

'A few years is a long time, and not our problem,' Crispinus declared. 'I may be envious of your good fortune last night, but you should not doubt my satisfaction with your conduct, centurion.'

Later in the day, the wind dropped and the Romans took a stroll around the high king's stronghold. People stared at them, but were generally friendly and obliging. Children, too young to remember the days when the Romans were here, followed them about, curious to see these strange creatures from the south. Ferox heard a little girl explaining to a younger brother that a Roman was made from stone fashioned to look like a man and that is why they were happy around stone and lived in high stone towers that reached up to the sky. He whispered an explanation to the tribune. The boy did not seem convinced, but was a bold lad and crept up behind Crispinus. Vindex nudged Ferox and they watched as the child took a big swing and kicked the tribune on the ankle. To his credit the aristocrat did not react, save to turn very slowly around as if his whole body were stiff. The boy scampered away howling in fear.

Gannascus and several dozen warriors were practising in an open space, throwing javelins and fencing with each other. All were big men, if only one or two as big as their giant of a leader, and they were markedly thicker set than the local tribesmen. A lot of them were blond or red-haired, but that was not uncommon in these parts, even if it was unusual to sport such thick beards and long hair. Every man had an army-issue sword at his belt.

'I understood that it is against the law to trade in weapons beyond the frontier,' Crispinus observed, sticking to Latin so as not to cause offence.

'It is, but people find a way.' Ferox thought back to the Treviran merchant they had met at Trimontium, and how the man had not wanted to say what he had sold to Tincommius. 'A lot of stores of all kinds went missing when we pulled out of the bases up here. It always happens. People make mistakes, or they try to cover them up, and there's always someone up to making a quick profit by selling contraband to the locals.'

'Why, think of that,' Vindex added sarcastically. 'A dishonest Roman, whatever is the world coming to?'

'Or someone is giving arms to the king already,' Crispinus suggested, ignoring the Brigantian.

'Perhaps,' Ferox said. 'Then there's always deserters. A man who goes over the wall with all his gear is a man likely to find a welcome up here. You saw the posts?' Earlier on they had passed another open patch and seen two posts like the one outside Syracuse. Army methods of training suggested former soldiers serving the king – no doubt men who chose to keep out of sight while the Roman envoys were here.

As they watched, a few more Germans appeared carrying a crude straw figure of a man strapped to an upright stake, which they drove into the ground at the foot of the rampart. The effigy was dressed in an old Roman helmet and the segmented cuirass sported by legionaries. A pair of tall warriors carrying bows as tall as themselves came to stand near them, while the rest moved to either side to watch. Each planted five arrows in the grass at their feet, before stringing their bows. They were simple, made from a single piece of timber, but Ferox saw the men strain to hook the strings in place. The army used smaller bows, with several types of wood glued together and reinforced with animal horn, and these looked crude by comparison.

One of the warriors plucked an arrow from the ground, drew back his bow and loosed, sending the missile straight into the target and there was a dull clang as it punched through an iron plate of the cuirass. The other archer fired a moment later with the same effect. Ferox thought back to the ambush and the Batavians shot down by hidden archers. He had never seen arrows fly with such force unless they came from a *ballista*. The next arrows went higher, the first clattering off the helmet to the mocking applause of the crowd. Then there was a cheer as the next one drove into the bronze and stuck there.

'This doesn't look too friendly,' Vindex said.

Gannascus acted as if he had not noticed them until now. 'Roman!' he called to Ferox. 'Want to try?'

The Silures were not archers. As a boy Ferox learned how to use a sling, but it was not until he went to Rome and trained with the Praetorians that he had been taught to shoot a bow. He had practised a little since then, especially when he was on the Danube, but had not even held a bow for years.

One of the Germans grinned as he handed him a bow. The warrior was taller than he was and so was his bow, but Ferox was surprised at how light and well balanced it felt. There were two arrows in the ground beside him, and after feeling the taut string, he reached down and plucked one. He nocked it, began to pull and felt the appalling strength holding the string back. Grunting, he used all his might to draw it. His left arm was straining to keep straight, his right hand juddering with the effort. He tried to steady it, breathing out before he loosed, but it all felt wrong and he was not surprised when the arrow went high and wide over the rampart and outside.

'Some poor bastard of a shepherd's probably having a bad day!' Vindex commented.

The Germans roared with laughter. Ferox reached for the second arrow, nocked it and drew all in one motion, doing his best not to think and just letting his muscles take over. One thing he had learned long ago was that if a shot felt right then it flew true and to the mark. As soon as he had the string to his chest he loosed and if the aim was not perfect it was better than before. It missed the armour and drove deep into the post on which the straw figure was mounted, piercing the straw just where it divided to form the legs.

'Ooh, that's nasty,' Vindex said and the Germans laughed again, but this time they were amused rather than scornful and they made squealing noises as if the target were a real man hit in the crotch. Gannascus came over and pounded the centurion on the shoulder in delight. The blow added to the ache in his arms and the sense that his ribs had almost been pulled apart.

'Now show us what you can do with a sword,' the big German demanded and to Ferox's surprise they produced wooden swords and heavy wickerwork shields. As he hefted the training equipment he could see that they were not army issue, but close copies. Gannascus' warriors were used to handling them, and to simple versions of the standard drills, and he guessed that the deserters recruited by the high king had brought with them ideas as well as their own weapons.

The Germans were good – not up to the level of a truly well-trained unit, but still better than he had expected, at least when they fought as individuals. He put his first opponent down quickly, surprising him with an immediate attack that knocked him off balance. The second man did better, but kept his shield too high, wanting to protect his face, and after feinting high, Ferox was able to slice low and hit him hard behind the knee, scooping the man's leg from under him. Gannascus cheered, but pounded the warrior on the back for doing well and grinned at Ferox.

Crispinus lost interest after a while, and took Vindex away with him in case he needed an interpreter, leaving Ferox to fight on. The Germans were enthusiastic and he knew that each man desperately wanted to be the one to beat the Roman officer. He was glad Gannascus stood back and watched, for he did not relish facing his speed and strength, at least not now that he was tired.

The third man was older, with streaks of grey amid his brown hair, and there was a good deal of watching and waiting in between each rapid attack. Ferox thought that he could beat the man, but reckoned that it was better to declare a draw and do him honour. The Germans cheered that, especially when he put down his sword and clasped the man's hand. After that he took a break, calling for water.

More warriors were appearing, some of them Germans, but also local men and a few wearing long tunics and bare-legged who were most likely Hibernians. Talking to the men, he learned that the high king had more than a thousand warriors in his household, although half lived at other settlements. These thousand were the best men, the ones who had no real occupation other than war, and they included the exiles. For a month before Lughnasadh, the great summer festival, each clan sworn to the high king sent him fifty men, along with all the lads who had turned fifteen. For four weeks they trained for war or laboured to restore the defences of this fort or helped to tend his cattle, then they shared in a great feast before returning home, ready to muster again in time of war. One of the Germans boasted to him of the storerooms full of shields and good spears ready to be given to men answering the king's call to arms. Tincommius was creating an army of a sort never seen before among the tribes of the north, and that raised more questions about what he planned in the longer run.

Soon – too soon – Ferox was forced to duel again, and he wondered whether Gannascus had deliberately saved his better warriors until the Roman was tired. Soon he had to start pulling out all the dirty tricks he could remember. He beat the fifth man by punching with the boss of his shield at the top of his opponent's shield, then slamming it up so that the edge caught the man on the chin. The warrior bit his lip and was left dazed and bloodied.

The sixth man was not a German, but was clearly in Gannascus' band. It seemed that he had bolstered his numbers with a couple of dozen eager local men, so that these days he led almost a hundred men, eleven of them archers. The new recruits were slighter than the Germans, but several sported beards instead of moustaches. The one facing Ferox had gone further, tying his hair in a knot on top of his head in imitation of some of Gannascus' best men. He was quick in his movements and wily, so Ferox let him probe his defence for a time while he looked for a weakness. He noticed a raven tattooed on the man's right wrist, which was a mark of one of the clans of the Venicones.

Trumpets blared, the sound a mix of the harsh carnyxes and softer horns, and the Briton's eyes flicked towards the gateway. Ferox pounded him with his shield, forcing the man back, and the warrior's guard dropped for a moment allowing the centurion to thrust with his practice sword. He stopped the blow with the tip just short of the man's throat.

Gannascus clapped the man on the back. 'Watch the man you fight. Forget everything else,' he bellowed, but looked pleased that his warriors were doing better when they faced the Roman.

The trumpets announced the return of the high king, who thundered through the gateway at the reins of a chariot. The car was painted bright red, and the harness on the two grey ponies pulling it was of red leather. Seeing the Roman, he turned on a denarius and galloped towards the training area, slewing the chariot to a halt at the last minute. 'So, are you teaching my warriors?' he called happily.

'And learning from them.' Compliments were rarely wasted and this one made Gannascus' men cheer. Ferox had to admit that he liked them. He had always felt most at ease among fighting men, finding them easier to understand than Romans like Crispinus, for whom the army was merely one short step as they climbed the political ladder.

'Talk with me,' the high king said and began walking off. Ferox followed.

'Did the hunt go well?' he asked.

'Well enough, although I lost a fine horse.'

'Boar?' Ferox had seen plenty of mounts brought down and gored by the tusks of a cornered animal.

'Spear,' said the high king. 'We were hunting men who dared to steal my cattle. I had thought yesterday's executions were sufficient warning, but these rogues must have thought that I would be too busy feasting to watch my own property. They were wrong, as I am sure they realised when my hounds found them.'

They were near the great hall and in a burst of yapping half a dozen puppies ran up to greet Tincommius, their tails wagging furiously.

'Ah, my children.' The high king scooped up one of the animals in each hand. They were only a few months old, and their legs looked too long for their bodies. 'You must leave tomorrow.' The abrupt change of subject took Ferox by surprise. 'Speak to your tribune, and we will have a council tonight and agree matters.' The high king made it clear that he expected the Romans to accept his offer.

'I will speak to the Lord Crispinus.'

'Good. You must go quickly and I will send some of my men with you as escort.' Tincommius' tone suggested that this was more than a courtesy. 'There may be danger.'

'The Stallion?' Ferox asked and the high king looked surprised at his directness.

'You do not like dogs, do you?' He offered one of the puppies to the centurion, and the animal stopped barking and stared at him with scepticism 'No, I thought not. They call the Silures the "Wolf People" so perhaps you do not care for creatures broken and trained. I hear that the Silures are queer folk. Yet there is an old saying that you cannot trust a man who does not like dogs, but I trust you so perhaps the saying is wrong or I am wrong. I like dogs because they are simple and the best ones are more loyal than any man. My hounds are like family to me and it gives me sorrow when I lose one.' He put the other dog down and held the puppy he had offered to Ferox up to his own face. A little pink tongue licked the king with great energy and enthusiasm.

268

Ferox said nothing, sensing that there was a point to all this.

'We had to kill one of my hounds today. She was a bitch, strong, sharp-nosed and fearless. Two years ago she saved me when I was trapped under a fallen horse and a boar charged at me. The bitch fought him alone until men came to help, and she was sorely hurt. I had her tended and nursed back to health. Her courage was undaunted and she continued to serve well until she became subject to rage. She bit a servant, and today she would not be called off and kept mauling one of the thieves until she got at the man's throat and tore it out. The man was no loss, but a hound like that cannot be kept. The madness and rage will grow and one day she will turn on a servant or a child and she will kill. So I killed her before that could happen. It was' – he struggled to find the Latin – 'necessary.

'There are men who have served me well in the past, men who boast that the gods love them and speak through them.' Tincommius nuzzled the puppy against his face.

'The Stallion and the great druid.'

Tincommius nodded and there was sadness in his voice. 'The one is his own man and not to be commanded by any chieftain or king. He will do what he will do, but I do not fear him. The Stallion is different and has made promises to those who follow him.' The high king sighed. 'It is a shame, for the man has persuaded many to accept my leadership. It was he who won me the druid's blessing.'

The high king turned the puppy on its back, and one hand closed around its neck. It struggled, but could not break free.

'You can be very fond of something that is simple, or someone who sees the world in a simple way,' he went on. 'I do not know where the Stallion came from, or who he really is, but there is a fire in his soul. He believes utterly, so that when he is cruel or savage he does not understand. It is simply his nature and that cannot be changed. This creature in my hands was born to hunt. You could not stop it from hunting even if you tried. If it is put in chains it will hunt as far as the chain stretches. The only way to stop him would be to break him.'

The high king stared at the animal as the rest yapped around his feet. His face was grim, until at last it softened and he took his fingers from around the puppy's throat and tickled its stomach. He smiled and set the animal down.

'The Stallion wishes only for flames and destruction, and for sacrifice.'

'Samhain is near,' Ferox said.

'Then you have heard. He promises a great and terrible sacrifice and he promises much more, for he says that the souls of dead warriors will come into the world and fight alongside his followers, and that men sworn to do his bidding will not be pierced by any blade. He promises blood and fire. He promises war and I believe he is ready to start one and trusts that I will join him.'

'And you will not?'

Tincommius turned and placed his hands on the centurion's shoulders. It reminded Ferox of how short the man was, and also the hard assurance in his eyes.

'I do not wish for a war,' the high king said, emphasising each word. 'It is up to you to make sure that I do not have to fight one. Get home, make the new legate of your province agree to friendship.' Tincommius smiled as he displayed his knowledge. 'I think you will find that the new governor has arrived. So seal our friendship with him and it will be better for us all. That is why I need to make sure that you get home, and that is why you will have an escort.'

XXI

GANNASCUS AND TWENTY of his men rode south with them. The Germans looked too big on the little ponies, but the animals had strength and stamina and they went at a good pace. With them also came Venutius, accompanied by a dozen warriors as well as Epaticcus, the son of the high king. It rained for the first few days with barely a break, and somehow that made the abandoned remains of the army's old bases seem even more forlorn.

In their last meeting Crispinus had presented the high king with a gift of three hundred denarii, newly minted and shiny and bearing the image of Trajan. The gift was a token of esteem and friendship, and the centurion had not even known that the tribune had brought it with him. He had known about the sword, a new, perfectly balanced spatha, and was pleased at the evident joy with which Tincommius accepted it, and his immediate gift of it to Epaticcus. In return Ferox and the tribune were given horses, a couple of greys so similar that they might have been twins, and had by chance been born on the same day. Their names were Frost and Snow and they were a generous gift.

The high king had spoken frankly to them, his great hall almost empty apart from a few servants. Galla was there, standing tall behind the royal chair, but she did not acknowledge Ferox in any way. Tincommius told them that he feared that the Stallion meant to start a war. A year ago at least a thousand men served him, bearing his marks on their foreheads and hands, and now there were surely far more because men kept coming north to find him. Most were strangers to these lands, vagrants, dreamers and runaways – not warriors but filled with faith in his magic. The priest had gathered them all in a long-abandoned fort on the borders between the Venicones and Selgovae. There were thousands of them there a few weeks ago, and by now there might be many more, all daubing the mark of the horse on their heads.

'It is a bleak spot, hard to access. I will no longer send food to him, and I do not know what stores he has. I doubt that he will stay there, for he must attack to show his strength.' The king suspected that many true warriors, men from the tribes, would answer the call to war, and so might some chieftains. 'Many more will come if victories show his magic to all.

'You must stop him soon,' he said, but the Stallion had left on the night of the feast and was more than a day ahead of them. 'He can travel fast.' With more reluctance, the high king explained that the druid had also gone, no one knew where.

They went at a good pace, but the sight of more than sixty heavily armed riders did not make villagers wary, for the presence of the Germans and the king's son showed that they travelled with his blessing. People gave them food and shelter for the nights and talked freely. They spoke of the Stallion, who flitted about from place to place, appearing when least expected and telling men of the end of Rome and the cleansing fire that would soon sweep through the land. Even folk loyal to Tincommius were in awe of the priest's powerful magic. Ferox spoke to one herdsmen and then repeated the story to Crispinus and Vindex.

'They say that at the great feast the Stallion confronted the Roman envoys,' he explained.

'Well, there is truth enough in that,' the tribune allowed.

'They also say that he raised his hands in the air, calling on the gods, and struck all three Romans stone dead.'

Vindex grabbed his own left wrist and flopped the hand back and forth. 'Should we still be moving about?' he asked.

Crispinus was unsure whether to laugh or take it seriously. 'How can we make the lie known? Tell the man that we are the envoys and we are as alive as he is.'

'I already have,' Ferox said. 'But he wasn't surprised. It seems that the great druid told the Stallion that the time was not yet ripe, and that he should respect the high king's hearth and hospitality, so the priest raises his arms, prays a bit more, and restores us to life.'

Vindex puffed breath on to the palm of his hand and nodded with exaggerated pleasure.

'Very kind of him, I must say,' the tribune said. 'But surely the fellow does not believe such nonsense?'

'Maybe yes, maybe no,' Ferox explained. 'But someone told him the tale and he told us. Word is spreading.'

Next day they met a group of half a dozen men trudging along wrapped in their thick woollen cloaks. They had round shields, a couple of throwing spears on their shoulder, and were going to answer the priest's call, even though they did not seem to know why. Epaticcus told them to go back home and with the big Gannascus looming over them they shuffled back along the track.

'Probably double back as soon as we have gone,' Vindex said and Ferox suspected that he was right.

There were more men the next day striding over the hills to the south as little groups or individuals, but all going in the same direction.

On the fourth day the skies cleared for a few hours, and a pale sun without warmth beamed down on them. An hour after dawn on the next day, the rain started and lasted throughout the day, now and again turning to sleet. They were cold and wet, but by the end of the day they reached the ferry and were taken across the river.

It was hailing as they crossed, the sluggish waters pocked with splashes. Ferox felt his face stinging from the blows. The people in the houses on the south bank were nervous, reluctant to talk, and they discovered the cause an hour later. At first they saw only the outline of the great yew tree, standing alone on the low ridge above the track leading south. When they got closer they saw the overturned cart, blackened and smouldering, the remains of a fire under the boughs of the tree and the two bodies hanging down from the branches. One of the men wore a Roman tunic, the dull white wool slashed and stained dark with blood from where they had sliced at him with knives as he slowly choked to death from the noose around his neck.

The other corpse was naked, and hung upside down, the rope around his ankles, his head downwards so that it was held just above the fire lit under the tree. He would not have been in the flames but kept in their heat, and Ferox imagined the men who had done this sitting and listening to his screams.

'I hope the poor fellow was dead when they did that to him,' Crispinus said, staring in horror at the corpse, the head burst open and its scorched contents in the fire.

Ferox did not bother to answer so foolish a question but jumped down to look at the ground properly.

'If he was dead they wouldn't have bothered,' Vindex replied when the centurion said nothing.

'It's the Treviran,' Ferox said at last, recognising the dead man's hands. 'The one we met at Trimontium.' There was little left to recognise of the man's face.

Crispinus glanced at him, obviously wondering how he could tell, but deciding not to ask.

There were three more corpses in the grass, all badly cut about, which meant that whoever did this had kept slashing long after they were dead. Apart from the burned cart there were marks from a dozen mules, which the attackers had taken with them.

'Whatever they were carrying, the Stallion's men have it now,' Ferox said. 'Come on, we'd better get them down and buried.' He called to Masclus and his men to help.

'Won't do them much good now,' Crispinus said, unable to tear his eyes away from the dead men, 'and it will take a lot of time. Why bother?' Then something occurred to him. 'How do you know it was the priest's men?'

'Who else? They were killed because they were Roman and whoever killed them had a lot of hate. They wanted their goods – whether it was food or weapons it was something of value. And it's a yew tree. That would have appealed to them.'

'Weapons?'

Ferox drew his dagger and started cutting the rope tying the Treviran's corpse above the fire. 'Someone has been giving or selling swords and other gear to Tincommius.' He glanced at their escorts, wondering whether any spoke Latin, not that it mattered now. 'I reckon the priest's men decided that they could put them to better use. And they've started killing any Roman they can find. These two and their slaves were in the wrong place at the wrong moment and this is what happened. We don't need to leave them up there as proof that Romans can be killed without fear, do we?'

'I see.' Crispinus dismounted. 'Let me help.'

They scraped a long shallow hole and laid all five corpses in it, before covering them with soil and any stones they could find. Gannascus, Venutius and the others watched with mild interest for a while, before attending to their horses and taking a bit of food. Only the young Epaticcus helped, eagerly following Ferox and doing whatever he did.

No one talked much for the rest of the day, and even the Germans were subdued, until the clouds broke up and they saw the sun for the last part of the afternoon. A clear sky meant a cold night, but they found enough kindling and wood to make a couple of good fires. Better still, they were given two sheep by the headman from the nearest cluster of farms. These were quickly killed and butchered, one of Venutius' men showing great skill in the task. Ferox enjoyed the meal, although part of him wished they had cooked them in the fashion of his own tribe, tossing the entire animal on to a hot fire, and cutting and butchering it after it was cooked. It had been a long time since he had eaten mutton roasted that way and he missed it.

The headman brought news that was not good. The two merchants and their slaves were not the only victims of the Stallion's rampage. He had heard of other traders caught and tortured to death, some of them local men whose only fault was to do business with the Romans.

'Men say that we all must choose,' the headman told them, 'to join with the gods and cleanse the land or to be slaughtered along with the Roman defilers.' He was old with leathery skin and little hair left on his wrinkled head. Two fingers were missing on his right hand from some old injury, and his left leg was stiff. 'I tell them that it is folly, but the young do not understand and they listen too well to the promise of a great magic. A king and a queen's blood will summon the strength of the gods and an army from the Otherworld to fight alongside them. It will happen at Samhain, so he says, and many believe him.'

Ferox felt a chill as he heard the man's assurance. The festival began at sunset in three days' time. As they ate he drew Vindex aside. 'If the tribune lets me, I want to do something very foolish.'

The Brigantian grinned, the lines of his face even harsher than usual in the glow of the fires. 'So naturally you thought of me,' he said. 'Lovely.'

'I will not command you to go.'

'Wouldn't take a command anyway. I am of the Carvetii. But I'll come as a friend, if you need me.'

'We're not friends,' Ferox began, and then found that he was laughing.

Crispinus was not keen when he heard that the centurion wanted to leave them and ride hard to get to Vindolanda.

'I can travel much faster if I leave the main tracks and go as straight as I can. They need to be warned,' Ferox insisted. 'Your letter may not be enough.'

'Letter?' The tribune looked puzzled and then seemed to remember. 'Of course, I had quite forgotten. It should have got there, though.' He began to waver.

'You do not need me, my lord, and if I can get there in time I might make a difference.' He lowered his voice to a whisper. 'Do you want to see her hanging from a yew tree like those merchants, or burned like this mutton?'

Crispinus stared in sudden distaste at the meat. 'Very well, centurion.'

They set out an hour later, as the camp began to settle down for the night, and they took Snow and Frost with them as spare mounts. They were close enough to the lands they knew well to find their way without much difficulty and when a waning moon rose the country was easy to see in its silver light. They rode for three hours, changed horses, and then rode for another three before they rested and ate a little food. As a red sun started to rise they set out again.

At first they rode through country dotted with farms, and everywhere there was the smell of blood and fire as flocks and herds were culled to provide meat for the winter. It was the smell of Samhain, the beginning of the lean and cold months, and for the first time Ferox found it to be sinister. People were nervous, and whenever they stopped they spoke of the older boys and younger men leaving to join the great war. They saw plenty of them striding away, heading in the direction of rimontium.

'Hope the tribune gets through,' Ferox said.

Vindex snorted. 'Yes, there's only fifty or sixty of them.'

'You did not have to come.'

'You did not have to ask me.'

Late in the day they realised that they were being followed. There was a lone rider on a shaggy pony, tailing them about half a mile behind. He was bareheaded and wore a drab cloak, but did not come close enough to be seen properly. They changed horses and cantered, flying over the spongy turf, and their lead grew.

'He might just have been going our way,' Vindex suggested when they slowed. Frost and Snow were panting, a foam of sweat making them look even whiter than usual.

'He might.'

An hour before sunset five horsemen appeared on the crest of a hill ahead of them and to the right.

'Must have had friends,' Vindex said. Their mounts were too tired to try to outrun them, so they veered a little to the left and pressed on. The riders kept their distance, watching them.

'Waiting for darkness,' the Brigantian suggested.

'That is what I would do.'

It was another clear night, frost adding to the silver light of star and moon. They lit a fire, and tethered the horses to some low birch trees. For a while they talked, knowing that the sound would carry a long way. There was not a farm or village in sight, for this was one of the barren patches used mainly as summer pasture and it was not where anyone chose to live.

As Vindex moved around and stood warming his hands on the fire, Ferox slipped away into the night. He left his mail behind, but kept sword and dagger because he was sure that there was killing to be done. With his face smeared with mud and the heavy hooded cloak around him, he should not be easy to see even on so bright a night. He went away from the camp for some distance, before looping around. They had chosen a site overlooked by a craggy hill because he reckoned that no attacker would ignore such a well-sheltered approach. Slowly and carefully, stopping again and again to lie still, watch and listen, he made his way to a steep-banked little gully on the far side of the hill. At the bottom was a brook, bloated with rain and running along noisily. All the while he could hear Vindex humming. 'I see a sweet country; I'll rest my weapon there.' The tune had become a great favourite with the Brigantian.

Ferox waited. The song made him think of Sulpicia Lepidina, and of Galla lying beside him. Such thoughts helped to keep away the cold, but he could not let them distract him or make him drop his guard. The moon rose and the stars turned as the hours passed, and it was not until sometime in what must have been the third watch that he heard a low scraping sound. He waited, eyes just above the lip of the gully, head covered by the dark hood. There were shapes moving up the slope of the hill. Three shapes, crawling slowly and with care. The leader stopped and hissed something back at the men behind. One shifted, sitting up, and Ferox guessed that he was adjusting the scabbard, which had scraped on the ground.

Three men meant that there were two more out there somewhere, but he could not see them and had to trust that Vindex could cope if they attacked from another direction. Ferox ducked back into the gully and edged his way along it, trusting to the chuckling of the water to mask any sounds he made. After a while he stopped, but could hear nothing apart from the brook, so peered over the bank. He was level with the hillock and could see Vindex sitting next to the fire, humming to himself. The horses shuffled and shifted in the way resting horses always did, and he could just make out the saddles wrapped in blankets that were supposed to imitate his own sleeping form.

One of the men was lying on the crest of the rise, while the other two crept around the side. These men were far more skilful than the ones he had met outside the camp weeks ago. Yet they were not Silures. The two men crawled along next to each other, making a larger, darker shape on the grass than if they had spread out. Metal glinted in their hands, which meant that they were carrying weapons, probably knives. Vindex sat still, now and then stirring up the fire. It must have taken a lot of willpower for him not to turn and notice the men creeping towards him.

Something moved, far beyond the camp, and Ferox saw the taller outline of horsemen, walking slowly forward. There were two long spears in their hands, their sharp points gleaming. Vindex pretended not to see and started to sing in a low voice. He did not have a good voice, and the sound was harsh and discordant. Ferox heard one of the crawling men snigger. They were level with him now, little more than twenty paces from the little camp, and he began to ease over the lip of the gully.

The attack came sooner than he expected. Up on the hillock the warrior rose into a crouch, swinging his arm around above his head. Something cracked as it hit the fire, sending up a shower of sparks. The horsemen surged forward, letting out high-pitched screams as they charged. Vindex sprang to his feet, raising the spear that had lain beside him. To his flank the crawling men pushed up and ran at him.

Ferox copied them, unclasping his cloak and letting it fall. He made no sound, and as he ran drew his pugio in his left hand and his gladius in his right. Only when the nearest warrior saw him did he start to yell. The man turned, dagger raised, and Ferox let him block a slash from the gladius, catching it on the blade of his knife, so that he could thrust his left hand into the warrior's throat. The stubby army-issue pugio punched through his windpipe and into his spine. Blood jetted over Ferox, the liquid warm on his hand, and he let the knife go and went for the next man.

In the firelight Vindex stood, spear raised and poised to throw. He waited and waited, until Ferox feared that it was too late, and then flung it at the nearest horseman. There was a grunt as it hit the rider full in the chest and pitched him out of the saddle. Then something whipped through the fire and the Brigantian cried out, clutching his leg, and was not ready when the second rider spurred at him, jabbing down with his spear. Vindex fell as the warrior's horse carried him past.

The man facing Ferox threw his knife at the centurion's face and he only just had time to swat it away with his gladius. The man drew his own sword, a long slim blade, and stamped forward, thrusting it out. Ferox jumped back because there was no time to parry, then had to go back again because the man followed, lunging.

Vindex was struggling to get up, drawing his own sword, while the horseman reined in hard to stop his mount, and then tugged to turn back and attack the Brigantian again. Another rider appeared, coming from the same direction as the others, galloping straight towards the camp, and it was all going badly wrong.

Ferox feinted a cut at the man's head and kicked him on the shin. The man gasped in surprise as much as pain, so the centurion jabbed the dome-shaped pommel at his face, just as he had hit Venutius, hitting him squarely on the forehead, where there was a dark mark that was surely a tattoo. The warrior was reeling, and Ferox slashed at his neck, felt the steel edge bite, wrenched it free and slashed again with all his strength. More blood sprayed across his face.

The Brigantian faced two horsemen and did not know which way to turn. Ferox saw him hesitate, and then raise his sword at the newcomer, who was already close.

'Get down you fool!' someone shouted in Latin and Vindex dropped to the ground. The rider went past, ignoring him, and then neatly chopped the other warrior from his horse. Momentum carried him past until he turned, heading towards the hillock. The man at the crest flung another stone from his sling, but missed, and then made the mistake of running. Ferox heard the horse's hoofs pounding across the turf, and saw the animal bound up the slope before he and the rider vanished after the fleeing man.

The centurion ran over to Vindex, who was pushing himself up and feeling his leg.

'Don't think it's broken,' he said. Ferox could see a gash along the scout's arm near his shoulder, but his mail had taken the force of the blow above that. 'It's nothing.' Vindex took a deep breath. 'At least we're alive.'

'So far,' Ferox replied, and then came a long scream of bubbling agony.

'We're better off than him, any road.'

The centurion began to bind up Vindex's arm.

'You in the camp.' It was the same voice in its accented Latin. 'I'm coming in.'

XXII

E WALKED TOWARDS them, leading his horse by the reins, his other hand empty and held up to show that he was unarmed. 'I want to talk,' he said, stopping five paces out from the fire. His cloak was back to show a cuirass of scale armour, the gladius at his right hip, with army-issue belt, tunic, breeches and boots. He was bareheaded and his dark hair was shaggy, his beard thick. 'I am a soldier of the First Cohort of Tungrians and I want to talk to the regionarius. Will you hear me out?'

'I'm Ferox. Come in and talk. I don't think there are any more of them about.'

'I killed the last one.' The soldier's tone was matter-of-fact. 'But I'll stay here until I am sure. My name is Gannallius. Some say I am a deserter and some say worse. I am neither.'

It was the missing man from the tower, the Trinovantian. Titus Annius had said that he was a steady man and had not believed the accusations.

'Tell me what happened. Stay there if you want, but I promise that if you come over to the fire you will be free to go unhindered if that is what you want.'

Gannallius tethered his horse next to the others and came over to sit by the fire. Vindex offered him some of their food.

'Never thought that I would get to miss army biscuits,' Gannallius said as he broke a piece off and swallowed it. 'I have not had much to eat for days.'

Close up they could see that he was dirty and his face – or what little could be seen behind his beard – looked thin and drawn.

'I am true to my oath,' he told them, eyes earnest as they stared at each man in turn, but especially at the centurion.

'Then tell me what happened.'

Gannallius hesitated.

'You were not there when the attack came, were you?' Ferox was guessing, for the tracks he had found were muddied and unclear, but the more he had thought about it the more likely it seemed.

The auxiliary started in surprise, but then his shoulder sagged and he shook his head. 'There is a girl at one of the farms a couple of miles away.'

'Big lass,' Vindex put in. 'Lot of tawny hair. I know her.'

'We were friendly,' Gannallius said.

Ferox ignored the Brigantian's dirty laugh. If the soldier had left his post without permission then he had broken regulations and earned punishment.

'I never went when I was on duty,' Gannullius said quickly, as if reading his thoughts. 'Never missed a watch or a fatigue. The others did not mind.' He stared into the fire, and Ferox guessed he was thinking of his dead comrades. 'I came back that morning in plenty of time to take my watch.'

'Bet you were yawning, though, and hadn't had a lot of sleep,' Vindex said.

Ferox waved a hand for the Brigantian to keep quiet. 'Go on, lad.'

'I saw the patrol come,' Gannullius continued. 'They didn't see me and I ducked down because I didn't want to be seen off the post. Didn't want to answer questions.'

'Was it the usual patrol?'

'No. They were early, and not anyone we had seen before. Strangest of all there was an officer with them. Just seven troopers and at their head this fellow with a great plumed helmet. You don't expect that.'

'Had you seen him before?'

'No, never, but I've been at the garrison or at an outpost for the last few years. Haven't really seen anyone high up. Another odd thing – they were legionaries. Not what you'd expect to see at all, and the fancy buggers were riding along with their shields uncovered.'

'Did you see the symbol?'

'Clear as day. They were Second Augusta – the Capricorns. Rode up as calm and casual as you like. Got down, returned the salutes as the lads were frantically trying to get dressed and put on a proper show. We weren't due for inspection for another week – at least that's what the detail we took over from had said. So they go in, and suddenly there's screaming. One of our lads – Julianus his name was, a great snoring brute from Pannonia, but a good comrade – dashes out of the door and the officer himself hacks him down from behind. It all happened so quickly. There was nothing I could have done,' Gannullius implored the centurion to believe him. 'Nothing. If I'd come out I'd only have died with them, but to be honest I couldn't have moved if I'd wanted to. It didn't seem real. They were our men – legionaries, it's true, but soldiers just like us. I couldn't understand. I still don't understand.' He stared at the fire for a long time, and Ferox waited.

'It was all over so quickly. Then I heard them shouting out a count. Must have been of the men in the tower and they knew that they were one short, and one of them starts walking up past the beacon towards me. He couldn't have seen me, but the bushes there were the obvious place to look. That's if he was looking. Maybe he just wanted a quick slash. But anyway he comes up the slope and I'm about to stand up and draw my sword when the officer calls him back. "Yes, my lord tribune," he says, and turns right around. They rode off soon afterwards, but not towards the road, which I thought was odd.

'Now I know I shouldn't have been away from the post. I'm guilty of that, I'll admit. But they were my *commilitones*, my mates, and I wouldn't have turned on them for the whole world. And I would never break my oath either.'

'Then why did you vanish?' Ferox asked.

'I was scared. Scared they might come back and finish the job, scared that no one would believe me and that I'd be condemned before I could say a word. I ran, just ran, and kept on running. Hid in the farm for a week. My girl, she said that I should go to you, that you were a good man and fair, said you'd helped her Da when someone stole a couple of his pigs.'

Ferox nodded. He had a vague memory of the incident, but dealt with so many cases that most did not stick out in his memory.

'I was too frightened, and it got worse as the rumours spread of druids and holy war. I thought they'd mark me down as a fanatic who had just become a barbarian again and turned on his friends like a wild beast. Truth be told, I thought that it was all over and that now I was over the rampart through no choice of my own, then I'd better stay there. If the lass would have come with me I'd have gone north as far as I could go, but she wouldn't, and in the end I decided to go to you at the burgus, but by this time you'd gone up to the Vacomagi, so I followed. Got myself a pony, but didn't find you until you were on the way back, and then didn't fancy riding up to a turma of Batavians and handing myself in. Heard that there was some fine officer in charge and I got scared that he was the one at the tower and, even if he wasn't, knew he would never take my word over one of his own class. So I followed, and you split off. You gave me the slip earlier, but I stumbled on these five and followed them. Reckon they're Selgovae – coming from their lands anyway.'

Ferox tried to work out whether Venutius could have ridden off and reached his own people in time to send them, but decided that it was unlikely.

'There's little groups of men wandering everywhere at the moment, loads of them,' Gannullius went on. 'Men are daubing the horse on their heads and going to war.'

'Can you describe the tribune at the tower?' Ferox asked.

'Not well, sir, I'm afraid. I wasn't close.'

'What can you tell me? It's important.'

'He wasn't a big man. Quite dark.' The soldier thought for a while. 'Carried himself as if he owned the world,' he added. 'Mind you, a lot do that, but there was something different about this one. Didn't waste any effort, even when he killed old Julianus.'

'Would you recognise him if you saw him again?'

'I think so, sir. Yes, I am sure of it, though I'm in no hurry to meet the bastard again, begging your pardon. You do believe me, sir, don't you? Every word I've said is the truth. Haven't hidden a thing.'

'I know.' Ferox hoped his smile was reassuring. 'I believe you.'

Gannullius' relief was obvious. 'Lass said you would. I should have listened sooner.'

'I believe you,' the centurion told him, 'but you know as well as I do that there are plenty who will not.'

The soldier's shoulders slumped and he stared into the fire, eyes glassy. Perhaps he was imagining the likely punishment, stripped naked and clubbed to death by his former comrades, his disgrace permanently recorded on the cohort's books.

'I will vouch for you, and I'll say how you saved us tonight. That will count for something.'

'I'll come back with you, if you want me to, sir,' the man said, voice glum. 'I took the oath seven years ago. Don't really know anything else anymore.'

'There might be a better way,' Ferox said, and saw hope in the soldier's face. 'Will your girl and her family still shelter you?'

The man nodded. 'Think so. I help out, you see.'

For once Vindex did not snigger.

'Come south with us for the moment, but then go and hide with these folk. Find me at the burgus in ten days. By then, I may have been able to sort things out. I shall do my best, at the very least.'

'Thank you, sir. I am grateful.'

'Grateful enough to stand guard for a couple of hours?' Vindex's eyes widened at this display of trust, but the Brigantian said nothing.

'Of course, sir. Happy to do it.'

'Good.'

They saw no one for most of the next morning, and then only a few groups in the far distance. It might have been a flock of sheep, but they moved with more purpose than that and Ferox was sure that it was a group of warriors. A little later they saw the ravens and other carrion fowl circling up ahead. They were nearing a trackway that could not be described as a road, but was a fairly clear route running east to west and was used by a lot of people, including the army.

The first body was stripped naked, the skin very pale except on the lower legs, arms and neck where the sun had caught it. Its head had been taken, but the man had a Roman eagle and the letters SPQR tattooed on his chest. Gannullius sighed, for it was obvious that the man was a soldier. There was a big wound in his back and at least he had died quickly. There were two more dead soldiers a little further along, their severed heads impaled on stakes next to the naked bodies. Their hands were bound behind their backs, there were scars on their arms and legs, pieces of flesh cut away as if by a butcher, and it was obvious that they had suffered a lot before they were killed.

'Bastards.' Gannullius spat the word, and spurred his horse over the low rise to reach the track itself. There were a dozen more bodies around a couple of carts. Two men had been tied to the wheels, spreadeagled and then carved up by their captors. They must have worked slowly, peeling off strip after strip of skin and flesh. Another man lay in the bed of the other wagon, and the priest's men had set it on fire and let him burn. The fire had been a big one, and there was a lot of newly cut timber strewn around the site of the massacre.

'Wood-gathering party,' Ferox said. 'It's that time of year.' Garrisons always needed wood, for building work but most of all for fires, whether to cook food or just keep warm.

A scream split the silence, startling the carrion birds from their meals. Three warriors charged down from the far bank at them.

Gannullius reacted first, slamming his heels into the sides of his tired pony and galloping straight at them. 'Bastards!' he screamed.

One of the warriors brandished an army-issue pickaxe as a weapon and was ahead of the others. Gannullius reached him, slashed low and across with the force of rage, and the man dropped, head cut off at the neck and flying through the air so that it struck the chest of the auxiliary's pony. It reared in terror, pulling away, and the other two warriors were on each side as the soldier fought for balance. One thrust a spear hard into his stomach, breaking through where four scales joined. Gannullius cried out in pain, but cut down, his gladius driving through the man's skull.

Ferox reached them just as the last warrior hacked at the soldier, nearly severing his left arm. The pony bit the man, ripping off his nose and part of his face, and bucked, throwing its wounded rider. It bounded away, knocking the man aside, so that Ferox's thrust missed and the centurion was carried past. Vindex finished the job, cutting down twice at the man's neck.

Gannullius was coughing up blood, gasping for breath as he lay on the grass. The spear point had broken off and was still deep in his belly. The man tried to speak, but Ferox could not make out any words, and then there was more blood pouring from his mouth and the eyes went dead as his soul left the body.

'Poor sod,' Vindex said and he sounded sad. 'I liked him, even if he was a southerner. What now? He was supposed to tell everyone the truth.'

'Same as before. We get to Vindolanda and hope we are in time.' Ferox sighed. 'I doubt they would have believed him – at least not at first. If I cannot persuade them then...' He trailed off. 'The only thing now is to get back to the garrison.'

'Then what?'

'How should I know?' Ferox tried to hide his bitterness. 'If we keep our heads above water maybe we can swim to shore or last a little longer before we drown.'

'Lost me there.'

'It's a saying among the Silures.'

'Cheerful lot, aren't you?'

Ferox swung back up into the saddle. 'What is there to be cheerful about?' he said, and set Frost off at a canter.

XXIII

T HE BATAVIANS DID not know Samhain, but they had
their own festival to herald the approaching winter. It
began earlier, at dawn instead of sunset, and the rites
continued after the sun went down so that for one night the
two festivals overlapped. Ferox and Vindex saw the glow of the
bonfires off the low clouds long before they could see the fort.
In the settlement outside, several locals gathered to sacrifice
a bull in the traditional way. The centurion saw one man had
even found a flint knife and watched as he delivered the first
cut to the animal's throat. Other people watched – Romans,
Spaniards, Pannonians, and the gods only knew how many
other races – curious enough come out and see the rituals and
sensible enough to feel that even witnessing them might bring
good fortune.

Inside the fort, the Batavians took over. Ferox saw one of
the Tungrians he had fought alongside in charge of the guard
at the porta praetoria. The man saluted and then offered an
acknowledging nod.

'Any trouble?' Ferox asked him, raising his voice to be heard
over the chants and shouts. 'Anything odd?'

The auxiliary shook his head. 'Just this lot trying to deafen
the gods!' He jerked his thumb at a Batavian, his fur-covered
helmet tipped low over his forehead as he leaned against the
corner post of the tower's lower platform. The sentry did not
move and although there was a glint from his open eyes it was

clear that he could see and hear very little. On any other day he would have earned a flogging for being incapably drunk on guard, but this was not any other day or night.

'If the enemy comes he'll just have to puke over them,' the Tungrian said. Vindex laughed, and then followed the centurion as he kicked his weary horse under the gate.

Fires were lit in two rows behind the western rampart of the fort, spaced out every six feet as the length of a man and left with just enough gap between for someone to run with care. If a man could race from one end of the course to the other in bare feet then it was thought lucky, and a good omen for all. If someone scorched himself in the attempt then that was not the end of the world, for it gave onlookers plenty to laugh at. Like most of the celebrations held by cohors VIIII Batavorum, it grew more festive with every mug of beer. Every man not on duty ran or watched and shouted, and tradition in this and every other unit of Batavians meant that very few soldiers were on duty – and even fewer in a fit state to perform their allotted tasks.

Frost shied and reared, nostrils flaring and teeth bared as a runner stumbled and fell into one of the fires, throwing up a fountain of sparks, and it took force to calm her as the soldier rolled away from the flames. Comrades rushed to throw a blanket over him and staunch the flames from his burning tunic, but they were laughing too much to do a good job. The man kept rolling until the fire went out and his tunic was in rags. His friends doubled over, unable to speak, while the scorched man started to sing tunelessly as he lay on the ground.

'Wonder he didn't go up like a barrel of oil with all that he's drunk,' Vindex said, but the centurion was not listening and instead drove the grey to jump across the line of fires, making the flames surge and wave as she passed.

'Oh bugger,' the Brigantian muttered, and let go of the horses he was leading so that he could use both hands to force his own mount over the fires. 'Oh bugger, oh bugger, oh bugger!' he yelled as the beast fought him and then finally bounded awkwardly across, throwing him out of the saddle before he slammed back down hard and just managed to regain his seat.

Ferox was looking for an officer, or anyone else who looked sober and responsible. He could not see one, apart from a centurion who was being carried along in a blanket by four soldiers. The little procession lurched this way and that, but if the men were barely sober it was obvious that nothing could be hoped for from the centurion for many hours.

Some children, the oldest a girl of no more than seven or eight, came over to stare at the two riders.

'Have you seen the prefect, little lady?' Vindex asked in Latin and then in his own tongue. The children just watched them until the Brigantian stuck his tongue out and a little boy giggled. The child cupped his hand around his mouth and did the same thing back at the tall, fierce-looking scout, until the girl cuffed him and started to chivvy them all away. Vindex chuckled and then realised that the centurion had galloped off again. Along the roadside were groups of soldiers preparing big effigies that they would carry in a procession out of the fort. They were made from timber, straw, wickerwork, cloth and anything else ingenuity could devise, and most were shaped like cows or deer. There were also a few shaped like people, two or three times life size, including one in armour, with a high plumed helmet and bright red hair, riding a mule deliberately made to look small and ugly. The whole thing was mounted on a cart with a dozen soldiers waiting to haul it along. Vindex grinned because it was obviously meant to be Cerialis, and he saw the centurion shout something to the men before spurring away when they just pointed at the effigy.

Ferox pounded along the via principalis, the horse's tread flinging up water and mud because this was Vindolanda and the ground was always wet. He swerved to the right when he reached the junction with the other road, ignoring the principia and riding straight up to the commander's house. He sprang down and ran to the main door. It was locked and he pounded on the heavy oak.

'Open up!' he bellowed. 'It's urgent! I need to see the master and mistress now!' There was no reply, although since the sound of the festivities rumbled on behind him he could not be sure whether or not anyone responded. It was almost the third watch of the night, so late without being so very late, and he could see light from behind some of the shutters on the upstairs rooms. It was hard to believe that the household was asleep. Who could sleep with all this going on around them?

Ferox pounded on the door, using his clenched fists like hammers. 'Open up!'

Vindex went past him along the side of the house to the alleyway and the entrance to the servants' quarters and working area of the praetorium. The door hung open, leaning at an angle because the top hinge had been ripped out of place.

'Here!' he screamed at the centurion. 'This way.' The Brigantian swung out of the saddle, wincing because his feet were cold and numb after so many hours riding and that made the ground feel harder than usual. He went to the door, one hand on the hilt of his sword, and waited to listen. He could hear nothing apart from the shouts, and started in shock when there was a great raucous blare of trumpets and horns. Someone began to beat on what sounded like drums made from tree trunks, a deep sound, pounding on and on. Before the Brigantian could lean around to look inside Ferox pushed past him, sword drawn and his face so full of cold fury than the scout hesitated before he followed.

The drums throbbed in their ears. The corridor was long, with doors opening off on either side. One was open a little, light spilling from it, and Ferox pulled off his cloak and wrapped it around his left arm to use as a primitive shield. His sword was up, ready to thrust, but he was fighting the despair that told him he had failed, and that brought an urge to charge ahead and hack into pieces anyone he met. He tried to breathe and to think, but it was hard. They had failed, the drums went on with the same relentless rhythm, and then he smelled the blood and the rage took over. He kicked the door in and screamed as he burst into the room and the stench of blood and butchered meat was overwhelming.

There was blood everywhere, dark pools staining the earth floor where the liquid had gushed out so quickly that it could not all drain away at once. A man lay on his back, but little of the blood was his because he had died from a neat wound that had gone under his ribs and into his heart. Whoever had done it was well practised, but there was no hint of skill in the rest. Ferox guessed that there had been three dogs – three of the big hounds the prefect loved so much – but it was hard to tell, because whoever had come here had chopped them into so many fragments. There were heads, paws, limbs, cuts of bone and flesh from a butcher's shop strewn all over the room. Amid them were a few fragments of torn clothes, and no doubt the hounds had given a good account of themselves, but they had faced cruel men with sharp blades and the temper of madmen. It was almost like angry children tearing their toys apart.

Ferox's rage eased, and it helped that the drums stopped amid another blare of trumpets. He guessed that the corpse was a slave, taken by surprise, but the slaughter of the enraged dogs must have made a noise and he had to hope that they had warned the rest of the household.

Vindex looked into the room and whistled in dismay. He was fond of dogs. Ferox went past him, calm again, and gestured for the scout to follow. Most of the doors along the corridor were locked, and the few that were not opened on to rooms that held tidily stored sacks of grain, amphorae and barrels. When they turned the corner they came to the places where slaves and freedmen lived, and the floors were covered in a mat of heather and straw just like the barracks. There was another corpse, this one slashed across his stomach and then cut several times on the head. There were scratches in the white plaster on the wall beside the dead slave.

Further along was the underside of wooden stairs leading to the upper storey, and Ferox sensed that this was the way the attackers had gone because the heather around them looked scuffed up by running feet. Someone had also gone further along the corridor and that made him wonder whether he should follow them or even whether he and the Brigantian should split up. Then he remembered Sulpicia Lepidina saying how much she preferred the upper rooms for their sense of space. She would be there and so would the children, and whatever had happened he must see because it was his fault for failing them and not returning in time.

The centurion stepped quickly past the foot of the stairs and turned, so that he faced up the stairs, left arm ready to ward off a blow, but there was no one waiting at the top. He started to climb, each creak as he placed his weight on the next step sounding as loud as a slammed door. He wondered if someone was waiting, arm poised to throw a spear as soon as he appeared up the stairs. He wished that he had put on his helmet rather than kept on the felt hat as its broad brim made it harder to see up to the side where the ceiling opened to lead on to the upper floor.

Ferox took another step and the drums were pounding again unless that was just the beat of his own heart. For the first time the next step made no noise when he put his weight on it. He could not see anyone's feet along the edge of the floor to the side of the stairs, but then the obvious place to wait was behind him. That was where he would be and it would be so easy to kill anyone climbing the stairs before he had any chance to fight back.

The centurion was nearly at the top and he flicked his head around and saw a pair of eyes gleaming, and then there was a yowl and something leaped past him, soft fur brushing his face. It shot off down the stairs and was followed by a second cat. He breathed out for otherwise the corridor was empty. There was light from around the corner ahead of him and so he went that way, beckoning Vindex to follow. The drums kept throbbing and every now and again the trumpets blared and men cheered and yelled. He edged towards the corner, the plank floor squeaking only a little less than the stairs.

Ferox swung with his left arm as he turned the corner and saw the glint of the blade. He pushed the thrust aside, felt his cloak being sliced, and the man was roaring at him in anger, a tall man, with a lined face and grey beard and flecks of blood on his cheek. Ferox managed to get his balance back and was about to stab at the man's face when he saw it break into a smile. 'You,' he said.

'Centurion.' Longinus raised his left hand in salute and then winced, clapping it back against his side. Ferox saw that there was a long rent in his mail shirt and that the fingers were covered in blood. 'I'm getting too old,' the one-eyed veteran said and leaned against the wall, the plaster brightly painted because this was the area where the family lived.

'Them two won't get any older.' Vindex had come around and gestured at the two corpses stretched out on the floor. They were both in army uniform, one in scale and the other in mail armour, although their heads were bare.

'Reckon they're legionaries,' Longinus said, 'or at least dressed up to look that way. That one's got the Capricorn on his brooch.'

'Where are the Lady Sulpicia and the family?'

Longinus grinned and obviously regretted it because it brought a spasm of pain. 'Safe,' he said. 'Leastways as far as I know. I've got the rest of the household in there, all locked up from the inside. The youngsters are in the principia playing hide and seek with a couple of good lads to keep 'em safe. The prefect is outside somewhere, that's his job tonight, and there's a few more men that I trust with him all the time. Hard to do much in the open with so many people about. The lads may be drunk, but they can still fight.'

'The lady?'

Longinus gave him a strange look. 'Safe. Safest place I could think of.'

'Any more of them around?' Vindex asked.

'Must be some. I heard the dogs, saw the door forced and came in here. Fortunately I found this room before they did and Privatus recognised my name. Good lad, that one – he'd done what he was told and got all but one or two somewhere safe. Then this pair appeared and I was busy for a bit. There was a third, but then someone shouted from down below and he ran off. Heard a scream, so I reckon one of the slaves had the bad luck to get in their way, but they all left. Thought that I'd better wait here just in case. Don't feel much like running, truth be told.' The old soldier slid down to sit with his back against the wall.

Vindex leaned down to help.

'I've had worse,' Longinus said. 'And I'm still here, although whether that's a blessing or a curse who can say.' He laughed until he started to cough and the motion must have brought more pain because he hissed and went still. '*Omnes ad stercus.*'

'How did you know?' Ferox asked.

'The letter from Crispinus. Himself didn't pay much heed, but she told me and so I did my best to protect them. Owe him that much, even if his father was such a bastard.' With an effort he stopped himself from laughing. 'We're Batavians. If we don't look after each other then who will? And she's special, and I knew her grandfather and owed him, so that was that. Whoever they wanted, they were going to find me.'

'You are him, aren't you?' Ferox said, wondering why he had taken so long to realise. 'There were always stories that he survived, was hiding in the army somewhere.'

'Everyone's someone.' The single eye watched him closely. 'Even you. Does it matter what we were?'

Someone shouted from inside the room asking what was going on, but Ferox ignored them. What did it matter? If Julius Civilis, former prefect, former equestrian, and former leader of the Batavian revolt, was now Longinus, a simple cavalryman here in the cohort at Vindolanda, then what did it matter?

'Not a damned thing,' he said, and then a thought struck him. 'I have heard that Civilis was of royal blood.'

'Worked it out, have you?' He pointed at one of the corpses. 'A couple of them came for me earlier on. Almost offended it was only two, but then I'm an old man, aren't I? They won't give any more trouble, but it slowed me down and let that one scratch me.'

'If this is a scratch, Father,' Vindex chipped in, 'then I'd hate to see what you call a real cut.'

'Why didn't you keep some men with you?'

'Not many I can trust to stay sober enough and to stick with their duty tonight. They were all needed elsewhere.'

'Where is she?'

'Flora's. She'll be safe there if she can be anywhere.'

Ferox laughed and could not stop, and soon he was leaning against the wall to keep himself up.

'Glad you are having fun,' Vindex told him.

At long last the centurion recovered. 'Look after him,' he said to the Brigantian. 'And get the alarm raised in case we can still catch them.'

The old man looked scornful and Ferox was sure that he was right, but the effort had to be made.

'I'm going to make sure that the prefect and his wife are safe.'

'Yes, both of them, of course,' Longinus said.

Frost was still outside, and Ferox hauled himself on to the back of the grey mare and was not gentle as he made her run again. For a moment she fought him, but then she jerked into an ugly canter which soon became smoother. He followed the road, soon catching up with the tail of the procession of effigies and men snarled at him when he went past and forced his way through them to go under the gate. He did not stop. The air was full of smoke and the smell of burning meat, but he ignored it and rode hard for the edge of the canabae, forcing people to jump out of his way. More shouts and curses followed him.

Only once did he slow, when he saw an old man with long white hair and hunched back coming from one of the alleys between the houses. He wrenched on the rains to turn the mare, but then the beggar looked up and he was a fatter, smaller man with a face scarred all across one side by burning. It was not Acco or the great druid or whatever the man called himself, and he did not spare him any more thought as the old beggar went and looked at one of the straw figures, this one of a great cow, tipped on its side and left by the side of the track.

He went on to the big stone house beyond the settlement. There were more guards than usual at the door, and to his surprise he heard Flora as he approached. 'Let him in.'

She looked grave, but showed him through the hallways. 'Not much business tonight,' she said, 'for Batavians hold it unlucky on this night of the year. Risks demons or evil spirits entering their bodies.' The brothel owner stated this as a matter of fact, something she needed to know in her line of work, and did not pass comment. 'There's a couple of others upstairs, Tungrians, but no one downstairs.'

Ferox guessed that Flora was explaining that the heavy guard was there for another reason. She wanted him to know that she understood everything. In his experience she usually did, and so he walked down the corridor as she pointed him towards her bath.

'You look like you could use a clean too,' she said, feeling a bit of his sleeve and grimacing. 'Go on. It's all right.' She smiled, looking older than usual, and almost maternal in her fondness.

He began to sweat as soon as he stepped into the room, for even though the bath was not heated to a raging temperature there was steam in the air that for a moment masked the erotic paintings on the walls and ceiling. Ferox blinked, heard the gentle sound of water being stirred and then a voice that was softer still.

'This is a strange night.'

Sulpicia Lepidina, *clarissima femina*, daughter of a consul and wife of the garrison commander, was floating on her back, now and then using her arms to push herself through the water. Its surface flickered in the light of many lamps supported on pedestals or bronze holders fitted to the wall. Her skin was pale, her limbs long and slim and her only covering was a red band around her breasts and a matching covering for her loins, the triangular material tied up with a thong on each hip. Once, during the months he was in Rome, Ferox had gone with some others down to Neapolis and the sea, and had seen the women dressed in the same way at the beach. It still baffled him that the Romans had devised a way to cover a woman's modesty and yet somehow make her seem almost more naked than when she was naked.

'You look as if you need a bath,' she said, and there was no hint of reproof or hostility in her voice. He was already fumbling with the left shoulder fastening of his mail cuirass. 'Did I tell you my family have estates near Bergomum? The country folk there have been Roman for centuries, but part of their hearts remain Cenomani. They celebrate Samhain, and when we were little we used to sneak out and watch. One of my nurses told me of how on this one night the dead walk among us and all the power of life and the world cannot prevent them, or hold sway with its laws and rules.'

Sulpicia Lepidina turned over and swam to the far side of the bath. Her skin was smooth, utterly perfect and looked very pale. 'A night without rules and laws,' she said, sitting on the shelf that acted as a step, and stretching her long arms out along the lip of the bath. 'A night like no other.'

Ferox knew that one of the murals showed Pan charging out from some trees to chase naked nymphs and faced with such loveliness he felt as clumsy and ugly as the goat-legged and horned god. His armour seemed even more awkward than usual; his hands fumbled with the straps, but finally he dragged it off over his head and began to work on the quilted jacket underneath.

'Lady,' he said, for she had fallen silent and he felt that he ought to say something, but he struggled for words and it was a while before he tried again. 'Lady, I am glad to find you safe.'

'It seems that once again I owe you my thanks.' She did not smile, and he struggled to understand her mood. She had not fled, like the nymphs from Pan, or grown angry and chased him to his doom like Diana, but she still seemed a distant vision, almost as if she was a dream in his waking mind. His jerkin was off, and the tunic came away far more easily. He sat on one of the wooden stools beside the wall to remove his boots and socks. Sulpicia Lepidina watched him, eyes unblinking. 'I am grateful.'

'Longinus did more,' he said, emphasising the name.

'Ah, Longinus.' She gave the same weight to the word and smiled to show that she knew his secret. 'He is a remarkable man. All of the Batavians would willingly die for him – even my husband, I think, and he is not usually a man to sacrifice for others. He tells me it is a great compliment that I was told. The clearest sign that the cohort accepted me.' She sounded puzzled by this glimpse into a strange and foreign world. 'But in truth he knew my family, and there are favours and friendship from long ago.'

Ferox thought once again how often that was true, and prominent people knew each other or found mutual friends even in the far corners of the empire. He also thought that his feet were the foulest things he had ever seen and felt even more ashamed and unimportant. She was like a statue come to golden life, even if her fair hair looked dark and slick from the water.

He stood up, still with his trousers on.

'If you think you are bringing those filthy things in here then you are much mistaken, Flavius Ferox.' The mockery was gentle, even if the tone was firm. 'This is the best bath I have had since I arrived here, and since I cannot in decency visit a whorehouse I intend to make the most of it.'

'Shall I go?'

She tilted her head slightly to one side. 'Are you truly such a fool?'

He met her eyes, and began to undo his belt. 'I think I am dreaming a hopeless dream,' he said, 'and fear that any wrong step will make me wake.'

'I told you, this a night when laws and rules do not hold sway.' She pushed herself back into the main pool and swam towards him. Her eyes looked bright and he could not tell whether it was fear or excitement.

With his clothes gone he rushed forward and dived in, sending water flying and making her shriek.

'You are a barbarian, are you not,' she said, as her fingers brushed water from her eyes. 'But at least that should tell you that you are awake. The dream does not have to spoil.'

He came towards her, and it was difficult to swim because the pool was not really deep enough for him, but he did his best, toes now and then scraping the bottom. They floated, only a little apart.

'I wish I had had a chance to shave,' he said.

Lepidina frowned. 'And I wish that tonight would last, that I was not who I am and could act as I wished.' She reached out and ran her hand over his cheek, grimacing. 'It is rough, and I am not one of those women who take pleasure in roughness and vulgarity, but it does not matter now. I think you love me.'

The change of subject shocked him as much as the directness, and he sought refuge in well-tried jokes. 'I cannot help what you think.'

'I also think you are a better man than you pretend to be,' she began, 'and I—'

'This is not the time to talk,' he said, interrupting, and he went forward, sliding his arm around her waist, pulling her to him. They floundered, heads dipping almost under the water, until they came up again and he kissed her. Her legs folded around him, gripping him tight, and they lost balance again, but it did not matter for they had each other and all that mattered was to hold each other close.

Later, Flora herself guided them to her most opulent room. It was Samhain, the lady was safe from harm and the laws and rules did not apply.

XXIV

SULPICIA LEPIDINA LAY on one side, head on a cushion, watching him. 'The sun has risen.' Her voice was sad. 'I guess that is no longer Samhain and the world will soon return to how it was.'

Strictly speaking the festival lasted until dusk, so it was still Samhain, but the daylight hours were a time for placating spirits set loose the night before and persuading them to return to the Otherworld and not haunt the realm of the living. There were more fires and more sacrifices and dances, but these were less of a celebration and the mood was always different, little better than that among the hundreds of hung-over Batavians who began the task of clearing up the debris of their own revels.

Ferox reached out to touch her hair. For a moment her smile grew warm, although there was something brittle about her in the pale light that came into the room through the cracks in the high, shuttered window.

'I am glad to have a good memory,' she said. 'Its sweetness will carry me through the days to come.' The lady took his hand and kissed his fingers.

'I am glad that you are safe,' he said. 'Last night I was...' He struggled to finish, but then she leaned forward and he pulled her to him. They kissed for a while, until more might have happened if she had not pulled away.

'You are a good friend,' she said. 'Someone I can trust.'

'I have been from the start,' he said, wanting to believe her in

303

spite of his instincts that told him no fine lady would bother with a mere centurion unless she needed him for some dark purpose. 'If you just want a friend, you did not need all that business last night.'

She sat up, the covers slipping down so that she was naked to the waist. Her face was a mask except for the anger smouldering in her eyes.

'What do you really want from me, lady? I am a nobody, and you have thrown yourself at me from the start.'

'Bastard!' she hissed the word. 'I must be a fool to bother.'

'As a matter of fact you are. I'm really not worth it.'

The slap caught him by surprise. The lady swung her arm and hit him across the face with enough force to sting. 'Bastard!' she said again, but now her eyes were glassy, and Ferox still did not know what to think.

There was a knock on the door before it opened and Flora appeared with the news that a carriage and escort was on the way to collect the lady. She hurried Ferox out, and he knew that there was nothing to be said even though he wished that there were. They left Sulpicia Lepidina to get dressed – her maid had appeared and must have spent the night in the place. From the next room Ferox heard Flora telling the soldiers that the prefect's lady would be with them soon, and informing the decurion in charge that Flavius Ferox had stood guard all night outside the lady's room, so that it was just moments ago that she had sent him off to sleep. The lie added to the sense of unreality, and it was already feeling like a dream save for the lingering taste of her lips and the smell of her hair.

He stayed at Flora's for an hour, for the sake of form and to help the story the brothel owner had told. One of her girls was a good barber and she shaved him, and it was strange that having a pretty and flimsily clad young woman fussing over him brought only mild arousal. He had not felt like this for many years, and even though any love was hopeless, even dangerous, it was still as if life was breathed into him, and all his suspicion and doubt could not quite hold it back. There was happiness in the world, even for him and even here near the edge of the world. It might be fleeting, already past, and was probably taking him down a dangerous road, but he had the memory to cherish and warm him. Better yet a vague hope of contentment was welling up within him, and when he glanced at the copper mirrors covering all of one wall he saw that he was smiling.

Flora provided him with clean tunic, trousers and socks, so that he was more presentable when he went to the fort, heading for the principia. He forced his face into its usual impassive mask, but suspected that he walked with a jauntiness reflecting his mood. The sight of pale-faced and nauseous Batavians standing guard at the main gate added to his high spirits. He could guess how they felt, but sympathy struggled with amusement and lost. Others responded in the same way. A party of Tungrians marched out of the fort to go on patrol and the soldiers stamped louder than was necessary, while their commander yelled with all his might when he asked permission to leave the base.

'You're up then?' Vindex appeared as he approached the big archway leading into the principia. He looked the centurion up and down and burst out laughing.

'What?'

'Nothing.' The Brigantian fell silent apart from the occasional snigger, but then stopped and clapped his hands on the centurion's shoulders. 'It is good to see you again.'

'Huh.' It was not a question. Ferox did not want to talk, but the scout ignored his mood and began to tell him what had happened. Three slaves and a freedman found dead in the praetorium, along with a sentry at the western gate. Another soldier wounded, along with Longinus, who was coming along well.

'Tough old bugger, that one,' Vindex said, and then explained that everyone else was safe. 'The prefect's got a bruise the size of an apple on his cheek from when he fell. Longinus' men carried him to a barrack room and watched him all night.'

'Attacked?'

'No, beer.'

'A couple of slave girls are missing, but that lad Privatus reckons they'll have been out with soldiers during the night, so they're probably just drunk or bow-legged by now.'

A thought nagged him for a while, and it was only as they walked across the courtyard that he remembered Flora telling him that the Batavians abstained from women during their festival. Perhaps the women were just too drunk to return to the house.

Morning reports were a good deal more subdued than usual, with less stamping and shouting. Flavius Cerialis sat at the table, chin resting on his hands, and apart from the bruise on his face his skin had a greenish pallor and his eyes were glassy and red-rimmed. His servants had done their best to tidy him up, but there were stains on his boots and trousers. Ferox wondered whether they had brought the commander directly from the barrack block to the headquarters. Of all the men assembled for the parade he looked the one closest to death. Several of the ordinary soldiers were turned out as perfectly as on any other day, even though he was sure they had drunk as much as anyone else. He had known a fair few soldiers like that, who could spend all the night drinking, get no sleep, and yet still look ready to parade in front of the *princeps* himself. What was the old tag? 'Iron stomach, iron head, iron heart.' Ferox wanted to smile at the thought, and it took an effort to keep his face rigid.

The bad news came in gradually, and it was as if enemy soldiers were undermining the rampart of his good mood. An optio from the Tungrians came first, marching smartly and noisily into the hall and shouting out a request to deliver an important message. Cerialis winced as if the sky had fallen on his head. He struggled to speak, then satisfied himself with a beckoning wave that was meant to give permission.

'The centurion Pudens regrets to report that cohors I Tungrorum has a number of men missing.'

Cerialis gave a weak smile and coughed to clear his throat. 'I dare say there are fifty or sixty of my men unaccounted for at the moment.'

The optio did not smile. They had found two soldiers killed, the bodies dumped inside a workshop. Three soldiers were gone. 'We fear that they have gone over the wall.'

'Deserted?' Cerialis was brutal in his reply, not sparing the junior officer's shame. 'I suppose you know who they are.'

'Yes, my lord. All from the new draft that reached us back in the spring.' The optio spotted the questioning look. 'Yes, my lord, all three are Britons.'

Cerialis nodded. 'As before.'

'I fear so, my lord. And the sentry wounded at the gate says that they were attacked from behind. Some men in uniform approached them. They were not men he knew, but he did think one was from the cohort. Then half a dozen men in trousers and tunics sprang out from the shadows. He heard them speak and thought that they were Brigantes.' There was a murmur at that. 'Britons at the very least.'

'My lord! My lord!' The shout came from the courtyard. Other voices answered in anger, but the man persisted. 'My lord! I must speak with you.'

Cerialis gestured to one of the soldiers. 'Bring him in.'

It was Privatus, the head of his household, and for once he did not display his habitual calm assurance. He ran past the soldiers and crouched beside his master, whispering in his ear.

'She is not an early riser.' Cerialis frowned as he spoke. The chamberlain whispered again, and although he spoke louder and with more force Ferox could not catch the words.

'I did not see her last night,' the prefect said, his face scanning the men around him in case they could offer an explanation. 'She can drink a lot. Probably sleeping it off.'

'She has gone, master. The Lady Fortunata is nowhere to be found.' Privatus must have decided that he needed to speak out loud if the message was to get through. 'You should see the room. Her slave is dead.'

'We're humped,' Vindex muttered under his breath, but Ferox was more concerned when the prefect turned towards him.

'I would be glad of your company, centurion.'

Cerialis said little as they went to his house, and only once was there real emotion in his voice. 'Do you know they slaughtered three of my dogs? Chopped 'em up. Bastards.'

Privatus led them through the entrance to the left wing of the house, where the rooms were better decorated and furnished. The wife of Vegetus had been given a room on the ground floor, away from the family. Sulpicia Lepidina waited by the door, wearing a spotless dress in the pale blue she favoured. The corridor was in shadow for the sun had not yet risen high enough to reach into the courtyard alongside it, and yet she glowed. Long ago Ferox had served with another centurion who was devoted to Isis and the man had spoken of the goddess appearing in visions, a perfect statue of ivory and gold, and for the first time he understood something of the man's ecstatic description. Seeing such splendour was thrilling and terrifying at once. Mixing with gods rarely ended well for a mere mortal.

'My lord,' she said to her husband.

'My lady,' he replied, inclining his head. 'It is good to see you safe.' He pecked her on the cheek with no great suggestion of warmth.

Yet there was even less hint of real affection in her brisk and formal 'Good morning, my dear Ferox. I trust you are well.'

'My lady,' he replied. 'You are most kind.' He looked for some sign to show whether she now hated or trusted him, but there was none, only the noble Roman lady and dutiful wife walking beside her husband.

Cerialis hesitated in the doorway, breathed deeply, and then went in. Before Ferox could follow, Lepidina stepped after him.

'My lady,' he said, 'it is probably better if you remain outside.'

She turned, every inch the high and mighty aristocrat. 'Centurion, I am grateful for your concern for my welfare, but this is my house and I am not one of your soldiers to order as you please.'

Privatus was standing behind her and Ferox saw the

chamberlain give an approving nod. The freedman could not see his mistress wink. He hoped that it was a sign of forgiveness and the simple gesture brought memories of the night flooding over him again. Ferox could tell that all his natural suspicion and scepticism would not be enough whenever he was near this woman, for there was something overpowering about her. As he followed her through the door he looked down at her shoulders, the smooth white skin barely covered by her light dress, and he longed to pluck off the brooches holding it up and see it rustle to the floor. As if she could read his mind, the lady turned her head and gave him a cold stare.

The smell brought him fully back to grim reality. There was the usual odour of a bedchamber in the morning, before the slaves had come to empty the vase of night soil. It was the scent of the human body, tinged with sweat, and if this was fainter with a woman it was always there. The damp, musty smell so common at Vindolanda and especially on the ground floor of the praetorium lingered in the background, even when Privatus got a pole and opened the shutters on the high windows, so that bars of sunlight speared into the room.

Over it all was the smell of death: not the violent butcher's yard stink of the dismembered dogs, but a subtle, insidious cloud that seeped into the nostrils and throat. The girl lay on the bed, and now that the windows gave them more light Ferox could see that what he had taken to be a necklace was a deep cut around her throat. Someone had covered her up in blankets, so that it would look as if the guest was asleep in her bed.

'It is her maid,' Privatus told them. 'Her name was Artemis and she was a silly little thing, but worked hard and was faithful.'

Cerialis sighed. 'I'll organise a search. Ferox, would you mind taking a look and seeing if you can work out what happened?'

'Of course, sir.' One thing Ferox knew had happened was that he had failed. He had saved the golden woman in this room, but the price had been the death of this unfortunate slave girl and maybe her mistress as well.

'I shall stay and assist.' Cerialis looked surprised when his wife spoke. 'In case the centurion needs to ask about the household,' she explained.

The prefect stared at her for a while and Ferox could not read his thoughts. Then Cerialis gave a gentle nod. 'That is prudent.'

After he had gone Ferox went to the side of the big wooden bed with its high canopy.

'Ugly old thing,' Lepidina told him. 'It was left behind by the previous commander and his family – and no doubt by everyone else back to the fool who bought it.'

The girl was young, fourteen or fifteen at a guess, and she had an unremarkable face. Her hair was dark brown and a little thin, her staring eyes small and grey in colour. Drained of blood her skin was white, but her lips were dark and mottled and stains on the bed beside her showed that she had frothed at the mouth. Ferox leaned over and sniffed, and heard his boot crush something. It was a piece of mistletoe, and when he smelled it there was the trace of other things as well. He guessed that one was nightshade, and that meant they had forced poison into the poor child.

The centurion pulled back the covers, grimacing at the stink of excrement. The corpse was naked, save for a bracelet of cheap stones, and there was no other trace of injury. Someone had drugged her, placed her in the bed and then slit her throat. She had not been dead when it had happened, so the cut had bled freely and she had fouled herself.

Sulpicia Lepidina had covered her eyes with one hand and sounded as if she was praying.

'You should not be here, my lady,' Ferox said.

She looked up, stern and proud again. 'This is my house. I must know everything that happens here. Everything. Privatus?'

'Mistress.'

'Go and find out who saw the girl and our guest yesterday. We will need to see them.'

'Yes, mistress.' The chamberlain left, and Lepidina began to look at the clothes and boxes on a table in the corner of the room.

Ferox wondered whether to talk to her about what had happened, but he did not know the right words, so got on with the matter in hand.

He drew the blankets back over the dead girl and closed her eyes. It was the least he could do and did not make him feel any better. He tried to look for signs in the room. There were some scuffs on the floorboards that looked fresh, which suggested the hobnailed boots of soldiers, but that might mean no more than a recent visit by the prefect to his lover. Nearer the window the boards were wet from damp seeping up from the ground and there was a print or two, faint, but showing traces of at least two boots – one markedly smaller than the other.

'Look at this.' Sulpicia Lepidina was holding up a writing tablet. As Ferox took it he saw that her eyes were moist. She must have gripped it tightly because her thumbs had left deep smudges in the wax coating on the surface of the thin wooden sheet – made from silver ash by its feel and colour.

Vegetus, assistant slave of Montanus, the slave of the
August Emperor and sometime slave of Iucundus, has
bought and received by mancipium the girl Fortunata,
or by whatever name she is known, by nationality a
Diablintian, from Albicanus, for six hundred denarii. And
that the girl in question is transferred in good health, that
she is warranted not to be liable to wander or run away,
but that if anyone lays claim to the girl in question or to
any share in her...

He did not bother to read on. He had seen hundreds of similar documents, recording the sale and purchase of slaves. Somewhere there was surely another document announcing her manumission. Until now he had not thought of Vegetus, who had also made the jump from slave to free man.

'Do you think that she is dead?' The question was direct and he knew that the lady was not asking about the corpse in the bed.

'I cannot say. We may find her.'

'You can forget trust if you lie to me as plainly as that,' she said.

'There is not much hope,' he admitted. 'We might be able to catch them.'

'And I might one day forget that you are a pig as well as a good man.' She waved him down when he tried to speak. 'I did not like the woman. How could I? Husbands stray and that is the way of the world. I do not take it personally. How could I after last night?' There was a thin smile. 'Nor did she commend herself to me in any other way. Just a foolish little whore who flung herself at men – even you if I remember that dinner last month.'

That was a surprise, for he had not thought anyone had noticed.

'It does not matter.' Lepidina's voice was sad. 'She was a guest in my house and that does matter. Murderers came over my threshold and they killed this child and abducted her owner. Perhaps they have killed her too.'

She began to sob, shoulders quivering. Ferox glanced quickly at the door, was relieved to see that Privatus had closed it behind him and he went and clasped her to him. Her head was on his shoulder and he felt her body shaking. One hand clasped her and the other smoothed her hair.

'It was not your fault,' he said. 'Never your fault.'

Sulpicia Lepidina lifted her head and he kissed her on the cheek and soothed her. 'It's all right, it was not your fault,' he repeated over and over again. Ferox still could not tell just what this clever aristocrat wanted, or what she really thought of him, but she was in his arms and at that moment all he wanted was to comfort her and make her smile again. 'It was not your fault. I am to blame.'

She stared at him, puzzled and unconvinced.

'I should have thought more clearly. They were looking for you, and all I wished to do was save you. Your husband as well, for that is my duty, but I could not bear the thought of them taking you, of them...'

'My husband told me why you think they attacked me in my carriage,' she said. 'I assumed they just wanted my jewels – and

312

perhaps my aged body.' The tears had stopped, and she tried to laugh at her poor joke.

'Then you know the horror of it all,' Ferox said. 'I thought only of stopping them, and when we arrived last night and found the praetorium raided all that mattered was to see you safe. It was my only thought.'

Her smile was a little warmer this time. 'You had other thoughts once you found me.'

'Yes, and while we...' He trailed off for the guilt engulfed him. 'I should have gone back to the fort. Checked that all was well. Instead I did not and they got away.'

'How could you have known?' She reached up and stroked his cheek.

'It's my job to know, and my job to think. I am tasked with keeping the peace in this region and I have failed. Do you not understand?' He was surprised at how much this wounded him, striking at a pride he thought long gone.

She gave a slight shake of her head.

'They thought they had you. It is the only explanation. Here is a big room, with a rich woman in it. They were sent to snatch the prefect's wife and they found a lady in a big bed in his house. "Blood of king, blood of queen." Just because you were safe did not mean that there was no more danger.'

She pulled free, as if to think more clearly. 'There was no attack on my husband.'

'There was on Longinus.' It all seemed so simple. 'If they knew who he really is then that is their king's blood – though in truth he was too dangerous for them.' One thought followed another. 'The mongrel!' he said angrily. 'It was him.'

'I do not follow.'

'Longinus, or Civilis, or whoever the rogue is. He knew what was happening, got you to safety, protected the children and your husband, but sacrificed the others.'

'He is a fine man and we owe him much.'

Perhaps the lady had known what he was doing? The idea

313

certainly did not appear to disturb her. Ferox stared into her eyes, but could not read what was behind them.

'That fine man also staked out Fortunata as a decoy,' he said. 'Made sure Privatus forgot to take her to safety, knew your husband would be too careless and then too drunk to bother. He used her to save you.'

'It is all because of me.' The tears came again.

'No, for you. Perhaps I would have done the same if I had to make the choice,' he said in grudging admiration. 'It was not your fault or his fault, but mine, to be so besotted that I failed everyone last night.'

A knock on the door ended the conversation. They spoke to the slaves, but learned little more and Ferox remained convinced that he was right. Prolonged searching discovered the remaining maid fast asleep and snoring in an empty box in one of the stables. There was no trace of Fortunata.

'How could they have got her out past the guards?' Cerialis asked of no one in particular.

'Easier last night than almost any other in the year,' Ferox said. 'No one saw a cart or anyone carrying something bulky in a sack, so my guess is that she was inside one of the straw figures.'

The prefect went even paler and sent men to look at the remains – before dawn all the effigies were burned as part of the ritual. He was relieved when the men returned to say that there was no sign of anyone hidden within the burned figures, but then another party arrived and said that they had found a big figure of a cow tipped on its side near the edge of the canabae. Ferox remembered it, which made him think that they had got away even earlier than he had guessed.

'I need to see if they left a trail,' he told them, but there were more delays before he set out with Vindex and half a dozen Batavian troopers who looked almost sober. They had to wait to leave the main gate as an officer and his escort clattered through into the fort. It was Flaccus and he gave a friendly wave as he passed.

The trail was easy to follow and it took them westwards.

Vindex was not happy. 'Ten of my lads were at the fort waiting for us to come back, just as you ordered,' he explained. 'Now they are told that they cannot leave Vindolanda until the details of the attack are established. What's up? Are they prisoners?'

Ferox had been afraid of this. He had not yet mentioned to anyone else the potion of mistletoe and nightshade or the double death inflicted on the slave girl. He wondered why they had not added the third death of strangulation to make this a proper sacrifice, but then these people were druids and many other things as well, who invoked Isis and used magic from the east and not everything they did followed the old rules.

'We really are humped, aren't we?' Vindex said when he told him.

Half an hour before they got there Ferox knew where the trail was heading. At last they saw the two standing stones, and between the Mother and Daughter there was a woman.

'Bastards,' Vindex gasped when they first saw her, and his anger grew as they came close. 'Bastards, bastards, bastards.'

Two of the Batavians vomited there and then, and another did the same thing a moment later. The soldiers cursed and swore and screamed out the vengeance they would wreak.

'Bastards,' Vindex said again.

Ferox said nothing. This was his failure and his fault. If the thought of this being done to Sulpicia Lepidina was a nightmare too appalling to admit, that was little consolation. He had let this happen. Samhain was not yet done, but he felt as if hope was slipping back to the Otherworld with the rest of the spirits. He had failed. These swine were butchering victims in his territory and he was not stopping them. One hand gripped the handle of his sword and he itched to use it.

XXV

FOR ONCE, CAVALRYMEN did not object to digging. Ferox rode to a farm half a mile away and borrowed two spades and a pick because they had no tools. The family living there were nervous, and happy to hand over anything as long as it made him leave. When he got back every man took off his cloak and they wrapped the mutilated body round tightly and buried Fortunata in a deep grave. Such sights needed to be buried away, out of sight. They gathered the local grey stones and piled them over the grave, while one soldier found a fallen tree trunk and carved her name into the wood. They dug another pit, and raised the wooden monument at her head. Vegetus would be able to find his wife's resting place with ease. Ferox hoped that he could be persuaded not to unearth the body for cremation. Better that he never know what they had done.

It took them several hours and barely a word was said as they all took turns working. It was almost sunset by the time they returned to Vindolanda and still no one spoke. Ferox tried not to imagine the freedwoman's screams, for she would not have lost consciousness for some time.

The fort was busier than when they had left, with working parties labouring away so that there was already little trace of the previous night's festivities. A long convoy of ox carts and pack mules was going through the main gate, so they went around through the canabae to find another way in. Sentries at the western gateway, the *porta principalis sinistra*, challenged them, accepted the password and then saluted with fervent precision, and Ferox had the sense of children caught out in mischief and now hoping to make amends. He began to understand when he saw the soldiers standing guard in front of the principia. Twenty of them were horsemen in highly polished scale armour and plumed helmets. Their shields were mixed – oval, hexagonal and rectangular side by side – and carried the symbols of half a dozen different units. They had on matching dark blue cloaks and this marked them as the governor's *singulares*, his bodyguard of picked cavalrymen drawn from the best of the army in the province. Alongside them stood a similar number of Batavians, who for all their size could not match the splendour of the governor's men.

'You're to go in straightaway, sir,' the optio in charge of the Batavians told Ferox as soon as he rode up. 'Provincial legate's orders,' he added, evidently relishing the prestige of their visitor. As Ferox went into the headquarters, a soldier led him to the room normally used as a classroom. Inside were Cerialis, Rufinus, Claudius Super and the Tribune Flaccus as well as a dozen senior officers he did not know. An even greater surprise sat near the back.

'Glad you are back,' Crispinus whispered as Ferox took the camp chair beside him.

'Surprised to see you, my lord.'

The young aristocrat grinned. His face was dirty, the grime giving it lines so that in his tiredness he looked twice his real age, and more like a man who ought to have grey hair.

'If you do not mind me saying, sir, you look terrible.'

'Better than the horses I rode, I can tell you. I've killed two getting here.' There was a pride in his voice that the centurion disliked. 'Only got here an hour ago. Didn't expect such exalted company.'

'Then why did you hurry?'

'Thought you might need my help.'

'Silence there!' The voice was deep and the speaker had not shouted, but even so it carried to the back of the room. Lucius Neratius Marcellus, Legatus Augusti, *vir clarissimus* and former

317

consul, was not a big man. He was thin-faced, thin-limbed and Ferox guessed that he was barely five feet tall, yet he dominated the room. Appointed to the post at the start of the year, the new governor had not set foot in Britannia until the autumn, but the impression this had created of lethargy vanished as the little man paced up and down, never still for a moment and always talking. He spoke first of the situation in the wider empire, of the hard work the princeps was doing to ensure peace and stability throughout the provinces. With the deified Nerva taken from us far too soon, his son would secure his legacy by his strength, justice and virtue. There would be no chaos, no civil war.

Then he turned to Britannia and most of all these lands in the north. Ferox was surprised to find great chunks of his own reports repeated, if admittedly in more rhetorical and elegant language. Some of this came from things he had written last year, a good deal from more recent reports, while some was astonishingly up to date.

'Bet you thought no one was listening,' Crispinus whispered.

Marcellus paused. He had reached the aftermath of the punitive expedition against the Selgovae, and begun to speak of the embassy to Tincommius. He beckoned to Crispinus, asking the tribune if he would be kind enough to tell them the outcome. With feigned reluctance the young aristocrat went to the front, and was soon recounting their journey north and the encounter with the high king, explaining the agreement they had reached.

'Good,' the provincial legate declared once he had finished. 'That is eminently sensible and I approve your decisions. I am sure that the princeps will confirm that judgement as soon as the matter is brought to him. Flavius Ferox,' he said. 'Stand up, sir.'

He did so, feeling awkward and unkempt and aware that the rage was seething within him and could burst out at the slightest provocation. There was something about the manner of this new governor, the self-confidence exceptional even for a distinguished senator, that annoyed him.

'Many of you know that the regionarius acted with the tribune on this mission. Do you have anything to add to his account?'

'No, my lord.' He wanted to shout out that a war had begun and that they should not be talking, but doing. Instead he said nothing.

Marcellus arched one eyebrow to show his surprise. 'Very well, perhaps as we proceed. Continue, my dear Crispinus, and tell us what happened after you left the king's stronghold.'

Ferox listened, and had to admit that the tribune gave an accurate report, including the provision of an escort and discovery of the murdered merchants. 'The yew tree is sacred to druids,' he said, and, if that was not quite the way Ferox would have explained it, it was good enough for this audience. The tribune spoke of how and why Ferox and Vindex left them, then described his journey to Trimontium, shadowed and then harassed by warriors on horseback. The garrison had lost a number of men to ambushes as detachments moved through the country. One wood-gathering party was long overdue and no news had come of them.

'They are dead,' Ferox cut in. 'We found the bodies and the burned carts.'

'I suspected as much,' Marcellus said, his tone one of mild regret. 'Continue please, Crispinus.'

The tribune did not have much more to say. Trimontium's garrison was well enough provisioned to survive a blockade for some time. At the moment the chieftain from the hill fort and other local elders were assuring the Romans of their goodwill. 'It is hard to be sure how long that will last,' he finished.

'As long as we show ourselves to be strong, and good friends.' Neratius Marcellus had forced himself to keep still while listening to the report, but once it was over he resumed his pacing. He spoke of the attack on the praetorium here at Vindolanda, ignoring the attempt to murder the trooper Longinus. Ferox wondered whether the provincial legate knew who the old soldier really was. As Marcellus told the story it was part of the greater conspiracy led by the two priests, men who wanted to rouse loyal provincials as well as allied tribes to turn against Rome. There were soldiers – or men dressed as soldiers – as well as some warriors among the attackers and they knew a lot about the fort. It was not known whether the Britons serving with the Tungrians were deserters, traitors or had been killed by the attackers and their bodies hidden.

'The aim was to kill or take the prefect and his esteemed wife, the clarissima Sulpicia Lepidina,' Marcellus said, his face grim. 'This prophecy of theirs, which relied upon a disgusting sacrifice of a distinguished man and woman, led them to carry out this impudent and vicious raid.'

Although he was used to it after all this time, Ferox was still surprised by the tendency of wealthy Romans to launch into rhetoric and turn everything into an oration.

'They failed.' Marcellus slapped his fist into his palm. 'The prefect and his wife are safe due to the courage and quick thinking of the garrison and the timely warning of the Tribune Crispinus with the aid of the regionarius. Alas, an innocent woman was abducted. We suspect in error. May I presume, Flavius Ferox, that there is no good news of the unfortunate victim?'

'We found Fortunata, the wife of the imperial freedman Vegetus, my lord.' Ferox may not have liked her much, or thought about her at all, but the dismissal of her abduction as a small thing fed his anger. The dead slaves did not appear to matter to them at all.

He took a deep breath. One of his tutors at Lugdunum had told him that the divine Augustus used to recite the alphabet in his head whenever he felt rage coming and did not wish to speak words he might regret. Ferox tried it now, and it did not help much. 'Fortunata is dead, my lord.'

Marcellus sighed. 'I had little hope. Such murderous hate made mercy of any sort unlikely. The poor thing.' He shook his head, his voice full of the well-practised sorrow of an orator. 'All we can hope is that she did not suffer.'

'It was a grim death, my lord,' Ferox said, struggling not to shout. 'A slow one and painful.'

There were murmurs from the assembled officers. This was not how anyone, let alone a centurion, was supposed to address the legate of the province. Crispinus gestured for him to calm down.

'The poor child.' Marcellus showed no sign of surprise or offence.

'They did to her what Boudicca's men did to the aristocratic ladies they captured.' There was a gasp of horror from the audience – someone who must have known the stories. 'She will have screamed as they began to cut her,' he went on, and took a step towards the small senator. 'Screamed as they sliced the ends off her breasts. She would only have stopped screaming when they started to sew the pieces of flesh on to her lips. After that she could only have moaned as they took her to the sharpened stake. If you wish I shall draw you a picture.' At that moment he hated them all, these great men who sat here secure in their power, worse than the crowd in the arena because at least spectators were interested in the fate of the people who died before their eyes.

Marcellus' skin was deeply tanned, and he had eyes so deep brown that they looked black. His dark hair was slicked down with oil so that not one strand was out of place. He looked up at the centurion as the big man loomed over him and he did not seem at all intimidated. Instead he reached out and patted Ferox on the arm, as a man would calm a horse.

'This shows us the inhuman cruelty and evil of our enemies,' the legate said, stepping past Ferox so that his audience could see him once again. 'It is our duty to our Lord Trajan to defeat his enemies. It is our duty as pious men who fear the gods and the laws of heaven and this world to wash this evil from the earth.

'Men always believe that a new governor will move slowly and be cautious. Today is the Kalends of November, and so men will also expect the campaigning season to be over until the spring. Most men will think these things and be wrong.' The legate had stopped pacing and stood very still, his right hand clasping his left wrist. Only his head moved, scanning the audience, looking at each man directly and then moving to the next. Ferox was behind the governor and could see the faces all focused on the little man.

'From the reports I received before I arrived I suspected that a show of force would prove necessary before the year was out. Therefore orders were sent to gather food and transport and to prepare a force to take the field.

'If these fanatics appear to be winning then others will join them. We must strike quickly and with all the force we can command to show the tribes and our allies that the prophets are liars, and their magic a fraud. Tomorrow we go to Coria to join the rest of the army. I want as many men as can ride or march and can be stripped from the garrison to accompany us. Detailed orders to be issued in an hour. Gentlemen, there is much to do and to arrange and I shall not detain you any longer. Thank you for your attention. Let us prepare to scour the land clean of this sickness.'

As the meeting broke up and the officers left the room, Neratius Marcellus pointed at Ferox, the gesture much like commanding a dog to stay. Crispinus glanced at the legate, looking puzzled, but the small man waved a hand for him to leave as well. Only one officer remained, a round-faced old man whose bronze cuirass did not fit him well and was traced with the lines of muscles that he clearly did not possess. His hair was white, but remained only as a thin fringe surrounding his dome-like bald head.

'I wish to speak with you, centurion, and I wish you to speak to me frankly and conceal nothing.'

'My lord.' Ferox stiffened to attention.

'Sit man, sit.' The legate waited until he obeyed, placing himself on one of the folding camp chairs. 'That is better,' he went on. 'This will take a while so you may as well be comfortable. Now Crispinus has told me about the gifts someone has been sending to Tincommius – the money and weapons. He suspects the same people encouraged the high king to lend his aid to this Stallion' – he said the world with distaste – 'and the druid. It was better that he not include such detail when he spoke to the other officers, but he told me the truth. It is also clear that the people who snatched that unfortunate lady and murdered her and the slaves – and who wanted to kill my wife's cousin, the Lady Sulpicia, and her husband – knew a good deal more than they should have done about this garrison. Without your warning they might well have succeeded.'

The legate paused and stared at his face. Ferox did not think that the man could have any idea that he and Sulpicia Lepidina were more than junior officer and commander's wife, but the announcement of a family connection was a surprise. For all its size, for all that senators – and now the princeps himself – had origins all over the world, the aristocracy of Rome still lived in a village where everyone knew everyone else and was related to almost everyone.

Ferox said nothing, and after a long silence Neratius Marcellus resumed.

'This attack followed the one on her carriage, and all that your report said about that incident – as well as much it did *not* say – shows that our enemies know our every move even before we make it. The massacre of the men stationed at the beacon confirms it. Only someone of high rank would know enough to give them so much information. That means at least one traitor. Perhaps there are several, and certainly others who follow their orders. My nephew has spoken to you about this and says that you have told him most of what you know and some of what you think.' The legate must have seen a trace of confusion. 'The Tribune Crispinus is my nephew,' he explained, and Ferox thought about the village again.

'There are men who wish our princeps to fail. I am not one of them. He is a decent man and the empire needs stability above all else. I serve the good of Rome and so I shall do everything in my power to serve Rome and serve him. That means that I must prevent this traitor or traitors from doing any more harm, and I cannot do that without your help. We must find this man and punish him.'

Ferox thought back to Domitian's rage at the conspirators who had backed Saturninus, of that mottled red face ordering him to seek them out, and his soul shuddered at the memory of the trials and deaths that followed. The men he found were all guilty, all oath-breakers, but the cruelty of the emperor's vengeance and the way it reached out to claim victims from the condemned's families and friends haunted him. It made it hard to trust yet another Roman demanding the truth.

The provincial legate seemed to sense his doubt, and again patted him on the arm. 'You saw that poor girl and what they did to her. Whoever helped them needs to suffer.'

The old man coughed. Ferox had almost forgotten that he was there for he had said nothing at all.

'I have not forgotten,' the legate said with a broad smile. 'I do not believe you have met Quintus Ovidius. He's a philosopher and a poet, but you must not hold that against him for he is a sensible enough fellow most of the time. He is also a very old friend of someone you know, whereas I can boast no more than acquaintance – if a very fond acquaintance, at least on my part.'

'He asked me to give you this,' Ovidius said, holding out his bony arm, his fingers enclosing a small leather bag. 'There is a message as well, but he insisted that you first see this token. Even I do not know what it is.'

There was something hard in the bag, but until Ferox opened it and tipped the contents on to the palm of his hand he could not guess what it was. When he saw it he gasped out loud, regretting it immediately and yet unable to restrain himself for he had not seen the necklace for many years. It was a simple leather thong with one stone hanging from it, a rich blue apart from a thick white stripe. A friend had worn it – a friend of his youth who had died in his arms, coughing up blood after a Sarmatian had run one of their great spears right through his body.

'The "tall tree that sways in the wind, but does not break"' – Ovidius intoned the phrase he must have practised – 'sends his greetings and asks that you trust his friends as you trust him. He would have written, but his eyes are weak these days.'

That was not surprising, for Caratacus was well over ninety and he had seemed frail years ago when Ferox had met him in Rome. One-time king of the great tribes of the south, long-time enemy of Rome and ally and friend of his grandfather, the war leader had lost in the end and been betrayed. The divine Claudius had spared him, keeping him in comfortable captivity near Rome. His grandson was a citizen and a soldier just like Ferox, and they had become friends and comrades in those grim days on the Danube, when the Dacians and Sarmatians had cut an army to ribbons.

Ferox began to talk. He could not refuse this request and no one else could have persuaded him so readily. 'A man does not easily say no to Caratacus,' his grandfather had often said. There was a power about the man that made anyone feel flattered to have his attention. Ferox told the legate and his friend everything, from the first doubts about the ambush, all that he had seen at the tower and everything that had happened since then. He talked for a long time and they did not interrupt, except once or twice when the legate asked short, direct questions to make matters clearer. Ferox spoke of Gannallius, his story and the man's death, and of what had happened when he and Vindex had reached Vindolanda, of his regret at thinking all was over once he had made sure that Sulpicia Lepidina was safe.

Most of the hour went as he told his story, and when he finished the legate asked his friend to fetch the sentry from outside the room. 'Say that the orders will be delayed, but not by long,' he told the man, and then asked Ovidius to stand by the door and make sure no one disturbed them.

Neratius Marcellus began to pace up and down, and had crossed the room half a dozen times before he spun around. 'A tribune?'

'Yes, my lord. Or at least someone pretending to be one. My guess is that the soldiers who slaughtered the men at the tower were real soldiers. Perhaps deserters, but they sound too well equipped for that. No doubt they were bribed, but to commit so great a crime there must have been more. The man giving the orders was able to convince them that they were safe from arrest and execution. Must have made them think that they were on the winning side and that rewards would come, and that he was well enough connected for them to trust him.'

The legate crossed to the wall and came back again. 'Who?' he asked, stopping and staring at the centurion, dark eyes hard.

'The evidence points towards Legio II Augusta, and hence your nephew.' Ferox had little doubt that the legate had already made the connection. 'He was there or at least nearby every time something happened, even when the Tungrians were left stranded on the day Titus Annius was cut down.'

'He is a man who will always want to be on the winning side.' Neratius Marcellus gave a thin smile as he quoted the centurion, and did not dismiss the suggestion. 'It is harder to say whether he thinks the tide has turned against our princeps.'

'My lord, would it change your actions if it proved to be him?'

'Not for a moment.' The face was now as hard and cold as the legate's black eyes.

'It may be him. I cannot be sure, not yet. But any tracker worth the name will tell you that it is not always wise to follow so obvious a trail. The Tribune Flaccus of the Ninth Hispana is also well placed to be our man, and he has been here in the north longer.'

'I hear he is a fool?'

'My people have a saying that a foolish man will never be lonely,' Ferox said and heard Ovidius laugh from the far side of the room. 'How clever does a traitor have to be? Especially if he is not alone.'

The legate came over to him and placed a hand on each shoulder. 'Find out. Whoever it is I must know. Find out the truth and bring it to me. Will you do that, Flavius Ferox, centurion of Rome and Prince of the Silures?'

'I will find him, my lord.' Ferox meant it. No doubt men got away with far worse every day, but they did not do it on his patch.

'Good.' Marcellus smiled and stood back. 'In the meantime we have a garrison to relieve and priests to hunt down. I need the rebels to fight me and fight me soon, and not fade into the hills

326

and force me to chase them as the weather turns worse and my food runs out. What is the best way to make them risk battle?'

'Give them a chance,' Ferox said. 'Make a mistake and let them scent victory.'

'I am glad to see that honesty is becoming a habit in your speech with me. A mistake? Not too big a mistake, I assume.' The legate's eyes softened just a little. 'I see we think alike. Well, let me explain that the force I plan to march north is not as big as it might be. Will that do the trick?'

'Perhaps, my lord.'

'A prudent answer, if not helpful. Well, like Caesar I plan to take fewer tents and pack the men in, while making our camps smaller than normal. That will make them think our numbers are even fewer.'

'Perhaps, my lord.'

Neratius Marcellus grimaced. 'Didn't Caratacus tell you that Silures gave nothing away?' he shouted to Ovidius.

'Run, my lord,' Ferox said, and saw the legate frown. 'What hound can resist a chase? If the right moment comes, order a retreat and they will follow. Then you can turn with the whole pack and tear them to shreds.'

'We shall see. For the moment I am drafting an order placing you in command of the exploratores. You will be my eyes and ears.'

'My lord.' That was another reminder of Dacia, when he had had the same job. He clutched the bead of the necklace tightly and prayed that this army would march to better fortune. Back then no one had believed him when he had reported that the enemy had massed and was waiting in ambush. He hoped Neratius Marcellus was as shrewd as he seemed.

'Let's kill these bastards.' The legate spoke with surprising vehemence. 'The traitors and the ones who torture women to death. I hear she was a dancer.' He shook his head. 'Such a waste of life.' Noticing the centurion looking at him he went on. 'The Lady Sulpicia told me a little about the poor girl. She blames herself. Still, I think it better that the details of what happened be kept from her. At least I do not have to write a letter to my wife telling of the death of her niece. That is something. Do not blame yourself for what has happened. You saved the lady Sulpicia Lepidina and she is worth saving. No reward could be too high for that deed.'

Ferox was not sure whether there was a sparkle of amusement in the legate's gaze.

'Well then, get some rest and be ready to have no more for as long as this task takes.'

Ferox stood up. 'My lord,' he said, and saluted.

XXVI

I T TURNED COLD overnight, and the next morning the grass crunched underfoot from the heavy frost and the breath of men and beasts steamed as they tried to stamp life into their bones. That night the stars were a vast field of tiny lights, made more bright because there was no moon to challenge them. Far too many soldiers had gathered at Coria to fit into its fort, so the bulk of the army slept in a camp beyond the civilian buildings. Neratius Marcellus had concentrated almost four and a half thousand men – over five thousand including the servants – and planned to lead all save five hundred of them up the Eastern Road the next morning. That plan changed when late in the day a contingent marched up from Bremesio and reported seeing buildings burning and small groups of mounted British warriors shadowing them. Four hundred additional soldiers, half of them cavalry, were instructed to stay at Coria and be ready to confront any signs of trouble in the area in case this threatened communications with the main force.

'The centurion in charge of the column coming up from Bremesio estimates the bands of horsemen as numbering several hundred,' the provincial legate told Ferox late that night.

Ferox was tired, for he and Vindex had spent the day riding hard, marauding across the land, taking care to be seen on the tops of hills by the troops going up the road. The Brigantian scouts had acted the part of rebellious warriors, and the task had amused them, especially when they were told to set light to any abandoned buildings they found.

'Imaginative fellow, that centurion,' Ferox said. It had taken a good deal of effort to persuade the legate to release the scouts held under loose arrest at Vindolanda, but in the end he had had his way and with the other warriors who had come in time there had been twenty-three riders out in the hills. 'Perhaps, my lord, it would be wise not to place him in charge of counting stores.'

The army marched an hour before dawn. Ferox and the advance guard of the exploratores set out two hours before that, although he left Vindex and his men behind to rest and catch up before the end of the day. The legate had given him eighty troopers detached from their units and it was a pleasant surprise to find Victor and the Thracian from his own burgus among them. They were good choices, active and intelligent, and his impression of the rest of his command was equally favourable. It seemed that Neratius Marcellus was a clever man, who liked to plan ahead and tried to prepare as well as possible. Ferox hoped that he was also lucky, for without that the odds were on a disaster and a wave of blood and ruin sweeping over the north.

Marker stones were already there warning of the approach of a large force. There were others put down by the Textoverdi, vaguer warnings of danger, and there was no hiding the wariness among the people they met. Ferox had already heard the rumours of a work of great magic made greater by the hideous sacrifice of a queen of the Romans and the killing of their king. It made little difference when he told them that neither had died, and that the actual victim was born a slave and not royal. People only shook their heads and talked of dark times and a blood-red winter.

For most of the first day Ferox stayed with his outposts. The men worked in pairs, spaced wide apart across the lands to either side of the road. He kept half a dozen troopers with him, half a mile back, and had similar groups on either flank. On the second day he was strengthened by Vindex and his men and placed patrols in the rear as well.

The army had made good progress, covering fifteen miles on the first day, helped by the frost-hardened ground and the restless energy of a provincial legate who rode up and down the columns, joking, encouraging and chivvying the men along. Nearly half the force were legionaries, and that was an unusual thing so far north. Marcellus had instructed both II Augusta and XX Valeria Victrix to provide a cohort each, led by their best centurions and reinforced with the fittest and ablest men so that each numbered over six hundred and fifty: VIIII Hispana contributed two cohorts who had spent the last year up on the frontier, but were reduced by sickness and other losses to some six hundred men between them. Marcellus told them to show the other legions what real veterans looked like, then he told the men of II Augusta that they were the emperor's own, named by the divine Augustus, and must live up to their reputation as the finest legion anywhere, and afterwards he reminded the Victrix that they were ones who had beaten Boudicca all those years ago, and said that he expected them to win more glory in the next weeks.

Flavius Cerialis had three centuries of infantry, the same ones that had gone on the punitive expedition, but, in spite of the losses they had suffered, the rush of volunteers to avenge the attacks on the commander and his wife had boosted their numbers to some two hundred and fifty men – more than their proper compliment. Sulpicia Lepidina and the children had travelled by carriage with them as far as Coria. Ferox had not cared for the idea, but they would probably be safer there than anywhere else for the moment. There had been no chance to speak, but he had glimpsed her several times, because the legate believed it was important for her to be visible as proof of the failure of the attack. The Batavians cheered whenever they saw her, and several times he had only known she was about when he heard the great roar.

Cohors III Batavorum, their sister unit, shared their anger and longing for revenge. Whatever the Romans said, Cerialis was from their royal house, and she was his wife or queen, and they would die for them both. The cohort provided another three hundred men, formed into five centuries, and these men also began to cheer whenever the lady and her husband came in sight, swearing to make those who had threatened them pay. The mood spread. Cohors I Tungrorum had begged to be included in the expedition and made up a century of seventy men, attached for the moment to Rufinus and his Spaniards who mustered one hundred and eighty infantrymen. The Tungrians knew the lady, the Spanish knew her by reputation and they too raised a great cry when they saw her. Soon even the century of eighty archers detached from a cohort based far to the south took up the cry as well.

Ferox had spent his adult life around soldiers from all over the empire. They could be brutal, ruthless, cruel, and were capable of stealing anything that was not nailed down – and often even that did not stop them. For all that they had a sentimental streak a mile wide and could be kind, even gentle when you least expected it. It helped that Sulpicia Lepidina was beautiful, the sort of woman a soldier dreamed about and knew that he could never have. It helped even more that she smiled at them, laughed at their jokes and even made a few in return. Ferox watched as a whole army fell in love with a woman and marvelled as the affection spread. He had left Coria long before the main force, but later he heard that she had sat on horseback to watch them go by and that rank after rank of soldiers had cheered her, legionaries and auxiliaries alike. Neratius Marcellus kissed her hand in farewell to yells of approval, and then pecked her cheek to a deafening roar of acclamation. Cerialis glowed with the reflected glory. In their few meetings Ferox did not get the impression of a man gnawed by sorrow for his murdered lover.

The army marched in high spirits, eager to smite a loathsome enemy on behalf of a beautiful woman. It was a theme fit for the bards to set to verse, but so far not even Ferox's scouts had seen a single one of those enemies. On the second day a bitter east wind began to blow, at times knocking the breath from men as they struggled along a route that was becoming steeper. They did not set out as early, for it took longer than usual to break up camp. On Neratius Marcellus' orders twelve were expected to sleep in tents meant for eight, and four more were expected to be on sentry duty or otherwise awake while the rest slept. He had also instructed that the roads in each night's camp and the intervals between the tent-lines were to be made narrower than usual. This meant that the ramparts enclosed a much smaller space and helped to make the force look smaller, but it also made it harder to form up ready to march on the next morning. They made barely ten miles on the second day.

On the third day the east wind brought in thick cloud to cover the whole sky. Not long after dawn the rain came, turning to sleet and then snow as the day wore on before switching back to sleet later in the afternoon. Men's cloaks became soaked and heavy as they plodded along. Neratius Marcellus had nearly nine hundred horsemen under his command, three hundred and fifty apiece from Aelius Brocchus' ala Petriana and his own singulares, and the rest made up of detachments from the cohorts, a contingent of mounted legionaries and the exploratores. Then there were six hundred pack mules and ponies, and a few oxen for the handful of carts carrying essential equipment too bulky to put in a pack.

The army marched expedita, with the minimum baggage, but that still meant hundreds of tents, and hard tack, salted bacon and other food to last nine days, after which they would have to rely on replenishing supplies from the well-stocked granaries in the forts along the road. All of the cavalrymen had sacks of fodder tied behind their saddles, the big bags making the animals look clumsy and misshapen. One and a half thousand ridden or led animals and twice that number of men on foot including the slaves soon churned the roadway into mud, getting worse as more and more passed the same spot. The infantry marched in a hollow square, with the baggage train protected inside, but this just spread the trampling over a wide area either side of the road. As always the men in the back had it worst, held up the longest by any delay ahead of them, and squelching through cloying mud heavy enough to trap a boot and rip it free. The legate let them stop and camp just beyond Bremenium, and men from the fort brought out enough dry kindling and timber for fires to be lit.

The fourth day saw gaps in the cloud, with tantalising glimpses of sun, before the next shower blew in across the hills. It was mostly rain apart from an hour's swirling snow in the middle of the day. Men slipped as they trudged up and down through the hill country, and when the legate stopped and joked with them they no longer laughed as loudly.

It was during the snowstorm that Ferox for the first time saw warriors watching them. His men had been reporting them all morning, and he did not doubt them, but the weather made it hard to see far. He was surprised that it had taken so long, and guessed that enemy scouts had been there for some time, although with the Stallion's men it was hard to know what to expect. They had seen Votadini quite a lot, but those little groups of armed men on ponies were never shy of calling to them or coming in to talk. They were locals, wanting to assure the Romans of their friendship – and keep an eye on the army to make sure that it behaved in a friendly way. They said that Trimontium was under attack, but holding out, and that the Stallion had promised his followers a great victory in the days to come, greater than they could imagine, and that this would be just the first. The Votadini shrugged when they repeated his claims, doubtful and cautious at the moment, but not so much that they were sure such a thing could not happen.

Ferox sent regular messages back to the cavalry vanguard and on to the main force, and once a day, usually in the middle of the morning, the provincial legate rode forward to meet him in person. Neratius Marcellus had a trio of stallions, all of them tall and black, and when he was in the saddle no one noticed his small stature. As usual his questions were direct for all the florid language, but his frustration at the ever-slower progress was obvious.

The rain stopped as the army began to dig its camp for the night. That was some comfort, but the brooding red glow off the low clouds ahead of them added to the grim mood among the cold and wet men as they carved out a ditch from the rocky soil and threw up a rampart.

'Too many fires just to be a burning fort, my lord,' Ferox said when the legate asked his opinion. 'Even two forts.' There was a smaller garrison ahead of them, about a dozen miles south of Trimontium. The few locals he had found during the day said that the Roman forts held out, but that both were hard pressed. More and more warriors appeared around the army as it advanced. Several pairs of scouts were chased. Two more came back, both men on the same horse, and one with a javelin wound to the thigh.

'You said *just*,' Neratius Marcellus held his gaze.

'Maybe they have fallen, maybe a few of the buildings have been set on fire, and all the farms for miles around. That's still not enough fires.'

'Then what is it?' the legate snapped, his patience worn thin.

'It's an army, my lord. A big army, not far away.'

Neratius Marcellus took a long breath. He was drinking from a silver cup and now offered it to the centurion, who shook his head. 'Tomorrow then,' the legate said.

'Probably, my lord. This is as good a place as any – for them as well as us.'

'And you saw them?' The legate's dark eyes never left the centurion's face.

'No,' he admitted. 'Only a few riders. But they are there, sir, and they are coming.' In the late afternoon Ferox had ridden to the north-west, searching on his own for the force that he was sure planned to swing around behind them and box them in. He guessed at least half of the Stallion's men would surround them, while the rest blocked their path. It was a guess, but it was what he would have done in the priest's place.

'Why are you sure?'

How could he explain the warning signs set out by the Votadini and the smoky fires men had lit, giving off thick plumes to signify danger, and expect even the sympathetic Marcellus to understand? Ferox did not need to see thousands of warriors to know that they were there.

'They need to fight us as much as we need to fight them,' he began, deciding that logical argument was more likely to convince this senator. For all his capability, Neratius Marcellus had never once seen battle, and up until now had spent his time on military service in the dull routines of peace. 'His men will be running out of food by now. Faith and the promise of miracles will keep them here for a while, but not forever. Eventually empty bellies will make the warriors drift home. Before that happens he needs to work his magic and win a victory. This is where he will make it happen. All you need to do, my lord, is give him the chance.'

'It's a gamble.' The legate turned away and paced up and down the small tent. Another man would have needed to duck his head under the low roof. There was silence for a long time and he must have crossed back and forth a dozen times. His friend Ovidius sat on a folding chair and watched him, now and again rubbing his dripping nose. The old philosopher had insisted on coming, and appeared remarkably cheerful in spite of the discomfort and danger.

'It's a big gamble,' Marcellus said at last.

'I thought that was why we were here, my lord.'

Ovidius chuckled.

'So be it.' The governor turned to his friend. '*Iacta alea est*, as they say. It worked well enough for him.'

'*Aneristho kubos*,' the philosopher corrected him. 'As I heard it, Caesar spoke in Greek.'

'That must have made all the difference. Well then, I shall roll the dice and see how they fall.' His smile was thin, his face taut in the flickering light of the lamp. 'And what do your Silures say when they play a game?'

'We do not think much of a man who plays, my lord,' Ferox said, trying to sound more confident than he felt. The Romans were an emotional people, ready to weep and cry out in triumph or frustration, and so many years spent among them had weakened the calm so important to his people.

Marcellus' face turned hard immediately.

'We admire only the man who wins,' Ferox told him.

'And care little for courtesy, I see.' The legate punched him softly on the arm. 'Well, true enough, and I doubt Caesar thought any different. Get some rest. Tomorrow we win.'

Halfway through the night the cloud cleared and the first faint outline of the moon rose across the sky. It was cold, turning sentry duty into a numbing torment as men stared out into the night and hoped not to see anything. A heavy sun rose blood red over the hills, but the morning brought only slow relief from the chill and the reds and pinks in the sky hinted at bad weather to come. Before dawn Ferox and his exploratores went ahead. One of the auxiliaries, an easterner by the look of him, chanted a low hymn to the god of the morning as they rode, and for once the others kept silent and listened to the strange words in a tongue they did not understand. It made Ferox think of Philo, who was back in the camp having insisted on following his master. With another slave, the boy helped to look after the tent that he shared with two of the Batavian centurions.

They did not see any warriors for the first hour, and that was strange, but Ferox kept his men in hand for it would be dangerous to get too far ahead of the supporting cavalry in the vanguard. The enemy were there, they were close, and he suspected that they wanted the Romans to press on. There were plenty of tracks showing where horsemen and quite a few men on foot had been on these hills before they had drawn back to the north.

The wind had dropped, otherwise they would have smelled them sooner, long before they saw them. There were plenty of piled stones warning of great danger, and it was no surprise when Vindex rode back and called to him, 'You had better take a look.'

Ferox followed the Brigantian up the long ridge, ignoring the road, which climbed in a series of laborious bends. A pair of scouts were waiting for them on the crest, sitting impassively, spears resting on their shoulders. Neither man paid him any attention as he rode up, both just staring out at the view. He could not blame them. When it crossed the ridge the road dipped down, following the valley until it began to climb again. It was too wide to be called a pass, but on the line of hills around three-quarters of a mile away the rebels waited. Most sat or wandered about without apparent purpose. There were clusters, some very dense, and elsewhere looser swarms of men. Ferox tried to make a rough guess at numbers, and quickly reached a total of well over ten thousand. More kept strolling across the crest to join them and he guessed that there were many, many more not yet visible.

'There's a few of them,' Vindex said.

'Won't be so many by tonight,' Ferox replied.

'And how many of us will there be?'

He sent a messenger back to the main force, choosing Victor from the half-dozen troopers with him because he knew and trusted the man.

The sun had gone, the sky once more an unbroken sea of dirty clouds, so that the day had become darker rather than lighter. Up on the ridge an icy wind gusted into them, making them lean into it to keep their balance.

'Least it's not raining,' Ferox said to Vindex as they waited and watched the enemy.

'Not yet.'

The Britons did not advance. Their numbers kept growing and over time the line more clearly became a row of dense masses. Even if they had answered the Stallion's call to war, Ferox suspected that most men were seeking out their kin to stand beside if it came to a fight. He fought the urge to go forward and take a closer look, and instead remembered the provincial legate's instructions. There were four or five hundred horsemen in plain sight on each flank, but almost everyone else was on foot. From up here he could see few chariots, which meant that not many important chieftains had joined the cause. That is if they were not simply waiting behind the ridge, ready to make a triumphant entrance just before the battle. The little he had seen of the Stallion and his followers did not suggest any great subtlety in the way the man did things, but if important leaders had joined him then he would not be in sole charge and some of them would be old and wise in war. Then there was the great druid, if he was over there somewhere, a man famed for his deceptions and magic. For the moment the Britons waited and Ferox wanted to do nothing to provoke them.

Others did not share his caution. The decurion in charge of the first turma to reach them was young and eager, and it took a direct order to stop him from riding forward on his own and challenging the enemy to single combat. Fortunately he was from the ala Petriana and Ferox knew enough about Brocchus to be confident that the prefect would frown on such glory-hunting.

Crispinus and Flaccus were another matter, and when the two tribunes rode up at the head of the main body of the vanguard, they looked like two boys who had just been told that their schoolmaster was sick and would not be back for a week.

'We have them!' Crispinus almost shouted the words, waving his hand along the great length of the enemy host.

'Yes, bet we've got them worried,' said Vindex under his breath.

Flaccus' eyes betrayed a moment of anger before he made the decision not to hear anything said by so insignificant a person as a scout from one of the tribes. 'It's almost like an arena,' he said. 'Just perfect.'

In the past, Crispinus and the other tribune had treated each other with courtesy and no more, but the prospect of action appeared to have created a wave of mutual affection. 'The legate will be delighted.'

If the fools expected Marcellus to advance and then attack straight up that slope then Ferox was not about to shatter their illusions.

'I feel that we should keep them busy,' Crispinus announced. 'We have a decent number of well-mounted men, so can disengage and withdraw whenever we want.' The two tribunes had arrived with the formed supports for the scouts. There were forty legionary cavalrymen, and three turmae, all from ala Petriana.

Ferox wished that Brocchus had come up. 'My orders are not to look for trouble, my lord.'

'I am not asking you to do anything,' Crispinus said with a smile. 'Your men have been in the field longer than us and are bound to be tired. What I suggest is that the noble Flaccus and I take the others and see if we can sting some of their horsemen. We can kill a few and that will show our men and the whole army that the enemy are not to be feared.' He turned to stare at the enemy for a while. 'The left looks closest so that is the place to strike. What do you say, Flaccus?'

Ferox thought he saw hesitation, doubt, and then resignation as the junior tribune agreed.

'Good,' Crispinus said. 'Then let us not waste any time.'

Vindex watched them ride back and give orders to the cavalry. 'Daft buggers. What about us?'

'Get everyone together. We might have to get away in a hurry.'

Ferox wondered about the two tribunes, and whether this reckless aggression would save him the trouble of finding out which was the traitor. As Flaccus went past at the head of the legionary horsemen Ferox could not help viewing their ranks with distaste. It was not fair, because at most a few were involved in the murders and all of these men could be innocent.

Crispinus formed two turmae in a line three deep and sent the other ahead in a loose line ready to skirmish. There were a couple of dozen men in each unit. Flaccus stayed back with the legionary horsemen as a reserve. The deployment was sensible enough, even if the plan itself was foolishness, and there was nothing to be gained by stirring up the enemy in this way.

The Roman cavalry went forward steadily, not going too fast and keeping good formations, and as they came over the crest and into sight of the Britons some of the warriors on the far side of the valley began to stir into life. Trumpets sounded, the noise thin in the gusting wind, and men waved standards in the air. The Romans pressed on, keeping to a walk, and the distance closed to less than half a mile.

'You have to admire brave idiots,' Vindex said, and then repeated the joke in their own language to his scouts.

'Why?' one of them said.

With a low cheer, the horsemen opposite the Romans began to advance to meet them. Two tight groups of fifty or sixty trotted ahead, and as many more galloped forward as a loose swarm. Ferox did not hear the order, but the leading turma split into two lines of horsemen who cantered straight at the oncoming Britons.

'Neat, very neat.' The comment came from one of the troopers behind Ferox, and he had to concur. The men leading each line of horsemen suddenly swung away, rode parallel for long enough to throw a javelin and then turned back towards their supports. Each man did the same, so that a stream of missiles struck the leading enemy, dropping several horses and men. By the time the last man in each file had thrown the leader had turned again and swung back towards the Britons to repeat the drill. More warriors were hit, and so far all of the javelins flung back had missed or struck harmlessly against shields.

The next time the turma went forward the Britons galloped away to safety, apart from the two denser knots of men that shook themselves into rough columns and pressed on.

'Look.' Vindex was pointing to the enemy right, where the horsemen were also beginning to advance. It would take them a long time to move around behind the Romans, but the threat should persuade the tribune to retreat before too long.

Trumpets sounded, clear across the valley, and then the notes became ragged as Crispinus led the two formed turmae forward into a trot, then a canter, heading straight for the closest mass of enemy. Watching a cavalry battle from a distance always struck Ferox like watching flocks of birds wheeling, diving and circling. When the auxiliaries went into a gallop the Britons started to rush at them, but then slowed and the whole group seemed to quiver. Crispinus was ahead of his men by two horses' lengths, plume streaming from his helmet, polished armour gleaming, and his sword held high. Before he reached the Britons they scattered like frightened sheep. One was too slow and fell as the tribune came past and slashed across his body. Another was hit in the back by a thrown spear, but the rest got away.

The other group of warriors had grown in size as more men joined them, including some of the retreating skirmishers. It wheeled clumsily, before heading towards Crispinus' men. The auxiliaries were no longer in neat ranks, for galloping always broke up a formation, and the enemy were coming from their left flank. Ferox saw the tribune waving his hand around, and the men responded to the order and followed him back. The legionary horsemen under Flaccus were there for just this situation, and once the auxiliaries fled past them they could drive off the enemy charge. That would give time for Crispinus to rally and re-form his men, so that if the legionaries became ragged then they could in turn be sheltered by formed supports. It was the way cavalry fought, and there was no shame in running as long as they stopped when ordered. Regulations said that at least half of the men should be kept back as a reserve, and although Crispinus had not used so many he ought to be safe.

Flaccus began to wheel his men until they were facing towards this threat. Crispinus and the auxiliaries were galloping back towards them, scattered but jubilant. The legionary cavalry kept turning as the Britons raised a great shout, taken up by the distant masses of warriors who yelled and blew their horns.

Flaccus' men broke. One moment there was a neat block of riders three ranks deep and the next there was only a stream of panicked men galloping to the rear. The junior tribune at their head looked around as if in surprise, and then followed. Crispinus and the auxiliaries heard the enemy cheers redouble and spurred to run as fast as they could.

'*Stercus*,' Ferox said. 'You' – he looked at Vindex – 'stick with me. The rest of you get back if you can as fast as you can and report this rout.'

XXVII

I T WAS A stampede, not a retreat. One unlucky man died when his horse stumbled and threw him, another when his gelding took him into a patch of thick mud and became stuck fast. Several more were hit by javelins, wounding their mounts or tipping them from the saddle. Ferox could see the two tribunes near the front of the main pack of riders, their expensive horses faster than the rest, so that they gained steadily on the troopers. The Britons chased them, a great scatter of individuals each going as fast as his pony could run. Their animals were small and fat-bellied from grass and they could go on all day, but they were not fast. Before long the rearmost Romans were safe from thrown missiles and the lead kept growing.

Ferox had hoped to shadow the retreat from the hills on one side, looking for an opportunity to watch the two tribunes and see whether there was anything more than folly behind this morning's rashness, but the two men never left the main group. He and Vindex soon attracted attention from the warriors, several of whom swerved towards them.

'Better shift,' the Brigantian said, but Ferox was not really listening.

'Look familiar?' he asked, pointing some way to the rear, where an ordered group of warriors came on at a gentle trot. They were half a mile away at least and he shaded his eyes as he strained to see. The leader was a big man with a red shield.

'Gannascus?'

343

'Reckon so.'

'Be a shame to kill him,' Vindex said. 'I liked that big lump.' He thought for a moment. 'Does it mean we're humped?'

Ferox did not answer, but if the high king had come with any great number of his warriors then the odds shifted even more in favour of the enemy. 'Let's go,' he said. 'Nothing more for us to do out here.'

It was a mile back to the rest of the mounted vanguard and the fleeing horsemen crossed the rolling moorland quickly. The head of the main column was already visible, resting for one of the short breaks given every hour. It took longer for Ferox and Vindex to get back, and by that time the provincial legate had issued the order to retreat. The instruction was easier to issue than perform, for the unit commanders were taken by surprise. Once they were convinced that this was truly what they were being told to do, it was simple enough to about face so that each detachment was still in a great rectangle, but now facing back the way they had come. It was harder to turn around the carts and strings of pack ponies and mules and, as always with the baggage train, nothing could be done without much shouting and beating the animals with sticks.

Just before noon the army began its retreat. Ferox rode with the legate, watching as he urged the men onwards. The soldiers were not as willing as they had been even when the weather was bad. To advance was one thing, for it held the prospect of meeting and smashing the enemy, which would bring glory, rest, and hopefully plenty of hot food. No soldier liked to retreat, and what made it worse was the feeling that it was unnecessary.

'So the cavalry got beaten?' Ferox heard a legionary of VIIII Hispana complain as soon as the governor was out of earshot. 'So what? Cavalry, I've shit 'em.' One of his comrades nudged him to warn him that an officer was listening, but the man was unimpressed by a centurion he did not recognise. 'Let's push on. We'll soon cut this daft druid down. See how brave he is when he sees his *mentula* on the end of a sword.'

'Hope it's bigger that yours or we'll never find it!' another man shouted.

'They're not happy.' Flaccus had appeared beside him. He looked flushed, but otherwise unscathed.

'Soldiers never are, sir,' he said. 'Or at least they're never happy unless they're bitching about something.'

'They do not like to run away.' The junior tribune's horse stirred and he made this an excuse to lean against its neck and pat the beast. Ferox could see that he was embarrassed by that morning's rout. 'It was not my fault,' he began, and the centurion let him talk at his own pace. After all, there was no reason for him to explain himself to a mere centurion. 'It all happened so quickly. We were ready to charge in support, the Tribune Crispinus and his men were coming back towards us, and then suddenly a voice shouted out, "Retreat! Retreat!" The men were turning before I could say anything.'

The legionaries had marched on and there was a gap before the next cohort would come alongside them. Flaccus fussed with his horse, avoiding the centurion's gaze. His voice was low. 'I may be mistaken, but I believe it was Crispinus who shouted. I fear that he panicked.'

A summoning call from the legate forced Ferox to canter away, but he sensed that the tribune had said what he wanted to say. The man had done his best to look embarrassed, but could not hide his delight in the failure of a superior.

Ferox saw them before he caught up with the governor – little clusters of horsemen over to the right. The valley was wide here, and the warriors almost a mile away, so that he could just tell that the bigger group that appeared a moment later were on foot.

Marcellus gave him a curt nod. 'It seems that you were right. They are following like hounds on a scent. It does not look as if they fear us, so we must make sure that they keep believing we fear them.'

There were a good five hours left in the day – if you could call the short hours of these autumn days in northern lands good.

The Romans pressed on, making little more than a mile in the next hour. To the west band after band of warriors appeared, still keeping their distance but steadily massing. There were not many horsemen, and even fewer chariots, some of which edged forward until they were almost within bowshot.

'Ten or twelve thousand, I make it.' Crispinus was riding with the legate and his immediate staff. The young tribune had nodded affably to Ferox, but not said anything about the rout of the cavalry.

Neratius Marcellus said nothing as he scanned the forming battle line. If anything, Ferox suspected that the guess was too low, for this was a bigger force than the one he had seen this morning.

'What about to our rear?' The legate's question surprised him, and he glanced back. So far there were only a few hundred cavalry, the ones that had chased the Romans away this morning. Faced with the entire ala Petriana as well as supports, they proved much more wary, and Brocchus' men were split into two halves, each one covering the other as they withdrew. Yet the warriors on foot could not be too far behind.

'Just horsemen, so far, my lord. Be a couple of hours before the rest are any threat.'

'Good. Then tell me, centurion, what would a wise general do now?'

Crispinus seemed surprised not to be asked, since he was senior, but made no protest.

The answer was simple, if the legate intended to follow the advice and instructions of all the emperors since Augustus. 'Pitch camp,' Ferox said, 'rest up, and be ready to fight a battle tomorrow with baggage safe and the refuge of a rampart in case things go against us.'

'"Do not go fishing with a golden hook," the divine Augustus commanded his generals. "For you risk more than you could possibly gain." Prudence is a virtue in a general, and what you have said is the prudent thing. Then tell me, centurion of Rome and Prince of the Silures, what would you do? What would Caratacus do? Would you gamble once more, with stakes as high as this?'

346

Ferox managed to stop himself from smiling when he heard the quote. He tapped the hilt of his sword. 'I'd win, my lord, and you won't do that by being prudent.'

'It really is all so simple in the end, is it not? Listen to this man, Crispinus. We may have beaten his people, but that does not mean we cannot learn from them.'

'But, sir, would it not be better to have a camp built? What if things go wrong?'

'If they go wrong then we are all dead and no camp will save us.' Marcellus smiled at the tribune. 'There is nowhere to go and no one to come and help us. So we win or die. If I recollect Hannibal told his men something similar when they first saw Italy from the heights of the Alps.'

There was a low hill ahead of them, and the baggage train was sent to the top of it. Ovidius half remembered a story of a general making a simple rampart from the pack saddles and baggage, so the *lixae* in charge of the animals were instructed to do this. They made a ring and just managed to squeeze the animals inside, but the rampart was no more than a couple of feet high.

'Perhaps my memory plays me false or the historian lied,' admitted Ovidius, who was placed in charge of the rough encampment, with only the slaves under his command, for every soldier was ordered to fall in with his own unit. Ferox and Vindex rode past and saw Philo, looking pale, cold and strangely excited as he held a staff he had sharpened into a point.

'If he doesn't stab himself with that we can call the day a success,' the Brigantian said.

The main line was in front of the hill, with the cohort from II Augusta as the senior unit in the place of honour on the right. Flavius Cerialis and cohors VIIII Batavorum were next to them on the left, then cohors III Batavorum and the men from XX Valeria Victrix. Each was formed just three deep, the minimum allowed by the drill book, so that the whole front line of infantry, with the gaps between the units, stretched for some eight hundred and fifty paces. The second line was smaller, with the two cohorts from VIIII Hispana on the right, and the Tungrians and Vardulli combined into one formation on the left, each stationed to cover an interval between the cohorts ahead of them. Each unit was formed six deep, and the gaps between them were far wider than those in the first line. Neratius Marcellus kept his singulares as a third line and ultimate reserve, and split the other cavalry with the ala Petriana on the left and the rest on the right. He had half a dozen scorpiones, and their crews carried these light bolt-shooters, and stationed them in pairs in the intervals between the cohorts of the first line. With them were the archers, told off to act as skirmishers.

'Does not look very many, does it?' Crispinus spoke softly. Ferox's exploratores were on the right wing, but the legate had asked him to stay with him for the moment until he had to take command of his men. There was far less order among the Britons, but the numbers now seemed even greater. They lacked horsemen, with Brocchus' men on the left flank facing barely more than their own number of mounted opponents. There were no cavalry on the other flank, at least at the moment. Instead there were men on foot, great blocks of them ten or more deep with barely a gap between each one. It was not a battle line capable of manoeuvre, but then they had no need for any subtlety.

'"I would name the fields on which a mere handful of Romans put to flight great hosts of enemies, and the cities fortified by nature which they stormed, were it not that such a theme would lead me far away from my theme."' Ferox was pleased to remember the whole line.

'Sallust again?' Crispinus managed a nervous smile. 'They sent him into exile for corruption, you know.'

'He pleaded innocence.'

'Don't we all.' The tribune seemed about to say more and then changed his mind. He offered the centurion his hand. 'Just in case that old sod was wrong about the odds not mattering. My apologies, I had forgotten that you do not like swearing.'

'Waste of good anger, my lord. And anger's a handy thing on a day like this.' Ferox had the odd feeling of being inside a song.

In the north he could see more and more enemies appearing, but it would still be some time before they arrived. For the moment the odds were three or four to one, perhaps more, and that was enough to keep them busy. 'Good luck, my lord. All that matters now is what happens in the next few hours, so we had better live them well.'

Crispinus gulped, his face pale. 'Wish I could think of a joke,' he said, but Marcellus was gesturing for Ferox to go to his men and the centurion walked his mount away. There was no point in hurrying, for the animal was tired enough as it was.

'You do not have to come,' he said to Vindex as the Brigantian followed him. 'You and your men are paid to scout, not fight battles.'

'Reckon scouting's done for the day,' Vindex said, rubbing his hand across the stubble on his chin. 'But I have taken a strong dislike to the mongrels over there, and so have the lads. Keep thinking back to that poor boy they buried.'

'Aye,' Ferox said, and it was not just the Goat Man and his boy, but poor silly Fortunata, the slave girl left murdered in her bed, and all the others. 'If ever people needed killing it is this Stallion and his rabble.'

A great shout went up from the enemy line and trumpets blared. 'Must have upset 'em.' Vindex had to shout the words.

The enemy surged forward a good hundred paces, before their spirit sagged and they slowed and then stopped. Chariots and a few horsemen went closer, the warriors screaming abuse at the Roman line, but the soldiers remained silent. It was never easy to make men charge at a waiting enemy, and Ferox had seen plenty of battles that started as gradually as this. The bands of Britons started chanting again and the trumpets still sounded, the deeper note of cow horns alongside the harsh blare of carnyxes.

Flaccus was in command of the cavalry on the Roman right, and ordered the exploratores to form up next to the cohort of II Augusta. Ferox had half his men, including all the Brigantes, back as a second line fifty paces behind the first. On his right, the decurion Masclus had two turmae of Batavians from cohors VIIII, supported by another from cohors III Batavorum in reserve. The legionary horsemen were in a third line.

For the moment most of the enemy were content to hurl defiance at the Romans. A few horsemen cantered closer to them, well within long bowshot, but for the moment the legate ordered all his men including the archers to wait. He wanted the enemy confident, wanted them to come on.

Opposite Ferox and the cavalry on the right wing were a few chariots, and some of them began to come forward as well. One, its car painted a bright green, rushed ahead of the rest, heading for the Romans, before it swerved and ran along in front of the massed warriors. The driver was small and hunched as he worked his team of a grey and a black – a combination Ferox's people always said was unlucky. He hoped they were right, for the warrior in the back was tall and stark naked apart from a torc at his throat. His skin was covered in tattoos and he waved a stag's head, complete with antlers, in his hand. It was the Stallion, and Ferox wished that there was time to pass the word so that one of the scorpiones could drive a bolt through the man while he was in range. The chariot drove on, sending up a spray of mud as the wheels hit a puddle, but none of the engines or archers shot and the priest drove past unscathed and was soon out of range. His followers shouted even louder, and they broke ranks and flooded forward another hundred paces before staggering to a halt again.

The Romans waited. Ferox could see the men of II Augusta as they stood in formation, shields on the ground resting against their legs, and pila held upright, butts on the ground. They had left their cloaks with the baggage, and even with breeches, tunics and padded jerkins he knew that they would be cold, for no armour, not even the banded cuirass that only legionaries wore, was ever any good at keeping out the cold. He did not know these men, for this cohort had not served in the punitive expedition, but their faces looked familiar, like so many other soldiers he had known.

Today those faces were taut, for no one liked waiting, and all of them could count. He wondered how many had never fought in a battle before, and guessed that that was most of them, even among the few older faces creased by weather and suffering. One man had taken off his helmet to adjust the woollen hat he wore underneath. He had a thick beard, the dark brown mottled with grey. An optio pacing up and down behind the line bellowed at him for being improperly dressed, and the soldier glanced at him and hesitated just long enough to make a point and not quite long enough for it to be insubordination before he put his helmet back on and retied the cheek pieces.

The Britons had stopped again, no more than two hundred paces away. Ferox saw much shouting and jostling as they were pushed back into an ordered rank. Here and there were groups of true warriors, as obvious from the way they stood and their bearing as their better equipment. These men had oval shields, a spear and often a javelin or two, all backed by a sword. Quite a few had helmets and some even armour. Yet most of the front rank was made up of simply dressed men carrying every sort of weapon – proper spears and sharpened sticks, axes, hammers or long knives, with just a few swords. They were the sort of men usually found at the back of a warband when an entire tribe went to battle, and they came because their chieftains demanded it, but they were of little account. Today they looked different, filled with the passion of their leader and all his hatred for Rome.

Ferox walked his horse a few lengths ahead of his men so that he could see better and looked to the north.

'There's plenty of them,' Vindex said. The closest were more than a mile away, but there were many thousand warriors coming towards them. Leading them were plenty of cavalry and more chariots than Ferox had seen earlier in the day. He guessed that there would be far more true warriors among that force, and wondered how many other kings had sent bands. Men like Gannascus might not fight unless it was clear that the Romans were losing, or the high king and others may have tricked the

Romans all along, in which case, as Vindex might say, they were royally humped.

'We need to get on with it,' Vindex said.

'Stay with your men,' Ferox told him. 'Just for once I need you to obey orders.'

The Brigantian's skull-like face split into a grin. 'Well, I suppose we're not being paid for this, so we could bend the rule just once.'

There was a sharp sound, like the crack of a whip but much deeper, and suddenly the enemy went quiet. Ferox had not seen a war engine shoot for some years, and had almost forgotten the violent force of its missiles. He saw a gap in the enemy's front line. A warrior was down, his shield pinned to him, the bolt having driven through his mail shirt deep into his body. The blow flung him back, knocking several other men over, and Ferox watched as they staggered up. More of the scorpiones stung, the bolts flying with great accuracy as the crews picked out men from the bands facing them and killed them. The legionaries cheered when one bolt drove through a man so hard that the point came out the other side and pinned him to a second Briton. The pair staggered about, men jumping out of their way as if they had some curse, until the first man collapsed forward, pulling off the shaft of the bolt as he fell.

Archers scampered forward and began to shoot. More men dropped, for most of the Britons carried only the small square shields used by the Selgovae and the Votadini. They were handy enough, but with no room to dodge because of the press of men, they offered little protection from missiles. The front of each warband rippled as men were struck, the quiver more savage whenever a bolt from one of the engines slammed into its victim.

With a low rumble like a distant swarm of bees, the Batavians began to chant the barritus. The legionaries remained silent, and Ferox knew that to the watching enemy the Romans would seem strangely impassive, almost inhuman. The Britons were screaming again and blowing their horns. Some started forward, but others called to them to stay. Then their yelling grew so loud that it drowned out the rising chant of the Batavians and Ferox saw that the Stallion was driving along in front of his men again. A *scorpio* spat out its missile, but the bolt whisked past the heads of the two ponies and slammed into a man standing in the front rank. Arrows missed and the man rode on until, at a gesture, the charioteer slowed down and the naked priest jumped to the ground. As soon as he was on the grass a bolt hit his charioteer in the head and pitched him over, while a second drove deep into the black pony's belly, so that it reared and screamed. A dozen arrows sped towards them, killing both horses, without touching the Stallion apart from one that stuck in the stag's head. Ferox saw him spit on the arrow and then pull the headdress on. Men appeared, handing him sword and shield, which he raised high as he yelled. The words were unclear, until the whole army took up the cry.

'Blood of king, blood of queen!' The Britons came forward, men flooding around the priest so that he was lost from view. 'Blood!' came the scream from thousands of voices.

'Silence in the ranks. Prepare to advance.' The centurion standing a pace ahead of the cluster of standards at the centre of the cohort of II Augusta shouted clear over the din. 'Keep in rank and follow the standards. Forward, march.'

The four cohorts in the first line stepped off, for it was always better to meet the enemy on the move. Ferox and the cavalry were ordered to hang back and protect the flank of the infantry, but he saw Masclus send one of his turmae forward to skirmish and that was the right thing.

'Good luck, men!' Neratius Marcellus had the rich, carrying voice of a trained orator. Ferox had not seen him come, but he was riding along behind his front rank and urging his men on.

'Blood!' screamed the Britons and charged.

XXVIII

I T DOES NOT take long for a running man to cover two hundred paces. Already the archers were pelting back as fast as they could to take shelter behind the cohorts, and Ferox hoped that the crews of the scorpiones were carrying the machines to safety. Ahead of him, the enemy were more cautious, not sure whether it was wise to charge horsemen. They came at a walk, hanging back, and he could see no true warriors or even the tattooed fanatics of the Stallion. Masclus' troopers began to throw javelins into the mass and as men started to fall the Britons stuttered to a halt.

All along the rest of the front, the enemy charged as fast as they could run. They did not come in a solid line because the keenest, bravest – and the most foolish – went far faster than the rest. Knots of men, mainly the fanatics along with a few groups of true warriors, outstripped the crowd. Others swung to the side to follow their lead so that instead of one great wave it was like the fingers of an outstretched hand jabbing towards the Romans. Ferox had seen the same thing happen many times, but today the mixture of inexperience and wild enthusiasm meant that it happened a lot faster. As always the groups of bold men aimed at the heart of the nearest Roman formation.

'Pila!' the centurion called out to the men of II Augusta and the front rank raised their slim javelins ready to throw. Already the space between the battle lines had shrunk so that the nearest group of Britons was no more than fifty paces away. They kept coming, and even the leaders were splitting up as each ran at his own pace. Ferox could no longer hear any words in their chant, just a scream where rage mixed with terror. The gap was down to thirty paces, then twenty, and the leading Britons did not slow, but if anything went faster. They were the Stallion's men, half of them stripped naked just like their leader, and all covered in tattoos.

Over towards the centre the Batavians' chant surged up into a roar and Ferox could see both cohorts charging, throwing their javelins as they went. The legionaries of II Augusta still waited, the nearest Britons within ten paces, and he was afraid that their senior centurion had left it too late.

'Now!' The centurion swung his arm down as his men jogged three paces and the front rank threw their pila with that familiar grunt of effort. The second rank waited a couple of heartbeats and then lobbed their own missiles, and then the third rank did the same, hurling them straight forward because they could not see well past the men in front.

Three great volleys, each of more than two hundred pila, hummed as they flew through the air and then slammed into the charging Britons and it was as if they were hit by a gale blowing hard off the sea. Their small shields were little protection and men were flung back as the heavy missiles drove deep into their flesh. Ferox saw one warrior manage to catch a pilum on his shield, and watched the man stagger as the point burst through the wood, pierced his arm and stuck out for a good six inches. Then a second heavy javelin hit him in the side of the head, sticking fast even when he was pitched on to the ground.

The Britons' wild charge had broken open their formation, and plenty of the missiles missed the mark and stuck into the grass, but dozens of men were dead, scores crippled, others wounded and all stunned. The chanting had stopped and there was no noise apart from screams of pain and moans of suffering. The charge had been broken, and the Britons reeled as they tried to recover their balance. In the centre the two Batavian cohorts had gone from a gentle jog into a flat run and hit the wavering enemy, punching with the bosses of their shields and stabbing at their opponents.

'Swords!' The legionaries of II Augusta reached down with their right hands, grabbed the hilts of their short swords and pushed down, sliding the blades free of their scabbards.

'Follow me!' The centurion started to run. 'Charge!' The order turned into a yell of rage and the legionaries joined in, so that they roared at the enemy as they went forward.

The Britons did not run. Many men, staggered by the volleys of pila and then faced by a rush of metal-clad, screaming soldiers, would have broken and fled. The boldest were down, for none of the men at the front remained on their feet, but the others were either too stunned or too stubborn to give way. They bunched together, a rough line forming quickly, and men raised their weapons. A few of them flung javelins and one of the legionaries was hit in the face and fell in a clatter of armour and equipment. The Romans ran at the enemy, but when they realised that the Britons were standing and waiting the legionaries slowed. Only a fool or a man too drunk to care rushed full tilt into an opposing battle line, for that was a good way to fall and a man on the ground was finished in this sort of fight. The Romans jogged into contact, although even this produced a crash like falling masonry as shield thumped into shield and blade met blade.

Both sides shouted, no longer in any ordered way, and the sound mixed with gasps of effort and pain. There were bodies on the ground behind the Roman line, most of them Britons and many still moving. One of the optiones stationed at the rear of the formation began jabbing down with the spike on the butt of his staff of office, until another of them yelled at the man to do his job and make sure that the men stayed in formation.

Ferox could not see the fighting clearly, just the backs of the Roman soldiers, but he could tell that they were going forward, step by step. There was a ripple as a Briton hacked down a man in the front rank and jumped into his place, so that the soldiers behind rained blows on him until he dropped. The gap was closed up as one of the men stepped forward, and the line pressed on.

Masclus led his second turma forward as skirmishers because the first had used all their javelins. Ahead of them the Britons were bunched together, crouching in the hope of gaining more shelter from their little shields. Some threw javelins, little axes or even stones at the fast-moving horsemen, but the missiles went wide or bounced off shields and none of the auxiliaries fell.

'A little more of this, and we charge, lads,' Ferox told his men.

'Better put your other hat on then,' Vindex said, and the centurion realised that he still wore his old felt hat. He reached back and unfastened his helmet.

'You go back to your men,' he told the scout.

There was a cheer from II Augusta as the Britons at last gave way, going back fifty paces before they stopped. Some were wounded or too slow and were cut down by the legionaries, many of whom streamed after the retreating enemy.

All along the front the same thing was happening. The Britons had held the Roman onslaught longer than Ferox had expected, but now they went back and both sides drew breath.

'Halt! Halt. Form up!' the senior centurion of II Augusta shouted at his men. Ferox could see the high transverse crest of the officer's helmet as he rushed up and down in front of them. The other centurions took up the cry, and after a little confusion the legionaries obeyed. Optiones in the rear helped re-form the line, and wounded men were sent back out of harm's way, apart from a few who refused to leave the front rank.

A single big flake of snow tumbled down and landed on the mane of Ferox's horse. It did not melt and sat there, looking very white against the rough black hair. Other flakes followed and there was a glow in the clouds that promised plenty more.

Masclus signalled to the trumpeter to recall the Batavians harassing the enemy and they took their place again in close formation beside Ferox's men. The decurion looked around for Flaccus, but could not see him and so walked his mount over to the centurion. 'We go on your order, sir,' he said. 'When they charge?' He nodded at the cohort of legionaries.

'We wait a little longer.' Ferox looked to the north. It was hard to see, but as far as he could tell the enemy coming from that direction were not yet close. 'There's time, and if we wait a bit the mongrels have longer to worry.'

Masclus looked unconvinced, and was no doubt wondering what an infantryman knew about such things, but Ferox was a superior officer and the habit of obedience was strong. 'The lads are doing well,' he said instead of challenging the order.

'They are indeed,' Ferox agreed and gestured over towards the centre where the Batavian infantry were charging again, not bothering with the drawn-out barritus this time, but simply screaming defiance as they took their blades to the enemy.

'Should one of us go to the Lord Flaccus?' The decurion asked the question, his expression formal, but not quite hiding the lack of confidence in Ferox that underlay the question.

'Come on, boys, let's show these dogs how real soldiers fight!' the senior centurion of II Augusta harangued his men. He began to bang the blade of his gladius against the side of his long rectangular shield. 'Come on the Capricorns!'

The legionaries copied him, drumming the swords in time, and then marched forward. Ferox did know his own legion, but could not help feeling pride as the men stepped smartly towards the waiting enemy. Part of him – and not just the part than remained a Silurian – disliked the banging of swords on shields, for it risked blunting a blade's edge and the noise was often less frightening than silent order.

The Britons were not cowed.

'Blood! Blood!' The chant was clear, and Ferox saw the Stallion near the front of this group, his headdress distinctive and a bloodied sword in one hand. There were more of his tattooed followers with him and they looked fresh as they pushed their way into the front rank. 'Blood!'

Romans and Britons began to charge at the same moment. This time there were no pila and only a few javelins thrown by the warriors as they closed the distance. Neither side flinched, until the last moment when they slowed as the two lines met. Men yelled and hacked or stabbed, shields pounding on shields, blades striking armour or flesh and bone.

'We go now.' Ferox patted Masclus on the shoulder. 'Straight at them and hope they break. Flaccus will follow if we win and cover us if we don't.' He hoped that was true, but there was no time to make sure, otherwise the warriors facing them might get some of their confidence back.

Ferox drew his sword and hefted the flat round shield he had borrowed from one of Vindex's men. 'Right, boys. We're going straight at those mongrels and we're not stopping. Advance at the walk!'

His horse responded readily, and he had to restrain her from rushing with a gentle tug on the reins. To the left II Augusta were still fighting and so far no one had given ground. The noise was slackening as men grew tired.

'Trot!' Ferox wished that he had a trumpeter to repeat each order, but none had been allocated to the exploratores.

The waiting Britons were close now, huddled together so tightly that they looked like a wall. They must have used up all their missiles against Masclus' skirmishers because nothing was flung at Ferox and the others as they approached, by now no more than thirty paces away. Neither were the warriors shouting, and that was a mistake, because horses did not like too much noise even when they were trained to battle.

'Charge!' Ferox yelled and was pleased when a trumpet sounded from one of the Batavian turmae. The snow was still falling and flakes struck his face as the horse leaped forward, at last free from restraint. The auxiliaries yelled and from behind he could hear the high-pitched yip-yip-yip war cry of the Carvetii as Vindex and his men followed. He heard the heavy feet of the horses pounding on the springy turf as they closed those last few yards. The enemy were still quiet, crouching, waiting, and it could all go wrong at this moment because if the warriors held their ground then no horse would ride into what seemed like a solid block. The horses would stop short, a length or more away, the riders almost bobbing in the saddle as they tried to kick the beasts on.

One of the Britons stood up straight, mouth open wide as if to shout, but Ferox heard no sound, and his horse kept going. The warrior turned, pushing at the men behind, and suddenly the mass broke apart, men running away. A gap opened and the mare flew into it. Ferox cut down, felt a momentary jar as the sword hit bone before biting into the skull, and his gladius was almost pulled from his hand before the speed of his horse wrenched it free. A warrior came at him from the right, spear thrusting at his chest, and he beat it aside and was past, running amid a loose crowd of fleeing men. He leaned into a thrust, caught a man at the top of the spine, saw him drop and kept going. There were cavalrymen close behind and on either side, slashing more often that they stabbed.

Ferox sliced down, the man sheering away at the last minute so that the triangular tip of the centurion's blade cut through one eye and the warrior's cheek. The Briton clutched at the wound screaming until Victor drove his heavy spear full into the man's back. Masclus was pushing his horse through the press, and Ferox watched as he drew level with a running man, cut back and took the warrior's head off with a single blow. A jet of blood pumped up into the air, and horses and soldiers alike were spattered with blood, but little of it was their own.

Not all the Britons were helpless. Two men came at Ferox, one from each side, and he yanked hard on the reins and made his mare rear, front feet flailing, and one man lost his teeth when a hoof slammed into his face. The centurion hacked through the right arm of the other warrior, the hand still clutching a workman's axe as it fell free. He raised the blade again and cut across his body at the first enemy, missing his head and biting into his neck. With the next blow blood was pumping and the man dropped.

Ferox pushed on, and the crowd was more scattered, and yet still there were ten or more Britons for every Roman riding among them. It was intoxicating to have so many enemies at your mercy so that a rider could choose which one to kill next. Alexander had led his Macedonians like this, and it was small wonder that the king soon felt himself to be a god, because there was an exultation and raw excitement about such slaughter that was like nothing else. The auxiliaries killed and killed, and there were still more enemies as the troopers grew weary, and their horses went faster than the men on foot and soon burst out of the back of the great mob of Britons. Ferox looked around him and there were no more warriors to cut down, for all had been left behind. His horse began to slow, but he forced the mare on until she was properly clear and only then halted her and turned her around.

Ferox tried to shout, but had to cough before any sound would come. His mouth was dry as dust, and his voice cracked as he called out, 'Rally, rally on me!' He waved his sword in the air and his arm felt like lead. Men came to join him, all wide-eyed, not quite believing what they had done. Vindex was with them, the blade of his long sword notched, and Masclus with some of his Batavians, even the fur on their helmets flecked with blood. The Thracian was there as well, and the man looked down at his thigh, puzzled because he was wounded, but not remembering how it had happened. Some forty men had made it through. Ferox did not know how many had fallen, although he could see a couple of dead horses among the crowd of enemies who now milled about, uncertain what to do. They had stopped running. Beyond them he could see a few dozen more cavalrymen, which meant that some had not broken into the enemy formation. The legionary horsemen were further back and it was hard to see them through the snow.

He looked towards the centre and there was another lull in the fighting. It was strange to see the backs of the Britons rather than the Roman cohorts. Second Augusta did not seem to have made any ground, but they had not lost any either, and instead the two lines had fought until they were spent and then shuffled back so that they were a couple of spear lengths apart. He could see the six *signa* of the cohort clustered together in the centre of their line, but could not see the legionaries. The Britons were massed, fifteen, maybe twenty deep in places, and if the Stallion was still with them he would be whipping them up into a fresh frenzy. Ferox wondered whether II Augusta could hold and was pleased when he saw arrows arching high over the cohort and landing among the dense mass of enemy. Someone must have seen the danger and sent the archers to support the legionaries. In the centre the Batavians had made a little ground, but were still hugely outnumbered, and as the snow flurries became heavier he could not see the left flank and could only hope that XX Valeria Victrix and the cavalry were holding their own.

'Right, lads, back we go to where we started,' he said, running the blade of his sword through the mare's mane to clean off the blood. 'Go again before they start counting.' A few of the men grinned, for there were hundreds of warriors in front of them and they were gathering together again, many of them turning to face the Romans who were now behind them. Yet if Flaccus sent the legionaries and the other horsemen charging in from the other side then they might still panic and flee.

'Sir!' Masclus pointed past the Britons to where the legionary horsemen were wheeling away to face north. For just an instant the snow slackened and Ferox glimpsed one of the cohorts of VIIII Hispana from the second line also turning away from the main battle. The reserves were shifting to meet a new threat at the very time the battle was balanced on a knife edge.

With a dull roar the Britons facing II Augusta went forward again, forcing weary limbs and fading spirits to try one more time. Ferox hoped that the legionaries could hold, for there was now nothing behind them.

'Come on, those people have lived too long already,' Ferox called to his men, his sword pointing at the re-forming Britons. Vindex laughed, his eyes wild.

'Charge!' There was no point building up the pace gradually. Horses and men were tired and it was just a case of getting them to go at the enemy as fast as they could. His men did not cheer, saving their strength for the fight, but they followed, a ragged line two ranks deep.

The mare jerked into a canter, stumbled, recovered and found new strength to go faster. The Britons were close, and among them were corpses, the snow settling quicker on them than it did on the damp ground so that they looked like little white mounds. Some of the Britons stood back to back, weapons ready, but Ferox ignored them and rode into the spaces where men fled from their path. The back of a warband was where the cautious and timid lurked, so there were few bold spirits and many more without the sense to realise that running was the most dangerous thing they could do. Ferox cut a man down and made for the next one, only to see the Briton fling himself flat so that he could not reach him. He hoped that someone behind him had a spear to finish the rogue off, but there was no time to worry and it was better to keep moving.

The Romans drove into the loose crowd of warriors, stabbing and hacking, pressing on wherever there was a space or one opened up ahead of them. They wounded and killed, but there was not the same surprise and momentum as the first charge and more of the enemy fought back. A Batavian took one man in the throat with his heavy spear, while another reeled back when his horse bit the warrior's face, leaving it a bloody ruin. Another Briton drove a sharpened stake into the animal's belly, and it screamed as it fell, throwing its rider who hit the ground hard and was hacked to pieces in moments.

Ferox pushed on, lunging to pierce a man's skull just where he bore the tattoo of the horse, but another man, more of a warrior this time, was on his left, and two great blows shattered the centurion's shield and left it weak and broken. He was about to turn and face him when another wild-eyed, tattooed man charged at him, his open mouth frothing, and it took all Ferox's strength to block the furious blow of an axe held two-handed.

Vindex saved him. The Brigantian came up from nowhere, and there were sparks and a sharp ring as his long sword met the warrior's blade and both came to a juddering halt. Ferox parried another wild sweep from the axeman, and had time to flick his blade up and jab into the man's throat. Blood gushed from the wound, but the tattooed man used his last strength to raise the axe again, slicing its blade across the shoulder of the centurion's horse.

Ferox turned to see Vindex beating the warrior down, wounding him on the shoulder so that the strength left his sword arm and then hacking again and again at the man's head. When he had finished the blade of his sword had even more notches and was bent back at a weird angle.

'You owe me a sword!' the Brigantian yelled, and slammed his heels against his horse's sides to force the tall beast onwards, using its weight to barge a path because his weapon was useless. Ferox followed, attacking any man who threatened the scout. His mare was bleeding badly, and he could feel her shudder. If he did not fight his way through to the far side then she would fall and he would have no chance.

Vindex found his path blocked. He caught a spear thrust and pushed it aside with his bent sword, and Ferox reached him and hacked down, taking off the back of the warrior's skull so that blood and brains splashed over him. The press was getting denser, but then there was a shout and Roman horsemen were charging in from the front. There were not many of them, for only half the men left behind were bold enough to charge, but it was enough to confuse the Britons. Some died because they were facing the wrong way, and the mass broke up again so that Ferox, Vindex and the others could push through and gallop free of crowd, riding for the Roman lines again. At least ten men had not made it, and half of the rest were bleeding from wounds or nursing broken bones. Ferox's mare sank under him as soon as they were clear, but he managed to spring from the saddle before she rolled over. Victor appeared, leading a riderless horse, its side stained with the blood of its former master, and Ferox thanked the auxiliary and hauled himself up.

The cohort of II Augusta had given ground. It was just a dozen or so paces and then the two lines had parted once more, men gasping for breath and with no strength left to shout. Each time men closed and fought they spent some of their strength and will, and no one knew how big a store of either he possessed until it was all gone. Each time the fighting lines separated it took longer to persuade anyone to go forward again. It was even harder when men sensed that they were losing and being forced back.

In the centre the Batavians were just about holding their own and might even have gained a few paces. As Ferox watched, the furthest group – that must be cohors III – shuffled forward, but with none of the enthusiasm of the earlier charges. The Britons met them and held on, refusing to give way. They had numbers on their side and the hot passion of a prophet in their midst who had promised them victory. Against that the soldiers had years of training and practice, better equipment, and pride in themselves and their units.

There were no reserves. Both cohorts of VIIII Hispana had wheeled round and marched several hundred paces to form a new line facing north. The Vardulli and Tungrians had been fed into the line to reinforce the Batavians – Ferox saw the last group of auxiliaries jog forward as a centurion led them to join the fighting. He could not see the singulares and had no idea where they had gone for they were not part of the line facing north. Flaccus was with the legionaries, and he wondered what the man was doing, but then Crispinus appeared as well and he could only guess that the Legate Marcellus had ordered the redeployment.

A couple of soldiers helped an officer back from II Augusta. The man shook them off, and Ferox recognised their senior centurion, even though his helmet was gone and a dirty bandage was wrapped around his head. There were wounds on both arms, he had lost his shield and his armour was rent and stained, but the man lurched forward, going back to the fighting, until he collapsed. Even then he tried to crawl back to his men.

'Keep them busy as long as you can,' Ferox croaked to Masclus. His throat was parched, in spite of the snow still tumbling down around them, and it seemed an age since he had had a drink. 'You help him,' he said as Vindex looked ready to follow him. 'Try to hold them back as long as you can.'

He trotted the horse towards II Augusta, jumping down beside the centurion, who was still pulling himself across the grass, leaving a trail of blood behind.

'Get him away,' he said to the soldiers. He turned to another man, a young soldier who looked to be no more than a boy. 'Who is in charge now?'

'Don't know, sir,' the man said, seeing Ferox's crest. 'Must be one of the optiones because all four centurions are down.'

'Wrong answer, lad.' Ferox grinned at the pale-faced youth. 'I'm in charge. Now come with me.'

XXIX

T HERE WAS NO trace left of the neat three-deep line in which the cohort had begun the battle. A lot of legionaries – Ferox guessed as many as two hundred – had drifted back so that men were scattered alone or in loose clusters as far as a bowshot behind where the line had once been. Most of these men were bloodied, and plenty of them had wounds to the legs, right arm or face, all the places a shield did little to protect. The handful of *medici*, the soldiers trained to deal with wounds, had long since been overwhelmed by the sheer numbers of casualties. They were doing their best to help any who could be helped on a snowy moor in the middle of a battle. Lots of other men, unscathed and reluctant, had used the excuse of helping the wounded back to slip away.

Ferox saw a couple of legionaries leaning on their shields, their heads bowed so that they did not have to meet anyone's eye. 'You!' he bellowed from a few feet away, his voice suddenly full of strength and with enough of a parade-ground tone to make their faces jerk up. 'What are your names?'

'Longus, sir,' one answered before he could think. His comrade glanced at him, but knew that he could not refuse.

'Terentius, sir.' He was younger than the other man, probably no more than twenty, but he had the sharp features of someone who planned to grow as old and rich as possible.

'Good. You are with me. Stay right behind me and if ever I lose sight of you, I'll make sure they have the skin off your back before the week is out. Understand!'

'Sir.' The voices were weary and lacked enthusiasm, but the habit of discipline was strong and his crest marked this man out as a centurion – and his tone as a right bastard likely to remember.

Everyone knew that the worst slaughter happened when a unit broke and fled, and as a fight drew on and on and everyone tired, they all knew, too, that the collapse could come at any moment. So men hung back and waited. No one wanted to be seen to start the panic and be blamed. No one wanted to die either, so they lurked well behind the fighting line until they could follow the lead of everyone else.

Terentius and Longus trailed after the centurion as he went forward, ignoring men who were wounded but yelling at the rest to follow. Ferox scooped up a shield that lay on the ground, hefted it to test that the handgrip was still firmly in place and the boards solid, and pushed on. There were a dozen archers nearby, waiting and not shooting.

'Running short of arrows, sir,' the optio with them reported. 'Down to four or five each.'

'Right. Every second man gives his to the soldier next to him. Then he draws his sword and follows me. You stay with the others.'

'Sir.'

He expected more show of resentment at being asked to fight hand to hand rather than do what they were paid and trained to do, but the archers' faces were impassive.

Ferox ran forward. The front of the cohort was now a row of seven or eight clusters of weary men. Some of them may have started out as the centuries of the cohort, but there was little regularity any more. Legionaries still determined to fight on bunched together because that made them feel safer. Most of the clusters were ten or twelve deep and there were big gaps between them. If the Britons had been fresh and eager then they could have swarmed through the spaces and overwhelmed the remnants of the cohort, but they were just as exhausted and their line looked much the same and was no more solid.

The six signa carried by the cohort were in the biggest group at the centre of the line and Ferox headed towards them, running through the gap to get in front. 'Form there.' He pointed with his sword to show that he wanted them to stand level with the standards in the space between this cluster and the next. 'Terentius, you're there as right marker. Longus next to you, then you and you.' He gestured to two more men. 'The rest in three ranks behind them. When I say go, you follow me. Understood?'

'Sir.' Terentius stamped to attention and clashed his sword against his shield. 'We'll be ready.'

'Good.' He turned his back on the enemy to face the other legionaries, praying that there was no one still with a missile and the energy to throw it into his back. The Britons were no more than four spear lengths away, but all looked spent – at least for the moment. Some were even on their knees or bent double as they gasped for breath. There were bodies of the dead and badly wounded strewn on the ground between the two sides. One was a Roman, just a few paces away.

'Water, please, water,' the wounded man begged.

Ferox ignored him and shouted with all his strength. 'Capricorns! You are Second Augusta.' Some of the men looked up to see who it was, but some were too tired to care. He could see that only one of the signa was still carried by a signifer wearing the usual bearskin over his helmet. The other five were held by ordinary soldiers, which meant that the standard-bearers were down. Ferox could see no sign of a centurion anywhere along the front, which meant that the report must have been right. He saw a soldier by the standards. The man's shield was gouged by two big cuts, the calfskin outer layer peeled back to show the boards underneath. The man had no staff, and his segmented armour was bent and dented on the shoulders, but a red feather stood up high on one side of his iron helmet and the stub of another showed that there had once been a second feather on the other side, marking him out as an optio.

'I am Flavius Ferox, *princeps posterior* of the third cohort, currently on detached service, and I am taking command. Optio, report!'

'Sir.' The man straightened slightly, but did not attempt any more formal show of respect.

'Water. Please, for the love of Diana, give me water,' the wounded soldier begged. Ferox still ignored him.

'Call that a salute, man!' Ferox was trying to get their attention, and was pleased to see a brief flash of anger before the optio raised his right arm, sword still in his hand. The blade was bloody.

'Sir. Beg to report—' Before the optio said anything, Ferox saw the alarm in his face and spun around. Two warriors were coming at him, eyes wild and teeth bared, although they did not scream a war cry. The first held a broken spear with only three feet of its shaft left and he lunged it underarm. Ferox swung his shield sideways so that the edge pushed the spearhead aside and lunged to take the man in the throat. The dying man's eyes widened, looking more surprised than fearful as the centurion yanked his blade free.

The second warrior had a sword and shield and came with more care, until the wounded Roman reached out to grab his ankles. The Briton swayed, fighting for balance, looking down angrily and raising his sword to cut this nuisance down. Ferox took two paces forward and thrust his gladius into the man's stomach.

'*Hoc habet*,' came a voice from behind him and there was a dull cheer from the legionaries at this cry from the arena. Ferox kept his shield towards the enemy and looked back over his shoulder.

'Come on, then. That's how to deal with these mongrels. Capricorns, follow me!' He turned his head to the front, took a deep breath, vaulted over the wounded legionary and ran straight at the Britons. This was not what he had planned. He had wanted to get the knots of men from II Augusta, or at least the ones around the standard, to re-form into something more like a line so that they could fight better, and he had hoped to spur them to make one last effort.

There was no time, and he just had to hope that cutting two of the enemy down would stir them to follow him even though he was a stranger. He yelled as he charged and did not look back.

They would follow him or they would not, and if they did not then he would most certainly die.

He jumped over a corpse, this time of a naked Briton with his belly slit open and steam coming off the coiling streams of innards around him. He could hear nothing apart from his own yell and it was almost as if the sound came from someone else. The enemy waited, and one or two were trying to get back out of his way. He saw a tall man with limed hair pushing through the mass towards him, and recognised the Stallion, who must have lost his headdress, and then other men jostled and were in the way so that all he could see was a raised sword. The glimpse was enough. He thought of Fortunata, of the other victims butchered by this man, and he thought of what could have happened to Sulpicia Lepidina. The raw hate gave him strength and he wanted only to kill the priest before he was himself killed. It no longer mattered whether II Augusta came with him or not.

'Mongrel!' His incoherent yell became a word, and still no one came to meet him, so he reached the line, punched with his shield, knocking down a warrior's little buckler, hitting the man in the face. The Briton staggered and the sword drove into his belly. Ferox twisted the blade free as the man fell, screaming, and a moment later he blocked a cut with his shield and slashed open the throat of a tattooed fanatic. He pushed into the ranks, and they all seemed to be slow and sluggish while he was as fast as a hawk. He punched again with the boss, felt the man's jaw break, and then jabbed with the pommel of his sword into the face of another because he did not have time to bring it back ready to thrust. The man reeled away. Ferox flicked the blade back down and lunged into the man behind, the long tip piercing an eye. He slammed his shield forward again, pushing into the mass, going forward, always forward, and he felt a blow strike his right shoulder and almost lost balance. His arm still worked and he was standing. He cut back, carving into a warrior's neck, the blade grating on a bronze torc before it reached the flesh. Blood spurted over him, and he pressed on, heading towards the

Stallion who was close now. Something slammed into the side of his head, denting the helmet and cutting his forehead as the iron edge was driven into his skin.

Ferox turned, eyes blinking as he tried to stay conscious, and he lifted the shield to parry another blow from a shaven-headed fanatic wielding a thick branch as a club. A sword took the man in the side, under the armpit, blood bubbled at his lips and Terentius drew back his blade and slashed, knocking the warrior down. One of the archers came after him, using the small round shield they carried and an axe rather than a sword. Other men were appearing all around him, and the optio yelled as he stabbed low, driving into a warrior's groin so that his high-pitched shriek mingled with the victor's cries. Beside him a legionary took a spear thrust to the face and sank down.

The Britons were edging back, even as the Stallion called on them to kill. Ferox saw an axe head burst through the back of his shield, throwing up jagged splinters, but the weapon stuck there and Terentius appeared and hacked again and again at the warrior's neck until his head was left hanging by a thin sheet of skin. Longus stamped his front foot down and pounded another man with his shield, knocking him down. The Roman leaned forward, stabbed once, but his friend's cry came too late for him to dodge the crude spear that pierced the cheek piece of his helmet and drove into the side of his mouth.

The Stallion let the spear go and clasped one hand tightly around the wrist of his sword arm. He raised the blade high, his pale skin a network of blue woad, and he looked like a demon from stories with his spiked hair and the burning savagery of his eyes. A legionary went for him, slipped on the intestines of a dying man, dropping his guard, and the priest slashed down. There was a dull clang as the blade cut through the iron helmet and the soldier fell.

Ferox barged Terentius aside. The priest was quick, his sword already back up, and he cut again, slicing through the bronze edging at the top of the shield and into the wood. Ferox fought for balance, saw the heavy sword going up again for the next attack, and cut wildly with his gladius. He felt the blade bite and dragged it across the priest's chest, pushing as hard as he could. The sword cut down again, weaker this time, but enough to carve another rent in his shield.

Men were dragging the Stallion away. With a howl one of his tattooed followers leaped up, flinging himself bodily at Ferox. The centurion felt the wind knocked from him and he was falling to the ground, the heavy weight of the man on top. He lost his sword and shield. The man's face was inches away from his, features contorted with hate as his hands felt for the centurion's throat. Ferox tried to roll and push the man off, but he was heavy and now the fingers closed around his windpipe. He felt for his dagger, found it and pulled it free from the scabbard, but it was getting hard to breathe as the man's hands tightened. He stabbed once, twice, and only at the third wound did the grip slacken. Ferox gulped in air, and stabbed the man again.

A trumpet sounded, then two more, and there were shouts. Ferox strained to slide the corpse off him. The pugio and his hand were sticky with drying blood, his mail bloodstained, but as he pushed himself up he saw that II Augusta were driving forward, killing the enemy as they ran. There were Roman cavalry riding among the Britons, the cloaks of the legate's singulares streaming behind them. They had won on the far left, driving away the enemy horsemen after a hard fight and then they had begun to attack the flank of the infantry. The Britons held on for a long time because there were so many of them. Only slowly did they weaken, and at almost the same time the remnants of the first Roman line were going forward with their last strength and the Stallion's great host collapsed.

Ferox's eyes kept closing. He was breathing deeply, but was finding it hard to stand. Nearby Terentius knelt by Longus, weeping over his dying friend, as an archer staggered past, his right arm missing below the elbow. The snow turned to sleet that somehow seemed colder and the centurion began to shiver. Most of II Augusta had stopped, exhaustion claiming them, and over their heads Ferox could see the cavalry riding among the enemy, killing at will, but there were so many thousands of Britons even after all this slaughter and the cavalry were few. He saw the tall figure of the Stallion being supported by several warriors. They were past the main crowd, and none of the cavalry seemed to have seen them. There was a chariot waiting, and a dozen horsemen, and one of them had long white hair and even though it was so far away he knew that it must be the great druid. The men lifted the priest into the chariot and it drove off, protected by the riders.

Ferox looked around for a horse, knowing that he must chase and finish the priest off while they had the chance. He saw one, the same one he had ridden to join the cohort, and it was standing amid the corpses, cropping at a tussock of grass.

Ferox tried to run and could not. He walked a few steps, but could not keep in a straight line. His eyes were heavy, wanting to close. He lurched a few more paces until the darkness came and he fell.

XXX

T HE TRAIL WAS faint, sometimes vanishing among so many other tracks of men fleeing from the defeated army, but the direction was clear and each time they lost it, Ferox was able to pick it up again. On the first day he suspected their purpose. By the second day he was sure. He had been unconscious for only a short time, before waking with a fierce headache. The *medicus ordinarius*, the doctor in charge of all the medical orderlies, had given him something to drink and he had slept through the night, until the legate's men roused him before dawn.

Neratius Marcellus was pleased with his victory, and was sensible enough to know how close they had come to disaster, and shrewd enough to write a report that would show how everything had gone to plan. They were saved by the high king, and the other princes and chieftains who had sent men to answer the Stallion's call to arms even though they did not go in person. All of those contingents were with the northern force, and they had not hurried to join the battle, but let the Stallion and his main force win or lose on their own. Even when they came in sight of the fighting, they had tarried, and their influence made many other warriors cautious. Only the most fervent, led by the tattooed fanatics, had pressed on in spite of this. Perhaps twelve or fifteen hundred Britons had attacked the improvised Roman line, and VIIII Hispana and the others in that hasty line facing north had fought these to a standstill and were starting to drive them back when the panic spread from the rest of the army and they broke. Tincommius' men and the other real warriors had watched from a distance.

'Our embassy to Tincommius has borne splendid fruit,' Crispinus told Ferox as they rode out on the morning after the battle. 'The high king proved true to his pledges.'

Ferox could not help thinking that the high king had kept a foot in each camp until the very last moment. He had sent Gannascus and several hundred warriors to join the Stallion. If the Romans had blundered into that force instead of retreating when their cavalry were routed then it was hard to believe that the German and the rest would not have fought against them, especially if the Stallion's bands had come round from behind and trapped them according to plan. The same was surely true if things had gone worse for the Romans in the battle. Tincommius' men were cautious, but either way they would have ended up on the winning side. Ferox suspected that the legate sensed this truth, but was happy to ignore it since everything had turned out well. He was less sure that the tribune understood, for Crispinus was a harder man to read.

Neratius Marcellus had ordered Ferox to hunt down the wounded priest and bring him back as a captive or his head as a trophy. 'Either way I want his head on a stake over the gates at Vindolanda,' he told them. 'That seems the right place, and it would be better if he was executed there, but it does not matter too much if you cannot bring him in alive.' He had nodded to Flavius Cerialis, who was nursing a nasty wound to the side. The prefect winced as he smiled at the compliment.

'The men would appreciate it, my lord. As would I.'

Ferox wondered whether the prefect was thinking about his murdered lover. Cerialis ought to recover as long as the wound did not turn bad. The centurion tried to dismiss from his mind a wild fantasy where the prefect died, leaving his widow free to remarry. It was nonsense and he knew it, for a senator's daughter could condescend to marry an *eques*, but never a man of lower rank and far less means. Sulpicia Lepidina was as far beyond him as the stars in the heavens and in truth he could not really wish her husband ill. Cerialis had fought well, leading his Batavians even after he had taken the cut to his thigh and a heavy blow to the chest.

Aelius Brocchus was also among the wounded, although not so seriously, and none of the senior officers had been killed. The centurions had suffered more, as they always did, for their place was in front. A quarter were dead, half wounded, and the remainder struggling to run the units. Overall there were one hundred and fifty-two dead and almost double that number wounded. The Britons had lost a thousand dead, and another thousand too badly wounded to crawl or be carried away, who would be killed as soon as they were found by the parties of soldiers sent out on that grim duty.

Ferox was glad to leave the stench and the cawing of ecstatic crows behind. Vindex came with him, refusing to stay in spite of a nasty cut to the head.

'If I leave you on your own you'll only get into trouble,' he insisted, and Ferox was pleased to have his company, for he chattered away and kept Crispinus occupied. There was also Flaccus and an escort of five legionary horsemen, the number agreed with Gannascus, who with ten of his warriors would accompany them.

'A prophet cannot survive when his miracle fails,' the Legate Marcellus assured them. 'You should not have any trouble, but the sight of the king's men will make you doubly safe.'

Ferox was much less certain, but was proved wrong for they met no parties of fanatics determined to kill any Roman they saw. The lands seemed unnaturally quiet, and for all the trails left by men going back to their homes they saw few people abroad, although since rain fell steadily from the very start it was rarely possible to see far.

Gannascus was in good spirits, seemed pleased to see him, and made jokes about how they were lucky his Germans had not led the attack on the Roman line. Ferox did not let himself be drawn, and was glad that the constant downpour dampened spirits so that most of the time they rode in silence. He did not want to speak, needing to think because he was not sure how to obey the legate's last, secret order.

'One of those tribunes is a traitor,' the legate had said, once again with only his intimate friend Ovidius as witness. 'Whoever it is, even if it is my nephew, I want you to make sure that he does not come back.'

Much of the time he rode ahead of the rest, claiming that he needed to search for tracks, and even Vindex left him alone. Ferox thought he knew the answer to all the riddles, was almost sure, but the battle had drained much of his hatred and anger, taking the hard edge off his desire for revenge. Instead he felt listless and empty. If he had been back at Syracuse he suspected that he would have got drunk, so maybe it was better that he had something to do, unpleasant though the task was.

'We will be at the ferry soon, will we not?' Crispinus had ridden up to join him.

'Two hours, my lord, but I do not think we shall have to go that far. "Some leaves do not fall, some trees do not die."' He sang the words softly.

'I am too cold and wet for mysteries, my friend.' The tribune was pale and looked truly miserable.

'Perhaps it would have been better if you had not come, my lord.'

Crispinus smiled. 'I had to be here at the end.'

'Not long now,' Ferox said. Under his cloak he felt for the bone handgrip of his gladius.

The trail ran straight the last few miles, and when they came to the spot it was easy to see in his mind's eye what had happened. They had unharnessed the two ponies from the chariot and then burned the car. The remains were scorched a deep black by a great heat, for they must have used oil to get the wood and leather to burn in all this rain. The ponies lay dead, throats cut and made to lie down on either side of the pyre.

'The Legate Marcellus was right,' Crispinus said, patting his horse to calm it as it tried to pull away. 'A prophet cannot fail.'

The Stallion's corpse swung gently in the breeze, suspended from one of the main branches of the yew tree. Ferox imagined Acco the druid supervising, probably placing the noose around the priest's head himself, then watching as the others hauled him up and made the rope fast. The naked priest would have jerked and twitched, struggling for breath, choking slowly as his own weight dragged his body down. They had cut him about the body, cut him time and again, and Ferox saw a broken flint blade on the ground, which meant that they had not used ordinary knives. A great scar ran across his stomach, sewn up and starting to heal a little, which was the wound the centurion had given him during the battle. It did not look as if it would have proved fatal. All the other cuts were neater, less deep, and the rain had fallen, washing away the blood, so all that was left was slice after slice cut into his white skin. It would have taken a long time and traces around his lips told Ferox that the man had been given poison as well. The triple death, the sacred death of a willing victim sacrificed to appease the anger of the gods.

Flaccus gave a nervous laugh. 'These Britons really don't like failures.'

Ferox did not bother to answer. The Romans would never understand.

Flaccus jumped down. 'You men,' he ordered the escort. 'Help me cut this fellow down. My Lord Crispinus, perhaps you would like to do the honours and take his head?'

The tribune seemed surprised, but realised that there would be something for him to boast about and shock his friends with when he returned to Rome, so got down.

Ferox gestured to Vindex to dismount as well. 'Do you trust me?' he whispered to the Brigantian.

'No.'

'Then just do what I ask. Have your blade ready. When I look away and say that I'm expecting someone to join us, that will be the signal.'

Crispinus had thrown his cloak back to get at his sword. He drew it, just as one of the legionaries rode over to the tree and sawed through the rope. The corpse thumped on to the soggy ground and somehow looked even whiter.

'Little bloke, wasn't he?' one of the soldiers joked.

Ferox drew his gladius and in the same motion brought it so that the tip quivered an inch from Crispinus' throat. 'Drop the sword,' he said.

'Have you gone mad, centurion?' Flaccus looked baffled.

'My Lord Flaccus, I must ask you to place the noble Crispinus under arrest on charges of treason.'

'What?' Crispinus' eyes flicked from side to side. 'This is absurd.'

'Drop the sword.' Ferox pressed so that the tip of his gladius touched the skin of the tribune's neck. 'Drop it.' Crispinus let the weapon fall.

'What is the meaning of this?' Flaccus was confused, but he gestured to one of the legionaries and the man came and took away the tribune's sword.

'I am acting on orders of the Legate Marcellus,' Ferox said, his eyes fixed on Crispinus. 'And I regret to say that the tribune has plotted with other senators to damage the majesty of the republic and our princeps, the glorious Trajan.'

The legionaries had all stopped and were watching and listening. Gannascus frowned and then shrugged, and his men sat on their horses showing only mild curiosity at the Romans talking in a language they did not understand.

'You!' Ferox nodded to one of the legionaries. 'Get some rope and tie the tribune's hands behind his back.' The soldier looked at Flaccus, who waved a hand to show that he was to obey the order.

'That is better,' the centurion said, even though the man had not yet returned, for Crispinus held his arms down and waited meekly for the bonds. 'Now I can lower my arm.'

Ferox stepped away and began to walk in a circle, waiting until he was behind Crispinus before he started to speak again. Two of the legionaries crouched down beside the dead priest, waiting for orders. One was next to Flaccus, another fetching the rope, and the last man, the one who had cut the dead priest's corpse down, sat on his horse, watching.

'The tribune wanted to start a war,' Ferox began, 'so he sent weapons and money to kings among the tribes, men who encouraged that fiend.' He pointed his blade at the corpse. 'With a priest preaching hatred and promising victory, the tribes were stirred up. He well knew that the garrisons up here are weak, so that we are seen as vulnerable as well as loathed. That's never good.'

Ferox gave a thin smile. 'When you look back it was really all so easy. The tribune had friends. He's the son of a senator with lots of connections, and he is an up-and-coming man, someone to watch and someone well worth doing a favour to earn his gratitude. There is all that even before he helps break one emperor and raise up another. Plenty of people were eager to help the noble Crispinus. Some were already tied to him or his family.'

Ferox had gone right round and was level with the tribune. The legionary came back with a piece of hemp rope cut from the one that they had used to hang the Stallion. He tied the young aristocrat's hands together.

'I recall an oath,' Crispinus said in a low voice, his words bitter. 'One willingly taken to my father.'

'You should,' Ferox said, glaring at him, 'because it's the only reason you are still alive. That oath is a burden, but I have a higher oath, a sacred oath that all soldiers take.' The sacramentum to obey and serve the princeps and the Senate and People of Rome was sworn when a man joined the army, taken in front of the standards, and then renewed at the accession of each new emperor.

'I serve Rome,' the tribune claimed. 'Always Rome.'

'But not Trajan!' Ferox yelled and twitched his sword up before putting his other hand on his wrist to push his arm back down. 'Noble Crispinus, I will not kill you unless I have to, but will leave that task to others. My oath to your father holds that far.'

'You have no evidence.' There was doubt in Flaccus' voice. 'It is no light matter to arrest a senior officer.' The protest came after he had let one of his men bind the tribune. 'How can I be sure you are right?'

'He has not denied anything, has he?' Ferox realised his tone was sharp – too sharp for words to a senior officer. 'My apologies, my Lord Flaccus, but treason is a dirty business and it is hard not to feel rage, especially since I am pledged to this man. But let me explain. Back in the summer the noble Crispinus met with men from the procurator's staff and arranged for them to demand a higher levy from the Selgovae, and demand it sooner than usual.'

Out of the corner of his eye, Ferox saw the captive tribune frown. He walked around behind him again, still talking. 'That provoked rebellion, as he knew it would. He got command of the smaller column and made mistakes. He was too slow to cut off the enemy's retreat, then left the Tungrians high and dry without support. Only luck and your interventions prevented an embarrassing defeat. Then he claims to deal with the king up north, and yet Tincommius' warriors still join the rebel army. If you had not acted fast and taken the Ninth to guard against attack from the north we might well have lost that battle.'

'You are too generous in your praise, centurion.' Flaccus looked pleased.

'The legate does not think so, my lord, for these are his words. If it were not for one thing, his joy would be untarnished.'

Flaccus said nothing and his face became hard. Two of his soldiers were close behind and he pointed to one of them. 'Draw your sword. It is clear that the tribune is a traitor, but I quite understand that it would be embarrassing for the governor to have to arrest and try him in public.'

'The legate was sure that you had the subtlety to understand. That is why you were sent with us.'

'Sent among the enemy the day after a battle?' Flaccus sneered. 'It seemed a strange order until now. And if the noble Crispinus fell in an ambush and did not return...'

Ferox nodded. 'Who could blame us, or the legate?'

'You'll never get away with this.' Crispinus was struggling to sound confident. 'Do not listen to him, Flaccus. My father will demand to know what happened.'

'And what did happen, soldier?' Ferox asked the legionary with the drawn sword.

'Barbarians, sir. Came at us from the woods. Terrible it was.' The man leered at the tribune and walked towards him. 'Now then, sir. Hurt less if you kneel and make it easy for us both.'

'A moment. There is one more thing the legate wishes to know. You can still serve the princeps and the state, noble Crispinus.'

'Which princeps? Trajan won't last a year and you all know it.' The tribune did not kneel, but stared at Flaccus. 'Not a good idea to be on the losing side. There's no gratitude or favours from dead men.'

Ferox strode over to him, raised his left hand and slapped the tribune hard across the face.

'Who helped you?' He looked back at Flaccus. 'We know about Vegetus demanding the tax early from the Selgovae to make trouble. Then you got his wife killed. Did he know about that? What about Cerialis? What did you promise him, for trying to hand his wife over for that mongrel to sacrifice?' Ferox hit him again, and the tribune staggered from the blow, falling on his bottom.

'Go hump yourself, centurion.'

Vindex chuckled. No one had paid him any attention for a while, and he had wandered around to stand next to the mounted legionary.

'Not until I get an answer.' Ferox kicked the tribune in the chest, knocking him on to his back. 'You let those bastards torture a woman to death. It was even the wrong woman. What was the matter, did you screw it up or was that your men?' He kicked again, making the tribune hunch up on his side.

383

'He had help from someone important,' Ferox went on, looking now at Flaccus. 'A senior officer in one of the legions. On the day of the ambush he betrayed the Lady Sulpicia, letting the rebels know about her journey. But someone else arranged for soldiers to go to the tower and murder our own men so that they could not light the beacon and raise the alarm. The men who did were legionaries, and they bore the symbols of the Augusta, but that was a ruse to throw us off the scent. Same when some of the men were at Vindolanda at Samhain.'

Ferox kicked Crispinus again. 'Talk, you mongrel.'

Crispinus moaned.

Ferox spat on him. 'I'm afraid that the murderers came from the Ninth.'

Flaccus' hand gripped his sword, but he did not draw it.

'Did you know they raped that poor woman before they killed her?' He invented the detail on the spur of the moment. Given the state of poor Fortunata's body, there was no way to tell. 'All of those Roman soldiers took turns and then handed her across to the rebels for them to torture.'

There was a flicker of surprise in the junior tribune's eyes, but although Flaccus glanced at the soldier with the drawn sword, he said nothing.

'I will need your help to find them, my Lord Flaccus. And to find the officer who led them. I suspect one of your centurions, although the man dressed as a tribune to confuse us. Will you help me?'

Flaccus' hand stayed on his sword, but he seemed to relax a little. 'Of course, centurion, although with so little to go on it will not be easy.'

'Ah, but we have a witness.' Ferox turned away and looked north towards the hills above the ferry crossing. 'He's late, but should be here soon. The survivor from the attack on the tower. No. No sign of him yet.' Ferox turned back and smiled. 'He did not get a good look at the officer, but he claims he saw some of the soldiers clear enough to recognise. We can find them, I am sure.'

Ferox strolled towards Flaccus. 'You may as well have your man kill him,' he said mildly. 'I don't think he is going to talk.'

'Do it.' Flaccus told the soldier with the drawn sword. 'Make it clean.'

Ferox watched the man pace over to Crispinus, who did his best to roll away. Flaccus sneered and shook his head. 'A nobleman,' he said sarcastically, and then Ferox swung his blade up and jabbed straight into the junior tribune's throat. Flaccus' eyes widened, blood jetting from the wound as the centurion pulled his sword free, stamped forward and drove the point through the eye of the legionary standing behind the officer.

Vindex grunted as he stabbed the one on horseback, using his knife and driving it upwards between the scales of the man's armour. The two men next to the dead priest sprang up, reaching for their swords. Ferox headed for the one standing over Crispinus, but the man ignored him and slashed down at the tribune. The young aristocrat just rolled out of the way, swinging his legs, trying to wrap them round the soldier's ankles and trip him. The legionary sprang away, and then turned as Ferox came at him.

Their blades met, and the centurion felt his arm jar with the shock. Both men jumped back, the soldier stumbling as he tripped over the tribune, but before Ferox could follow up one of the other soldiers came at him from the side. Vindex was fighting with the last man, which left him to deal with two. He gave ground, making room for himself.

A spear hissed through the air so close that he felt its wind. It struck the soldier attacking on his right full in the stomach, punching through his mail cuirass and flinging him on to his back. The other man was struggling to free himself from the tribune's legs, and raised his sword to deal with the annoyance. Ferox bounded forward, screaming, and slashed at the man's head, heard the clash of iron on the bronze helmet, saw the man stagger, and then sliced low, hitting him below the knee with such force that he severed the leg. The legionary fell. He was still trying to hold his sword up protectively. Ferox kicked the man's arm so that he dropped it. He leaned forward, took careful aim, and drove the tip of his sword through the legionary's left eye.

'Mongrel,' he said under his breath.

There was a grunt as Vindex cut down his opponent. Ferox turned and saw Gannascus sitting on horseback just a few paces away. The German was smiling.

'Good throw,' Ferox told him.

'Only if I was aiming at him.' The big man roared with laughter. He did not seem interested in an explanation. His men just watched.

'Thank you,' Ferox said. 'Those men needed to be killed.'

The German shrugged, then walked his horse over and retrieved his spear. 'The horses?' he said. 'They don't need them any more.'

'You can take three.'

Gannascus leaned down and offered his hand. 'We go now.'

Ferox took it, and felt his hand being crushed. 'Thank you. Send our greetings to the high king.'

The German shouted something and a couple of his men came to lead the horses away. Ferox saw them pick out Flaccus' stallion, but did not stop them. Expensive though it was, there was no harm in letting it vanish along with its master.

Vindex had helped Crispinus to his feet and cut him free.

'I guess we are all on the same side,' the tribune said. He was bruised and bloodied, but his anger subsided when he saw Ferox's expression. 'Did you know all along that it was him?' he asked.

'I needed to be sure. You could not have been at the tower and out hunting with Cerialis on the day of the ambush, so that was in your favour. When he didn't ask questions and just let me order your arrest and death I thought that he must have a lot to hide. The threat of the witness made him nervous.'

'What if he was merely stupid?'

'That was a risk I had to take, my lord.'

'*You* had to take!' Crispinus rubbed his sore wrists. His tongue flicked out to touch his cut mouth. He spat and there was blood in it.

'Well, I could have just killed you both to be sure.' Ferox patted his sword against his trousers. 'If you like, I still can.'

'Thank you, centurion, that will not be necessary. And your oath to my father?'

'Still binds me. Unless it clashes with the one to the princeps.'

'Why didn't you tell me your plan?' The tribune stared at the corpses all around them. 'I guessed something was up. That's why I babbled all that about Trajan not lasting the year. I could have helped more if I'd known what was going on.'

'Was not sure I could trust you, my lord. Might have been hard for you to act surprised. This way it was natural and you were very convincing.' Ferox rubbed his knuckles and smiled. 'You take a punch well.'

Crispinus shook his head and did not seem to know what to say.

'Do you want to bury this lot?' Vindex did not sound enthusiastic at the prospect.

'Leave 'em.' Ferox waved to Gannascus as he and his warriors trotted away. 'Now our protection has gone we had better not hang around. Let's take his head and go. Do you want to do it, my lord?'

Crispinus found his sword and walked over to the pale corpse of the priest. He flexed his sword arm, looked down for a while and then stopped. 'I am not sure how to do it.'

Ferox grabbed the body by its limed hair and hauled it up so that the dead priest was sitting. The body was no longer stiff, but it felt heavy and clumsy. He knew that the fighting would have taken the best edge off his sword and wished that he had an axe. It took three cuts using all his strength to do the job, and they were all flecked with dark blood, even after all the wounds the man had received during his slow death.

'There you are. A keen edge and a strong arm,' Ferox said. 'They solve a lot of life's problems.'

'Not all,' Crispinus replied. 'Not the ones that really matter.'

Vindex brought a sack and he dropped the head into it and tied it up.

'We had better move,' Ferox said. 'That is, with your permission, my lord.'

'Of course, centurion.'

They mounted, Vindex taking the reins of the three spare horses.

Crispinus turned in the saddle, looking at the tree and the bodies of the Romans surrounding the priest. 'I am just glad that it is all over at last.'

Ferox thought about the sacrifice of a triple death, of the power that brought to the great druid who had hallowed this offering to the gods. If the Stallion was beaten and dead, the druid Acco was still at large, stronger than ever, and there was an ambitious and clever king in the north, and more traitors in the army, at least one who was senior and had given Flaccus his orders. Trajan was not yet secure, and from all Ferox heard showed no sign of leaving the frontier armies and heading to Rome.

'Over, my lord? It's only beginning.'

HISTORICAL NOTE

Claudia Severa to her Lepidina greetings. On 11
September, sister, for the day of the celebration of my
birthday, I give you a warm invitation to make sure that
you come to us, to make the day more enjoyable for me
by your arrival, if you are present [?]. Give my greetings
to your Cerialis. My Aelius and my little son send him
[?] their greetings. [*2nd hand*] I shall expect you, sister.
Farewell, sister, my dearest soul, as I hope to prosper,
and hail. [*Back, 1st hand*] To Sulpicia Lepidina, wife of
Cerialis, from Severa.

Vindolanda Tablets II. 291.

This text excavated at the fort of Vindolanda was the spark that
first inspired this story. It was written around the turn of the
first to second centuries AD, and the second hand in the text was
surely that of Claudia Severa herself, adding a personal touch to
the invitation. This makes it the first surviving piece of writing
by a woman in the history of Britain. The original text, written
in ink on a thin wooden writing tablet, can be seen today in the
British Museum.

We will talk more about Vindolanda and the texts discovered
there in a moment, but it was this glimpse of something as routine
as a birthday party in a frontier zone on the edge of the Roman
Empire that made me want to create a story around it and bring

that time and place to life. *Vindolanda* is a novel, and much of the story is invented because we know very little about what was really happening in northern Britain at this time. However, given that I have spent my adult life studying the Roman world and the Roman army in particular, I have done my best to place the story in as accurate a setting as possible.

Ferox and Vindex are inventions, although a later tombstone records a Brigantian soldier in the Roman army who was the son of someone named Vindex and in my imagination this is our man. Many of the other characters are also inventions, or people about whom little more is known than their names. Sulpicia Lepidina, Claudia Severa and Flavius Cerialis appear in other texts, but even so are only a little less shadowy. I have done my best to invent nothing that clashes with what we do know about them, but as characters they are essentially fictional. The same is true of the other people plucked from the texts found at Vindolanda.

Much more detail on the historical background can be found on my website – www.adriangoldsworthy.com – which also includes suggestions for further reading. In the meantime, it is worth looking at a few topics.

Before Hadrian's Wall
The story occurs at the start of the reign of Trajan, whose successor Hadrian came to Britain and ordered the construction of Hadrian's Wall around the year AD 122. Our sources have little to say about major events in Britain under Trajan, although there is talk of major conflict, which may well have prompted the decision to build the Wall. The fort at Vindolanda (modern Chesterholm) lies a few miles south and within sight of the Wall and clearly was incorporated within the network of garrisons serving it. Much of our story takes place in what would become Wall country.

Vindolanda is set in AD 98, the first year of Trajan's reign, and at this time the province of Britannia was just over fifty years old. Although Julius Caesar had landed in Britain in 55 and 54 BC, no permanent Roman presence was maintained, and it was not until AD 43 that the Emperor Claudius sent an invasion force across the Channel. In AD 60 Boudicca's rebellion devastated southern Britain, but after her defeat there is no trace of any serious resistance in the Lowlands. This is not true of northern Britain, which was garrisoned by substantial numbers of troops for the remaining three and a half centuries of Roman occupation.

In AD 98 few would have guessed that the Romans would stay for so long. Their presence in the north was more recent, for it was mainly in the seventies and eighties AD that this area was overrun. During this time Roman armies marched far into the north of what would become Scotland, while a naval squadron for the first time circumnavigated Britain, confirming that it was an island. An entire legion – one of the four then garrisoning the province and one of twenty-eight in existence – built a base at Inchtuthil in Perthshire, the biggest site in a network of garrisons on the edge of the Highlands. Around the same time, a system of observation towers along a military road was constructed along the Gask ridge.

All of this activity, which to a great extent is known only from the archaeological remains, makes clear the Romans' intention to occupy this region more or less permanently, but in the late eighties AD priorities changed. The Emperor Domitian, faced with serious trouble on the Danube, withdrew Legio II Adiutrix from Britain and did not replace it. It is probable that substantial numbers of auxiliaries were withdrawn at the same time, so that the provincial garrison was cut by at least a quarter. Inchtuthil and many of the other bases were abandoned, and the same thing happened a little later to the remaining sites and the Gask ridge line. No Roman base was maintained north of the Forth–Clyde line, and soon the northernmost outpost was at Trimontium or Newstead.

Several forts were maintained or built close to what would one day become the line of Hadrian's Wall. A couple of years after our story, a proper road running between Carlisle and Corbridge was constructed and more forts and smaller outposts added. Today the road is known by its medieval name, the Stanegate or 'stone road', and archaeologists continue to debate its composition and purpose. By about AD 106 Newstead was abandoned in another withdrawal. Our paltry literary sources make no mention of any of this, so it is left to us to guess from the archaeology just what was going on.

A novelist has more freedom, and once again I have done my best to reconstruct these years for our purposes in a way that never conflicts with any hard evidence. At the very least I hope that our story is something that could have happened. Something made the Romans station significant numbers of troops in this area at the end of the first century AD, and then made them increase these numbers and develop the deployment along the Stanegate just a few years later. All of the forts mentioned in the story existed and were occupied in AD 98. (Precise dating is rarely possibly through excavation so it may be that the fort at Magna or Carvoran dates to a year or two later, but it is not impossible that it was there in 98). Syracuse is an invention, but typical of the many small outposts set up by the Roman army as needed. I see it as a predecessor to the excavated sites at Haltwhistle Burn and Throp, which were built alongside the Stanegate, although these were stone structures and larger than the fictional Syracuse. In the late first century AD most of the structures built by the army in Britain were in turf and timber. Some sites were being rebuilt in stone, and in the second century this became ever more common.

Vindolanda and the Writing Tablets
Vindolanda is one of the most remarkable Roman sites in Britain. The first fort was built there in the seventies AD. The fort from our period was the third constructed on the site, and I have stretched the dating by a year or so to have it there in AD 98. The remains visible today are of the later stone fort and the civilian settlement or *vicus* (a more organised version of the *canabae*) outside it. A level of laziness in demolishing the earlier forts when the new ones were built, combined with the waterlogged nature of much of the site, created unusual conditions that have allowed the preservation

of wood, leather, textiles and other material usually lost. Over 5,500 shoes have already been found at Vindolanda, more than from anywhere else in the Roman Empire. For more information about the site and the Vindolanda Trust visit the website at http:// www.vindolanda.com.

Although less impressive as objects, even more remarkable are the wooden writing tablets, hundreds of which have preserved some text. Papyrus was known and used in Roman Britain, but was expensive, and much everyday correspondence and record-keeping was written in ink on thin sheets of wood. Some were covered in thin wax, so that this could be smoothed down again and reused, but these tend to be impossible to decipher since scratches from numerous different texts overlap. The most useful were the plain wood sheets, which had been rubbed with only a thin layer of beeswax to prevent the ink from spreading and were then used only once. Even so, little of the ink survives, and it requires careful analysis of the scratches made by the nibs of the stylus pens to trace the outlines of letters. Deciphering the texts and then reconstructing and understanding them is a painstaking business. More detail and many of the texts themselves can be found online at http://vindolanda.csad.ox.ac.uk.

The contents of most of the texts are mundane: private letters, accounts, daily reports of the units garrisoned there, lists of men allocated to various duties, etc. A significant number of the tablets are associated with Flavius Cerialis and his household. His name suggests that he or his father gained citizenship at the time of the Batavian Revolt in AD 70, presumably for loyalty. In one text, the decurion Masclus refers to him as 'his king'. The editors of the tablets are inclined to see this as no more than sycophancy by a subordinate, but it is possible that he was from the Batavian royal family. Neither he nor his wife, Sulpicia Lepidina, are recorded outside the tablets. The editors suggest that her family became Roman citizens through the favour of the short-lived Emperor Sulpicius Galba, who reigned for several months after the suicide of Nero. This is possible, but she could equally have come from a family whose citizenship was far older. There is no evidence that she was the daughter of a senator, but once again this is not impossible. A generation or so later, such a woman is recorded as the wife of an auxiliary prefect commanding the garrison of High Rochester.

Commanders of auxiliary units usually served with them for three or more years, and Cerialis and Sulpicia Lepidina seem to have been at Vindolanda for at least as long as this. Texts give us some idea of the food they provided for guests – with poultry and eggs common – and his taste for hunting. They also tell us of the social life of garrison commanders – in one letter Claudia Severa speaks of coming to visit Vindolanda, but requiring her husband's permission to do so, and probably his assistance in arranging transport and, most likely, an escort. Elsewhere Sulpicia Lepidina appears supporting an appeal for assistance made to her husband, and it is clear that an officer's wife behaved much as she did in more settled provinces, not simply running the household but trading favours in a very Roman way.

There are references to children in the households of commanders, and Cerialis appears to have had at least three. However, no letter specifically names Sulpicia Lepidina as their mother, so that I was able to make them offspring from an earlier marriage even though this is pure fiction. Shoes found associated with the *praetorium* from this period are of such high quality that they surely belong to the prefect's family. This suggests that there were two boys and a girl, the older boy's shoes wearing out in a strange pattern that may well indicate some physical disability, albeit one that did not prevent him from walking. Among the shoes likely to have belonged to Sulpicia Lepidina is one slipper that would not be out of place in a shop window today. On the whole the footwear from Vindolanda consists of enclosed shoes rather than the sandals we automatically associate with the Romans. Judging from finds of similar styles elsewhere, patterns in footwear changed throughout the empire every couple of decades. It is also clear than the majority of people owned more than one pair – something rare until the modern era.

Tribes and Druids

Iron Age Britain was occupied by many different tribes and other groups, many of them only ever mentioned in Roman sources. It is likely that Roman and Greek observers misunderstood many aspects of the indigenous population's sense of identity, but we have little more to go on. All of the groups mentioned in the book lived in the areas described, and as far as we can tell all shared a version of the same language. These days, some archaeologists are reluctant to use terms like Celtic or to assume that this linguistic group shared a common culture, and therefore that traits described in Gaul or elsewhere were also likely in Britain. This approach can be too dogmatic, and as a novelist I have drawn upon evidence from other regions as well as cultures from other lands and other periods to create a picture of the tribes. I have done my best to make sure that none of this material conflicts with what we do know.

Judging from the environmental evidence, in AD 98 the climate in the north was a little milder than it is today, closer to that of southeast England. This may well have changed and grown colder during the second century. There is evidence for widespread cultivation as well as pastoral activities. Several sections of Hadrian's Wall were built on ploughed land. The population was considerable and this was far from being a wasteland, but most people lived in small settlements, often a few huts on their own, with larger villages and hill forts much less common. In spite of some attempts by scholars to pacify Iron Age Britain, all the evidence points to societies in which warfare, usually in the form of raiding, was an ever-present threat. This is true of most of the ancient world. The Roman Empire imposed on a large chunk of the world a much higher level of peace than it had ever enjoyed before. The famous Pax Romana was real, but it was maintained by force, and in some areas, especially near the frontiers, it was far from unbroken by outbursts of violence and warfare.

Archaeology is not well suited to charting political change among Iron Age peoples. Tincommius and his growing empire are both inventions. There is no evidence as yet for the appearance of so powerful a leader in this region, or for any reuse of an abandoned and slighted Roman fort in the way described in the story. However, his career so far and in the stories to come is based on similar charismatic leaders who appeared at other times in the lands around the empire. At the close of the first century AD, most observers in northern Britain would have surely seen the Romans as in retreat. In such circumstances, other forces quickly emerge to fill the power vacuum.

The druids have attracted a good deal of interest over the centuries, most of it highly romantic. Julius Caesar depicts them as important figures in the Gaul of his day, acting above and outside the tribes. He does not portray them as anti-Roman or as able to control the tribes. Under Augustus and the other emperors the druidic cult in Gaul was restricted and later suppressed, although it survived covertly. In Britain the Romans attacked the centre of the cult in AD 60, invading the island of Mona (or Anglesey) and destroying the sacred groves there. This does appear to have ended the formal structure of the druidic cult. In spite of this people called druids appear in Gaul and Britain in the centuries to come, but lack the status of the aristocratic priests of earlier years.

Conquest and occupation by an imperial power has often caused serious dislocation to the society and beliefs of indigenous peoples, and it is tempting to see the periodic appearance of druids with apocalyptic prophecies as similar to religious movements in more recent times. Among the most famous are the various Ghost Dance movements in North America in the late nineteenth century, but other examples include the various mystics who appeared among the Xhosa in South Africa, or what was popularly known as the Hauhau movement among the Maori. Very often, such leaders preached a mixture of imported beliefs alongside traditional ideas. This is the basis for the story, and I have presented the Stallion's followers as using a mishmash of magical words and invocations, as well as Greco-Roman deities alongside old beliefs and gods.

The Silures lived in what is now South Wales. Tacitus described them as darker and different in appearance from other Britons. They first came into conflict with the Romans in the late forties AD, and were keen supporters of Caratacus, the leader from the southeast who kept fighting the invaders for years after his homeland was overrun. The Silures were known for raiding their neighbours, and exploited the hills and valleys of their homeland, using stealth, surprise and ambush in their long struggle against the Romans. It took at least twenty-five years to defeat them and substantial Roman garrisons remained in the area for some time. Ferox and his grandfather are fictional, but it was common practice to take hostages from defeated leaders, educating them within the empire. Many became Roman citizens and served in the army, so there is nothing implausible about Ferox and his career.

The Roman Army
This is a vast subject, but it is worth making a few points for those new to the topic. In AD 98 the Roman army consisted of twenty-eight legions – two more would soon be added by Trajan – each with a paper strength of some 5,000 men. Each one was divided into ten cohorts of heavy infantry and had a small contingent of some 120 horsemen. Legionaries were Roman citizens. This was a legal status without any ethnic basis and by this time there were over four million Roman citizens scattered throughout the empire. We may think of St Paul, a Jew from Tarsus in Asia Minor, but a Roman citizen and entitled to all the legal advantages that brought.

Supporting the legions were the auxiliaries who were not citizens, but received citizenship at the end of their military service. These were organised as independent cohorts of infantry and similarly sized cohorts of cavalry. There were also the mixed cohorts (*cohortes equitatae*) like the Batavians, which included both infantry and cavalry in a four to one ratio. Legionaries and auxiliaries alike served for twenty-five years. Most were volunteers, although conscription did occur and was probably especially common with some auxiliary units.

We know a good deal about the Roman army, about its equipment, organisation, command structure, tactics, ranks and routine, although it must be emphasised that there are also many gaps in our knowledge. As a historian it is my duty to stress what we do not know, but a novelist cannot do this and must invent in order to fill in these gaps. Some aspects of the depiction of the Roman army in this book may surprise some readers, but often this will be because some of the evidence for it is not well known outside academic circles. I have invented as little as possible, and always done my best to base it on what we do know. As an introduction to the army, I am vain enough to recommend my own *The Complete Roman Army* published by Thames and Hudson. I would also say that anything by the late Peter Connolly is also well worth a look. Once again, for more specific recommendations, I refer readers to my website.

GLOSSARY

ala: a regiment of auxiliary cavalry, roughly the same size as a cohort of infantry. There were two types: *ala quingenaria* consisting of 512 men divided into sixteen *turmae*; and *ala miliaria* consisting of 768 men divided into twenty-four *turmae*.

auxilia/auxiliaries: over half of the Roman army was recruited from non-citizens from all over (and even outside) the empire. These served as both infantry and cavalry and gained citizenship at the end of their twenty-five years of service.

Batavians: an offshoot of the Germanic Chatti, who fled after a period of civil war, the Batavians settled on what the Romans called the Rhine islands in modern Holland. Famous as warriors, their only obligation to the empire was to provide soldiers to serve in Batavian units of the *auxilia*. Writing around the time of our story, the historian Tacitus described them as 'like armour and weapons – only used in war'.

Brigantes: a large tribe or group of tribes occupying much of what would become northern England. Several sub-groups are known, including the Textoverdi and Carvetii (whose name may mean 'stag people').

burgus: a small outpost manned by detached troops rather than a formal unit.

canabae: the civilian settlements that rapidly grew up outside almost every Roman fort. The community had no formal status and was probably under military jurisdiction.

centurion: a grade of officer rather than a specific rank, each legion had some sixty centurions, while each auxiliary cohort had between six and ten. They were highly educated men and were often given posts of great responsibility. While a minority were commissioned after service in the ranks, most were directly commissioned or served only as junior officers before reaching the centurionate.

centurio regionarius: a post attested in the Vindolanda tablets, as well as elsewhere in Britain and other provinces. They appear to have been officers on detached service placed in control of an area. A large body of evidence from Egypt shows them dealing with criminal investigations as well as military and administrative tasks.

cohort: the principal tactical unit of the legions. The first cohort consisted of 800 men in five double-strength centuries, while cohorts two to ten were composed of 480 men in six centuries of eighty. Auxiliaries were either formed in milliary cohorts of 800 or more often quingeniary cohorts of 480. *Cohortes equitatae* or mixed cohorts added 240 and 120 horsemen respectively. These troopers were paid less and given less expensive mounts than the cavalry of the *alae*.

consilium: the council of officers and other senior advisors routinely employed by a Roman governor or senator to guide him in making decisions.

curator: (i) title given to a soldier placed in charge of an outpost such as a *burgus* who may or may not have held formal rank; (ii) the second in command to a decurion in a cavalry *turma*.

decurion: the cavalry equivalent to a centurion, but considered to be junior to them. He commanded a *turma*.

equestrian: the social class just below the Senate. There were many thousand equestrians (*eques*, pl. *equites*) in the Roman

Empire, compared to six hundred senators, and a good proportion of equestrians were descendants of aristocracies within the provinces. Those serving in the army followed a different career path to senators.

gladius: Latin word for sword, which by modern convention specifically refers to the short sword used by all legionaries and most auxiliary infantry. By the end of the first century most blades were less than 2 feet long.

legate (legionary): the commander of a legion was a *legatus legionis* and was a senator at an earlier stage in his career than the provincial governor (see below). He would usually be in his early thirties.

legate (provincial): the governor of a military province like Britain was a *legatus Augusti*, the representative of the emperor. He was a distinguished senator and usually at least in his forties.

legion: originally the levy of the entire Roman people summoned to war, legion or *legio* became the name for the most important unit in the army. In the last decades of the first century BC, legions became permanent with their own numbers and usually names and titles. In AD 98 there were twenty-eight legions, but the total was soon raised to thirty.

medicus: an army medical orderly or junior physician.

omnes ad stercus: a duty roster of the first century AD from a century of a legion stationed in Egypt has some soldiers assigned *ad stercus*, literally to the dung or shit. This probably meant a fatigue party cleaning the latrines – or just possibly mucking out the stables. From this I have invented *omnes ad stercus* as 'everyone to the latrines' or 'we're all in the shit'.

optio: the second in command of a century of eighty men and deputy to a centurion.

pilum: the heavy javelin carried by Roman legionaries. It was about 6 to 7 feet long. The shaft was wooden, topped by a slim iron shank ending in a pyramid-shaped point (much like the bodkin arrow used by longbowmen). The shank was not meant to bend. Instead the aim was to concentrate all of the weapon's considerable weight behind the head so that it would punch through armour or shield. If it hit a shield, the head would go through, and the long iron shank gave it the reach to continue and strike the man behind. Its effective range was probably some 15 to 16 yards.

praesidium: the term meant garrison, and could be employed for a small outpost or a full-sized fort.

prefect: the commander of most auxiliary units was called a prefect (although a few unit COs held the title tribune). These were equestrians, who first commanded a cohort of auxiliary infantry, then served as equestrian tribune in a legion, before going on to command a cavalry *ala*.

procurator: an imperial official who oversaw the tax and financial administration of a province. Although junior to a legate, a procurator reported directly to the emperor.

scorpion (*scorpio*): a light torsion catapult or *ballista* with a superficial resemblance to a large crossbow. They shot a heavy bolt with considerable accuracy and tremendous force to a range beyond bowshot. Julius Caesar describes a bolt from one of these engines going through the leg of an enemy cavalryman and pinning him to the saddle.

seplasiarius (or *seplasiario*): military pharmacist working in a fort's hospital.

signifer: a standard-bearer, specifically one carrying a century's standard or *signum* (pl. *signa*).

Silures: a tribe or people occupying what is now South Wales. They fought a long campaign before being overrun by the Romans. Tacitus described them as having curly hair and darker hair or complexions than other Britons, and suggested that they looked more like Spaniards (although since he misunderstood the geography of Britain he also believed that their homeland was closer to Spain than Gaul).

spatha: another Latin term for sword, which it is now conventional to employ for the longer blades used mainly by horsemen in this period.

stationarii: soldiers detached from their parent units and stationed as garrison elsewhere, often in a small outpost.

tesserarius: the third in command of a century after the *optio* and *signifer*. The title originally came from their responsibility for overseeing sentries. The watchword for each night was written on a *tessera* or tablet.

tribune: each legion had six tribunes. The most senior was the broad-stripe tribune (*tribunus laticlavius*), who was a young aristocrat at an early stage of a senatorial career. Such men were usually in their late teens or very early twenties. There were also five narrow-stripe or junior tribunes (*tribuni angusticlavii*).

Tungrians: a tribe from the Rhineland. Many Tungrians were recruited into the army. By AD 98 a unit with the title of Tungrians was likely to include many men from other ethnic backgrounds, including Britons. In most cases, the Roman army drew recruits from the closest and most convenient source. The Batavians at this period may have been an exception to this.